IN CONCERT PERFORMANCE

Nan A. Talese
DOUBLEDAY

New York
London
Toronto
Sydney
Auckland

In Concert Performance

a novel

Nikolai
Dezhnev

Translated
from the Russian by
Mary Ann Szporluk

PUBLISHED BY NAN A. TALESE
an imprint of Doubleday
a division of Random House, Inc.
1540 Broadway, New York, New York 10036

DOUBLEDAY is a trademark of Doubleday,
a division of Random House, Inc.

BOOK DESIGNED BY TERRY KARYDES

All of the characters in this book are fictitious, and any resemblance to actual persons, living or dead, is purely coincidental.

LIBRARY OF CONGRESS CATALOGING-IN-PUBLICATION DATA
Dezhnev, Nikolai, 1946–
[V kontsertnom ispolnenii. English]
In concert performance: a novel / Nikolai Dezhnev: translated
from the Russian by Mary Ann Szporluk.
p. cm.
I. Szporluk, Mary Ann. II. Title.
PG3479.6.E98V213 1999
891.73'44—dc21 99-20438
CIP

ISBN 0-385-49326-6

Printed in the United States of America
November 1999
FIRST EDITION IN THE UNITED STATES OF AMERICA
1 3 5 7 9 10 8 6 4 2

List of Characters

KOVALEVSKAYA — an old Bolshevik, Anna Alexandrovna's aunt

TELYATNIKOVA, Anna Alexandrovna (Anka, Anya) — director of a TV news program, Sergei Sergeyevich's wife

TELYATNIKOV, Sergei Sergeyevich (Serge, Seryozha) — assistant professor of physics, Anna's husband

LUKARY (Luka, Lukin, Lukash) — an evolved human, who is sent back to earth to Moscow as a *domovoi* (hearth spirit)

SHEPETUKHA, Semyon Arkadievich (Syoma, Sem) — by nature a *lẹshii* (forest spirit or goblin)

MARIA NIKOLAYEVNA (Masha, Mashka) — Anna Alexandrovna's friend

DIOGENES of SINOPE — Greek philosopher of the Cynic school

MILADY (Lucy) — an apparition, resembling a *rusalka* (water sprite)

YEVSEVY — childhood friend of Lukin's, later an inmate in an insane asylum

SERPINA — childhood friend of Lukary and Yevsevy, senior privy councillor in the Department of Dark Powers

NERGAL — also the Black Cardinal, Serpina's superior in the Department of Dark Powers

BUROV, Nicholas (Kolka) — a shepherd

TELYATIN, Sergei Sergeyevich — a physicist in Moscow in the 1930s

ANNA ALEXANDROVNA (Anechka, Anyuta, Anya, Anka) — his niece, an actress

LYUDMILA NIKOLAYEVNA (Lucy) — a prostitute, the Telyatins' neighbor

RED, SLANT-EYE, SAILOR — gang members

GRISARD — gang leader

ZAKHAVA, Boris Yevgenievich — stage director

AKIMYCH — studio head at the theater

SHCHUKIN, Boris Vasilievich — actor

SERPIN — secret police investigator in 1930s Moscow

ERGAL — Serpin's superior, member of the Central Committee

SHEPTUKHIN — informer for the secret police

EVGENIA IVANOVNA — a nurse in Moscow

ANAEL — an angel

LUKIN — a historian in contemporary Moscow

NERGAL — editor-in-chief of the journal of the Academy of Sciences

ANNA — Lukin's wife

SERPINOV — member of Parliament, friend of Lukin and Yevsei

YEVSEI — a friend of Lukin and Serpinov

MASHA — Anna's friend

LUCY — a colleague of Masha's

IN CONCERT

PERFORMANCE

1

In March, during the first days of spring, the old woman Kovalevskaya died. Some might say she made up her mind and then died, but had she been alive Kovalevskaya would never have agreed. She'd been a member of the Communist Party since 1932 and didn't believe in mysticism. She had spent her life in the objective world of matter, perceived through the senses, and it was proper for death to come to her in an equally simple and lucid way. "May our dear country live on," Kovalevskaya had sung along with the rest of the people, and the country lived, but she never aspired to such a luxury for herself. She didn't have time—she was too active in the struggle. And even though her husband, a fellow Party member, went to the grave straight from prison, and even though she had never made any distinction between personal life and civic duty, Kovalevskaya had an unconquerable thirst for life, a childish interest in its absurd and exhausting process. She kept her sharp analytical mind into old age; she read all the newspapers she could get and understood the fine points of the confusing political situation, which significantly contributed to her untimely end, by the way. When you've been accustomed to clear-cut goals and predictable events your whole life, it's hard not to lose your mind when you encounter the madness mistakenly called modern-day politics. The old woman couldn't bear it. On the day of her death Kovalevskaya listened to the morning edition of the latest news and then she phoned Anna, her only relative, and dryly informed her that she would probably die soon.

Later, it became clear that she had no longer trusted the state and had bequeathed her only property, a two-room apartment, to her niece. Kovalevskaya looked tall and withered in her coffin, wearing the same calm and stern expression she'd had while alive. Frank to the point of rudeness, she had made few friends. Some six or seven people came to bury the old Bolshevik, all equally severe and stiff, dressed in modest but clean clothes in the style of the fifties. The painful job of funeral arrangements fell to Anna Alexandrovna—Telyatnikova by marriage—and partly to her husband, Sergei Sergeyevich, though he was extremely busy at his institute. The deceased was buried in her husband's plot in Vagankov, and afterward a service was held in the church there.

Snow fell abundantly that year; it lay in ragged drifts on the roof of the kiosk with pictures of Vladimir Vysotsky and on top of the hall for civil ceremonies; it covered all the small side paths leading off the cleared avenues. The mourners made their way to the grave through a maze of fences, trying to stay in the track of footprints ahead. Tired out, the gravediggers from the state funeral agency demanded one more bottle of vodka than they'd agreed on earlier. Quietly twilight began to fall. The gray mist of the bleak Moscow thaw thickened between the bare branches of the trees. The mourners returned the same way—in single file. When they reached the central avenue, Anna shook the snow off her coat, and as she cast a farewell glance at the distant fresh grave, she saw a tall man with a wreath in his hands standing beside the dark mound. Anna was bewildered.

She left the old people to her husband's care and went back. She felt obligated to invite the stranger to the wake, but oddly enough, when she reached the grave no one was there. Nor were there any footprints, except the ones the funeral procession had made. There was a small wreath of fresh red roses tied with a black ribbon on which someone had carefully written in old-fashioned script: "We got along well." All the way home, shaking in the cold half-empty bus, Anna couldn't stop thinking about what she'd seen, but she didn't tell anyone about it.

There was little drinking at the gathering; instead the old people all reminisced about their youth, their work in the prewar state agencies, and the war itself. They criticized the decline of public morality and the lack of ideals among today's youth. But they didn't complain about the constant rise in prices—they were above that. The old women smoked. The only man among the survivors watched everything in wonder with lusterless moist eyes and was silent. The fork in his hand trembled slightly. Anna sat pensively at the table. From time to time she looked up at the photo of her aunt on the sideboard in a black frame, and strange thoughts began to float in her head. She wasn't picturing the life of the deceased—it was the man at the cemetery who occupied her imagination, and it seemed to Anna that not only did she know this man but—and this was completely absurd—he was near and dear to her. A strange languor came over her and touched her heart with a presentiment of joy and a fullness of life which seemed out of place at a wake. But she didn't want to let go of this sensation, so like a sweet morning dream full of hope and promise.

After everyone had left and the dishes were washed, Anna stood at the window for a long time and stared at the Moscow courtyard flooded with cold moonlight and at the coal-black tree shadows that sliced the yard into pieces. She was sad, but a sense of something fleeting, surprisingly gentle and pleasant, promised happiness to her apprehensive soul. The only person Anna told what had happened was her best friend Mashka. She didn't even try telling her husband—he was preoccupied with his research, he wouldn't have understood.

Life went on, however, and very soon Anna's feeling faded and she only remembered it as something pleasant which, alas, bore no relation to dreary reality. Her thoughts were more and more consumed by completely practical matters. The apartment she inherited from her aunt had come at just the right time: despite the fact that they were no longer young the Telyatnikovs were cooped up in a communal apartment with no possibilities for moving out. Sergei Sergeyevich was respected at his institute, but not enough to help him get a better position or anything more than vague promises. True, the inheritance turned out to be no easy matter, and it took a good deal of persistence and energy, not to mention time and bribes, before the legitimate heiress could come into her own. But finally Anna's victory was secured. After waiting for a proper period of time, the Telyatnikovs moved to their new apartment and, still euphoric from their victory over the bureaucracy, they decided to exchange it immediately for a good three-bedroom apartment somewhere in a quiet and respectable part of the capital. It was the end of April, the second month of spring, a time of hope and expectation . . .

You'd think Lukary wouldn't have cared about any of this fuss. But these events in the lower, three-dimensional world of man had roused him. He lost his peace of mind, and from his place in the astral plane he would often catch himself thinking, not of the nature of time, as was his habit, but of something very different.

The death of the old Bolshevik had occurred in March, and by the beginning of May so many strange incidents had taken place that Assistant Professor Telyatnikov was forced to stop and analyze things. Such an analysis fully corresponded to his natural inclination, for Sergei Sergeyevich had reached the age when a man begins to feel the need for reflection, or, more to the point, the need to convince himself that his life has meaning. At this age ambitions are still alive and hope may stir the soul with an errant youthful dream, but the blurry silhouette of old age is looming on the horizon, and when the sunset of life begins you occasionally feel a cold breeze of indifference toward yourself, not to mention the world. It's then that a man begins to understand a lot of things he's only glimpsed before. He begins to see that nature, with a maniacal persistence, reproduces the very same types of people, mixes them up in different combinations, and pretends that this constitutes the diversity of life. Then the day comes when with autumnal clarity you see the superfluousness and mediocrity of what's going on, and this knowledge makes you want to bury your head in the protective bleakness of ordinary life, walk around half asleep, and slowly and inconspicuously slip into a different world. The soul calcifies with age and you no longer have the strength or hope to respond to feelings. Getting no answer, love passes by. You watch it go and, echoing the Hindus, whisper: love is a great misfortune, love is a distraction from the quest for perfection, love . . . You keep trying to believe this. Still, all would be well, everything would be peaceful, except for the hidden danger that exists at this age. The beast of vanity, which until now has fed on hope, suddenly goes on the warpath. Everything has fizzled out, everything is past its prime, and what's left is the one thing you can't accept—you're nobody and you haven't *lived* at all!

As for the troubles that had fallen on Telyatnikov—Sergei Sergeyevich was sure that they had all begun with the move to the new apartment. He didn't accuse the old woman herself, even though when she was alive his relations with her were extremely cool. As a physicist and scholar, Telyatnikov flatly discarded the possibility that a ghost or apparition had interfered—evidently he didn't take after Pushkin's Hermann, but at times, in a moment of weakness, he too was visited by the thought that not everything going on here was innocent. As a joke, and mostly for amusement, he dropped in at the library and looked through some material on witches but he didn't find anything that resembled the deceased. Kovalevskaya's character was better suited for the role of Inquisitor.

Turning his thoughts back to when the troubles had started, Sergei Sergeyevich remembered that on the very first day a sheet of water had rained down on him from the new apartment's ceiling. Just like that—for no reason at all, and without any provocation on his part.

Immediately thereafter the Czech glass chandelier began behaving strangely. Defying the law of gravity, it slipped off its hook and almost hit him in the head. For a long time afterward Telyatnikov walked around with his neck extended and glanced uneasily at the ceiling.

In due course it turned out that all of these strange natural phenomena, including the arbitrary flight of objects and the fact that the refrigerator worked like a microwave, were somehow tied to the theme of exchanging the apartment, which was clearly beginning to seem a mistake. But even after he stopped talking about it, Telyatnikov would get electric shocks as a warning, and not only from the wall sockets, which would have been understandable, but also from such confirmed insulators as his own toothbrush and condoms—and often at a bad moment. These spontaneous natural phenomena clearly had nothing to do with fairness, for the punishments were exclusively imposed upon the apartment's master. Only once, when Anna first started to discuss the move, did an object fly at her—and it was a pillow. On the other hand, the buttons on all of her dresses and housecoats began to pop off with the sound of gunshots, and various belts and ribbons were incessantly coming undone.

"He has fallen in love with you! He's in love with you and he's making my life miserable!" the raging Telyatnikov bawled. But to Anna's question, "Who's he?" Sergei Sergeyevich couldn't answer and just glanced around from side to side with a badgered look. Now, before opening his mouth, he carefully weighed everything he meant to say—a benefit to him in all respects.

They tried to discuss the matter of the apartment exchange metaphorically, even using broken English and sign language, but all of these tricks were deciphered right away and punishment followed inevitably. As a light, friendly warning all the gears on the wall clock would whirl off like fleas, and the television would suddenly begin to speak in Chinese. That was fine—they could have adapted to it, had there been anything on television besides ads for an American laxative. Life had become absolutely unbearable, however, and he knew they had to make the exchange and move quickly.

They decided to go live for a while in their old room in the communal apartment building in order to get some rest and calm their nerves, but that was not to be. Just as they showed up at their old apartment they were met with the smell of burning—a meticulous little fire had engulfed their entire room, sparing neither the furniture nor the wallpaper, and then had quietly died out by itself on the threshold of the common hall. Sergei Sergeyevich sat on a stool in the kitchen and laughed and sobbed until the building manager, who'd been called to the scene of the action, made him gulp down a full glass of vodka—this took away the stress but didn't change the situation one bit. After this their friends all stopped inviting the Telyatnikovs to stay with them, and from a human point of view you can understand why. Anna cried too, yet felt there was something flattering in what had taken place.

It's probably not even worth mentioning how they tried to discuss the notorious matter over the phone or outside their home. When they did, the telephone turned an ordinary seven-digit number into a connection to Brighton Beach in New York, where everyone spoke Russian, though without an American accent. The arrival of astronomical bills for international discussions came as a great surprise to the Telyatnikovs and was a heavy burden on their modest family budget. As for their attempt to talk about things in the open air, well, Sergei Sergeyevich's legs were bitten all over by stray dogs—and completely respectable ones as well, who kept running after him until he stopped them with a few curses about their doggone business.

In addition, there were hardships of a different kind that made intimate contact between the spouses impossible. Nothing abnormal, in the doctor's opinion, but something just didn't work and that was that! It even started to be funny and they laughed, but the inner tension mounted and Sergei Sergeyevich seriously began to worry about his mental health.

Assistant Professor Telyatnikov was thinking about all these troubles as he was walking one day past the main building of the institute. It was lunchtime and the student population was outside bathing in the sun and reclaiming life outside of the classroom. There was more than an hour before lectures began, and Sergei Sergeyevich took pleasure in exposing his pale face to the warm rays. Intelligent-looking students greeted him respectfully, and some female students who were still attractive smiled sweetly, secretly hoping that it would count for something during the coming exams. Telyatnikov proudly swam in this sea of universal respect. Sergei Sergeyevich was well aware of the reputation he'd earned as a mean ogre and pedant. But he liked his own image, and all would have been well in life, had it not been for his domestic troubles.

"Something must be done! Measures must be taken immediately!" Sergei Sergeyevich thought while on the move, giving his neat little doctor's beard a pinch and frightening the timid first-year students with his expression. "Maybe all of this is only the theory of probability run amok?" How many times had he asked himself this and right away, scientist that he was, he'd come up with some groundless hypothesis. Considering the variety of unruly incidents, he could only divine that a malevolent being was connected to the crazy apartment. "We have to move! We have to move at all costs! So I simply go home, take Anna by the arm, and leave as if for a walk. And don't return! As for a place to live—something will turn up!"

Having come to such a clear and logical decision, Sergei Sergeyevich cheered up and even began to whistle something not unlike the aria of the toreador. He even thought with animal pleasure of the lunch that awaited him, his appetite now whetted by his walk in the fresh air. He climbed the steps of his beloved institute and was just putting his hand on the massive door when he suddenly noticed a commotion and the students below crowding around a frail, strangely dressed man. Wearing a padded workman's jacket that had seen better days and clutching a cloth cap, the man gave the impression of an alien body that had somehow wormed its way into the colorful crowd of young people. The little man was pushing the students aside and, as if riding a wave, making straight for Telyatnikov. His destination was so obvious that Sergei Sergeyevich even took a step toward the stranger. "Probably some blockhead's parent," Telyatnikov guessed. "He'll intercede for the little fool, go on about his old mother and his worker-peasant background. He might even offer a bribe," the lecturer presupposed, getting ready to rebuff him, but this time he was mistaken. Staring with impudent eyes, and twitching the tip of his rosy rabbitlike nose as he moved, the tiny man suddenly broke into a radiant smile and, with open padded arms, literally threw himself at Telyatnikov.

"My dear Sergei Sergeyevich! How delighted I am to see you!" he said rapidly, for some reason winking the playful eye that slanted toward his nose. The little man took hold of Telyatnikov's hand, grasping it with both of his, and began to shake it as though he intended to tear it off.

"Excuse me"—Telyatnikov arched his brows stiffly—"but have we actually met?"

"No, of course not, but that doesn't matter! Shepetukha, Professor Shepetukha, Semyon Arkadievich!" the man in the padded jacket introduced himself and made several attempts to embrace the assistant professor. When he saw it was futile, he finally let go of his hand, reached into his pocket, and offered Telyatnikov a glossy card with a thin gold border. Sergei Sergeyevich took the little card and read that the frail Semyon Arkadievich standing before him was not only a full professor and doctor of science but a State Prize winner and Director of the Coordinating Center of Bio-Equilibristics. Overwhelmed by the number of titles and ranks, Telyatnikov put the card in his pocket and took a look at the doctor-director. The man's eyes seemed keen and lively now and his thin animated face had a look of importance. Even the sharp nose with its rosy tip in some strange way signaled its possessor's uniqueness. Telyatnikov was confused.

"I'm sorry, I don't have one with me. I must have left it in my office," Sergei Sergeyevich said—he'd never in his life had business cards, but he was embarrassed.

After the usual introductions, when questioned about the nature of his work, Telyatnikov simply answered that he was a physicist. "Assistant professor in the department of general physics" was too long and somehow degrading. It sounded academically dull and common, whereas the shorter "physicist" recalled the days when the profession was still revered. In spite of the job's security and his seniority Sergei

Sergeyevich still couldn't reconcile himself to his fate and continued to dream that his talent would be recognized nationally.

"It's OK, it's no problem, my dear fellow," the professor reassured him. "Why would *you* need business cards! Who hasn't heard of Sergei Sergeyevich Telyatnikov! Right now the entire scientific world is talking about you!"

Sergei Sergeyevich was stunned when he heard this and didn't know what to say. Not that he was being asked anything, however. Taking the initiative, the professor briefly reported that he'd come to Moscow on a flight from Toronto and was heading for a congress in Montreal, where he was expected to give a paper on methods of oxidizing microleptons.

"But I kept hearing so very much about you, my friend, and—I won't deny it—I've dreamt of meeting you for a long time!" Taking the assistant professor by the arm, Shepetukha unobtrusively began leading him to a passage on the side of the institute. "And I read your article with the greatest attention, with pencil in hand!" he said, taking prim little steps while adjusting to Sergei Sergeyevich's gait. "A fascinating little piece! Simple in form, but revealing such depths to the scientist! I have to say it reminded me of one of Albert's first publications—Einstein, that is. They should give you a doctorate for that alone! Would you have any objections to defending your dissertation in my institute?"

Shepetukha looked up at Telyatnikov's face and saw the assistant professor had no objection.

"Splendid, then! As soon as I return from Canada! And don't pay any attention to this outfit—I was on the way to my country house. Let me just stop by and take a look, I thought, maybe I'll be lucky enough to meet Sergei Sergeyevich! And it turned out I was lucky!" he said, gaily laughing, and then quickly added in a serious tone, "At times I terribly want to have a talk with someone intelligent and learned! I'm tired of unstated hypotheses—it's the same as lack of intimacy with a woman!"

Sergei Sergeyevich was struck by the boldness and profundity of this comparison. "What a brilliant man! What a subtle, sophisticated mind!" he marveled to himself, afraid to miss even one word that Shepetukha uttered.

"Creative and sexual energy are of the same nature!" the professor said in the meantime. "Both sweep you away and compel you to be engaged in life. For example, you work on unified field theory, am I not correct?"

"Yes, to some degree . . ." Sergei Sergeyevich mumbled, continuing to be amazed at the State Prize winner's sagacity. "You see, I'd like to arrive at some kind of fundamental conformity to law . . ."

"I understand, oh yes, I understand what you mean!" Shepetukha said with delight. "Every scientist, but why just scientist—anyone with the slightest bit of intelligence tries to construct a unified picture of the world and find his own place in it. Though it may be that the search for one's own place, like the search for the meaning of existence, is simply Russian masochism!" The director of the coordinating center became silent and looked thoughtfully into the distance where the Kashira Highway was smogged over with car exhaust. "Maybe beauty really will save the world, you know! I have in mind the beauty of mathematical formulas! It seems to me that we scientists still don't completely understand the true importance of the elegance and symmetricality of mathematical formulations! Well, we'll come back to this—I've got a present, you might say, just made for you."

Shepetukha cast an intriguing glance at Telyatnikov.

"How confidently and sincerely he speaks!" Sergei Sergeyevich thought and from the corner of his eye observed how beneath their cover of long gray hair the professor's large ears moved in time with his words. Shepetukha's thoughts corresponded with Sergei Sergeyevich's own findings down to the smallest nuance, and this fact, together with the mysterious promise, made his head spin lightly and pleasantly. In the meantime, still being led by Shepetukha, Telyatnikov suddenly saw his reflection in the glass wall of the Dream Café, which stood right opposite the institute and tempted the souls of students who had not yet been sufficiently hardened by the sciences.

"You haven't eaten yet, Sergei Sergeyevich, have you? So let's stop in here, sit down like civilized people and talk!" Shepetukha suggested. "A business lunch! The other day I was in Paris, and there . . ."

With these words the professor pushed the glass door of the establishment and gently but insistently guided the assistant professor's weakly resisting body through the space he had made. Sergei Sergeyevich protested sincerely, even muttering something about the responsibility of the professorial and teaching staff before the broader circles of the scientific community, but he kept walking and did so not without anticipating the pleasure awaiting him. A mysterious force drew him into the bar, and he immediately found himself in half-horror, half-joy sitting on a metal chair at a round marble table. Shepetukha, who'd seated himself on the opposite side, was already whispering something to the waitress leaning toward him. Her powerful body, barely held in by her uniform's flimsy fabric, hung over him; her generous red lips smiled. The cunning professor wasted no time and while giving his order kept casting indiscreet glances into the depths revealed by the slit in her blouse. He had undergone some strange transformation and now seemed to be a natural part of the shabby restaurant-bar.

"A gifted person is gifted at everything," Telyatnikov concluded with some envy. Suddenly something inside him awoke—a Hussar-like, devil-may-care boldness. He wanted to put his arms around the beauty's plump waist and drink *Bruderschaft* then and there with a bottle of Moselle. Words about herring with a fur coat and cold chicken wafted over to him, rousing his imagination and appetite. The singularly strange thing was the fact that the professor was constantly winking and making faces, and at some point Telyatnikov suddenly felt sad and even wondered if he shouldn't leave . . . But at that moment the appetizer came—fresh moist slices of ham—and the desire to leave vanished by itself.

"And another thing, Marusechka," the irrepressible Shepetukha amused himself, "take that funeral arrangement of yours off the table, the assistant professor and I don't eat such things!"

"Oh, what naughty little children these scholars are, the things they say." Marusechka, the picture of health, giggled seductively and brushed Telyatnikov with her breasts while trying to take the dusty artificial flower from the vase.

"So . . ." said Sergei Sergeyevich, after the waitress had left the hall, swinging her hips, and he caught himself rubbing his hands out of inner elation, something he'd never before noticed himself doing.

"Let's drink to our acquaintance and to sacred science!" The professor had caught the drift of Telyatnikov's soul and poured two generous glasses of port.

"No, I can't, I have a lecture," Sergei Sergeyevich made his last attempt to refuse, understanding full well the complete futility of his insincere efforts.

"You're hurting my feelings!" The State Prize winner spread his hands, and Telyatnikov saw that Shepetukha was telling the truth. "With your experience and skill! A hundred grams of port for inspiration never hurts!"

He raised his glass, and Sergei Sergeyevich was astonished to see that his own hand was moving on its own toward the vessel standing in front of him and then he felt a heavy sweet taste of wine in his mouth. For an instant an unearthly light sadness brushed his soul with its wing, then disappeared, and in his suddenly vacant head there remained only the likeness of a thought: I haven't drunk port since I was a student. Following the professor's example, Telyatnikov emptied his glass, made a spirited snort, and wiped his moist lips with the napkin. Meanwhile Shepetukha was courtesy itself: regaling his new friend, he'd first push him the herring covered with the fur coat of beets and cream, then heap onto the cafeteria plate some stale bluish chicken, which looked like it might have been stolen from Aeroflot, their national airline. Fussing and constantly blotting the sauce spilled on the marble table, the professor became flushed and took off his padded jacket and greasy cloth cap under which there turned out to be a cement-gray bald patch, which looked like a landing strip, with scattered clumps of khaki-colored hair. To Telyatnikov's amazement, the director of the coordinating center's outer clothing was worn straight over a rather dirty striped sailor's shirt. But on the other hand Sergei Sergeyevich was momentarily uplifted by the frivolous picture tattooed on Shepetukha's cachectic forearm—beneath which was written, in the same typeface as the title of the newspaper *Pravda*, "Love Semyon—the source of knowledge!"

"Remembrances of youth!" sighed the State Prize winner, having noticed the glance from across the table. "Who of us has not sinned! Distant raids by sea and frenzied nighttime landings!" He reached for a second bottle, which had somehow made its way to the table, and leaning his head to one side, he poured the port. "To us, Sergei! I tell you, middle age has its delights too. Wisdom and brains!" The professor sniffed and spit on the floor. "And for all that it's pleasant to know you're a person who's made it."

Sergei Sergeyevich made a wry face, but Shepetukha insisted. "Come on, Serge, don't be stubborn, a little wine is good for your health! Remember our lively student drinking bouts! Whoever hasn't done his share of drinking in life is a failed scholar! To you! No, no," he cut short Telyatnikov's attempt to feign drinking, "the person being toasted must drain the cup!"

Sergei Sergeyevich winced and swallowed his wine with a suffering expression, then hastily neutralized its excessively sweet taste with the *Stolichnyi* salad. If earlier his thoughts had been confused, then after the second glass his picture of the world fell into focus and with a sixth sense he knew that the time to talk about science had arrived.

"What field are you in, as a matter of fact?" he asked, concentrating in order to hook his fork into some jelly that shook like the waitress's breasts.

"I'm into women!" The professor laughed loudly. "All right, I'm kidding, Serge! I work in cross-disciplinary research and I've been focusing increasingly on man! But it's about time for you to call me Semyon." Shepetukha's body had suddenly become covered with mossy green spots, and he began to hiccup sonorously. A distinct smell of cheap eau de cologne drifted over to Sergei Sergeyevich. "Excuse me, old man, I've been a little out of sorts since morning, but now I'm better," he explained, and took a crumpled pack of cheap cigarettes out of his jacket pocket.

"You're a biophysicist, then," Telyatnikov pursued his own line.

"Could be!" Shepetukha agreed, lighting up. "But the name doesn't matter. Science is as unified as the world! It is we ourselves with our poor imaginations who have divided everything into various chemistries, physicses, and other geographies!" For emphasis he minced the remains of the ham on the plate with the tip of his knife. "But in the larger scheme of things there is a unified nature, a unified science, a unified field!"

"He speaks eloquently, the dog," thought Sergei Sergeyevich, repeating some line from the movies that had stuck in his head. "An analytical mind. And how cleverly he's moved to unified field theory! You sense it right away—a big-shot academic. But it's odd that he goes around in a worn jacket and tattered shoes. Aha," Sergei Sergeyevich conjectured, "he's trying to shock our decadent society. Confront the philistine with his outlandishness. All the same I'd wash the sailor's shirt." For some reason Telyatnikov had reached for the cigarettes, lit up with the match Shepetukha extended, and was coughing and gasping for air. His eyes bulged and instinctively he reached for the conveniently refilled glass of port, which he drank in small gulps for a long while. In the samovar he could see the reflection of Shepetukha's face; he was leaning toward him from the other side of the table, and his lecherous and slightly intoxicated eyes and large protruding lips seemed unexpectedly close.

"Serge! Do you hear me, Serge?" the professor whispered ardently, covering Sergei Sergeyevich with a smell of onion and cheap tobacco. "That article of yours told me a lot! Hell, you're an ambitious fellow, greedy for fame! That's good! That's right! There are only thieves and losers around here. Yet you hear that this one became a member of the Academy, that one became a professor . . . While someone with a mind like yours just rots! I'm heart-stricken, Serge, I can't bear to see it!" Out of indignation Shepetukha bashed his small fist on the edge of the plate with such force that Sergei Sergeyevich found himself covered in sauce like the herring. "Mediocrity is flourishing in scholarship and so is opportunism!" the State Prize winner continued, thoughtfully removing a finely sliced onion ring from Telyatnikov's forehead.

"Thanks," the assistant professor said, and hiccuped loudly.

"Don't thank me. I haven't done anything yet! But we'll show them, just wait till I return from Honduras! Amidst the others, Serge, you're a Colossus of Rhodes!"

"Semyon, please, there's no need . . ." Telyatnikov was embarrassed. "There are some smart people even in academia. Two or three. But they stuck my article in a journal for young idiots . . ."

"That's what I'm saying—they're suppressing talent in the Russian land! But you guard your dignity, Serge!" In a burst of noble anger Shepetukha half rose and grabbed the bottle as if it contained some inflammatory mixture and he was about to throw it at the presidium of the High Academic Council. "The most important thing in scholarship is not to diminish your own accomplishments," continued the professor, who'd calmed down a bit by now. "Members of the Academy are elected exclusively depending on the number of talented scholars destroyed . . ."

Swaying and biting the tip of his tongue in his zeal, the State Prize winner unsteadily poured out the rest of the port and looked with deep feeling into Telyatnikov's eyes. "I'll become a snake. There's no freedom in sight, but I'll help you, Serge!"

He beckoned the assistant professor with his finger. Unhappy to part with the back of his chair, Telyatnikov collapsed forward, bumping his chest against the marble of the small table. The center director's insipid red-rimmed eyes looked straight at him.

"I'm drunk as a shoemaker," Telyatnikov said to himself, but he didn't feel any embarrassment or remorse, only a pleasant lightness and a freedom hitherto unknown.

"I've made a great discovery!" Shepetukha uttered in the whisper of a theatrical villain, and took furtive glances around the room. "A great one! And I'm giving it to you!"

"No need to do that." Telyatnikov wagged his finger in front of Shepetukha's nose. "In this life I've done everything on my own."

This pleased Sergei Sergeyevich, and he decided to repeat the exercise with his own finger and someone else's nose, but this time it went badly and he almost lost his balance on the chair, which had skirted somewhere to the side. Nonetheless Telyatnikov kept talking. "You're a swine, Semyon, if you dare propose such a thing to me."

These mental and physical efforts caused sweat to appear on Sergei Sergeyevich's forehead, and he wiped it off together with the remaining traces of herring sauce.

"Shhh! Don't make a fuss!" the professor interrupted, scolding the assistant professor, who had gone too far. "First of all, everyone steals, and so it's not plagiarism these days but a modus vivendi! Second, every discovery is related to revelation and more often than not doesn't come to the person who's worked for it! You've labored your whole life, perhaps, but I partook of a glass one night and in a state of drunkenness I had a dream! It was like taking a card from the extra pile—it went to the wrong person! But after I read your article I immediately understood that the celestial office had made a mistake—I was sent your dream! You understand?"

"I understand." Telyatnikov shook his head. "Tell me!"

"Do you remember Maxwell's equations?" Shepetukha asked with a professorial squint in a taunting voice.

"Ask me," the assistant professor urged, starting like a cavalry horse at the sound of the horn. "It's my trick exam question, students fail by the dozens on its account. Do you want it in the differential form?"

"Go ahead!" Shepetukha agreed graciously, pushing Telyatnikov the ruled slip containing the bill and sarcastically observing how he diligently made flourishes of some sort on it. "I'm self-taught, you know," Shepetukha continued, and unexpectedly a complaint against fate and a barely concealed envy were in his voice. "I didn't graduate from any fancy academies, did everything on my own. Drove stuff into my head like a woodpecker, and came out a professor!"

"Finished!" Sergei Sergeyevich pushed the scribbled-upon paper with the bill away from himself. "The rotor of the electric field strength vector," he began repeating like a schoolboy, "is equal to the partial time derivative . . ."

"Enough!" Shepetukha interrupted in an examiner's tone of voice. "But why is that derivative of yours only partial? Are you saving something for yourself? Selling mathematics to the black-market dealers? Well, don't be afraid of me, I won't rat on you, but be a little more careful with others, Serge, keep your tongue in check! It's a bad time, you'll be locked up before you know it! And get a term . . ."

The professor looked at Telyatnikov, who listened to him with his mouth wide open, and then started scratching the sunken chest beneath his striped shirt.

"Oh, all right, you don't know anything about life, and I can't explain it to you on my fingers! Better listen here! You remember I carried on about all kinds of symmetries there? Well, in those scribblings of yours"—Shepetukha pointed to the bill—"there just aren't enough of the symmetries!"

Telyatnikov nodded, demonstrating comprehension. Most likely he had lost the divine gift of speech by this time. A visceral anguish seized Sergei Sergeyevich. He suddenly saw himself from the outside, collapsed over the table and foolishly drunk at the height of a bright and cheerful May day. People rarely get pleasure from seeing themselves from the outside, and so, as it was especially hard for him to move, the poor man simply had to relax and participate in the delights of this transitory life.

"Sem, oh, Sem, give me a little more to freshen my mind," Sergei Sergeyevich suddenly proposed, and the ability to form words into sentences made him speechless. They drank without toasts, quickly, businesslike, and then the professor got down to explaining.

"Right here, between these two little hooks"—he poked one of the equations with his finger—"we have to put in dependence on time! That will be both more beautiful and in general . . ."

The professor didn't elucidate what he had in mind for the "in general," but wiped his greasy fingers on the sheet of paper with the bill and, peeping like a student at notes he'd just taken from his pocket, he drew several hieroglyphs on the bill.

"That's im-impossible . . ." For a brief moment the drunken haze in Telyatnikov's head dispersed. With a child's amazed eyes Sergei Sergeyevich looked back and forth between Shepetukha and the formula he'd been given, and a cry of delight burst from his chest.

"It is possible!" Shepetukha assured with authority. "Absolutely possible!"

"But that means that . . . the past depends on the future."

"Would I talk mumbo-jumbo to you?" Mercy replaced the State Prize winner's anger. "You see that little bridge there"—he pointed to the equals sign—"from left to right you go to the future, and from right to left into the past. Everything in this world is relative, old man! Symmetry, Serge, is a fu . . . is a thing of terrible force!"

"Excuse me." The assistant professor suddenly became indignant. "But this contradicts the basic laws of nature!"

"Oh, Sergei"—Shepetukha let out a heavy sigh—"you're still young and inexperienced! Laws are written by people! I'm personally naming this formula Shepetukha's double loop: one loop for catching the past, and the other to catch the future!"

"But if the equation is true, it completely changes our conception of the world!"

"Don't search for truth in the world, but I'll give you the formula!" With a regal gesture the director of the coordinating center threw the crumpled bill over to the other end of the table.

Furtively looking round, Telyatnikov gathered the paper ball into his fist and shoved it quickly into his jacket pocket. His hands were trembling, perspiration appeared on his forehead and all over his body.

"Semyon," he said, full of emotion, and tears of gratitude appeared in his eyes. "Can I kiss you?"

But the Shepetukha sitting in front of him for some reason had suddenly lost all interest in his drinking companion. The striped sailor shirt covering his body no longer seemed to be a striped shirt, but looked something like gray hide buried beneath thin hair, and the State Prize winner's expression was conventionally dull. All of a sudden he yawned with wide-open jaws and offhandedly announced, "Let's finish the bottle and then I'm off!"

Sergei Sergeyevich wanted to say that he'd never let his new friend leave, they'd go to his home now and talk about sacred science, but instead the assistant professor's hand instinctively took hold of the glass and brought it to his mouth, which was already wide open. With furrowed brow and full of suffering, into the waiting aperture he poured the thick, sickly sweet liquid, made heady by the southern Azerbaijan sun. It didn't all go down at once, but remained stuck in his throat. Only a little later, when something else in there had moved down, was it all flushed into his stomach, where lying in wait was the herring in its own juice, the unlucky mutilated son of a chicken, and still something else, whose name Telyatnikov couldn't remember, but which now threw itself out in desperate waves.

"Too bad," Sergei Sergeyevich said, and made an effort to record this likeness of a thought in his failing consciousness. "It's too bad that so many years went by senselessly without port . . ."

At another time he'd have been amazed by a conclusion like this that had turned up who knows how in his poor head, which donged like a copper bell, but this time he wasn't able to be amazed—he'd reached his edge.

"Spring! The sun is shining," said Telyatnikov, hiccuping loud enough for the whole bar to hear. "Sem, why am I so sad? Is it true that much knowledge engenders great sorrow? I know what I'll do—I'll go right now and take my life to the dry cleaners!"

But no one was listening to Sergei Sergeyevich. From some corner the waitress was relentlessly moving toward him, swinging her fantastic hips like the train in the Lumière brothers' film. In her hand she held a gigantic bill, on which instead of abacus balls the first time derivatives were merrily rolling from side to side. Sergei Sergeyevich pondered if it was possible to encompass Marusechka's breasts with an integral, though only a double one. The waitress smiled, though quite unhappily by now. Her other hand was being covered by kisses from the center director, who trembled slightly and made irreverent winks. From time to time he interrupted what he was doing and bleated, pointing to Telyatnikov with his thin crooked finger and tittering in a vile way.

"He's like all the rest—keeps on asking for another bottle! But when it's time to pay he'll head for the hills! I know these scholars—high-and-mighty, but not a penny in their pockets. The bums!"

"I'll pay for everything." Sergei Sergeyevich proudly straightened up in his chair and made a broad sweep with his hand, but at this moment something happened in Descartes's three-dimensional world—and without any warning the force of gravity changed the direction of his movement. Unprepared for this base trick, Telyatnikov, like any other normal man in his position, spun onto the floor and immediately began to sail like an ocean liner into a foggy distance the color of undigested port wine. Smiling blissfully, he peacefully curled up like a round loaf of braided bread and soundlessly withdrew into the world of dreams. The last thing Sergei Sergeyevich saw before the curtain was lowered was the formula for Shepetukha's double loop, written in gold and black—of paramount importance and still unknown to anyone.

2

No one knows and now no one will ever know what happened to Sergei Sergeyevich Telyatnikov's body during those several hours his wife was making the rounds of shops. When she returned home, she found her lawful spouse lying at the door of his own apartment. The body was breathing, but the immortal soul, which presented itself in the form of consciousness in this case, was clearly absent. Despite his average height and good nourishment the assistant professor was positioned entirely on a small rug reserved at other times for wiping the feet. Smiling blissfully, he lay in the pose of an infant who hasn't yet managed to leave his mother's womb. Thus, during long winter nights, do huskies sleep and dream of icy fish, their leathery noses covered with their furry tails. Refusing point-blank to abandon his breeding ground voluntarily, Sergei Sergeyevich passively resisted the transporting of his body by portage, but then quieted down on the couch inside. At some point, his smart gray suit of some worth was picked up by two fingers and thrown, as one piece, down the garbage chute. Having fulfilled her wifely duty in this odd way, Anna sadly sat down next to the phone and started calling her best friend. Before half an hour had passed the short signals became long and Anna heard the familiar voice in the receiver.

"Mashka," Anna said, and started to cry, "come over here! Tell the taxi to wait so you can take me to the nuthouse."

Knowing her friend's stoical character, Maria Nikolayevna was seriously alarmed by what she'd heard, and after giving her husband orders on how to manage the household chores, she rushed through the city to the Telyatnikovs'. She began clearing up the matter at the door.

"What is it, did you mess up your program again? Were you called in to the boss? Oh, just spit on them, Anka—spit on them all and get out of that madhouse! Just think, the television center . . . You're young, beautiful, energetic—I'll find you some work you'll love.

Maria Nikolayevna pulled off her raincoat and stuck her feet in the house slippers provided for guests. Anna was silent. Without saying a word, she took Mashka by the arm and led her into the room. The expression on the face of the man who'd passed out and the strong smell of alcohol left no doubt about what had happened to the master of the house. The friends stood in sorrowful silence over the fallen hero's body, then went off to the kitchen to drink coffee and discuss a plan of action.

"Stinking drunk," Anna certified, as if she couldn't rely on Maria Nikolayevna to have her own impression.

"That's it?" The guest shrugged her large shoulders. She lit up a cigarette and leaned her back against the carved sideboard that Anna's aunt had left her, then crossed her legs and began shock therapy. "I don't quite understand you, Anna. First you complain about Sergei, that he's not like other men and is up to his ears in work, and now when he's started to act like a regular guy you're still dissatisfied. There's no pleasing you, my dear!"

"He didn't have to drink himself senseless," Anna objected, but Mashka immediately interrupted.

"I read that doctors recommend getting drunk once a month. It removes nervous tension and gives you a new perspective on life. In this country, after all, there's nothing more natural and organic than getting plastered! Our government is well aware of this, by the way. Every presidential decree, every resolution proceeds from the fact that people are certain to squander everything that hasn't been stolen on liquor."

"Don't quote me international statistics, please," Anna said. She had sat down at the kitchen table, and was looking at her friend meaningfully. "I haven't told you anything yet. This binge of Sergei's is by no means the beginning—it's most likely the conclusion—of our drama. And, you know something, I can understand him . . ."

With this Anna began her story about the events that had rained down on their heads during the last weeks. When Telyatnikov burst into the kitchen some three hours later with a feverish glow in his eyes, she was still in the middle of her tale.

The women shuddered at the sight of him—Sergei Sergeyevich was a fright! Tousled vestiges of his once luxuriant head of hair tossed in all directions, his broad chest heaved impetuously, barely covered by his bathrobe, beneath which his hairy legs stuck out in touching light blue socks. Spiritual torment had distorted Sergei Sergeyevich's face, the horror expressed on it had battled and conquered the timid remains of hope.

"Where is . . . ?" Telyatnikov said in a voice fraught with doom, throwing the women a look that froze the blood in their veins. So might the wild Moor have looked at Desdemona, had he been a little more temperamental.

"Where is who?" mouthed Anna soundlessly.

Maria Nikolayevna in the meantime quietly rose from her stool and attempted to take a strategic position between the spouses. She'd kept an eye on the cutting board hanging on the wall and now was considering the most clever way of reaching it. At the critical moment her voice did not tremble.

"Seryozha." She spoke in the tone spies use in the movies in times of mortal danger. "No one's here and no one's been here. I swear to you . . ."

Sergei Sergeyevich wasn't listening. He stepped forward, staggered, and clutched his heart with his hand.

"My suit! My gray suit!" His lips were white.

"Oh, Lord." Anna let out a sigh. "How you frightened me! Just lie down and don't think about it, we'll buy you a new one."

"Where is it?" Sergei Sergeyevich straightened up. His eyes gleamed coldly.

"I . . . it . . . try to understand." Anna began to stammer. "It was so . . . dirty that I put it down the garbage chute . . ."

"You idiot!" Telyatnikov began to yell with all his might, and the chandelier on the ceiling started to sway.

Maria Nikolayevna saw that it was time for her entrance. Rage and anguish on behalf of insulted and injured women of all ages and nations boiled up in her breast. She slowly advanced on Sergei Sergeyevich, whom she surpassed in size. The demonstration of force proved to be unnecessary, however: a moment later Telyatnikov was running down the stairs like a boy, taking two or three steps at a time. Fearing the worst, the women followed him as fast as they could, but only caught up to him in the basement. In a state of frenzy the assistant professor was digging into a pile of garbage. In less than a minute with a cry of victory he pulled out what had once been his good gray jacket. Holding his breath, his neck twitching nervously, Sergei Sergeyevich thrust his hand into the pocket with the cautiousness of a sapper and pulled into the light a crumpled ball of greasy paper and crushed rectangular white card with a gold border. Holding them in his open palm, he turned to the women and began to sob soundlessly. Big slow tears, like those of toddlers, rolled from his eyes; Telyatnikov was both laughing and crying. They returned in the elevator. Back in the kitchen, Sergei Sergeyevich clumsily sank onto a stool, wiped his wet face with his free hand, and wistfully asked Anna to please get him a pencil and some paper.

Trying hard to keep himself in a vertical position, Sergei Sergeyevich unfolded the paper with the bill on it as neatly as he could, and after smoothing it out lovingly with his palm, he painstakingly began to copy the equation onto a fresh piece of paper. He did this so selflessly it seemed the external world had no significance for him at this moment. When he'd finished, Telyatnikov folded the paper several times, put it in a drawer in the sideboard, and carefully lowered the crunched original into the deep pocket in his robe. Sergei Sergeyevich's face bore an expression of deep satisfaction. Apparently feeling the need to explain his behavior at least in part, Telyatnikov looked at the stern and silent women graciously, and articulately pronounced, "My best friend Semyon is the most generous of souls."

Wincing from his own alcoholic breath, Sergei Sergeyevich opened his left hand, where lay the crushed rectangular card with the golden border.

"Those with whom you drink," noted Maria Nikolayevna patronizingly as she took the business card from the master's shaking hand, "are called drinking companions, and if you're not lucky, then they're fellow inmates as well."

"My best friend Semyon is a great scientist, his field is mankind!" There was pride in Telyatnikov's voice.

"That's not hard to figure out." Maria Nikolayevna took the little card over to the light and read, "Semyon Shepetukha—prosector. You were probably guzzling alcohol somewhere in a columbarium. Oh, Sergei, you're taking a risk—your friend in insobriety will freeze you instead of the deceased . . ."

"We were drinking port," Telyatnikov corrected her. "From sunny Az . . . Azr . . . in short, from Georgia."

Sergei Sergeyevich stood up, indicating that the audience was over, and he left the kitchen, steadying himself against the wall. He stopped in the doorway and turned around.

"Anya!" Telyatnikov spoke sincerely. "It was necessary for science!"

"OK, go to sleep, you drunk." Mashka chased him out. "You see, it's nothing special," she continued, turning back to Anna. "They weren't drinking with any profligate, but some person who can afford to hand out business cards to his drinking companions."

"You don't have to pacify me." Anna wasn't going to listen to her friend. "You can see for yourself he's had a nervous breakdown. Running off to the garbage dump to look for some kind of formula!"

"You're a fine one yourself! To go and throw out a perfectly good suit when it could have just been cleaned. And besides it's not worth taking everything so to heart, be more mindful. In general men should be treated with condescending sorrow. Under no circumstances should you pity them or sympathize, because that implies that they have emotions. It's enough that we fabricate an inner world and feelings for them, but then to believe in our own fabrication is really too much. You should feel that you're the director of life and he's just an actor in your play. I tell you, smart women like us can't really be happy. If a man's beneath you intellectually, then life becomes a mockery, a game of giveaway. You're supposed to go into raptures whenever he utters some commonplace banality or laugh at his stupid jokes. If the guy's your equal, then he's most likely an inveterate egoist, and, if not, then he's a simple person for sure—who bangs his tools at night or, God forbid, is preparing to do mankind a great favor by inventing something. And please note that I'm only speaking about the ones who can be called respectable with some reservations."

"What if there's love?"

"Love?" Maria Nikolayevna shrugged her shoulders. "A forgotten word from the school curriculum. Since nature made all women and all men identical, she clearly didn't consider a phenomenon like love. Anna, I'm afraid it's all only a ruse people resort to while trying to escape the drab monotony of life. Although on the other hand . . ." There was a dreamy look on Maria's face.

"Wait," Anna broke in. "I still haven't told you everything—that incident in the cemetery at the time of the funeral had a sequel!"

"Ah, you kept quiet about it . . ." Maria sighed. "And you still consider yourself my best friend!"

"Well, I wasn't able to tell you," Anna repented. "Try to understand, it was unreal! Not long ago I was coming home from work, it was already late and dark. I walked under the arch and saw two men standing there. If I'd noticed them earlier, then, naturally, I wouldn't have gone, but I thought it was too late to turn back. I kept walking. My heart was beating like a sheep's tail and my eyes were blinded by fear. I thought I just have to get through to the courtyard where there's a light; if I shout from there someone will hear me . . . But then I saw that one of them, the shorter one, had detached himself from the wall and was coming at me. He grabbed my purse and then slowly, lazily even, shook all my stuff onto the pavement. 'What's your hurry, lady? You've got nowhere to hurry to,' he says. Can you imagine that? My heart sank, of course, and even if I'd wanted I couldn't have shouted—I couldn't breathe. The second guy, who was a little taller and younger, was coming up behind me . . . Well, this is it, Anka, I thought—your last hour! But just then I saw a man suddenly come from the courtyard. Something about him seemed strange to me; only later did I understand it was his clothes. Just think, in our dirt, where you have to make your way between piles of garbage, out comes someone in a dark suit with a bow tie, wearing a hat and carrying a cane. What struck me most were his patent-leather shoes, just perfect for a ball. I noted all of this later—at the moment I wasn't up to it. He was walking with his hands in his pockets; only his stiff shirt cuffs and dickey shone in the light. The gangsters noticed him too and sidled away from me. The man approached and said very politely, 'I hope I'm not disturbing you.' And he smiled.

"The shorter bandit strode over to him and I saw his hand slip into his coat pocket.

" 'Get out of here, twit, and you won't get hurt!'

" 'I'm afraid, I'm very afraid . . .' the man began, but the bandit interrupted, 'We know you're afraid, so beat it!'

" 'It's a pity, Bunhead, you didn't let me finish,' the man smiled, but in a peculiar way somehow, with just his lips. 'I *wanted* to say, I'm afraid you're not in luck this time.'

"At these words the bandit shuddered and I saw that he really looked like a bun.

" 'All right, bastard, say your cop prayers to your Holy Mama!' Bunhead pulled a knife from his pocket and lunged at the man. What happened next I don't know, just that Bunhead flew toward the wall and banged into it with enough force to shake the building."

"So what happened then?" Mashka took a deep breath, and out of excitement kept breaking matches while trying to light up. She leaned forward, hanging on to every word.

"Nothing. He walked me to the entrance . . ."

"And what about the second gangster?" Disappointed, Maria Nikolayevna leaned back against the sideboard. "Did he really leave?"

"Actually I didn't tell you the most interesting thing! Remember the tall one coming up behind me? I quickly turned around and in one motion kicked him in the balls with the toe of my boot. He bent over and I hit him again—this time on the neck with the edge of my hand."

"You? You hit him?" Maria brought the cigarette to her lips, but forgot to inhale. "But you faint at the sight of a mouse!"

"Well, he didn't look anything like a mouse." Anna put on a new pot of coffee. "So he ended up taking a rest on the pavement next to Bunhead."

Maria Nikolayevna gave her friend a perplexed look.

"And what about the man?"

"He helped pick up things and put them back in my purse, and when he stood up he looked at me very thoughtfully and said, 'May I give you some professional advice? All in all, things turned out well and they will in the future too, but please don't wear such narrow skirts—they restrain movement, and when you kick someone lean forward with your hip first and only then extend your leg. It's less dangerous and also more elegant.' "

"Hmmm . . ." Maria Nikolayevna reflected uncertainly. "And what about him, what's he like—good-looking?"

"I wouldn't say he's the picture of beauty," Anna began thoughtfully, "narrow, but intense eyes, his face either suntanned or dark, and very calm. What else? Taller than average, and pretty gray already . . . And, you know, he walked me to the entrance, took off his hat, and kissed my hand. Then he asked . . ."

"To see you again?" Mashka sighed.

"Not quite. He asked me to move that still life somewhere"—Anna pointed to the wall—"because its tastelessness annoys him."

Maria Nikolayevna raised her head and looked at the picture carefully. A clay plate with two inexplicably blue pears painted in rough strokes on the canvas.

"You know," she said with the air of an expert, "maybe he's right! There is something annoying about the pears, something at variance with ideal harmony."

"What do pears and harmony have to do with it?" Anna said, suddenly upset. "How did he *know* about the still life? Incidentally, since that very evening the picture has been sliding off the wall regularly. I even put a cushion against the baseboard . . ."

Anna didn't manage to finish before the still life did a somersault, fell over the cushion, and crashed onto the floor. The clay plate on the canvas shattered into pieces, and the strangely colored pears turned into a jellied mush and dropped onto the linoleum. Maria Nikolayevna watched her friend silently, her cigarette trembling in her hand. Anna just shrugged her shoulders and went for the broom and dustpan. After removing the remains of the still life, she collapsed onto the stool and said, as if establishing a dry scientific fact, "Sergei and I also started to have problems with . . . well, in short, with sex."

"Well, that happens," Mashka calmed her friend, "people aren't machines."

"No, that's not it at all! You're going to laugh, of course, but just at the moment in question either we start to hiccup in synch or, say, one of the bed's legs will break. One time Sergei suddenly started to sing, 'Arise, ye prisoners of starvation.' Isn't that funny? It's funny. But that night he just sang the 'Internationale' twenty-two times at the top of his voice, not stopping for a minute! Imagine what our neighbors thought about us? I know that amuses you. At first we laughed too . . ."

Maria Nikolayevna was quiet for a while and then said, "So it seems he follows you all the time."

Anna sighed and looked at her friend.

"You don't understand anything, Mashka, even though you have a Ph.D. It's not just that he follows me, he loves me! Sometimes when I enter the apartment I feel streams of tenderness embracing me."

"I don't know if he's following you or he loves you, but if you called me here to talk about streams of tenderness I'm leaving. I have to cook and do the wash—and in general the apartment's such a mess the devil would break a leg there."

"Mashka, dear Mashka!" Anna went over and hugged Maria Nikolayevna. "Don't be angry at me. Who could I tell everything to if not you? I really don't know what to do. There've been times when I've gone into the bedroom and found a bouquet of flowers."

"Well, flowers aren't any proof," noted Mashka, still being intentionally querulous. "Even Sergei can bring flowers. Men have these relapses of falling in love—it's not quite senility but something like it."

"Oh, Mashka, why are you such a cynical bitch?" Anna leaned over and kissed Maria Nikolayevna. "It's all the fault of your dissertation—those finicky Cynics of yours with their rude tricks and jokes! You could have given me better advice about what to do. If things go on this way Sergei and I will end up in the nuthouse for sure."

"Listen, have you been run-down lately or maybe you've been reading too much of something?" Maria Nikolayevna searched her friend's face. "There are times when a person loses contact with the world around and begins living in a fantasy world . . ."

"Are you asking if I've cracked up? Then just say it and don't go beating about the bush—'loses contact with the world,' 'fantasy world,' " Anna mimicked.

"No, answer me, Anna. It could be very important."

Anna looked at her friend and shrugged her shoulders. Something in Mashka's face convinced her that she really was waiting for an answer.

"No, nothing like that, unless, of course, you take into account the usual outbursts of hysteria at work. As for reading, I haven't been reading anything of the sort and I haven't joined the Hare Krishnas. Although, I confess to having had dreams in color since childhood, so you're fully entitled to suspect me of latent schizophrenia."

Maria Nikolayevna hesitated. Her smooth forehead, like that of a Greek goddess, knit with a surge of doubt. "OK," she finally decided. "Make some more coffee, I'll spend the night. But everything that I'm going to tell you is strictly confidential. You're my dearest friend, Anna, and I haven't been able to be open even with you. I was afraid . . . you'd think I was mad." Maria Nikolayevna started to smoke, and, while musing, she made circles around the edge of the crystal ashtray with the tip of her cigarette. "Sometimes I have doubts that it happened—but in my heart, with some inner knowledge, I know that it did!"

She was silent as she watched Anna put on a new pot of Turkish coffee.

"I've thought about this a lot recently and I've come to the conclusion that everything I experienced has happened with others too—but either they don't recognize the reality of what's taken place or, like me, they're afraid to talk about it. In any case, one can establish a direct correlation between similar situations and a person's psycho-energetic state and intense inner life."

"Listen, Mashka," Anna interrupted, "you've hardly begun and I'm already tired from your scientific talk. Can't you be a little more simple and human?"

"All right, what could I expect from you," Maria Nikolayevna agreed. "It happened a month and a half before my dissertation defense. You and Sergei were vacationing in the south, I had sent my family to the country and I was working all night long. There was very little time left, my supervisor was hurrying me, and I sincerely believed that my three years of work on the topic had been a wild-goose chase. I had nothing new to say about the Cynics' philosophy and no matter how hard I'd tried to find my own approach, I could only rehash old ideas. It felt like I'd read and reread everything I'd written thousands of times and it was absolutely boring."

"Then why did you choose such an exotic topic?" Anna took the coffee off the stove and got clean cups from the sideboard.

"It's not exotic at all. I've been interested in Diogenes of Sinope since my undergraduate days. We're overcrowded with people who denounce human vices, but only a handful live according to the truth they preach. I wanted to understand such a person, to find out the reasons for a behavior that respectable society found shocking. But my efforts were going nowhere, my dissertation was a just a collection of generalities. At some point I decided to give up the defense—I felt so depressed and empty.

"I remember it like yesterday—a sultry August evening. Red heat had hung over the city since early morning. And the wind—a strong southern wind—was driving me crazy, forcing a numbing stuffiness onto the empty streets. Imagine, you could literally feel the nervous strain in the air physically; it seemed just a little more and the world would split open and end in myriads of little lightning flashes. The air cried for rain, for a tropical storm, and the anticipation alone was enough to drive you mad. My nerves were on edge, my fruitless quest had exhausted my mind. The worthless dissertation I'd concocted lay before me on the desk, and I was ready to tear it into shreds. I even got up from the desk with this intention, and looked out the open window as I passed by. The exhausting endless day was finally dying, and suddenly I knew that I was spiraling into sleep. The only thing I could do was stumble over to the couch and sink into it. The next moment I was asleep . . . But, no, it wasn't a dream!" Maria Nikolayevna put out her cigarette, and brought the steaming cup of coffee closer. "At first I thought I had died," she went on, taking sugar with her spoon. "My head was about to touch the pillow, and I felt such an amazing lightness in my entire body, it seemed I could fly. And indeed, I did rise to the ceiling, smoothly, almost imperceptibly, while at the same time I saw myself lying there deeply oblivious. I felt no fear at all or no sorrow for myself; on the whole I didn't have any emotion for that woman on the couch. I was overcome with joy.

"The walls of the room ceased to exist; I was flying, enjoying a sense of freedom, and I didn't even notice that a new sort of world was starting to surround me. It became solid and palpable, and all of a sudden I saw that I was walking along the shore of a quiet, azure sea. My feet wallowed in the damp sand, licked by lazy waves. The strip of virgin beach was wonderfully wide, and beyond it, replicating the curves of the bank, stood pine trees on a small rise, bright red in the sunset. The smell of the sea mixed with the smell of needles in the warm air, awakening an intense and avid desire to breathe and to live. Marvelous pebbles polished by the ages sparkled in the clear emerald water, and a small crab ran sideways in front of me, as if guiding my way. About a hundred meters away I saw a hull that had been tossed up onto the bank, part of a ship that had settled in the sand. Its steep wooden boards recalled the ribs of some prehistoric animal that had collapsed on its way to the sea. I was completely alone beneath the endlessly deep sky, already saturated with the thick colors of evening. In the distance seagulls squawked, waves splashed softly onto the shore, and in some marvelous way these sounds strengthened the feeling of calm enveloping me. I accepted the harmony of the surrounding world with my whole being and I knew that I must live in it very simply and belong to it with each moment of life.

"I'd barely walked past the remains of the ship, however, when I saw a man sitting on the sand looking out at the immense sea. He was thin, and dark from the sun, his thick beard had patches of silver, and long curly hair fell to his shoulders. When he noticed me, the man turned and started to look at me the same way he had looked at the sea. I sank to my ankles in the warm sand and dropped to my knees. The thin light tunic I wore didn't keep the warm breeze from caressing my body. The man continued to watch me in silence. It was surprising to see bright blue eyes on a face darkened by the sun. His eyes enjoyed an inner life of their own. Finally, he smiled and said simply, as if we had parted only the day before, 'I'm glad that you came. I was waiting for you. Did you notice how calm the sea is today?'

"I didn't answer. My silence was completely natural. The waves behind my back rustled with sand and the smell of the sea was like the smell of time. I felt I was free.

" 'I am Diogenes of Sinope,' the man continued, still smiling. 'People who follow Plato call me a dog, because they're not as honest and free as I am. I don't pity them. Happiness consists of being full of joy all the time and never grieving, but they don't understand this. They tell a lot of indecent stories about me and most of them are the dirty truth. You can leave if you want—I'll understand.'

"I didn't move. I thought I caught a glimpse of gratitude in his clear blue eyes.

" 'Maybe it is nasty, but how do you tell a beast that he's a beast—you can only show him the beast in the mirror. I am that mirror, and they are furious—they want to destroy me. Naked truth is a repulsive thing, like a naked old woman. But it's not my fault that corruption loves power and all power is corrupt.'

" 'Is that what you think?' I sat next to him on the sand. We both watched the sea.

" 'Axioms don't require proof. Power is corrupt, if only because it attracts those without talent who don't know any other way to ascend. The philosopher and the poet avoid it, they pave a path through the work of their own soul. Whoever aspires to power acknowledges it as something higher than himself. As the son of a money changer, I've reappraised values my whole life and thrown aside whatever is false . . .'

" 'And that scar?' I reached out my arm and traced my finger along his thin cheek.

" 'Oh, that's nothing . . . One time in the market square I yelled: "People!" The masses came running. I chased them off with a staff, saying "I called for people, not scoundrels!" When the son of a concubine began throwing stones at the crowd I stopped him: "Be careful you don't hit your father!" But for the most part scars are internal.'

" 'Aren't you afraid to live? There's so much grief and misfortune in the world.'

"This is exactly what he said, while keeping his eyes fixed on the horizon as it vanished into the mist of the sea:

" 'When you anticipate misfortunes they are always more terrible than the grief that comes when they actually appear. The fear is so great that the weak often rush out to meet what they are afraid of. Thus, men who are caught in a storm don't wait until the ship goes down—they take their own lives. I'm not afraid to live.'

" 'Tell me—are you free?'

"Diogenes paused, as if the question had caught him napping. The sun's scorching red disk touched the edge of the sea. The philosopher smiled at his thoughts.

" 'Yes, I'm free. There are no impediments for me on earth.'

"He stood up, threw a short cloak over his shoulders, and picked up the staff that was still lying there.

" 'Will you come with me?'

"Imagine, Anka, a completely serene stone face and fathomless dark blue eyes focused on me. And in them, in the form of a silent question, was hope. No, not exactly hope—it was a supplication!"

"And did you go?" Anna fastened her eyes on her friend's face.

"Of course! As your drunken husband would say, it was necessary for science!"

"And?"

Maria Nikolayevna smiled mysteriously.

"You know, my dear, a barrel's edges are curved and through the slits between the timbers you can see the bright southern stars clearly," she said, arranging her hair with a nimble movement of her hand. "As I left in the morning I asked him the same question—are you free, Diogenes?

"The sun, cleansed by the sea, invoked the day's joy. Diogenes remained quiet for a long time before answering.

" 'A man can be free if he doesn't know what love is,' he said at last. 'But then he's not a man.'

"And, you know what?" Maria Nikolayevna finished her now cold coffee and lit another cigarette. "He cried at night. He didn't complain—his pride wouldn't allow it—but I understood: an ordinary decent guy, whom life had driven into a corner, who found it painful to see the nastiness going on everywhere . . ." She gave a deep sigh and ground the cigarette she'd just lit into the ashtray. "I don't want to smoke! It turned out that I was away no more than fifteen minutes. I spent the whole night rewriting my work, which, in fact, almost got it rejected at the defense. The defense chairman stated that to an *astonishing* degree the dissertation bore the mark of personal experience rather than being a considered and sober analysis of the problem raised. At first I wanted to explain everything to the men of learning, but I changed my mind—in light of their advanced age they wouldn't have approved of my method of gathering information . . ."

Maria Nikolayevna looked up at her friend and smiled sadly.

"Do you know what I'm thinking about? Here in Russia there's simply no one to deal with all the people who are cowed into a corner—like Diogenes, tired of the glut of injustices. We're silly girls, Anka. Since we've had to act like men, we have a false idea of our own importance, but life is a simple thing."

Anna nodded in agreement, her eyes became misty, there was regret in her voice. "No, Mashka, I fear that's not my case—it's not my fate to fly . . ."

They sat facing each other for a long time that night, and a strange indeterminate smile wandered over their faces and quivered on their parted lips.

3

When evening descended onto the earth, a cosmic cold oozed from a fissure in the astral plane and a starry wind, flying from the depths of the universe, raged and howled like a blizzard in the chimney of a hut lost in the vast expanses of Russia. At times like these, sitting with a book in hand in a deep comfortable armchair, one can think well. In the semi-darkness the green light from the table lamp illuminated a desk piled with papers, the gleaming gold spines of folios, and part of a wall with an original El Greco. Somewhere in the depth of the studio there was an easel Lukary couldn't see, and sketches lay scattered in disarray. The beloved smell of oil paints blended with the smell of good English tobacco and the soft music drifting by carried you into other worlds and spaces.

Through the thickness of a thousand years clouded by the ripples of war, Lukary peered into the beginnings of human history, trying with all his senses to feel the course of time in those distant ages. Something very important had been lost since then—human life had lost its meaning, the readiness to accept the world as it is. In those days there was still hope that as it traveled the path to manhood young humanity would not become embittered and lose the spirituality it had been given. In the depths of hoary antiquity the path to the light for all of the living seemed shorter and more direct. But Lukary peered in vain at the reflections of fires extinguished long ago. Proud Aryans, dark-haired Sumerians, happy inhabitants of the rich land of Mesopotamia were silent as they dissolved into eternal darkness; they hid their knowing eyes, and only mysterious Egypt, a colossus wrapped in layers of the past, wore a trace of a smile . . . A secret—it possessed the secret! Its keeper, the legendary sphinx of Giza, looked impassively into space and in its head a procession of the absurdities of human history was formed into a harmonious picture of the world. Somewhere, in the foggy distance, beyond endless sands and boundless seas, the sphinx saw the great answer to the riddle of existence, which stands above life and death because it is both life and death, and it saw many other things that remain for man to know and accept. The sphinx of Giza and the stoical priests of Hermes-Thoth possessed the secret. Shrouded in veils of mystery, concealed in tales, distorted by copyists hundreds of times, the secret lived on through man's hope of touching upon the highest knowledge and finding a way to ascend to the highest truth. The path for all men is the same, but each must make the ascent by himself . . . Lukary smiled and put aside the book. The path of enlightenment is long and agonizing, and it's extremely difficult to drag oneself out of the quagmire of vain desires and trifiling passions. But there is no other way. While you are alive your soul must work: the great secret of existence can only be read in yourself . . .

Lukary rose from his chair and went to the shelves filled with books. Behind the closed doors of a small cabinet lay the most valuable documents in his collection. They had been taken from libraries and archives all over the world, and they warmed his soul; the prospect of touching the real evidence of human history made him happy. He opened the doors and blinked upon seeing the incalculable wealth displayed before him. Papyruses and scrolls lay in neat rows on the shelves, and as he looked at them Lukary was willing to swear that time has a smell. Infinitely changeable and always new, it imparted an agonizing, sweet scent, like memories of a woman he once loved. The smell of time excited him and awoke his imagination. The tablets of the Sumerians smelled of damp Mesopotamian swamps; the papyruses of the ancient Egyptians, of scorching sand and fragrances. He detected the powerful perfume of wild grasses and the sharp smell of horses' sweat: there went the cavalry of the Golden Horde, spreading over the vast expanses of the steppes.

After he had reflected for a while, Lukary took out one of the yellowed Egyptian papyruses and unrolled it. Following a sequence of hieroglyphics, he read:

And the priest went to the maker of destinies and when he had bowed respectfully, spoke: "O great Pharaoh, the troops are drawn up, the soldiers are thirsting for battle—why do you delay?"

The young Pharaoh turned his proud head and looked submissively at the priest standing before him. Sadness filled his eyes even as the Nile had flooded the Egyptian land in the autumn.

"O Priest," said the Pharaoh, "you must know that my heart grieves. Death awaits my best, most brave and faithful servants in this battle with the Syrians. I am mourning for my soldiers."

The priest lowered his shaven head, he clutched his white garments with his hand. "Then let it be known unto you, great Pharaoh, that wise men do not mourn the living or the dead. For every human being has existed, exists, and will exist in all the ages to come!"

Lukary put down the papyrus and picked up a collection of incantations and religious hymns written on parchment. When the ancient Egyptians read *The Book of the Dead* they learned how they should conduct themselves after death and how they would return to the world of people. The incantations, either written down on papyrus or drawn on the walls of burial halls, accompanied persons of importance after they died. The wisdom of the ages was concentrated in this text, but it couldn't help Lukary with his troubles. The ancient writings didn't say anything about how human life is related to the movement of time. Such a relation existed, he had no doubt about that, but in order to continue his work he needed proof, new food for his mind.

"Wise men do not mourn the living or the dead," he repeated the words he'd just read. "Death only scares immature souls!"

Lukary put his treasures into the cabinet and closed the doors. The priest was right in his instructions to the young Pharaoh, but that was only one man's truth. With both hands behind his back, Lukary began pacing up and down the semi-dark studio. A person's fate is predetermined by his karma, everything he has done and the things he could have done but didn't do in his previous incarnations on earth. When masses of people are slaughtered, the cosmic law of cause and effect must operate differently . . . He was engrossed in his thought. Is each person responsible for the time in which he lives or is the course of time determined by the masses?

Lukary suddenly saw a sea of human heads and heard the rattling of weapons and the guttural shouts of commanders. The Pharaoh's troops were gone—he saw Hellenic battle formations, followed by the precise geometry of Roman legions and then the standards of Russian regiments waving in the wind. The sun sparkled on the armor and the brass of military bands sounded a call to battle. Do the people marching set the rhythm of the time, or does the time, through qualities they cannot sense, drive them into regiments and battalions and bring dictators to power? In any case, people's karma must necessarily be related to the process by which the time is created. A critical mass of the evil people create sets the Moloch of war and revolution into motion, and like a steamroller it travels through countries and peoples until it bogs down in a bloody mash.

Lukary stopped and listened carefully. Everything was quiet, even in the lower, three-dimensional human world that adjoined his studio. Yet he stood and strained his ear; he was hoping to hear the slight squeak of a door opening and then he became angry at his own inability to concentrate. His comfortable world, regulated like clockwork and so accommodating to his studies, suddenly collapsed, and anxiety and alarm burst in. Attempting to recover the train of his receding thought, Lukary began to pace his studio floor again. He stopped in front of the easel. A sweet woman's face looked at him from the gray canvas. A subtle smile barely brushed her lips, the pure forehead had the slightest frown, and her eyes half questioned, half laughed.

"Solitude," he remembered, "is a natural form of existence for animated, conscious matter. Solitude reconciles man with the illusions and disappointments of life and forces him to carry on with the ascent to his higher self, to become an enlightened spirit free in time and space. Solitude is the one way you can leave the prison walls of your self through the work of your soul."

He was still standing before the easel. The woman's smile was barely noticeable. Lukary sighed deeply and turned the portrait to the wall. The only thing to do was to go for a walk—his tried-and-true method of putting his thoughts and feelings in order. Preferring to live in human form even in the astral plane, he would take his hat and, depending on his mood, enter the human world on some quiet street in the Sokolniki district or in the Vorobyov Hills.

On one of these trips into the world someone had even talked to him—a small, gray-haired old woman wearing white knit gloves and a prehistoric hat with a veil. Her eye had been caught by his somber suit and bow tie and the way he carried his cane. He listened for a long time to her recollections of life before the war—the marvelous slippers they wore then, with a thin white band and small heel—and suddenly he asked, "Tell me, in your opinion, what is time?"

The old woman looked at him with transparent eyes and moved her head in such a way that her gray curls began to shake. "You're not happy, it's clear!" She placed her light knit glove on his sleeve. "Why is that? You're still young, live while you can—you'll still find time for the eternal. The eternal will never leave you!"

He remembered how they had sat on a bench in the warm rays of a rare autumn sun . . .

Lukary took a raincoat off the rack, threw it over his arm and was reaching for his hat when Shepetukha all at once emerged from a fissure in the astral plane. He turned his bald round head from side to side, and after convincing himself that the master of the studio was alone, he leapt to the floor, shook all over like a dog, and with his small palm smoothed the gray hair that had been sticking out in all directions. His sharp animated nose twitched.

"Going out?" he inquired casually, in no particular hurry, and waddled up to Lukary. He stopped about a couple of feet away, propped his thin paws on his waist, and tapped on the floor with his foot as if beating out time. "Very nice! You've acquired a brand-new suit and a raincoat from Paris! By the way"—Shepetukha raised his thinning colorless eyebrows—"a *domovoi* isn't permitted to take on a form that's human! Just a little creature's—like a cat. Only in exceptional cases can you take the form of a building super, but then only one who's half-crocked! You're committing a violation, Lukary, it's a violation!"

Lukary was silent. Shepetukha strode along the book-lined walls and stopped in front of the El Greco in the pose of a connoisseur.

"A good artist!" he approved. "Lots of green! I'm so homesick for green! From time immemorial we forest spirits lived in swamps and forests, but now we've had to move to the city for lack of work. The countryside's deserted—there's no need for forest folk to frighten the old people left behind there! In the old days . . . in the spring," he continued dreamily, "there were delicate trees and in the glades an emerald mist spread over the earth. The birds sang, some creature who'd gotten scrawny over the winter rejoiced with every cell . . . And then for good sport you could frighten a lost little man to death! Or grab the girls in a grove and tickle the good-for-nothings till they had fits! But now? Phooey! The folk have gone soft, they don't know how to drink anymore, and you don't know where to find them!"

Lukary was silent. He hung the coat back on the rack and settled down in his favorite armchair, from whose comfortable depths he observed Shepetukha. The *leshii* had a frail body and a drab appearance, but carried himself so confidently and proudly it made you think twice. Knowing the unscrupulous nature of his uninvited guest, Lukary came to the conclusion that something had happened to make his own unenviable position even worse.

"You're disgusted! You won't grant me the honor of a conversation!" Shepetukha asserted without waiting for a reaction. "But it's to no avail by the way! I'm a *leshii*, you're a *domovoi*; according to the table of ranks we're equals, devilish spirits on a small-fry scale. Forget who you were before, that's no one's business! You're a prisoner, in exile now, under open surveillance, and I can do whatever I want with you!" The *leshii* sat down in the facing armchair and crossed his legs. "Incidentally, a little memo from up there arrived"—he couldn't resist—"concerning your soul! The bosses want to know how you are and what you're up to, they ask about your behavior! So listen, Lukary, don't put on airs, I'm here on duty!"

The *leshii* took a toothpick from who knows where and absent-mindedly set to pick at the gaps between his teeth.

"You're brushing me off," he said, spitting on the floor, "but I understand you, like no one else! With my whole soul, you could say! I did drudge work in the camps too, served a whole stretch there. In my youth I had a crazy notion—I'll do good for people, I thought. I look around and decide they need to have their spirits raised! Life is tough as it is, but then the poor creatures go to the cemetery and see the dead ones resting in their graves—and ofttimes they're younger than themselves. And humans—they're like this—tally up everything and get upset. I turned this over in my head—what about making off with the gravestones from the cemetery at night and changing the dates of birth and death. I'll let this guy live till a hundred, that one a hundred and twenty, and in my spiritual generosity—I was heated up—to one nice lady I forked out two hundred and sixty little years! Well, what do you think?" The *leshii* jumped to his feet in indignation. "No one even said thank you! The relatives of the deceased should have rejoiced for their dear ones, but they went to the police—defiling graves, you see! The second week of work they caught me red-handed. Then a trial. Five years of hard labor! They didn't see I was a *leshii* . . . So it goes—not one good deed goes unpunished!"

Still in a state of excitement, Shepetukha paced up and down the studio and puffed on a cheap hand-rolled cigarette.

"Of course, we're petty demons"—a note of insult stayed in his voice—"but even we can do something! For instance, I can inform the top that the person under surveillance—that means you—is modest to the point of bashfulness and behaves like a good boy. Or I can paint such a picture of your tricks that they'll drive you to Tmutarakan and you'll rot there till the end of time. Yes, and where is it written that a *domovoi* gets his own studio and scribbles on this and that." Shepetukha walked over to Lukary's desk and casually shifted several pieces of paper around. "Your place is behind the stove—lie down and warm your belly. But instead you philosophize and dab in oils!"

Lukary restrained himself. A door in the lower world squeaked. The *leshii* took heed and wriggled a hairy ear.

"Must be the old lady dragging her bones home from the store!" he conjectured. "The old hag—your punishment—is still alive! Instead of playing the fool," Shepetukha admonished, "you'd do better to serve! A worthwhile business! Take me! I may be an insignificant being, but I'm a useful cog in a big machine, and I'm proud of that! Even if there are millions of creatures like me in the Department of Dark Powers, the very fact that I belong to the system makes my existence meaningful. People have to be watched so that they don't think up something extra, and for criminals like you we need more eyes. To feel you're a part of power is a wonderful thing! The organization will feed you and provide you with drink, and if there's a need they'll give you protection. Yes, to serve there is a fine thing!"

Taking his time, the *leshii* headed for the wall with the clear intention of looking out of the astral plane into the lower world. Lukary tensed. Keeping an eye fixed on Shepetukha's movements, he asked in as friendly a way as possible, "So, what is it you want from me?"

"Very little!" Shepetukha came to a stop and moved his shoulders slightly, as though his skin had suddenly become too tight under Lukary's gaze. "Talk to me like a human being! It's every creature's wish that someone will listen and show some attention. Let's sit down, share a bottle, play a little game of cards. All just like people do! Show me respect." With his small fist he pounded his sunken chest covered with thin hair. "And I'll respect you! We're all made of the same dirt, we're all rotten inside, so why put on airs! Don't be so affected, Lukash, be more accessible to ordinary folk!"

Lukary shuddered. Meanwhile Shepetukha was just a yard from the wall. Wincing with disgust, Lukary impeded the *leshii*'s movement, tore him off the floor with a willful look, and left him hanging in the air in a restricted state.

"Hey, you, be careful! Put me back!" Shepetukha began squealing. "You're forbidden to use your resources when you're under surveillance!"

Lukary paid no attention to Shepetukha's wails; he waited until it was quiet in the apartment below, and only then did he loosen his grip. The *leshii* tumbled to the floor. After crawling to the wall, he began to pat his body with his paws.

"That's how I get treated," he whimpered like a puppy, wiping his bruised rear end. "The bosses use me to egg on others—an errand boy: beat this one senseless, scare that one, and then I get spit on myself. Maybe I should go join the vampires, at least they have a rich diet!" Groaning, Shepetukha stood up on shaky legs and gave Lukary a malevolent look. "All right, you'll see, tit for tat! My day will come! You'll regret your vileness, Lukary. Out of the goodness of my heart I came to warn you, pull you out of the noose, you might say, but now the bet's off! You'll pay for your arrogance. I'll report everything about you, describe all your artsy doings!"

The *leshii*, lame in one leg now, hobbled to the fissure in the astral plane, then suddenly sprang to the wall and stuck his head into three-dimensional space. What he saw there clearly amazed him. When he drew his head back in, Shepetukha looked at Lukary with a crooked grin and, staring blankly with his insipid red-rimmed eyes, asked mockingly, "Where's the grandma? Dead, is she? But you didn't report the change in conditions! After all, she was assigned to you as an extra burden, to make your punishment harsher!" The *leshii* smugly rubbed his paws. "And now we have another little violation! Well, as a male I understand." Shepetukha smacked his lips, an oily shine appeared in his eyes. "A beauty—the old grandma she's not. You probably spy at night and pretend to be a loofah in the bath. I know you, you only look like an angel!"

The *leshii* met Lukary's glance and stopped short. The roguish little smile sloughed off his lips, and Shepetukha's face was contorted with fear.

"OK, I guess I'll go!" He moved toward the fissure in the astral plane. "Really, I see it for myself—the woman's praiseworthy in all respects!"

Shepetukha made a pleading smile, but it was too late—his little body suddenly began to shake and jerk around, and, once torn from the floor, it started crumbling into a ball like plasticine that is being warmed up before modeling.

"I . . . I won't do it again!" the *leshii* cried at the top of his voice.

"No, Shepetukha, I don't believe you. Does it make sense to set you free when you're about to run off and inform? I need time to think." Lukary took his pipe from the desk and stuffed it with tobacco.

Invisible forces continued to work on the *leshii*. Constantly changing form, he would broaden into something like a pancake, then lengthen and dangle from the ceiling like a rope.

"You . . . someone's come to see you!" Shepetukha figured out how to free an arm and pointed to the far corner of the studio. Lukary turned. In streaming light blue waves a delicate form was materializing there, wrapped in a long cloak. The woman smoothed out her clothes, as if shaking off little sparks, and turned back the hood. There was something tragic in her enormous eyes, which were like a *rusalka*'s; her gaze was hypnotic.

"Milady?" Lukary rose from his chair. "Pardon, Milady, my friend and I here have a little business matter. I'll finish it momentarily and then I'll be entirely at your disposal."

He turned to Shepetukha. He was hanging half a yard from the floor, straitjacketed by invisible energy. Like a surgeon with a scalpel, Lukary cut space into strips with a sweep of his hand. Following his motions, it curved and began to suck Shepetukha's resisting hairy body into its depths, as if into a funnel. Twisting like a corkscrew, the *leshii* circled like a chip of wood into the tunnel that formed; his head sank into his shoulders and only an enormous mouth was left on the surface.

"I shall return!" the thick protruding lips promised before disappearing. "I'll get even for everything!"

Space closed over Shepetukha like water over a drowning man.

Milady rushed to Lukary and started to speak, pressing her thin, semi-transparent hands to her breast. "What have you done to him? I always knew you were a terribly cruel man!"

"Nothing special!" Smiling, Lukary looked into the radiant eyes that were still fixed on him. "My acquaintance cultivates a secret passion for cosmology, so I decided to dispatch him to the depths of space in order to give him some fresh air and cool his ardor. The beauty of the universe has an ennobling effect on the soul. I think with his energetic potential he'll return to earth in two or three years, and in the meantime I'll be without spies for a while. But he's not worth discussing!"

Lukary gave a passing glance at a candle standing in an old candlestick—it was crackling and smoking. Such behavior made sense while Shepetukha was in the studio. But now that he'd disappeared, it meant some other being belonging to the dark powers had been secretly present during their conversation. Slowly, like a hunter afraid of scaring off the prey, Lukary examined his living quarters. Overcoming the resistance of some force, he made out a barely noticeable glimmer behind the easel in the far corner of the studio. The reddish-brown tints were releasing a dark energy equal in force to his own. Lukary took a step forward and tensed, but the luminescence immediately vanished; he only managed to see a shadow slipping out of the studio. The candle flame flickered a last time and then quieted; earlier it had burned with a steady light, like a church candle, but now its flame died out.

"Did something happen?" Milady looked at Lukary with fright. "You turned pale so suddenly!"

"Nothing special—I'm just not always prepared for eavesdroppers. There's no time to reflect now . . . You see, when you've been leading an active life and then suddenly you find yourself in a quiet phase, you begin to relax against your will. The pursuit of philosophy disposes one to a state of spiritual kindness, it lowers the barrier of caution that protects against a scoundrel's deeds." He took his coat and hat, and turned to the woman. "If you have no objections, I suggest that we pass through the astral plane together. You always appear so unexpectedly and take me unawares."

He took Milady by the arm and they stepped out of the astral plane onto Tverskoi Boulevard in the direction of St. Nicholas Gate. The corpulent black body of night lay on the city—there was a sharp, springlike smell of damp earth. Rare passersby were hurrying to their warm apartments. A fresh wind high in the sky chased the light layered clouds, and the full moon would hide behind this gliding veil and then show its face again.

"Tell me, what makes you so attached to this unhappy country?" Milady's small feet stepped carefully on the street's moist gravel. "We could just as well be strolling along the banks of the Seine or taking part in the carnival in Rio."

"When you love, it's impossible to say why."

"You say that to me?" Milady's voice sounded a challenge and she smiled sarcastically. "From my own experience and with your help I know that one doesn't love for something, but in spite of!"

She gave her companion a meaningful look, but he ignored her words.

"Vienna, Madrid, Paris—they're all part of my past. In their tranquillity they are like elders who live through memories. Though I confess I have nothing against walks through their museum collections—that's where the paintings in my studio come from."

"You speak as though Moscow were different . . ."

"Not Moscow—but Russia! In this country everything is more meaningful and intense, even if it's for the reason that almost no one here is living here in a first life. I don't know the reasons for God's choice, but it's the souls of sinners that return here, people who during previous incarnations on earth lived immorally or even criminally and who still have a chance to change their karma and begin the path to enlightenment. Not only criminals come here, however—sublime and bright spirits also choose to return, enlightened beings who are able to lead others through their own example. The way the world is made, only a few such beings exist, but there are crowds of followers." Lukary took a sidelong glance at Milady. "By the way, if I were in your place I'd look carefully at this land of contrasts. Sooner or later, like every apparition, you will be given absolution, and then you'll have an excellent chance to be born again as a Russian!"

She held him back by the sleeve, and turned him around to face her. Her wild *rusalka* eyes stared from the half-darkness of the cloak thrown over her head.

"Listen, I don't want to return to the human world!"

"But why?" Lukary wondered. "Many dream of being born again in order to redeem their sins. In the end, it's the only way to lighten your own karma, to throw off the incredible burden that you carry with you from life to life. You know as well as I do that after death the soul is compelled to continue on the path it chose during its existence as a human in the mortal world."

"Yes, that's so." Milady lowered her head, and having suddenly come to a decision, she looked him straight in the eye. "Why hide it, you know very well that I love you. And I don't want to lose you! Someday you'll be granted forgiveness too."

"To be honest, I have every reason to doubt that now!" Lukary said with a smile.

"I know it for sure, I can feel it—they'll forgive you! You're a guest on earth, and, despite your exile, even here you remain a spirit of light. A return to the heights of the heavenly hierarchy awaits you, you'll take your place in the Department of Light Powers. You'll never fall so low that you must begin your ascent again from the level of a simple human. If I'm born again, the distance between us will be vast—you'll live within the boundaries of light!"

Lukary shrugged his shoulders. "No one knows the book of fates. But in the meantime we must fight off each punishment of ours. You're an apparition and I'm a *domovoi*—a great pair, aren't we!"

He burst out laughing, but in his laughter there was no joy. They started leisurely walking along the avenue again.

"Are you permitted to say what your crime was?" Milady tried to look into his face but it was hidden in the shadows of his wide-brimmed hat.

"The usual trivial matter," Lukary laughed. "To put it mildly, no hierarchical structure has ever encouraged doubt in the correctness of actions taken by the top. Such disobedience has always been branded as apostasy. Different faiths exist, but the punishment is the same—the unruly one is banished. On earth the unfortunate one is at the same time deprived of life—just in case, that is. As for me, my punishment was limited to exile. I don't want to talk about it. Let's go take a look inside the theater instead!"

They returned to the astral plane, then immediately left it again and stepped out onto a quiet deserted little street. Straight in front of them stood an enormous gray block building that housed a theater. The lights were out, the doors behind the massive rectangular columns were closed.

"Everything's closed." Milady was upset. "We're late!"

"Oh no, we're just on time! Of what interest is it to go to a theater when it's open?" Lukary asked in surprise. "There's just the standard set of human feelings and situations. It's boring. Do you know why people love chess, for instance? Because in life they're denied a significant choice of moves."

They walked into the lobby through the massive closed doors and climbed the carpeted stairway to the foyer. The enormous building was filled with resonant quiet to its very roof. A small light burned above the entrance to the auditorium. Lukary reached for the brass handle and the door opened soundlessly, letting them into the semi-dark orchestra. A diffuse hazy light came from the stage and gradually mixed with the darkness as it approached the last row of seats. The stage itself, exposed all the way to the back brick wall, resembled an aquarium. There was something mysterious and sad in the bareness on show.

"An empty theater at night is totally different." Lukary walked down the aisle and sat on one of the armrests. "It lives in the echoes of feelings and words. Here languages and peoples have mingled and you can still sense forgotten epochs. But the stillness of a theater at night is deceptive. Let it pass through you, like a ray of white light through a prism, and you'll feel a rainbow of passions. People say that 'the theater begins as soon as you hang up your coat,' but that's a pompous cliché. The theater begins with us; like an eternal and incorruptible judge, it divides people into those who can feel and share the feelings of others and all the rest, for whom you can only feel sorry."

Milady walked over to him.

"Were you an actor in one of your past lives?"

"You're mistaken. By nature I'm a storyteller, but my theater is different. It stages plays whose last act even the playwright doesn't know."

A transparent green light streamed from the stage and fantastic shadows thickened in the boxes. Somewhere deep within the theater a clock struck midnight.

"Well, in that case you might be interested in a certain story." Milady looked at him without a trace of a smile. Her beautiful austere face was thoughtful and sad. "It's about you and me, and, as you've already guessed, this story . . . Yes, it's the story of my love! The drama of one actor for one spectator."

Milady turned and mounted the stage as a queen might have mounted the scaffold. Lukary sank into a chair. High in the third tier of the balcony a bright front light flared on its own, plucking out from the murk a slender and graceful figure with chestnut curls scattering down her back. As she began to talk, Milady's voice seemed muted in the empty theater.

"I was born long ago in Languedoc. The small town where I spent my youth nestled at the foot of the Cévennes. My father's house stood right in the town center, its windows overlooking the square. The massive cathedral hovered above it and all the other houses in town. The mountain slope was covered with oaks and higher up grew beeches and chestnuts, and I often ran off to the forest and spent whole days there far from people and crosses. On Sundays, standing under the sounding cathedral vaults, I would experience a primordial animal fear. I felt like a grain of sand, an insignificant midge thrown into an enormous hostile world, and even the colorful patch of the stained-glass window didn't console me.

" 'Heretic' was the most terrible word at that time. The founder of the Order of St. Dominic had gone to the grave long before, the 'poor Catholics' who became Dominicans and Franciscans spread to all corners of Europe, and in Languedoc bonfires continued to blaze. In the name of Christ, the Inquisitor, hiding a hypocritical smile beneath his cowl, would ask God to show His grace to the souls gone astray. Some asked for mercy, others for alms . . . Lepers walked down the narrow canyons of streets, their approach announced by the blows of sticks; they held out the ulcerous stumps of their hands to the townspeople. Toward night they returned to their cold homes, terrifying people with their uninterrupted moans, and collapsed onto the floor. The very same Dominicans waited on them, those most terrible and inaccessible brothers-in-Christ who sent thousands of people to the stake. Such was the bitter taste of the time, this was the way they tested their faith!"

Milady wrapped herself more tightly in her cloak, as if suddenly feeling cold from her memories.

"On holidays a crowd would gather in the square in front of our windows. People stood silently in expectation of the auto-da-fé, and only little boys would dart into the crowd, searching for small coins.

"Finally a wave would roll through the sea of heads, and in the ensuing quiet orders rang out sharply and the soldiers in the cordon pressed together in a tighter ring around the condemned. My mother would take me from the window and we cringed in the furthest corner of the house, praying ourselves into a frenzy and imploring the good Lord to accept the unfortunate souls. A candle burned in the small low-ceilinged room, it was hot and the smell of wax was sickening. An eternity elapsed. The door would squeak. Father stood in the doorway. It was over!

"Once, on the holiday of St. Simeon Metaphrastes, the crowd in the square had begun to gather early in the morning. On such days I was forbidden to leave the house, but I disobeyed. I wanted to run away to my oak grove and breathe the early spring air. I remember that day well. The sun's bright light caressed the earth, which was tired from long winter twilights, and the deep, incredibly blue sky called me into its depths. I thought that people could learn how to fly. Seizing the moment, I slipped out of the house and ran along the street to the town gates, where my path into the forest began. Even now my skin feels that morning's cold, which crept beneath my cloak where I'd hidden my dinner—flat cakes made of rye. The street wound downhill and I was running and trying not to meet the eyes of the people who were coming toward me, when suddenly something compelled me to raise my head and I saw her. It was like a blow! I suddenly realized, though still an absolute child, that what was happening would change my whole life.

"On the other side of the street, in the interior of a dirty courtyard, a cage stood on a cart near the fence adjoining the inn. Traveling circuses conveyed their beasts in such cages. This time a creature that was barely recognizable as a woman sat in the cage. A crowd of gapers fidgeted nearby, poking fingers into the side of the cart and baring gap-toothed mouths. I felt my legs stiffen and the next moment a mysterious force irrevocably pulled me toward the unfortunate woman. Someone was trying to hold me back. He grabbed the edge of my cloak but I tore myself away and went right up to the cage. The woman watched the crowd's crazy behavior impassively. Her face was framed by long hair flecked with gray and was amazingly calm. I reached out and offered her the flat cake. She merely shook her head and her baked, parched lips had trouble smiling. Sticking her arm through the bars, she stroked my hair with her palm. I can still see her eyes—dark and remote, with a feverish shine. The dirt on her face mixed with bruises but nothing could have spoiled her beauty.

" 'You're a child,' the woman said, opening her mouth with difficulty, 'you can't understand, but remember my words. When you grow up, I'll no longer be here but the world will remain as before. It's worth living in for one thing only—to know love. If you love you won't fear anyone.' She licked her parched lips. 'I shall give you my love, I bequeath it to you!'

"Two slow tears rolled down her hollow cheeks. With her hand, which was callused with dirt and blood, the woman caressed my face, as if she wanted to remember its features by touch.

" 'You will be beautiful . . . I could have saved my life at the price of betrayal, but I wasn't able to do it . . .'

"I don't know if she could see, but her eyes looked straight into my soul. I realized that she expected confirmation of her righteousness from me.

" 'Dear Lord,' I whispered, 'merciful Father! I beg you, I'll give you my silver ring—save her!'

"She shook her head. 'It's too late, it's too late for me! Now you'll be the one who will love!'

"She wanted to say something else, but just then a drunken lot of soldiers stumbled out of the inn. They threw me back into the crowd of gapers and started to mock her, poking the blunt ends of their lances through the bars. She bore her suffering silently, and when the cart started out on her final trip her eyes found me. She tried hard to smile but couldn't.

"They burned her at noon in view of a large gathering of people. The Dominican Inquisitor refused her the last mercy and she was raised into the fire alive. I was later told that her beloved had informed on her. She had known about it and still thanked God for her love."

Milady lowered herself onto the stage floor and grasped her knees with her hands. A patch of bright light followed her, then suddenly vanished as if feeling no longer needed. The tiny figure froze on the edge of the enormous open stage in the hazy aquarium-like light.

"What happened after that?"

The woman looked into the semi-dark orchestra and continued.

"After that came life. An unhurried dream, which by some misunderstanding is called adult life. Not one day passed when I didn't remember her and say a prayer for her. The only thing I couldn't understand was what had happened to my legacy—the love she'd bequeathed to me. My husband, though of noble birth, was little better than an animal, just like those around him. To say that I found him unpleasant is to flatter him—I hated his stupid vanity—the defects of his mind and crudeness of his feelings. Add to that pathological miserliness, violent drunken behavior, and a craving for strumpets and you'll understand why one day I could no longer control myself and put a good portion of rat poison into his food. I had already been poisoned by the expectation of love. Afterward, I denied everything, but this did not stop them from treating me as tradition demanded, and, as a lesson to others, they immured me in a wall . . .

"After I became a ghost, I didn't stop searching for what belonged to me by right, but I only found the man who had betrayed her. He lived in another city in a large house by a warm sea. One sultry southern night I went to that house in order to carry out revenge. Hiding behind a shutter, I watched the old man sitting by the fireplace. For a second I thought he was dead, but, no, he was alive, and an inhuman joy seized me when I thought that in a moment he would lose his mind. Gathering all my powers I began to make terrifying moans. I started to spin like a whirlwind and galloped swiftly around the room, sending the furniture flying and toppling dishes. My insane dance was horrible—frightening black shadows rushed about the walls. I embraced him with my icy arms, laughing loud and wildly, sobbing and howling like a wolf, but he just sat there impassively, watching me with empty unseeing eyes. His lips moved very slightly, he was praying. He prayed for her. Then I sank down into a chair opposite him and listened. The old man was praying to God to take his life and send eternal grace to the woman whom he had never stopped praying for during all these years. Finally he grew quiet.

" 'Why did you kill her, old man?'

"He didn't answer right away, he sat with his gaze fastened on the flames in the fireplace. Suddenly his head jerked and two vacant dead eyes looked at me. Only the black holes of abandoned mines can stare like this, mines with no living soul at their bottom.

" 'They made me.'

"He lowered his head and raised it quickly. His eyes revived, two dim restless flames began to burn at the bottom of the mine. The old man moved in his chair, you could feel strength in his emaciated body.

He got up and took several steps, not taking his eyes off the rectangular black window.

" 'Love killed her!' he began barely audibly. 'Every day for a quarter of a century now I wake up and fall asleep to these words, if I can sleep at all. I repeat them day and night—love kills, love destroys everything, including itself. As soon as it opens, the bud of love already smells with betrayal and oozes the poison of jealousy. Afraid of losing love, we run toward the abyss, driving ourselves with the lash of imagination. Love is dirt, love is cruelty and madness! I've repeated these words for twenty-five years and I know that they're a lie from beginning to end. I loved her as I love her now. I killed her myself, I secretly desired her death because I could no longer bear the torment of love. There is no pardon for me on earth just as there is no forgiveness in heaven. With these words I handed her to the executioner; I dragged the wood for her fire on my own back.'

"He turned unexpectedly and his glance fell onto the fire in the fireplace. There was something elusive and completely insane in his crooked form, in the way he turned his head. A grimace distorted his face. He started to titter and flapped his arms and, skipping and singing, he swayed unsteadily around the room.

" 'They made me, made me, made . . .'

"He fell to his knees and covered his face with his hands.

" 'Every night, I had only to close my eyes and I'd see her in the embraces of another. A nightmare was haunting me. I forgot what it means to live because life had become the fear of losing her. Often, tormented by hallucinations, I would run around the house with a sword in my hand, threatening to stab each and all at the least provocation. I stopped going to church, afraid I would kill the priest when she went up to kiss his hand and receive his blessing. I had no strength left—I was burning in the fire of my own love.

" 'That night I woke from fear. It poured from my body and I could smell it. I got dressed hastily and slipped out to the street. Black lumps of houses bent over me like giants and only the light of the moon beckoned in the heavens. I started to run, and my steps, pounding dully over the roadway, reverberated in my poor head. It seemed she was calling me, begging me to return, but I kept on running, I rushed through the sleeping town until I collapsed. I must have passed some time in a semi-conscious state, and when I opened my eyes, the spire of the cathedral directly over my head was piercing the deep sky, splitting the moon. I understood where I was. Unexpectedly I caught sight of a dark figure on the steps of the neighboring house. I knew him. The black, humped spine of the Dominican prior flashed in the aperture of the doorway and disappeared. He didn't call me, I followed him on my own. It was a delusion. I climbed the steps, which were flat and dented by time, and found myself in a large room, in the middle of which stood a massive table on which a candle burned. The piece of paper seemed unnaturally white in its light. The walls of the room drowned in darkness.'

" 'The Dominican's voice rang out from somewhere in the corner. "Write!"

" 'Barely understanding what I was doing, I sat down at the table and began to write. My fingers were numb, my hand would refuse to obey, but gripped by memories, I continued to guide my pen over the paper, with no power to stop. I wrote about her, about the happiness of seeing her descending from heaven, about veneration and the bliss of possessing an angel in the flesh. I wrote about myself, about what love can drive a man to do. Dazzling pictures of happiness and pleasure, the fear of losing her, and all my suffering rose before me, and I wrote, choking with feeling and experiencing true relief from the chance to tell what I had lived through. The smell of frankincense affected my head, and whenever I tore myself from the page, searching for a worthy comparison, my eyes would meet the Dominican's fixed glance, and I had no strength to draw them away from his bony face. The flame was dancing as it died, something left my life and I could feel it. Finally my head fell onto the table, my hand let loose the pen, and the paper slid out from underneath.

" 'He was reading. He read slowly and sonorously. He was reading as if he himself had experienced everything the words told. The even sound of his voice was lulling me to sleep, and I fell back into a semi-conscious state, but as soon as he became silent, I awoke.

" ' "Sign it!"

" 'I didn't understand, and he repeated, "Sign it!" and forcefully pressed my hand to the sheet of paper.

" 'I signed. I signed the denunciation.

" ' "That's all!" The Dominican raised a chalice of wine to my lips. "I knew you would come sooner or later. One of us three had to die—it fell to her! I'm the Inquisitor, you're the informer, she's the victim—it's a triangle of love!"

" 'He smiled with lips only. I jumped up, but the next minute I was lying on the floor. He stood over me, his back hunched as usual, dangling his long arms.

" ' "Only a witch is capable of possessing a man in such a way. Don't regret anything, the memory of her will stay with you, and in this world what can be better than memories? Honor can be lost, and money, but what you have lived through can never be taken away. You will possess her eternally . . ." He became quiet, then added, "And so will I."

" ' "I'll kill you!" My lips moved soundlessly, but he understood.

" ' "I know. But what does it matter? Everything has already taken place. She's not here, to you she's dead!"

" 'I crawled after him on my knees and stomach like the lowest beast, grabbing at the hem of his cassock, and I invoked all the saints to return me the paper. He smiled sadly and sympathetically, the way he always smiled to parishioners from the pulpit, and he praised my religious fervor. Then blackness fell upon me. I would have given everything to have died that night, but dawn found me lying on the steps of the cathedral. Above my head the Dominican Order's standard, lit by the first rays of the sun, quivered in the breeze. From the cloth a good-natured monk was gazing at me strictly and almost cheerfully; a dog reclined at his feet in the clouds.

" 'I killed him the night after the auto-da-fé. He didn't resist. And during the day, I stood in the square, squeezed on all sides by the crowd. The Dominican denied her the last act of mercy and they burned her alive. I have felt cold ever since. Wherever I am, people light a fire for me.'

"He grew silent and looked up at me with eyes full of pain and despair. 'Did you come to kill me? Do it! There's no horror more terrible than what I feel in my own company.' He handed me a knife. 'Or I'll kill myself if you want.'

"The reflection of the fire fell upon his face and burned with madness in his eyes.

" 'They made me, made me.' The old man began to wheeze and he tottered, then took a step and collapsed at my feet. The knife fell and rolled across the wooden floor, its round handle toppling over and over. God protected the unfortunate man from his last sin and mercifully took his soul.

"That night I sat for a long time and watched the outstretched body, then lit a candle from the fire and quietly walked around the house. It was empty, dark, and strikingly sad. I carried the flame of the candle up to the heavy portiere and it burned immediately with a bright, cheery fire. Then the walls and ceiling caught fire. No one had the right to live in this house where a man had been dying for a quarter of a century. When the flame took hold of the roof, I flew out the window, and as I turned back I saw a man slip out to the street and run in flashes of fire along the crooked street that was flooded with moonlight. He ran toward her whom he had not stopped loving his whole life . . ."

Milady stood up and walked down the stage stairs into the orchestra. Her face was pale, her enormous eyes shone coldly and threateningly.

"That night," she continued, looking at Lukary with narrowing eyes, "that night I understood that the feeling bequeathed to me lives within me and will live there forever! Through the centuries I've carried my love and . . . only when I met you did I understand what it means for me. I love you! You belong to me!"

She drew near to his face. Her features became sharper, her expression was rapacious. Slowly her eyelids lowered, damping the furious shine of her green eyes, then immediately flew up. It seemed to Lukary that with every stroke of her lashes black thoughts broke free like a flock of bats and swirled beneath the vaults of the theater for a long while. A smile brushed her beautiful lips and she whispered, "Be careful . . . I won't give you up to anyone! And don't call me Milady—my name is Lucy!"

4

In the new television center building built for the 1980 Olympics the halls run along the perimeter. An ostentatious stairway cuts through the center of a space divided into numerous TV studios and auxiliary rooms and ends at something like a winter garden. But no one uses the stairway or that marvel of the country's botanical ideas. The inhabitants of the television branch of this madhouse simply have no time to contemplate decaying nature, and as for the formal stairs, they're lit so cleverly as to be life-threatening—if you only broke a leg on them, it would be considered great luck.

After passing the door to the news studio, where the policeman on duty was suffering from nothing to do, Anna turned a corner and entered the control room. The clock on one of the TV monitors that covered an entire wall showed 7:45. Fifteen minutes until airtime. Behind the thick glass separating the studio from the control room technicians were adjusting the show's lead story and the cameraman was busy with one of the lock-down cameras. Anna passed by a long row of control panels, sat down in the technical director's chair, and looked up to check the television monitors as usual. It was all systems go, as the cosmonauts say. On any other day Anna would have come in here with the whole crew, they would all have burst into the control room ten minutes before airtime, but today she felt like being by herself. For just a while, just five minutes. In the flurry of the day's events, no one would remember a minor anniversary, of course, and these five minutes were her only chance to mark this humble event in her life. Anna put down her work folder and leaned back in the revolving chair. Ten years in a woman's life is a long time. She had spent all these years in this building loaded with electronics, and—she was surprised by this thought—it had become her second home. Or was it her first?

Anna forced herself not to think about it or anything except the broadcast about to begin. She took the rundown sheet of the news program out of the folder and skimmed one more time through the columns of figures, the sequence of subjects and their airtime. It began with the lead story, then a session of Parliament, cut to the anchor, program identification . . . So, nothing unusual. The broadcast was well planned and logically arranged, although in a live broadcast there's no guarantee against mishaps. Anna smiled. She remembered the power outage that had recently occurred just several seconds before airtime; it had knocked out the teleprompter. It only seems that it's easy for an anchor to ad-lib—in fact, he's diligently checking the prepared text that runs line by line on the teleprompter in front of him. It was funny to see one of the famous journalists in the country open his mouth eagerly and then just stop: there was no text. It caused a medium-scale scandal, of course.

Anna looked up from her rundown sheet. On the central monitor the inscription APB-10 appeared, designating the section of the station responsible for this edition of the news. Her colleagues arrived and began taking their seats noisily. The captions editor took his place in front of a panel with a keyboard, the audio technician and audio editor stood behind a large control panel with dozens of knobs and levers. Sasha, the assistant director, quickly sank down in the armchair next to Anna's, said, "You look terrific," in his boyish manner, and in the same tempo spoke into the microphone: "Semyonych, what's wrong with your camera, it looks out of focus."

Anna pressed a knob on the control panel.

"Allochka, the 'Around Europe' story—after the picture starts to fade bring up the light for the program ID. Misha, write down—on page six—next item, spring in Tokyo, Japan."

The anchor appeared behind the glass in the studio and fussed with his thinning hair. He sat down in his chair and tested the microphone—"one, two, three." A loud signal gave notice that the fourteenth and fifteenth items were leaving the video cassette. It was very close to eight o'clock, the news program's logo appeared on the control monitor.

"Attention!" Anna ordered. "Don't touch the clocks!"

With a final spring the second hand reached a vertical position.

"Action. It's eight! We're on!" She saw the number of the channel flash on the screen and prompted the anchor, "Close-up."

Something incomprehensible happened then. On the monitor, instead of the somewhat arrogant face of a journalist known to millions of viewers, there appeared a middle-aged man in a fashionable evening suit with a bow tie under a stiff bright white collar. The man casually ran his hand through the gray waves of his hair and gave the viewers a friendly smile.

"Good evening, ladies and gentlemen," he said in a deep, pleasant baritone. "I'd like to ask you for a small personal favor. Turn off your television sets for a few minutes. Incidentally, it will give you a chance to think about whether it's worth turning them on at all."

The man stopped talking and as he waited he looked into the lens of a television camera whose location was uncertain. Anna sat there petrified. She recognized him, but how he had managed to enter the Russian airwaves in place of the news was beyond her understanding. She imagined the many millions of viewers, the thousands of furious pensioners who were now at their phones dialing, and she knew that this was her last day on the job. A scandal was unavoidable, its dimensions and consequences hard to predict. In ten seconds the program's producer would call, in thirty seconds the network president. In the meantime the man took a turnip-shaped watch from his jacket pocket, snapped the cover shut, and put it back.

"Good evening, Anna!" His voice and smile changed; they became warmer and she suddenly sensed the weariness he was concealing. "You're incredibly beautiful today. I've noticed that you look good in blue. Unfortunately your beloved violets are nowhere to be found in this city . . ."

Anna squinted as she followed his glance. On the table in the corner of the control room an enormous bouquet of fresh roses stood in a crystal vase. The faces of her colleagues who sat next to it were strained; everyone was intently watching what was happening on the screen. Anna forced herself to blink several times, but it didn't change anything.

"Excuse me, Anna, I would never have dared to disturb you, but circumstances compelled me to do it." To her surprise Anna heard a note of uneasiness in his voice and she became nervous too. "I'm asking you to meet me. I could wait for you at home, of course, but it turns out that I have a pile of urgent matters. A great deal depends on your decision—all things considered, my entire life."

Anna swallowed with difficulty. She waved her hand as if she were chasing a neighbor's wayward chickens from her flower bed. "Go away," she said.

"Not until you agree. You still don't know, but perhaps you feel, that our fates are entwined . . . my life is totally in your hands."

"All right, I agree," Anna whispered, glancing sideways at the assistant director beside her, but Sasha hadn't heard a thing. "But leave, for God's sake!"

"Remember you promised!" The man smiled. "I'll wait for you after work tomorrow evening—though the word 'tomorrow' hardly makes sense . . ."

Without taking his eyes off her, he bowed and at the very same moment the anchor surfaced from nonexistence and appeared on the screen. With an arrogant smile he began methodically pouring out the country's latest troubles on the heads of the masochistic viewers. Anna looked at the clock—from the time the broadcast began the thin, threadlike arrow had moved three seconds. Was it really a hallucination? With some effort she pulled herself together and by the start of the next segment she was in full control of the situation. The weather forecast was traditionally the last news item. After she'd given the order to run it, Anna turned and took a look at the camera room: behind the control panel her colleagues were gathering up papers and talking animatedly.

"Anna, what's wrong? Do you feel ill?" Sasha started to get up from his chair. "You're a little pale."

"No, no, it's nothing, everything's OK. I feel a little dizzy. Did you notice anything wrong?"

"Nothing criminal." The assistant director shrugged his shoulders. "If we ran over by just twenty seconds"—he thought for a minute and continued—"well, that's . . . nothing unusual. Why, was there a slip-up? When?"

Anna sighed with relief. "No, maybe I just imagined it. Most likely, a little screw-up with CNN news."

"Hey, guys, look—roses!" Svetochka, the teleprompter editor, leaned over the bouquet as she wound a column of text onto a reel.

"Today is our Anna Alexandrovna's anniversary!" The program manager came into the control room and walked over to the director's panel to kiss Anna's hand. "You're all invited downstairs now," he continued in the voice of a popular entertainer, "where champagne and cake await you!"

As always happens in a group of colleagues, after the first toast conversations shifted to professional matters, reminiscences of all sorts. Anna laughed and remembered with the others, but somewhere in her heart she knew that it hadn't been a hallucination, and that knowledge was extremely pleasing.

5

Lukary looked around in all directions.

"The world is a theater and the people in it are actors—and the mentally ill are actors in a theater of shadows . . ."

The psychiatric hospital's tall white fence stretched along a quiet rural road lined with old linden trees. He took the road down a small hill to where a river sparkled in the sunlight. Washed by the fresh spring air, transparent distances of all shades of green spread beyond the river. In the sun it was almost as hot as in summer; a light breeze rippled through the young leaves and whispered something simple and affectionate. The sharp smell of spring grass rose from the earth and piles of fluffy white clouds sat in the high, infinitely blue sky. Everything breathed lightness and peace—it seemed that nature had taken it upon herself to heal the troubled human souls.

Squinting in the bright sun, Lukary climbed the slope and stopped in front of an iron door that had been painted white. The doorbell, the only black spot, stood out against the whitewashed brick wall. Lukary pushed it several times and waited. Minutes passed while unhurried rural life went on. There was no sound from behind the wall, just a breeze stirring in the tops of the old lindens. Convinced that his delicate rings were getting him nowhere, Lukary picked up a match from the road and jammed it into the bell. This time it worked. Before five minutes had passed heavy steps thumped behind the iron door and a small window opened behind the grille. Lukary saw an ugly brick-red face, covered by a thick red beard. Heavy bags hung beneath the man's eyes, which had a sharp and unfriendly look.

"What d'ya want?" the man asked in a voice hoarse from tobacco and drink. "No visitors now!"

"But why? I'm an obliging person, after all, so before I came I made an inquiry—there couldn't be a better day than today for visiting." Lukary gave a friendly smile, sincerely expressing his warm feelings toward his interlocutor. The man looked him over from head to toe; neither the suspect stranger's good city suit nor the provocative freshly shaved face escaped his grave stare. Redbeard didn't catch the French eau de cologne because of his own strong odor: in addition to the persistent smell of many days of drinking, an air of fresh garlic wafted from him and the devil knows what other things you're not likely to find in nature. But Lukary stood his ground.

"Closed for inventory," the man growled offhandedly, intending to slam the small window. Lukary stopped him by sticking out his index finger. Redbeard pushed hard with both hands but to no avail.

"Tell me"—Lukary was curious—"are there many men in your family?"

"There are . . ." the hospital orderly answered, not quite sure what this city fop was driving at.

"That's good!" Lukary said approvingly. "You've guzzled away some two hundred and fifty pounds, and it's a long haul to the cemetery."

At this critical moment the orderly displayed a surprising quick wit. Not only did he stop trying to close the window in the impudent visitor's face, but he reversed himself completely.

"Wait, I'll go announce you. What's your surname?"

"Lukin," Lukary answered eagerly. "Tell the head some Lukin's arrived, about a personal matter."

"All right, I'll tell him," the orderly muttered. "But take your finger out, that's against the rules."

He was gone for some time, then numerous bars began to squeak behind the door and Lukary knew he'd estimated the man's weight correctly—he was a cube. Escorted by the orderly, Lukary proceeded through an immaculate park designed in an English style. Judging by the clear sound of bounces, there was a tennis court somewhere nearby, and the smooth blue surface of a swimming pool sparkled between trees. Some people in regulation uniforms, which were well made, but out of a standard dark blue fabric, strolled on the clipped lawns in a dignified manner, engaged in unhurried conversation. Lukary and the orderly turned behind a pavilion, where a billiard table flashed in the open doorway, passed a greenhouse, and entered a small detached house, such as you might find on a country estate, with columns and tall sparkling windows.

"In here," the orderly said, the words sounding almost polite. They stood in front of an oak door with the sign "Head Doctor," above which hung a banner with the mysterious slogan: "If you've already lost your own mind, help your comrade!" Lukary was just about to ask his escort the meaning of this visual propaganda when the door opened and a short energetic man with amazingly cheerful eyes appeared in the doorway.

"Ah, I've been waiting for you!" he exclaimed almost playfully. "Am I right that you're the one named Lukin? That's a very fine, a very fine name! One can envy you, old man. Professor Lukin, for example—that has a ring to it."

He straightened his white smock, took Lukary by the elbow, and directed him into the office.

"I'm very glad to meet you! And doubly glad that you didn't show up on our blacklist." The head doctor rubbed his plump hands, very pleased with everything.

"You have blacklists?" Lukary asked with surprise. He took a fruit drop from the box being offered him, and in response to the invitation sat down in an armchair.

"How could it be otherwise?" the head doctor asked, for his part surprised. "In our frenzied times!"

Settling down across from his guest, the doctor shoved several candies into his mouth and in between munches inquired, "Well, to what do I owe this visit?"

"Listen, Doctor"—Lukary looked at him intently—"I'd like to speak with one of your patients."

"Who? If it's not a secret." The head doctor raised his eyebrows.

"His name's Yevsevy."

"Yevsevy . . . Yevsevy . . ." The man in charge grew thoughtful. "Yes, of course, you may talk to him, but I have to warn you your choice is most unfortunate! We have many brilliant conversationalists here, and listening to them is pure delight! There's the Ambassador Plenipotentiary to Paris—a clever man and a connoisseur of the fine arts!" The doctor closed his eyes with pleasure. "Or, if you'd like, there's a master of ceremonies! He tells risqué stories in such a way that even the ladies aren't offended! But Yevsevy? He's a silent creature, a misanthrope; sometimes you can't get a word out of him and you certainly can't talk about the racehorses! Depression, old man, he's deeply depressed."

"Nonetheless he's the one I'd like to speak to."

"So you're already offended! I can see from your face that you're offended!" The head doctor almost laughed, but stopped. "But what relation are you to him, actually? What will you be talking about? We medical personnel of the clinic are obliged to protect our patients' interests." He rose to his feet emphatically, put his hands behind his back, and began pacing around the office. "Yevsevy has never mentioned his relatives or friends."

"Yevsevy is a childhood friend, you see, and when I learned that he'd been struck by such . . . trouble, I considered it my duty . . ."

"Well, all right"—the head doctor gave in—"but remember that in our clinic treatment is carried out in absolute peace and quiet!"

The doctor turned around abruptly and fixed his eyes on Lukary suspiciously. "Lukin? Didn't we meet in the Ministry of Health? Of course, in the special department that treats the Central Committee? Don't deny it—you're a physician, aren't you?"

"Oh, no, God forbid!" Lukary smiled.

"Well, well." The head doctor sank down in his chair behind the desk; his whole manner expressed doubt about the uninvited visitor's truthfulness. He sat quietly for a while, casting guarded looks and frowning even more. "I hope you won't find it too much trouble to answer," he finally said, nervously twirling a thick office pencil between his fingers, "whether or not you have a certificate from the psychiatric clinic with you." He got up quickly and walked over to Lukary. "Look me in the eyes! Are you schizophrenic? Are you afraid of closed spaces and women in black tights?" He waved the pencil in front of the visitor's nose, then suddenly slapped him on the shoulder in a jovial manner. "Don't be offended, Lukin—I was joking! It's my job! Here, take the pen, fill this out, and sign it legibly. And write the date—in figures and words . . ."

The head doctor took a printed form from his smock pocket and handed it to Lukary. The text read: "I ______ hereby swear that under no circumstances or pretexts whatsoever will I attempt to obtain a place for myself in the psychiatric hospital."

Lukary signed. The head doctor studied the signature with clear satisfaction, then neatly folded the paper in two and put it in the safe standing nearby.

"That's just wonderful! Just excellent! I regard your step as a real sign of friendship. You up and signed without any arm-twisting." He drummed his fingers along the iron top of the safe. "But remember—not in the guise of medical personnel or as a person who's ill! Because I know you and later you'll allege that I didn't warn you."

"Do so many people want to get in here, then?" Lukary asked, somewhat surprised.

"Many? Every last one!" The doctor clasped his hands. "There's no getting rid of them. You know how bleak it is outside these days, but here we have peace, enough to live on, civilized human relations—in short, communism within the borders of one insane asylum. Plus the people we accept are more refined—better, you might say—they won't take just anyone off the street."

"You mean to say that the patients themselves decide who's admitted?"

"Of course! They're the ones who have to live with the newcomers. If you land in here, it's like getting into the Academy of Immortals—life membership. You know what it takes: three letters of recommendation plus a trial period. In recent times everyone's become so crazy they're pushing their way in without any shame. The ministry has become even more brazen—if they don't come to us as doctors, they come as patients. A few days ago two directors from general administration wanted to worm their way in as epileptics, and one real crackpot defected from the Writers Union and requested political asylum. He bit almost all of our patients. But we keep two lunatics on hand for such situations. The defector spent one night with them and asked to go back; he said there were also lunatics where he came from but not as violent."

"So you don't treat your patients at all?"

"We treat them, I'll say we treat them!" the head doctor replied indignantly. "Our medicines are peace and a superior quality of life. It's not like on the other side of the fence—there's no reason to go crazy here. Sports are a must and formal receptions and romantic intrigues—all to help keep in shape. By the way, we tried shock therapy the other day, but it was unsuccessful—it turned out to be an overdose, I confess. First thing in the morning we distributed the latest newspapers, and in the evening, without warning, we showed the news. We thought lots of patients would ask to be released, that they'd rush out of the clinic with open arms. No such luck!" The doctor waved his hand in a sign of despair. "At night no one slept, and in the morning at an emergency meeting we resolved to ban shock therapy as cruelty to humans. Finally, we decided to give up the annual masquerade ball and use the savings to make the fence higher and hire a guard patrol with dogs . . ." He became silent, walked over to the window, and stood there for a long time with his hands behind his back. "Still, it's strange that Yevsevy never said anything about you!"

The head doctor turned around, gave a quick, penetrating glance at his visitor, and walked out of his office with a nod. Lukary prepared himself for a wait, but literally the next moment there was a timid knock at the door and it opened to admit the same head doctor, without his smock and dressed in the regulation blue uniform. The change that had taken place was not just in dress, however—the man who entered was sullen and gloomy and the formerly cheerful eyes exhibited suspicion and ill will. Even his gait and posture had undergone a transformation: the man shuffled his feet and slumped in uncertainty.

"You wanted to see me?" he asked quietly. "I'm Yevsevy!"

"What?" Lukary stood up in confusion.

"Today's my day to be on duty," Yevsevy explained, looking up at the guest distrustfully. "The clinic's budget is small, they've had to save money on medical personnel. And, to be honest, who knows our shortcomings better than we?" He sat down modestly on the edge of a cot covered with oilcloth and looked at Lukary questioningly.

"You don't recognize me? We were such great friends in our youth! You and me and Serpina . . ." Lukary smiled, inviting him to share in the joy of a long-awaited meeting.

Yevsevy continued to look at him with the same attentiveness and gloom. "No," he said finally, "I don't remember. You've come here in vain." He turned and looked out the window indifferently. "We know about these schemes. The clinic isn't made of rubber, and I won't give you a recommendation to get in. Like it or not, call it egoism, but such are the times we live in—it's everyone for himself!"

"You didn't understand me. We were friends in another life."

"You see, now you're going to play the part of a madman." Yevsevy shrugged his shoulders. "A well-known scenario! Leave by yourself, I don't want to have to call the orderlies, inasmuch as that service here is staffed exclusively with lunatics."

He started to reach for the alarm on the wall. Lukary realized his mistake—Yevsevy couldn't remember because he didn't have a memory that saw back to past lives. Lukary smiled and focused his will. Yevsevy's expression began to change. Before his finger touched the alarm he sat up and stared at Lukary.

"Luka? Wait, wait! Yes, of course, Luka! Why didn't you say so right away?"

Yevsevy's strained face looked almost happy. By some inconspicuous sign Lukary recognized in this broken man the cheerful and resourceful boy who had been his friend during his first childhood on earth.

"Why didn't I recognize you?" Yevsevy wondered in the meantime. "You've changed very little. So many lives have passed since that time, so many years!"

And yet—Lukary saw this clearly—the tension and feeling of awkwardness hadn't abandoned the friend of his youth. Yevsevy wanted to rejoice at their meeting, but for some reason was afraid.

"I'm glad to see you, I'm really glad," Yevsevy said, not knowing what to do with his hands and evidently burdened by the split in his feelings. "You know what?" He suddenly cheered up, as if he'd found a way out of his difficult situation. "Let's drink! It's even encouraged here as one form of therapy."

He began to fuss about and got a tall dark bottle and two large glasses from the medicine cabinet.

"Calvados!" Yevsevy poured the brandy. "We have wonderful ties with Spain. The other day a delegation from America came. They walked around and asked all sorts of questions—they want to apply our experiment. It turns out that even in an affluent society there's a need for oases of abnormal life. And, you know, they were especially amazed that we completely manage without hired medical personnel. They can't even dream about that in their America, and here it's already very popular. Oh yes, there's still something to be learned from Mother Russia."

He raised the glass, indicating with a gesture that he was drinking to Lukary. The brandy was excellent—pleasant, with a subtle bitterness.

"By the way," Yevsevy said, more at ease, "we made an agreement to exchange our insane. I'm not pushy, I won't make it into the first group, but with time, I think, I'll get a turn too. If I'm lucky, I'll go to Germany or Sweden. I don't want to go to the Americans, they're much too noisy."

He looked up at Lukary and the suspicion in his eyes was as heavy as mercury.

"How did you manage to find me? Ah, yes," he remembered, "I completely forgot. I heard that you'd reached great heights in your ascent. They even said that your bright spirit was not inferior to the angels in power!"

Lukary smiled. "The nature of human power is different, and there are no heights on the path of enlightenment, only work . . ."

He decided not to tell Yevsevy about his banishment, nor did he tell how much trouble he, a spirit in disgrace, had gone through to find Yevsevy in the clinic. With his thorough knowledge of human nature Lukary understood that this news would not truly grieve his childhood friend and he didn't want to hear insincere words of sympathy. Besides, it might spoil his plans, and so he hurried to change the topic.

"So, how did you end up here?"

Yevsevy was in no hurry to answer. He poured himself a drink and, raising the glass to eye level, looked at Lukary through the glass.

"I'm hiding."

"From whom?"

"From myself." Yevsevy took a large gulp with visible pleasure. "Yes, from myself! It's not so easy to explain . . . You're following your path, you see, while Serpina made a career serving the dark powers, and I, sinner that I am, decided that my place is the madhouse, and that's not without a certain logic."

Yevsevy finished the brandy and put the glass down on the table. His face was sad, his eyes thoughtful. Lukary suddenly remembered their distant childhood and his heart filled with compassion for his friend. Through the murky distances of the ages he made out a small tow-haired boy, always barefoot and dirty, but happy with the simple happiness of being in the world. He saw the high bank of a river, the graven image of the god Perun, and an open view of endless woods. Ships with sharp prows sailed beneath their white sails to the distant sea, and the three rascals watched them from the hillside and dreamed about life in the future.

"Can I help you with anything?"

Yevsevy shook his head. "I know you feel sorry for me. Don't feel sorry! I've chosen my own road. You were always good and strong and you have power over many things now, but you can't do anything for me."

"I'd like to try . . ." Lukary put his arm around his friend's shoulder, but Yevsevy just smiled.

"Can you change the great law of cause and effect, the law of karma?" he asked. "No one can, you see, not even He."

"But why the insane asylum?"

"I'll explain it right now." Yevsevy looked like a person who's resigned himself to his life. "Each one of us, you see, carries the seeds of paradise and hell in his soul. As you know, through his earthly actions, thoughts, and desires, a man determines which road he'll travel after he dies—whether he'll prolong his ascent to the light or face descent into the underworld. Under the law of karma people keep returning to earth until it becomes certain which of the two worlds they belong to. When it becomes clear and all doubts are discarded, the chain of incarnations ends." Yevsevy licked his parched lips. "I realized this very early on because I'd been reading the ancient books since I was knee-high, and, honestly, the prospective choice didn't make me happy. I love earthly life too much to leave it for the afterlife. I love to watch this joyous and colorful world in spite of its imperfections. After all, there's nothing wrong with finding pleasure in lying in thick grass and watching slow, majestic clouds sail high over your head. I know you'll understand me if I simply say that I love living on earth as a man." Yevsevy quickly looked out the window where the park's new foliage was rustling in the warm breeze.

"Then I started to think—how could you live so that the inexorable law of karma would compel you to be born as a human time and time again? And I found the answer! If you don't execute any actions, if you have no intentions, then it means you're not ready for any decision about which path to follow after death. If that choice isn't made, you can never be admitted to the world beyond death and so you'll keep living as a human until the day of His Last Judgment. The most important thing is to keep a balance between good and evil. Thus, the madhouse—here no one expects you to perform any actions, and absence of thought and desire is considered absolutely normal. Here I'm neither kind nor bad, neither good nor evil—I'm nothing."

"So you've renounced life in order to live?"

"Exactly, Luka, exactly! And that's no easy feat. We don't know anything about the world when we're born; we don't even suspect the existence of the law of karma and reincarnation. So in order to avoid determinative actions I had to work on my own subconscious. And I succeeded! From my very first steps in my next life it repeats: be nothing, nothing in this life should concern you. Call it fate or destiny if you'd like . . . The only thing that surprises me—and I've just understood it during our conversation—every time, without exception, I've been born a Russian. Don't you find that strange?"

"Not at all!" Lukary took a pipe from his pocket. "Moreover, to me it seems to be part of the natural order of things. You only think that you're living so uniquely, but in fact a good many people who call themselves Russian intellectuals have been professing the same philosophy of existence for a long time. Don't get involved in anything, don't desire anything, live in order to live . . . In their time they let their own home be plundered and defiled with astonishing ease and then lived for dozens of years without taking any action. And now, like cockroaches, they've gone even deeper into their corners. No, my dear friend, you're by no means alone! The discovery of refuge in a psychiatric clinic is indisputably yours, but believe me, very soon they'll come to the same conclusion—in essence, these people are on their way to the madhouse."

Lukary raised a match to his pipe and drew in air. The smell of good tobacco uncoiled throughout the office. He watched Yevsevy from the corner of his eye and couldn't help but see that Yevsevy was frowning and staring down at the floor as he'd done at the start of their talk. Everyone likes to think he's exceptional and to destroy that myth is always unhealthy and dangerous for a friendship. Lukary saw that he'd made a mistake and he was about to make amends but Yevsevy suddenly jerked his head and asked, "Why did you come?"

There was more than simple resentment in his voice. "Do you need something from me? Keep in mind that I won't do or say anything! Just think, because of some whim I could upset the fragile balance and lose eternal life on earth!" Yevsevy warily moved to the far end of the couch. "Go away, I feel you'll be my ruin!"

"What gave you that idea?" Lukary smiled and slowly finished his Calvados. "I simply wanted to see you, and to remember our childhood. Just think about it—with all my resources what would I need from you?" He shrugged his shoulders. "What harm can memories bring you? Everything's in the past, it can't act on your karma in any way." He took the bottle and poured more brandy in the glass. "Wouldn't you like to be immersed in that distant time once again? It was a happy and serene period . . ."

Lukary's words and calm took effect. Yevsevy softened right away, the guardedness in his eyes gave way to mild sadness. He sat down at the table and picked up his glass. Lukary decided it was time.

"Do you remember how you saved us?" he asked offhandedly. "Serpina and I—we both essentially owe you our lives and perhaps something even greater. Who knows how the chain of our incarnations might have changed had we been murdered in our first childhood . . ."

"Yes, those days were truly happy and carefree!" Yevsevy sighed and smiled dreamily. "I remember the day was windy and cold, the earth chilled our bare feet. In the forest drops of water hung on the branches, and the river looked leaden gray beneath its white swirls. Spring came late that year and was rainy . . ."

"It seems I was the first to see the prince's retinue," Lukary remarked.

"Yes, you yelled, 'Run,' and we rushed into the forest thicket. They came fast on our heels and if they'd caught us they'd have buried us alive in the fortress's foundation. It seems absurd now"—Yevsevy smiled—"but in those days it was a sacred belief that a citadel could be made impregnable that way."

"What happened next? I only remember that all at once we found ourselves in some other world where an old sorcerer was waiting for us."

"You've forgotten." Yevsevy finished the brandy and wiped his mouth with his palm. "It wasn't a sorcerer at all—the old man's name was Cronus. I dragged you off into an ancient temple that I'd noticed long before when wandering in the forest. But I doubt even that would have saved us from the prince's knights had we not stumbled upon the idol."

"Was it Perun?"

"Oh, no, even more ancient still—it was Rod! But he's beside the point: we had come to a passage into a different space. I had no idea that it existed—we were fantastically lucky. When we stepped into Cronus's world we were completely safe. Imagine how amazed our pursuers were when they couldn't find us anywhere." Yevsevy laughed like a child, but immediately became serious again.

"You know, I never found anything so beautiful again. If I close my eyes now, I can see enormous age-old oaks floating in a mist which is pierced by the rays of ten multicolored suns. You feel as if you're surrounded by revolving mirrors that reflect a quivering world of magical beauty. And the greenery! True emerald! What crystalline purity and clear air! The old man appeared to be waiting for us; majestic and grave, he sat on an enormous boulder overgrown with moss. Dressed in white clothing, like the druids, with hair as white as snow, he seemed to be from the time of the world's creation, and perhaps he was. When we drew near, he raised his clear blue eyes and looked at us from beneath bushy brows.

" 'Who are you, children? How did you get into my space?'

"After hearing our story he remained silent for a long time, looking straight ahead. He was very old. It seemed an eternity before his lips began to move and he started speaking again.

" 'I am Cronus. The keeper of world time. Through my own labor and the work of the spirit, I made all that you see around you. The entrances into my world are guarded by powerful idols, who in their earthly lives dared to slow the course of time or tried to reverse it. As punishment for their audacity, until the end of time they must protect the work of my hands—the Kissoeides, the machine that produces the world's time. The cosmic law of cause and effect punishes all those who in their fuss and flurry refuse to delight in the lives given them, who turn life into a senseless race and so cause others to suffer. The Lord commanded, and I created what He desired. I am the great Cronus!'

"The old man slowly got up from the boulder. Balancing with difficulty and leaning on a walking stick, he headed into the depths of the oak grove. We followed on his heels. When he reached a large glade filled with the light of suns, Cronus stopped and pointed to an enormous structure that was revolving slowly a yard above the emerald carpet of grass.

" 'There it is—the Kissoeides of all world time.' Turning back to us, the old man continued. 'What is time? The product of the war between good and evil, the two great forces that set everything into motion in the world of sufferings, dreams, and hopes. God instructed me and I arranged these two universal forces, like the eternally opposing plus and minus, to sustain my Kissoeides. When evil accumulates in the world, time speeds up its flow, making a man's life seem like a mayfly's. When good gains the upper hand, time flows in a smooth comforting stream, which brings wisdom and acceptance of the world to man. I, Cronus, made it all!' "

Yevsevy became silent.

"But why did he banish us from his space?"

"It was because of Serpina." Yevsevy sighed. "He called the old man a fool. He said, 'You're old and foolish, because after you made the machine that produces time you didn't take care of yourself. You launched the mechanism of your own death and became the victim of your own invention. You're a double fool, old man,' Serpina repeated. 'Because after you made your machine you should have produced enough time for your own profit right at the start and later sold it to the people. Now you're old and poor as a church mouse, and you could have been young and unspeakably rich—you could have ruled the world.'

"Cronus watched Serpina intently for a long while, and finally a quiet, gentle smile touched his lips. 'A great future awaits you, young man, but you'll hardly be happy at any time or ever learn that true riches exist in this world. You and I are on different roads and it's not because you're young and I'm old.'

"The next moment we were standing on the river's high bank, watching the ships as they left for sea."

Yevsevy looked up at his visitor, his eyes were sad. "I'm thinking about how our lives might have evolved had Serpina not spoken those words. No one can know, and we're left only with memories. By the way"—he smiled—"sometimes it seems to me that the only reason people live is in order to have memories later."

"You said that afterward you never saw anything as beautiful as that fantastical world. Haven't you ever wanted to return to the oak grove filled with the light of the suns?" Lukary held Yevsevy's gaze and asked gently, "Maybe you've forgotten where the temple is?"

"No, I haven't forgotten." They looked into each other's eyes. "You see, a departure into another space is an action—a serious action; it might influence my karma."

"So, you've been living circumspectly your whole life? Your whole life you've trembled at the thought that something might happen?"

Yevsevy wasn't listening. He looked as anxious as a snared beast.

"Luka! Did you come here to destroy me? I understand everything—you're looking for the entrance into Cronus's space. You need the Kissoeides of world time!"

Lukary was silent.

"I know you can force me to tell," Yevsevy continued. "I feel your power."

"Try to understand it's very important! Not only for me. The powers of light . . ."

"Don't bother," Yevsevy interrupted. "I don't care if they're light or dark—for me it would be the equivalent of suicide. The soul of a suicide never returns to earth, as you know. Tell me, is that what you want?"

Lukary got up and looked Yevsevy over from head to toe. He was clenched as if expecting a blow.

"Forgive me, I shouldn't have come here. No matter what may

happen, it's your fate, and I don't have the right to change it." He took a step toward Yevsevy, embraced him, and held him tightly. "Farewell!"

For some time they looked into each other's eyes. Yevsevy's lips were trembling and tears rolled down his cheeks.

"I know how important it is to you!" His voice broke off, he could hardly hold back sobs. "But I can't! I love this vile life too much."

He rushed toward the office door and turned around. "But in the place of that temple perhaps there's just a temple . . ."

Lukary drank the rest of his brandy in solitude and took his hat from the hook, but just then the door opened again and the head doctor flew into the office, adjusting the fluttering flaps of his smock on the way. His eyes burned with the indefatigable energy of an administrator and a businessman's professional smile floated on his face.

"So, did you have your talk? I warned you that your Yevsevy was not much of a conversationalist . . ." He curled his lips scornfully and threw up his hands in helplessness. Taking Lukary by the elbow trustfully, the head doctor led him to the door and detained him for a moment. "Not a word to anyone about our institution! Times are painfully hard and don't forget that we have your signature! That's if anything should come up!" He banged the top of the safe with his palm and shouted into the hall.

"Hey, orderly, please take the trouble to see Mr. Lukin to the gate! Goodbye, Mr. Lukin, goodbye!"

Close to midnight a black cloud crept toward Moscow from the east. Thunder growled in its midst like restless dogs and vivid zigzags of lightning pierced its bloated body. The first spring storm was approaching the city and, as its harbinger, sparse rain began to drizzle against the background of a bright sunset. It drummed on the glass roof of the main department store, GUM, and splashed on the square's stone blocks. The searchlights, which had been turned on early, were reflected on the wet surface. Lukary walked under the arch of the entrance to the store that was always closed and lit a cigarette. To his left stood the cupolas of the Cathedral of St. Basil the Blessed, the symbol of Russia. Behind his back someone fussed and then cleared his throat. Lukary turned around. On the top step of semi-circular stairs sat a thickset bald man. He was wearing a dark blue disheveled peasant's blouse and a padded jacket was thrown across his shoulder. In one hand he held a bottle; the other was petting a puppy which was cuddling up to him.

"I'm a defrocked priest," the man said, and turned to the puppy, "but not an atheist. God dwells inside you, you just need to feel Him. But it's so nice in the church!" He paused dreamily and raised the bottle to his throat. "The candles burn, the choir sings, and there's something like peace in your soul. Be thankful! It's almost as if there's no human rubbish around . . ."

The man rose to his feet and walked down the steps. "Gimme a smoke, brother!"

They stood shoulder to shoulder, smoking and quietly watching the reflections of the lights on the wet stone blocks. The golden streak of sunset narrowed above the distant roofs.

"Were you really defrocked?"

The man nodded and offered Lukary the bottle of vodka.

"Have a swig, you'll feel better! Helps you forget your own brutishness . . ."

Lukary wiped the top of the bottle with his hand and took a couple of large swallows. The puppy yawned sweetly, opening its rosy mouth and showing its small teeth.

"Did that help?" the defrocked priest asked kindly. "I can see you're in bad shape, all clenched up like a ball. Be easier on yourself . . ."

Lukary gratefully threw his arm around the man's shoulders and gave him a hug. "Listen, Father, you should know about this. There's a special place in Moscow said to have a spell cast over it . . ."

"I used to be Father, now it's brother!" The man smiled into his beard. "In our glorious Moscow there are places like that to spare. Time passes but they don't change a bit. Where Saltychikha's town house once stood you see the Lubyanka with its secret police, and the

Cathedral of Christ the Savior is now a swimming pool and that's all because no other building could stand there. It only seems like Moscow is changing, in fact everything remains as it was."

"Did you know," Lukary interrupted, "that in past times an idol stood there!"

"A temple, was it?" the ex-priest guessed. "Then they put a church in its place for sure."

"No, the temple ought to be there even now!" Lukary remembered Yevsevy's words.

"Hmmm . . ." the ex-priest drawled out thoughtfully, but suddenly he rejoiced. "My word! We're standing right opposite it!" He pointed across the square. "There's a temple for you! A little building like some cabin and an idol lying in there . . . But it's his comrades-in-arm who made him an idol, in truth he's a regular criminal! He ravaged Mother Russia. People had a bright dream of brotherhood and equality and he perverted it. But what's there to say!" He raised the bottle to his mouth again and went on. "Here's what I think: he'll answer for all he's done, but we'll have to answer too! There aren't any side stops in history, you can't step off and watch. When someone calls you, you don't have to go, but the people followed him—some out of vainglory, some for profit, though they had to know that it wasn't for God! Lenin should be buried in the earth, let people drink at his grave, let them pity the lost soul, but we just can't stop ourselves—we keep on groveling!"

Lukary trampled his cigarette, and looked at the ex-priest. "Tell me, do you believe in good?"

"You know," the man answered after a while, "I just live. In a world of crazy people it's best to be blessed."

Lukary raised the collar on his coat and crossed the square. Stepping over the heavy chain, he walked through the closed double doors. Inside, a dim night light burned, as if the corpse was afraid of the dark. When he got to the coffin, Lukary pressed his forehead to the glass and studied the shining pink face. There was neither cruelty nor vice in its features and he sensed sorrow there.

"You can't force time," Lukary said. "Everything passes, and therein lies God's great mercy! Nothing is eternal—not the torments of conscience, not repentance, and some day everything will be forgiven."

He stood up beside the coffin, not knowing whether what he had just said was true.

The next morning the night guard motioned for his wife to come into the bathroom, where he turned on both faucets full force, bent down, and with trembling lips whispered into the woman's ear that with his own eyes he had seen the leader of the world proletariat cry and smile in his coffin. Of course, he hadn't reported to the bosses about what had happened, just as he had kept quiet about the man who had walked through the dark marble walls as if they were water. Who would want to be thought crazy in a society that does not openly admit its own madness?

6

On a map of Spain, yellowed from age and frayed around the edges, a greasy cross marked the spot north of Madrid where the Cordillera Central stretch their peaks to the sky. From frequent use the map was covered with faded reddish-brown spots that looked like coffee and the paper was worn in the folds. A drop of candle wax the size of a small coin covered the outskirts of Guadalajara. Deep in thought, Serpina was picking at the wax with a long yellow nail. As he did, he drew in on a pipe whose bowl was shaped like a bearded goat's head. The courtier's velvet doublet fit his stout body a little too tightly: he kept wanting to loosen his splendid cravat and breathe with a free chest. The tall boots he was unused to wearing pinched his feet and the heavy hat with an ostrich feather kept slipping down on his forehead, obscuring the light, so that he couldn't locate that place on earth to which he had been ordered to report. This whole masquerade with the dressing-up and need to coordinate the place and time of the meeting irritated him no end.

Serpina scowled, he puffed on the pipe angrily, but he would never have dared disobey the Black Cardinal. Far too fresh were his memories of what happened to his colleague Pleshivy, who whether from negligence or an excess of pride had appeared before Nergal's dark eyes without having troubled to create a human form for himself. At the gate of the ancient Russian city of Smolensk even today tourists can see a large boulder that remotely recalls his bald head and large ears. Town dwellers who live nearby swear that the stone has the strange habit of hopping, and on moonlit winter nights it emits such heartrending moans that the hair of drunken passersby stands on end and dogs take refuge in distant corners where they shake and shudder. The people have tried breaking it into pieces and they've sold it to rich foreigners, but it always returns to its place, bringing more horror to the peaceful residents.

"Clothing and being in tune with the times are trivial matters," Serpina thought, "but ones that can have a significant effect on your fate." His own brilliant career served as a fine example. The ability to be natural, an excellent, never-failing memory, and, of course, unquestioning obedience enabled him to stand out from the general crowd of graduates of the Academy of Knowledge and to attract the attention of the high leadership of the Department of Dark Powers. Add to this unquestionable loyalty, an inborn deference to superiors—and you've got a ready formula for success! He smiled at his thoughts and began to fold up the map along its well-worn creases. Needless to say, intelligence is essential in any situation, but likely it was precisely his deference that allowed him—a man who'd worked his way up in the ranks of the demons—to occupy such a prominent position in the department, one deserving of his colleagues' envy. "Don't neglect work on your image, fashion it every day and every hour"—this place in his workbook *Methods of Applied Hypocrisy* was underlined twice—"never neglect the most trivial details and it will soon become clear how the image begins to work on you." This would seem to be a basic ingredient of success, the most absolute of rules, one which many do neglect, however, and then are still surprised at their own stagnation.

"Love people," Nergal once said, echoing the Bible, and added, "They are a fertile ground for sin! Cultivate their imperfections like delicate plants in need of love and care, and they will bear you fruit.

When you work with people, you have to live the way they live and always remember that the human soul is the only beachhead where our battles can take place." With these words the head of Secret Operations in the Department of Dark Powers began his introductory lecture on virtual human psychology, and Serpina, who was then still an insignificant student, scrupulously remembered the words of the teacher, who in time became his patron. Let Nergal amuse himself with this whole masquerade, to each his own, but he, his true student and subordinate, would play the game strictly by the rules.

Yet, Serpina thought, none of this in any way explains the reason for the urgent summons to the high command. Fidgeting in front of an enormous Venetian mirror and adjusting the various laces and bows, he tried to understand when and where he'd made a mistake and to prepare a reasonable justification ahead of time. Of course, one couldn't exclude the possibility of a false denunciation—something that was encouraged in the Department of Dark Powers as a way of keeping in shape and staying alert, but in this case he could only rely on his own resourcefulness and also on the good luck that almost never left him. The only thing Serpina didn't doubt was that a difficult and unpredictable meeting lay ahead. The choice of time and place where he was instructed to appear was proof. The atmosphere of a medieval Spanish castle hardly encouraged relaxed social conversation and the patron was an aesthete who always painstakingly selected the setting to fit the subject of the drama, of which he was both author and director. Sometimes Serpina thought that he, Serpina, was really just an actor whose lines Nergal had thought up earlier. One of their last meetings had taken place in Paris, in the intoxicating atmosphere of the early twentieth century. There were young women, music, and wine in abundance, and then the Côte d'Azur, a warm southern night and an outing on a yacht—that's how the Black Cardinal had congratulated him on his advancement in the service. But medieval Spain? For this he needed all his self-possession and mental faculties.

With these unhappy thoughts Serpina wrapped himself in a floor-length mantle, pulled his hat down over his forehead, and resolutely stepped out of the astral plane. As it turned out, his preparations were hardly excessive: a thick wet snow fell in the mountains and the wind swept down in gusts as it tore through the peaks, howling like a hundred hungry wolves. With his back pressed against a hollow in the stone, Serpina looked around and caught his breath. As he had supposed, the castle stood on the summit of a cliff. Its walls seemed to grow out of it naturally. The austerity of the architecture suggested that it had been built before the first Crusade. Serpina thought he saw a soft rose-colored light in the depths of the stone mass, but the thick veil of snow and the falling dusk transformed his vision into a conjecture. With a heavy sigh Serpina tore himself from the safe hollow and climbed along a barely noticeable path, risking with every step that he would be blown into the abyss. Clinging to stunted bushes, he would wait out the gusts of wind and finally he reached a small area that had been carved into the thick of the rock face and partitioned off by massive iron gates. From a rusty surface corroded by time and weather, two lions watched him, their bronze mouths open wide. A bell hung on a hook beaten into the rock face. Serpina struck it three times. The lone sounds echoed from the mountains and faded away, the white fog thickened, and everything around was spattered with sticky snow, but still he stood there, his back against the rough stone wall.

Finally, there was the light of a torch, one side of the gates creaked opened slightly, and directly before him Serpina saw a huge black man, whose dark bulging eyes regarded him indifferently. Snowflakes melted on the giant's naked torso; he was silent. With icy fingers Serpina undid the fastenings on his mantle, and a golden five-pointed star gleamed in the torch's fluttering flame. When the Moor saw the supreme sign of diabolical power, he bowed respectfully and stepped aside, letting the guest into the interior of the small courtyard. The gates clanged and the heavy oak drawbar slid back onto the massive brackets. Serpina and the Moor climbed in silence onto the drawbridge's ice-covered ramp and for a long time they wandered through passages cut into the rock, which smelled of dampness and mice. The roughly hewn steps on the narrow winding stairways were grown over with moss, and Serpina's boots slid on them. One of the stairways led to a small semi-dark room, lit only by an oil lamp covered with soot.

Making a sign for Serpina to wait, the Moor pressed on the stone wall and disappeared through a secret passage. He returned immediately, and with a deep bow invited the guest into the knights' hall, which Serpina could now see.

"Your Excellence." Serpina made a deep bow, and the feathers on his hat swept the stone floor and touched his boot's square toe.

"I'm glad to see you, Serpina!" An elderly man of almost frail build rose from a massive chair with a high carved back. The Black Cardinal remained true to form: the human appearance he'd chosen once and forever hadn't changed, only the various costumes for different periods. In Paris, at the beginning of the century, Nergal had preferred a long jacket and cape, and he wore his hair combed back smoothly, but now his feeble body fit snugly into a black velvet doublet with a white lace collar, and he wore black hose and soft short boots of singular beauty. In the light that came from the torches on the wall and the fire behind his back, the Black Cardinal's long shoulder-length hair radiated pure silver. His proudly held head and aquiline nose gave him the look of a bird of prey.

After the chilling dampness of the underground passages and the piercing wind in the high mountains, the large hall felt warm and cozy. A reddish reflection lay on the oak planks of a long banquet table and sparkled on the polished plating of armor hanging on the wall. The smell of burning birch wood spread a precarious sense of peace and well-being in the air. But Serpina was too experienced to be relaxed. After he bowed a few more times, he stood up straight and paused in expectation, keeping his eyes on the head of Secret Operations. Serpina knew this perfectly: if you start to relax your control over a situation, a mistake is inevitable. Nergal had intentionally chosen this image of an aging, sickly man: by dulling his interlocutor's heightened sense of danger, he meant to provoke him, if not into candor, then at least into a carelessness typical of dim-witted natures. And, needless to say, his image did not fit the colossal power possessed by the Prince of Darkness's closest attendant and comrade-in-arms.

Serpina took advantage of the pause graciously granted him and removed his coat; he took a perfumed lace handkerchief from the doublet's cuff and wiped the snow from his face. In the meantime Nergal slowly turned to the fireplace and began to poke the coals until they blazed up with a blue flame.

"Fine weather, isn't it?" He turned back and looked at Serpina with his burning eyes, which somehow resembled the muzzles on guns. His voice was deep and strong; a quiet, almost childish smile danced on his thin pale lips. "On such an evening there's nothing better than to sit by the fire with friends, sip a warmed red wine, and have a pleasant conversation. Yes, on the whole"—he made a vague gesture with his frail white hand—"nothing should sadden or spoil the mood. The logs are crackling, outside snow is falling . . . All very much in harmony with human nature . . . So please have a seat, Serpina. Sit down here, close to the fire."

Serpina drew nearer, carefully moved his chair closer to the fireplace, and only after the Black Cardinal had sat down on his soft leather seat, did Serpina permit himself to take a seat across from him. Relaxing and stretching his thin legs toward the fire, Nergal snapped his fingers and immediately the Moor came into the hall carrying a silver tray with two glazed mugs steaming with hot wine. This time the Moor wore a snow-white livery, embroidered with gold, and snug white gloves.

"Thank you, James. Put the tray on the small table and give our guest the larger mug; as you can see, he is thoroughly chilled to the bone from having clambered up to our little alpine nest."

The Black Cardinal smiled at Serpina in a most pleasant way, and with the nail of his middle finger he neatly tidied his wispy mustache. Serpina took the mug from the Moor's hands and gladly took a sip of the hot spicy wine. He didn't hurry to join in conversation, but shifted his gaze to look at the portraits of the castle's proprietors that were hanging on the opposite wall. Their faces were just as heavy and massive as the picture frames. "Robbers' mugs," Serpina thought to himself, "take your pick—you could pin something on the first bastard you see and you wouldn't be wrong!"

As if reading his thoughts, Nergal noted, "Such were the times, my friend! Only the strong were right. Little has changed from those days, by the way. But perhaps you're of a different opinion—I wouldn't want to force mine upon you."

"Oh no, Monseigneur! I agree with you completely! Time makes few changes in character or relations between people, and in any case it teaches them nothing. There have been seventy or eighty generations since the birth of Christ . . ."

Serpina looked at the Black Cardinal, meeting the stare of his closely set gimlet eyes. They bore not the slightest trace of the civility one heard in his words.

"Right you are," Nergal said. "I'm glad that we're of the same opinion. On the subject of art, today I asked James to acquire from Germany a portrait of Hegel by one of his contemporaries to hang in a conspicuous place in this castle. It will be a pleasant reminder of the successful operation. As far as I remember, wasn't it your idea to expose the philosopher to the idea of the unity and struggle of opposites?"

"Partly, Monseigneur, partly!" Serpina smiled politely. "I was only working out the details of your conception concerning the schematization of human thought and linking it to what, for laughter's sake, you then called the dialectic. I especially liked your thesis about the negation of negation! If you remember, I further suggested introducing the law of the negation of negation, but you correctly expressed doubt in the intellectual capacities of the students on whom would fall the fundamental burden of learning this gibberish."

"Now, now, don't be modest, Serpina! The law of the unity and struggle of opposites is exclusively your contribution. With the German's help we succeeded in instilling in the human mind the idea that evil is necessary in the same degree as good, making people think that, dialectically speaking, sins are as necessary as good deeds!" The Black Cardinal seemed pleased. "I remember very well that you were elevated into the ranks of the senior privy councillors precisely for executing this operation. Or am I mistaken? You need not answer, I know that you did not terribly want to answer my summons to come here!"

"Monseigneur, how can you!" the privy councillor exclaimed in an outburst of feigned indignation.

"Don't trouble yourself with the Pharisee act now, Serpina—it will come in handy later!" The head of Secret Operations twisted his thin lips in the likeness of a smile. "Accept your visit as an objective necessity. In the end, none of us is free, each of us has a superior. By the way, a long time ago I started a joke among people on this theme. It basically goes: the happiest subordinate on earth is the Pope because every day he gets to see his immediate superior crucified! So tell the truth—after all, I don't summon you very often . . ."

"The matter's really bad," Serpina thought. "Nergal is in an ugly mood." Everyone knew for certain what lay behind his habit of showering praise on his own subordinates and recalling their career successes.

"As for your secret unwillingness to appear at my summons," the Black Cardinal continued with a sigh, "we don't expect adoration from you! Our dark world, in contradistinction to the light world, is not built on hypocritical 'thou shall not steal's and 'thou shall not covet's, nor on an abstract love for your neighbor, but on real strength, fear, and a striving to crush that neighbor by any means. Be self-confident and brazen, if you can, but don't get angry if someone else throws you from your pedestal and tramples on you. Practice shows that in such circumstances it's safer and easier to be polite and civilized. You've learned that lesson well, Serpina. Those who see how society is constructed on the principle of force can understand the secret sources of power that are hidden from the view of simpletons. The law of the strong and intelligent is the most just and reliable law in the world!"

Lost in thought, Nergal drummed his thin fingers on the polished arm of his chair. Serpina waited respectfully. He'd heard all these platitudes many times and now he was waiting for Nergal to get to the heart of the matter. Nergal was in no hurry, however. "As for our meeting today, your displeasure is absolutely in order! You might consider it an old man's caprice—I simply wanted to spend an evening conversing with an intelligent partner. I almost said 'with an intelligent person'!" Nergal laughed. "Although this would have been partially true. You did begin your career as a person and, as I remember, you like to repeat that when you work with people it's necessary to live the way they live." The gimlet eyes turned on Serpina. Outside the narrow embrasures snow was piling up.

"I confess"—the Black Cardinal's voice sounded sad—"sometimes I'm sorry I wasn't born a person. No, no, Serpina, don't smile, I'm being completely sincere! Unfortunately, neither you nor I can experience the lifting and soaring of spirits which every ordinary mortal is capable of doing. I've brought this half-forgotten word 'mortal' to light for a purpose—it contains the solution to a secret, an explanation of both human baseness and the heights that people have achieved. Yes, Serpina, we can be great masters of temptation, we can arrange things so that some wretch follows us to hell with a bright smile of thanks, but we can never experience his rapture or the fullness and sharpness of his emotions. It's all because he is mortal and we are not. It's nonsense, but that's precisely the case. Only mortality accounts for the expansion of human emotion and potential, the delight they feel in living, their ability to rise above circumstances, above their very selves, and become spirits of light. Time limits people, they have to rush in order to feel and achieve, they have to understand the nature of good and evil in a short insightful moment. But the grim reaper around the corner has already lifted his scythe and is breathing cold air on the back of the skull. There, you're smiling again, but I'm intentionally using a graphic image. Thoughts about death pursue a person throughout life, but they also allow people to achieve greatness in their work. Take art, for instance. Feeling the course of time, the artist selects a singular moment and with all the power of his feelings seals it to the canvas with oils. Through fantasy and their heightened sensitivity musicians and poets transform themselves into tuning forks: they express the music of the time. When you think about it, Serpina, you'll understand that human art is but an attempt to arrest the course of time or to live life differently. To an amazing degree the speed of the flow of time indicates the intensity of human emotions, but people don't understand what time is and they're happy that way! You and I have been denied this experience, Serpina. The sense of life lies in the willingness to sacrifice it, but what can we sacrifice when we're immortal? He who said 'He who increases knowledge increases sorrow' was a thousand times right. This thought makes me sad, I feel deprived of my fair share . . ."

The cardinal covered his eyes with his hand. During the ensuing quiet one could hear the sudden sound of bad weather outside the castle's thick walls. The privy councillor waited; not a muscle on his face moved.

"You can see I'm joyless today!" Nergal looked over the top of his hand at Serpina. "Say something, cheer the old man up a little . . . What do you do when melancholy suddenly comes over you?"

"There's a well-known medicine." Serpina sipped from his mug. "Wine, cards, women!"

"Always the same thing!" The Black Cardinal sighed. "Aren't you sick of it? Although, it can't be denied, you're still young and don't know how tiring and monotonous this eternity can be. I was one of those who shared the master's fate in the underworld from the first day. To say it was a long time ago is to say nothing!"

Nergal took a long pipe with an ivory stem from a stand. Beating James to it, the privy councillor instantly jumped up and brought him a candle in a massive silver candlestick. The head of Secret Operations lit the pipe and leaned against the chair's hard back. His mood changed abruptly.

"Listen, Serpina, you're said to be a great connoisseur and lover of women." The Black Cardinal smiled subtly, sparks flashed in his eyes. "If I'm not mistaken, your examination for admission to the Academy of Knowledge was directly connected with this exciting subject. With such enormous competition how did you make your way into the Department of Dark Powers? There are plenty of petty scoundrels, after all, and most of them want to become major ones . . ."

"It wasn't that difficult," Serpina said, shrugging his shoulders and showing that he was extremely flattered by his superior's attention. "The first question on the exam was theoretical: 'Woman as a weapon in the work of the Dark Powers.' I was able to prove to the masters on the examination committee that Bernard Shaw's play *Pygmalion* was one of the greatest provocations in the history of art. Thanks to it, men got the idea that they could take a primitive and crude woman and raise her to the level of their own emotional and cultural development. This great lie of the playwright cost the stronger sex's best representatives dearly. Their attempts, which were condemned to failure, at best ended in drunkenness and complete despair. I also succeeded in showing what an important role the vogue for beautiful women plays in bringing men to a condition of complete prostration. When a man sees a woman who is made to look like the current ideal, he has a right to expect that a complete range of human feelings exists beneath the mask, the rich inner world of his chosen one. But, alas, the copy is crude, undeveloped, and far from the imagined original, and it's too late to step aside, Hymen's manacles are closed!" Carried away by his memories, Serpina took his short pipe from his doublet pocket, but remembered just in time. Noticing his movement, the Black Cardinal graciously nodded, giving his permission to smoke.

"What kind of practical assignment were you given?"

"It was the same for everyone." Serpina took the candlestick from James and lit up. "Each of the new students, after they married, had to drive his spouse to the point where she would destroy her soul on her own. Although at first glance the assignment seems simple enough, its execution demanded a certain inventiveness and, I would even say, artistry. Most of my less successful comrades, not having managed to get out of the marriage, took up drinking and brawling, trying to attract their wives to it too. A method as old as the world, but it works terribly. What's more, the essential goal isn't achieved: the woman must throw herself into the embraces of the Dark Powers! After reflecting upon it, I took a different approach. My scenario, which I called 'The Defenseless Victim,' called for a great deal of self-control and cold-bloodedness. It's a great art—to act naive and inexperienced in all life situations and at the same time keep her from leaving you. Anyone who had been present during our bedroom scenes would certainly have choked with laughter and tears. I was always walking around in bandages, with something broken or dislocated, I was fired from work on a regular basis, all the drivers in the city skirted your humble servant by a mile, knowing my tendency to fall under their wheels, blind old ladies with bad hearts helped me to cross the street, and that's not to mention such trifles as broken dishes and chronic diarrhea and colds. But my wife truly loved me. Steady as a tin soldier, she only started to smoke half a year later; after a year she began hitting the bottle; and she took lovers on the eve of our second wedding anniversary. In short, I won't tire you, after about three years the poor thing completely went to pieces, spoke blasphemously, and during the holidays dealt me a mortal blow . . ."

"Yes, I now see that you've truly mastered the problem of women." Nergal laughed. Then suddenly, with no forewarning, he asked, "So what have you been doing lately?"

Serpina composed himself. The prelude had ended, the conversation had turned to business. Straightening up in his chair, he changed the expression on his face.

"Evaluating the situation on earth," he began, after clearing his throat, "I came to a conclusion that it's necessary to strengthen discipline and control over the work of the rank-and-file operatives. The morals of human society are corrupting our personnel in the field. There is no longer any need to tempt people or set them against one another: people do these things on their own! If matters keep on like this, the personnel assigned to earth will lose their professional qualifications."

"What measures do you suggest?" The Black Cardinal raised his eyebrows.

"With your permission, Monseigneur." Serpina pulled out a scroll from the sleeve of his doublet. "This is a plan for retraining personnel, including the establishment of a museum of human stupidity and an attached teaching cemetery of human hopes. In the project's second stage we envisage the founding of a scientific center for integrative research into human depravity. Would you be so kind as to look at it?"

The senior privy councillor handed Nergal a scroll tied with a ribbon. Nergal took it and without unrolling it set it down on the small table beside him. "I'll look at it later. What kind of exhibits are being planned for the museum?"

"You're exceptionally kind, Your Excellence!" Before continuing, Serpina took a gulp of wine from the nearby mug. "Monseigneur just now spoke about the capacity of humans to rise above themselves . . . I don't dare cast doubt on such a wise opinion, but nevertheless I'll permit myself to note that such a flight of emotions is granted to only a few. My own experience as a practicing scoundrel testifies to the stupidity and spiritual underdevelopment of the majority of people. They have primitive desires, their thoughts and actions are predictable, and from the professional point of view they are of no interest. It's boring and tiring to work with them."

"You simply don't know the power of revelation that He gave to man!" Nergal noted sarcastically. "But go on."

"I'm sure that's so," the privy councillor was forced to agree, but went on with his talk. "I'd like to create a working model of human destiny as one of the museum exhibits. As with children's blocks, you could assemble a model of the life of a high-level bureaucrat with all his fears and torments and his early death from a heart attack, or you could make a model of the fate of a talented youth who was blocked by careerist professors and ended his life in the gutter, after becoming a total drunk . . ."

Serpina looked at Nergal, who wasn't concealing his boredom.

"But the museum's just a minor thing," he said, hurrying to improve the impression. "It may be great boldness on my part, but literally a few days ago I began a new experiment with a group of scientists. After their pride had been excited, they came very close to understanding the laws of so-called nature. Such things have happened before, and each time a new discovery is made, we've had to expand the limits of knowledge by one more step. At first they explored the atom, then its nucleus, and now they've gotten to elementary particles. It's become much more troublesome and costly for us to think up newer and newer laws for them and to split up the entire mass of matter again, not to mention that this work diverts our personnel from their real duties."

"Yes, yes." Nergal became interested. "That is really important. And what did you think up?"

"I decided to play on their sick pride and to direct the sharpest ones in the wrong direction. I dug in my memory and found a formula that we still used at the Academy for rough calculations concerning the course of history. The correlation is highly approximate and inexact, but it's attractive because it connects the events of the past, present, and future into one chain. It even creates the impression that the future can be predicted. Once astrologers offered something similar for the entertainment of the broad public, but this time the stakes are much more serious. To play it safe, my agents have worked on about a dozen scholars in different countries of the world. All their irrepressible energy will now go to waste and they'll leave us in peace for a hundred years or so. In addition, as always a rivalry about scientific priorities will start up and that will open a new field for us to intrude upon. Envy, unwarranted hopes, intrigues—I can guarantee that eight of the ten will forget to think about the discovery itself and will just become engaged in the struggle for their own authorship. Of course, in five years or so in order to stir up interest we'll have to throw out some experimental thingumajig for them, but one of my assistants will take care of that. Young people's interest in science still hasn't cooled, and they'll create such excitement that all the academicians on earth will tear at their bald heads in despair!"

"Well, that's a very worthy beginning," Nergal praised him. "I also like to play games with great minds. I remember I followed Einstein's research with great interest—it gave me pleasure comparable only to a great concert performance. Just think about it, Serpina, without any prompting, he came by himself to the understanding of the unity of space and time. Yes, indeed, you're being unfair to human genius! What a nice little piece Einstein wrote about the relativity of people's understanding of the world surrounding them. He was on the verge of discovering parallel worlds, and at the end of his life he was thinking that not only gravity but human will is able to exert an influence on space and time."

The Black Cardinal got up from his chair and walked around the hall. His enormous shadow followed him on the far wall. Serpina stood up and respectfully remained in a pose of great humility.

"Well, your project, let's call it that, is really quite good!" Nergal continued, his eyes cast down. "I've always valued situations that have an element of play. Human pride must be restrained: He has spoken about this openly, and if your venture succeeds I'm prepared to send a special report to His committee in charge of supervising the Dark Powers. Let them know they're not the only ones who are concerned with implementing His commandments in life."

Nergal smiled and went over to the fireplace. He stretched his thin ash-covered hands toward the fire.

"All my initiatives are only applications of your own idea of human happiness." Serpina cast a devoted and flattering glance at the figure bent over the fire grate. "That is the best operation our department ever carried out. On earth there's no person who would not thirst for personal happiness before striving for enlightenment and ascent to Him. You succeeded in replacing a clear and distinct goal with something illusory, which no one living can make any sense of. An absurdity, a mirage . . ."

But Nergal was not listening to the flattering speech. Serpina saw that his thoughts were somewhere far from this castle, lost in the mountains of Spain. Afraid to disturb him, the privy councillor stopped talking and tried to make himself inconspicuous. The fire crackled as it burned out. The wind outside the windows quieted down and, as often happens in the mountains in spring, the sky cleared and big bright stars appeared. The enormous yellow disk of the moon rolled onto the black velvet stretching above the snow-covered mountains. Straightening up and wiping his hands as he walked, the Black Cardinal crossed the hall and climbed up the steps leading into one of the recesses cut into the thick wall, from which one could look outside through the narrow embrasures. The light from the torches turned deadly white and they all burned out together, joining the spectral semi-darkness of the moonlit night. Softly stepping along the stone slabs, Serpina drew closer and came to a stop at the foot of a short, semicircular stairway.

"Serpina," Nergal said, looking through the window slit at the mountain slopes sparkling with snow, and the privy councillor shivered from the cosmic cold in his voice. "Something that no one could have expected has occurred. Einstein was close to the truth and would have come even closer if, instead of dead matter, he had examined the world of people. In their vain pursuit of illusory goods they have approached the speed of light—in accordance with the theory of the great physicist; the weight of their sins has grown beyond limits and that could not fail to have an impact on time. Do you remember, in the Revelation to John: the mighty Angel came down from heaven with an open scroll and swore by Him who lives forever and ever that 'there should be time no longer.' Time stops when the end of the world comes, His Terrible Judgment . . ."

The Black Cardinal turned and with empty unblinking eyes looked his councillor in the eye, and from that dead stare something inside Serpina snapped.

"Serpina"—Nergal's voice was steady and cold as ice—"time has come to a stop."

7

They had exceeded their allotted airtime by more than twenty seconds, and consequently they ran the weather forecast so quickly that the names of cities and villages just flashed by on the screen. After a day the roses on the table in the control room not only hadn't withered but had blossomed even more, releasing a delicate and gentle scent into the air. Anna gathered her papers and walked down to the editor's office along with the rest of the team, but she didn't hurry to leave for home, despite the late hour. She found some urgent matters, which could have been left unattended for another month or year without any harm, then sat down at her work desk and started to sort through papers. Anna knew all too well that she was wasting time, but she couldn't help herself. When the last of her colleagues had shut the door behind him, she grabbed the telephone and dialed Maria Nikolayevna.

"How can you be such a fool?" Masha said, after hearing out her friend's fears and misgivings again. "She gets lucky one time in life, and here she goes and blows it! In the midst of our wretched, dull life! Well, let's say he's really waiting for you! He's not a monster, after all.

Besides he gives you flowers and—as for the other things—who's not a little strange these days! Any woman with a husband like your Sergei would consider it good fortune!"

Maria Nikolayevna's last words were spoken in vain. When the conversation was over—if you could call Mashka's reprimand a conversation—Anna got her coat and walked through an underground passage to the television center's night bar. Deep in her heart Anna knew that she was trying to cheat fate with this maneuver, for in this case she'd be able to leave the building by a different exit from the one she usually took. She ordered a cup of coffee and sat for a long time, taking occasional sips of the liquid brown swill and looking through someone's abandoned newspaper. The half-dark bar was empty except for two guys who sat at the next table, smoking and swigging beer from tall glasses.

"Not bad," said one of them, nodding in the direction of her table—a fat man with a few hairs plastered to his bald scalp.

"Yeah, she's OK," agreed the other, with the look of a connoisseur and an experienced Lovelace. A greasy smile appeared on his face.

When Anna finally got up and headed for the door leading out of the bar, they stared after her for a long time.

"I wouldn't mind . . ." The lecherous one started to say something obscene, but wasn't able to finish it. Later, when the policemen on duty were separating the two as they rolled across the floor, each of the scufflers insisted that he was the one who had defended the woman against indecent attacks on her honor. The words they now used, and their combinations of words in the style of the best nineteenth-century poets, amazed not only the lieutenant making up the report, but the duelists themselves. This grandiloquent style remained with both men for another two or three weeks and then somehow unnoticeably turned back into everyday dull Muscovite speech. Anna didn't know about any of this, however, and couldn't have known: she was walking through the long halls toward the exit from the television center, trying not to think about the meeting that might take place. Her thoughts rushed back and forth between the elegant stranger and the miserable Telyatnikov, who had become completely unbearable in recent days. After calling in sick at the institute, he spent days and nights without a break at his desk, using up paper by the ream. For some reason she also remembered that the telephone had to be paid the next day or else it would be cut off: bills for the mythical conversations with New York continued to arrive with deadly regularity.

Giving the policeman on duty an automatic smile, Anna pushed open the glass door, and at once saw the white Volga come to a stop under the overhang of the entrance. A sporty man in a dark evening suit ran lightly up the steps. Him. Everything that followed was like a dream. As young women staff from the TV center watched with curiosity, Anna walked down the steps and got into the car. The door shut gently. He was already beside her, behind the wheel.

"Good evening, Anna." The man smiled. The headlights beamed at the windows of the building. The Volga made a turn in the square and headed toward the center of town. "The evening's so pleasant . . ." He spoke as naturally and simply as if they'd parted only the day before. "You probably didn't notice but there was a storm in the city. Feel how warm it is and how fresh the air is." He stopped the car at a light and turned to her. "My name is Luka."

"Apparently you know what my name is." Anna smiled sarcastically. "I just don't understand why you decided that gives you the right to interfere in my life!"

"If it's a matter of rights"—they were rushing along dark empty streets again—"if it's a matter of rights," Luka repeated, "then the question remains who is interfering in whose life! Before you appeared I was at peace, I had a clear goal . . . You took everything away from me and, what's more, incited me to commit a crime."

"Oh, that's such nonsense! You appeared live on TV . . . I almost died from fright!"

"Believe me, I didn't want to, but at that time it was my only opportunity . . . How can I explain it? I had to see you again in order to make a final decision. I made it. Besides, no one noticed a thing."

"What about all the outrageous things going on in the apartment?"

Anna remembered that she'd told Mashka and turned red. "Well, in general . . . Was it your doing?"

"To say otherwise wouldn't be truthful. But if you'd been in my place I hope you would have acted the same way. I love you, Anna, and I can't escape that feeling."

Anna was silent. The tires swished over the wet asphalt, the bright apartment windows had moved back in the distance, but they would sometimes flash through the delicate crowns of trees beginning to blossom.

"You said you committed a crime."

"I did. I'm on the run now!"

"Are you psychic? How did you know about the still life in the kitchen?"

"I'm not—I'm afraid to disappoint you. People who call themselves psychics are very often harmful. Particularly to themselves." He stopped the car and got a pack of cigarettes from his pocket. "May I smoke?" He kept on talking while he smoked. "The Lord made sure that higher or secret knowledge would only be revealed to those who through the work of their souls traveled some part of the path to enlightenment in their lifetime. Such knowledge is hidden, encoded, and covered by a veil of mysteries. Egyptian priests and the highest Tibetan priests once possessed it. It came to us from ancient times and informs us of the structure of the world and the destiny of man. If this knowledge, even a small, insignificant part of it, falls into the hands of people who are unprepared or, even worse, into foul hands, then it becomes truly dangerous. But as with every rule, there's an exception. However, your still life doesn't merit a good word." Luka started the car again. "I mentioned it on the street only in order to say something unusual so that you would remember me. Diogenes used this device too. Don't you have a friend in common with Diogenes of Sinope?" While keeping his eyes on the road, he smiled and added, "Don't feel sad about the still life! I'll give you another picture someday. One with two dancing birds—pink flamingos. If I'm ordered to return, of course . . ."

"Are you leaving?" To her surprise Anna heard a note of regret in her voice.

"That depends on you. Everything in my life depends on you now. And my life itself."

The city was going to sleep. Only the blinking traffic lights kept vigil, their yellow cat eyes winking at the carousing cars. Anna wasn't afraid, she only feared that now they would arrive somewhere and the mirage would dissolve and everything would forever be like it had been.

"In this bustling city there aren't many places you can hide from pursuers," Luka said, anticipating her question. "We're going to one of them, where they won't dare to bother us even if they find us."

"Is someone following you?"

"I think so. If the chase hasn't yet begun, it means I had too high an opinion of them." The car went up Tverskaya Street and turned at a light. After passing a high arch they plunged into the depths of a poorly lit street. "I always knew I would meet you, I knew it but didn't believe it. One should believe in oneself."

The dark bulk of an apartment building blocked the sky. The Volga came to a halt at the entrance. They took a rumbly old elevator to the fifth floor. Luka unlocked the door. Anna froze on the threshold. She had the strange feeling that once she crossed it she would enter a totally different world, one she had never known and which was full of dangers. She still could leave, she could utter some meaningless, unnecessary words and leave, and nothing would happen. She looked at Luka. He was quiet. He understood everything and wasn't pressing her to make a decision. Anna sighed deeply and with a smile gracefully stepped into the dark apartment.

It was a strange apartment. A light smell of dried flowers mixed with the smell of dust and old things that hadn't seen sun and fresh air for a long time. Luka took Anna's hand and led her down the mazelike hall. He pushed open the door to one of the rooms. Only a glimmer of light from the street came through the drawn curtains. They were surrounded by piles of furniture: enormous cabinets crowded against one another in the semi-dark, looming like cliffs over a narrow passage. Luka struck a match and lit a candlewick. A tiny flame leapt up, illuminating an old table spread with a lace tablecloth and a pair of very old cumbersome armchairs.

"This is my friend's apartment. No one lives here. I made certain people forgot about it and now it's something like a museum of his things."

"Did he go somewhere?" Anna rubbed her hand over the fabric on the back of a chair. The carved sideboard, an old water pitcher—everything here reminded her of her childhood.

"He died." Luka took a step toward the window and drew open the heavy curtains. Below, on the other side of the street, there stood a small church. Its gold cupolas shone in the moonlight above its azure walls. "There's our protection! Churches are always built in sacred places . . ."

The old cracked parquet floor squeaked as Anna went and stood next to Luka. Beyond the dirty window she beheld a clear moonlit world of fairy-tale beauty.

"My friend's heart was made from matter just as delicate as that. He'd been sent to earth on a mission of good and love for people, though he probably didn't suspect that was the case. Through our inner knowledge many of us know that we don't just simply appear in this world, but, unfortunately, far from everyone manages to realize what he is meant to do. I'll tell you about him, if you like." Luka helped Anna take off her coat and sat her down in a chair.

"He was a bright person and a gifted writer, but his talent went unnoticed. Naturally, he worried; he worked hard and in a state of confusion until finally he concluded that writers had to write according to public demand. And, to give him his due, he succeeded. He quickly became, if not famous, then well known, and his books, which were filled with violence, horrors, and sex, began to be hawked on the street. He began to churn out books mechanically, and perhaps because of this we saw each other less frequently. But one day—and the meeting took place right in this apartment—I warned him that a

Creator is responsible for all the images he makes . . . Do you know what hell is?" Luka sat down in the chair opposite Anna and began to smoke.

"Why do they keep criminals in solitary confinement? He didn't know either! The most terrible punishment is being left alone for eternity with the inner world you've created. It's worse than any torture—there's no need for cauldrons with boiling tar. I told him everything I thought, but he just laughed in my face. Then he went off somewhere for a while and reappeared only years later—famous but tired of life. He called me and asked me to come over. After such a significant break we weren't able to have a real talk. Either he'd start bragging or else drink vodka and start attacking someone. But one time he grew thoughtful and said sadly, 'You were right. They've come for me!'

" 'Who?' I didn't understand, and my friend didn't explain. He merely sat there, just as you are doing now, and looked at me without speaking. I don't know how much time passed before he continued.

" 'I tried to get away from them by writing a novel. About love. Something I hadn't done for many years. Just a novel about love. But apparently it was too late. Everything began with this novel. I was so captivated by it that after I put in the last period I couldn't stop. From force of inertia, you understand, I invented a love for myself! I picked one of the women I knew and sincerely fell in love with her. This love didn't last long: as soon as we had a conversation I realized it was just a self-made mirage . . . That's another story. But from this time on whatever I wrote began to pursue me, as if a dam had opened up and a stream of events that I had invented swept over me. Ah yes, I lived precisely what I had written. As if a producer-director was at work behind the scenes. Some small excerpt from one of my novellas or novels would be selected and staged—just one scene from each work. I don't want to tire you, I'll just say that once a car knocked me down in exactly the way I described it in my next-to-last work; later, in accordance with my texts, I broke a leg and then someone tried to kill me with a knife . . . Well, you know what my works are about! Today I understood that only one novella has not been touched, the one that brought me my first success. It contains only one episode—it describes in detail how a monster disposes of his victim.'

"He looked up at me and I still remember the paralyzed expression in his eyes.

" 'But we live in a civilized time.' I tried to calm him, but he wasn't listening.

" 'I've told you this so at least someone will know the real cause of my death.'

"He didn't touch upon this topic any more. When I left he was in a strange mood.

"They found him dead the next morning. The official diagnosis was a heart attack, but in response to my request they examined the retina of his eye. The last thing he saw in life was the mask of the monster he had lovingly described in his book . . ."

Luka stopped talking and looked around the room.

"He died here, at this desk, but his mission on earth wasn't finished. He'll return. That's why I'm trying to keep everything the way it was when he was here. Someday, in his next incarnation, he'll come back here for certain and this will give him the chance to remember and understand what his mistake was. A sad story?" He looked at Anna with a wide grin. "Not at all! What's bad is that my enemies used it as a pretext to send me into exile . . ."

Luka got up from the chair and picked up a bottle that was between some books on a shelf.

"I know I've tired you and probably frightened you as well, but such is the world we live in. I need to tell you many things—let the story of my friend serve as a prelude." From somewhere out of partial darkness he rolled a little serving cart up to Anna's chair. On it were two cups of hot coffee and cookies and candies in crystal and silver bowls. "Try some old Finnish liqueur—in such matters my friend knew what he was doing."

Luka poured the thick liquid into small cordial glasses and took his chair.

"Drink a little, you'll like it! The enormous world around us won't go anywhere, even if we're not watching it. It's possible, of course, to sit in your three-dimensional space and ignore everything that doesn't correspond to man's meager understanding, but all the same sooner or later all people have to come up against the laws of the cosmos."

Luka lit a stick of sandalwood incense. The sweet Eastern scent floated throughout the room. Anna's head was spinning, she felt that all this was happening to someone else, that she was merely a spectator watching an extremely fascinating movie and nothing more. Any moment the lights would flash on and the story would be over . . . Who was that man sitting in front of her? He had gentle manners, laughing eyes, and such rigid, bitter lines around his mouth. What was he doing here? How old could he be? Anna thought of Mashka's story, and she smiled.

"You're smiling?" Luka picked up a cup of coffee from the table. "You don't believe a single word of mine, of course. That's fine, you don't have to believe, as long as you listen. There's just enough time—more precisely, there's no time at all—and at the very latest you'll have to make your decision by morning. It can completely alter our future fate—that's right, yours and mine! But before you decide let me tell you about myself. It won't be very easy." He grew quiet, as if he didn't know where to begin.

"It's in man's nature to seek to understand the world he lives in and to define his own place in it. I didn't escape this ordeal either. An incident in my early childhood determined a great deal in my development and forced me to think about the meaning of time. As I passed from life to life along the chain of reincarnation, I strove to find the links between them and the fate of man on earth, to correlate the boundaries of the Lord and the depths of hell. Later, as my mind developed, the number of problems disturbing me multiplied. I asked myself: what is the meaning of human life and why does the implacable cosmic law of cause and effect return the soul to earth with mechanical regularity, compelling it to travel a transitory and sorrowful path over and over again? Intuitively I felt that everything that disturbed me and excited my imagination was essentially connected, parts of a single whole, but no matter how I tried to fit them together, nothing held—the mosaic remained in pieces.

"Then I turned to the ancient books and very quickly I understood that my failure lay within myself. Long and intensive contemplations convinced me that there is a universal law which prohibits the uninitiated, still a slave to his own passions, from seeing even briefly that the world is a unified whole. I told you that secret knowledge is concealed from those who haven't set foot on the path of enlightenment. A long, hard road was ahead of me . . . The solution to the secret lay within me, in the depths of my self—a small particle in the universe. Once you have come to know yourself, you can see in your true self, as in a drop of water, the ocean of the world surrounding you—and in this way come to God. 'Save thyself,' Jesus said, 'and round about you thousands will be saved.' I walked along the path of true knowledge that had opened to me and this path ran through my soul. I sought to unite with the harmony of the world; sorrow and joy were my teachers and will was my guide. This path was not simple or easy, and I managed to travel only a small part of it, but I won't speak of that now. With each step more of the world was revealed; I was fortunate to see and to understand what I'd seen.

"Then one day I discovered that I knew why the law of karma keeps returning man to this tragic, moving, and funny planet. This knowledge gave me faith in my own powers. No, it wasn't arrogance—it was the joy of knowing that God is merciful, that He places no limit on human perfection: if you desire it and are able to go—then go! I went, and the meaning of heaven and hell was revealed to me. I saw that they are only the extreme points toward which people head after they have left this world for good. After death the soul cannot change its karma, it simply moves along the path the person has chosen during his stay on earth. Whoever is bright and pure continues to ascend toward Him, carrying paradise in his own soul. Whoever bears malice and hatred, who has lived as a beast among beasts, carries the hell of what he has done in his soul; the weight of these thoughts and deeds draws him downward into the netherworld. On earth there's a way out—one can go insane; but in the world that exists on the other side of death the human doesn't receive such mercy . . ."

Luka looked at Anna. She sat, gripping the arms of the chair with fingers that had turned white. He knelt down before her, took her hand, and brought it to his lips.

"Don't be afraid, Anna, there's nothing terrible in any of this! The cosmic law of cause and effect is the highest justice man can receive. We are all sinners, but He is merciful! A human is capable of fighting the beast within him as he ascends the path of knowledge to become a bright spirit. Believe me—I belonged to that world once, I was a small particle in the infinitely mighty hierarchy of the powers of light." Luka kissed her hand, got up, and began walking around the room. "Now I'm going to say something blasphemous, but nonetheless true—I understood the Creator's design! I understood the higher purpose for man on earth. And even now that I'm nobody, and in exile for a crime, I have no doubt about the correctness of my guess. Its essence is this: that once—and we know this from the holy scriptures—the Creator saw that He was surrounded on all sides by evil, and the source of the evil was man. Imagine, Anna, there was an ocean of evil, the boundless dark of night, and within it, like a weak flame, was good . . . And the Lord found a solution worthy of His wisdom! To man, who wallowed in vanities and was consumed by his pursuit of false values, He granted the ability to multiply good through the work of the soul. Yes, He decided that by nature people are petty-minded and lost to sin, but in each life there are times when one's spiritual powers are uplifted and man's paltry essence aspires to what is most pure and radiant. In brief moments of love and self-sacrifice, of compassion and grief, the man-beast becomes like God in the power of his feeling and the acuteness of his senses. In these moments of human ascent God gathers the harvest of good. He tends it; He amasses good grain by grain as a thing of supreme value, the result of long and persistent work on the part of the human soul . . . The essential part of my insight is understanding this gift the Mighty made to mankind." Luka spoke with such passion it seemed he was reexperiencing the brilliance of the revelation that had illumined him.

"But I went further," he continued in a muted voice. "Long ago a wise man spoke about good and evil and said that the course of time depends on their correlation in the world. I always remembered those words and, comparing them with my insight about man's destiny on earth, I reached an astonishing conclusion. Time is the eternal slave of man: it depends on man—on how and by what he lives. Suddenly the depths of the universe opened to me: I knew I had stumbled upon one of its most hidden secrets. But very soon it became clear that such liberties of thought are not forgiven man even if he has a bright spirit. I was punished for this higher knowledge because by virtue of possessing it I came to understand the essence of a certain criminal agreement. I understood that the fall of an angel is not something that happened only once—it's an ongoing process. I don't want to go into details—and it's not so important in order to understand what happened—I'll just say that the purity of His idea was perverted by some who had been entrusted to pursue it. I couldn't endure that! A feeling of justice and love for the Creator incited me to act, and in my ignorance of life I erred. Driven by indignation, I told one of the highest beings in the Department of Light Powers about my discovery of betrayal. I thought it was necessary to inform Him of what had happened. I hadn't the slightest idea that the hierarchies to whom I'd turned were already informed! From then on everything developed according to a familiar scenario: they praised me and then immediately found cause to accuse me of the most terrible sins and to send me to earth as a *domovoi*, under the open surveillance of the Secret Operations branch of the Department of Dark Powers. In order to make the conditions of exile more severe, I was strictly forbidden to leave the territory of your deceased aunt's apartment—she was renowned for her coldness and her strict old Bolshevik personality."

"Why did you say that I had incited you to commit a crime?"

"Because that's far from all that I did, Anna! To my shame I must confess that I quickly resigned myself to my new position as a hearth spirit. In a certain sense exile even suited me, insofar as it didn't stop me from continuing my work on my self. In the good company of your aunt, under the pleasant light of a green lamp in the quiet of my studio I worked on the essence of time, trying to understand its properties and to discover the nature of eternity. I even became attached to the old lady's resolute character and her uncompromising and frank opinions. My existence was bearable: I was living with my ideas and rarely turning my attention to the external world until suddenly you burst into my life! Your arrival compelled me to look at my own life through different eyes and see its poverty and lowly nature. All the disgusting and trivial things that had seemed manageable became unbearable in the twinkling of an eye. You stirred the sense of human dignity in me and I came alive! After I found love I couldn't allow circumstances to take you away from me. I decided to draw His attention to me, no matter what the cost. Justice had been trampled on—I wanted to restore it and defend my love at the same time."

Luka got up from the chair. Anna followed him and they looked into each other's eyes. "Probably I'm crazy," he said. "Of course, I'm crazy, but I had no other solution than to stop the flow of world time. If He doesn't intervene now, they'll grind me into dust. The only thing left is to hope . . ."

"What if He doesn't hear you?" Anna looked straight at him.

"I gave myself until morning. If nothing happens, I'll have to make one final attempt to attract His attention, but you'll have to make a decision in this event."

"Me?" Anna was surprised. She smiled. "You have a wonderful imagination and you're a great storyteller. Now tell me none of this is true and I'll forgive you!"

"Of course, it's not true"—Luka smiled in reply—"rather, it's not the whole truth. I still haven't told you about one cosmic law that you should know. It goes: no matter how bad a person has been in life, no matter what he has done, much will be forgiven him if there was real love in his life. Thus did He create this world: everything passes and there remains only love—the subtle primary substance from which the soul itself is spun."

"You mean love is material?"

He drew her close to him and kissed her. "I know you don't believe me, but I can show you the materiality of love, thank God."

8

"**Time has stopped.**" The Black Cardinal's voice was as even and cold as ice.

"That's impossible! Do you mean He decided to begin the Last Judgment?" Serpina immediately felt himself trembling like a leaf in the autumn wind.

"No, Serpina, I said precisely what I intended to say. Cronus's Kissoeides, the machine that makes world time, has stopped. The consequences cannot be predicted. He might consider the moment right to begin His Last Judgment—in that case everything will come to an end. It will mean the end of the individual fate of every being who ever appeared in the world. If that's so, our conversation is simply absurd because neither you nor I will, in fact, exist any longer. What will come next, only He knows, of course—if anything will exist, that is. Needless to say, we've taken all measures necessary to prevent information leaks. The boss personally contacted someone from the Department of Light Powers, and, like us, they aren't ready for Judgment Day to begin. At this time, if that concept has any meaning, a team of the most trusted beings from both departments has been put together and they've begun work. There's some hope that they can start up the Kissoeides again. However, the machine's of such subtle complexity that no one can guarantee success . . ." Nergal stared at the privy councillor standing at the foot of the stairs. "We'd like to know who stopped the Kissoeides and how it was done, and you've been charged to clear things up. I have the right to expect that you'll be efficient and tough! Just as my fate is at stake, so is yours! You'll be helped by the fact that only a few individuals know about the generator's existence, not to mention its location."

"You need not continue, Your Excellence." Serpina made a half-bow. "I know the criminal's name. As I've reported to you, in my very young days, as the fates decreed, two of my friends and I found ourselves in Cronus's space and we saw his machine. One of us subsequently achieved a certain eminence in the Department of Light Powers, and you may be pleased to remember that in accordance with your instructions he was provoked, sentenced, and sent into exile on earth. He was charged with arrogance and disrespect toward the higher powers."

"Yes, yes, I remember, his name's Lukary," Nergal said, limply gesturing with his hand. "Do you know the real reason he was removed from the hierarchy of the Powers of Light?"

"I can only guess, Your Excellence!" The privy councillor bowed again.

"Tell me, Serpina"—the Black Cardinal stepped from the recess in the wall onto the stone floor—"wasn't this Lukary your friend at one time? Didn't you want to hide this from me? And why was it he and not your other friend?"

"How can you say that, Excellence?" Serpina exclaimed indignantly. "Hide it from you! As for Yevsevy, he's incapable of such things. Besides, at present he's in a psychiatric clinic that he checked into by himself. He's not ill—it's just a form of internal emigration . . ."

"All the same, Serpina, why do you dislike him so?"

"Yevsevy?"

"Don't be an idiot! You know very well that I'm asking about Lukary." The Black Cardinal returned to the fireplace and looked back at his privy councillor. "Well?"

"Why do I dislike?" He started trying to talk his way out of it, but suddenly changed his tactic. " 'Dislike'—that's putting it too mildly. My feeling for him is one of friendly hatred."

"Be so kind as to explain yourself!"

"I don't know what you suspect me of, Monseigneur . . ."

"Of everything," Nergal interrupted. "I suspect everyone of everything, and that's completely natural. If I suspected you of something concrete, we'd be continuing our conversation in the castle's cellar, where we've installed a very cozy torture chamber. On such occasions James changes his snow-white livery for a leather apron . . . However, I've no doubt you have a rich imagination, so let's return to our friend." Nergal sat down in the armchair, his once-burning eyes were indifferent and sleepy.

"You see, Monseigneur"—Serpina moved closer but did not dare to sit—"in many ways Lukary's career resembles mine, but from the opposite point of view. At the Academy of Knowledge, though we studied at the same time, we were in different departments, and, as far as I remember, we always took opposite positions. He counteracted me in everything—in every operation I conceived I encountered the presence of his power . . ."

"And his power surpassed yours." Nergal smirked.

"Yes, Monseigneur." Serpina lowered his head. "At least often enough. Our last conflict ended with his exile, but you ran that operation yourself—I only did the support work. We managed to seduce a messenger of good, who was then living on earth, with money and fame, and we played a little comedy with him. You may recall that we painstakingly projected onto his own life everything that he'd written for the sake of profit. It proved to be very amusing. Lukary tried to fight us, but his warning wasn't heeded. Lukary didn't bear any personal responsibility for what happened, so they accused him of apostasy—an ideological crime—for having allowed the messenger to deviate from his path."

"You did the right thing by telling me. I get rid of associates who can't tell me or themselves the truth. Let me add that I welcome personal scores between my subordinates—they work more maliciously then. You may leave, Serpina, but remember how much depends on the success of your mission. If you emerge victorious from this struggle, you won't be rewarded, if only because the shutdown of the machine will never have occurred." Nergal smiled. "But your service will not be forgotten."

The privy councillor struck the feather of his hat against the stone floor and looked expectantly at the castle's master, but he had nothing further to say.

"Monseigneur, perhaps you may wish to tell me something that might make my job easier?"

Nergal's thin lips hardened into a smile. "Why? You know about the existence of the secret protocol, although you shouldn't. However, if you hadn't learned of this on your own, I'd have dispatched you long ago to the provinces to work as a local vampire in some godforsaken place. Go, Serpina, go—don't waste time, if only because there isn't any. And remember that in the case of need you can rely on all the forces of hell."

"Your Excellence!" Serpina made a low bow and clicked his heels. Sweeping his hat back and forth, he backed up to the door and, permitting himself a rare liberty, stepped straight into the astral plane.

The ringing of bells woke him. The sun, which had risen above the roofs of the apartment buildings, flooded the room, and outside the window sparrows were chirping and chasing after one another. Anna was sleeping. He looked at her, freed his arm, got up from their bed, and went into the next room. Outside, an invalid was warming himself on the church porch, his stump exposed. Luka turned away from the window and stepped over to the icon hanging in the corner.

The face of Nicholas the Miracle Worker in this old painting was unusual—there was something Mongolian about it.

"St. Nicholas, help me!" Luka said, placing his palm on the icon. "I need your protection here and now. I'm a sinner, I will answer for everything. But save and protect her—you know she is innocent . . ."

When he turned around, Anna was standing in the doorway watching him.

"Why are you praying to the saint just for me?" She came up to Luka and clung to him. "Both of us need his help." Anna stepped back and looked into his eyes. "I'm afraid, Luka! I'm afraid to wake up and find myself again in that drab daily grind that was my life. I'm afraid of whoever is following you. Tell me, who are they and what do they want?"

"It's hard to explain." Luka drew her toward him and embraced her. "The human language is ill equipped to describe the energies that unfold in worlds parallel to this dense three-dimensional one. Don't take everything I say literally, but don't think that it's pure abstraction. In the world that He created there is a hierarchy directing universal evil, which in human terms is called the Department of Dark Powers. People have heard about bacchanalia and the escapades of evil spirits, about all kinds of satanic balls on Bald Mountain and witches' Sabbaths—and it's all true, but only as the external manifestation of what is taking place; behind everything, as if behind a screen, black forces are doing their work. They are professionals who don't yield to emotion and balk at nothing as they sow evil in the world. So, special scores arose between me and them. I had been destroying their plans for too long—spoiling all kinds of dirty tricks. Now they will do everything possible not to miss their chance!"

"Are you afraid of them?"

"No, it's not that! It's too late for me to be afraid." He kissed a curl on her temple. "Until now I've been hoping for His mercy, I wanted Him to listen to me, but that hasn't happened. I took an extreme measure when I stopped the flow of world time, but even that has turned out to be in vain . . ."

"What can you do now?"

"I don't have much choice!" Luka grinned. "There's one last chance—I'll have to drop back blindly into the past, as into a deep whirlpool, and once I've hidden myself there, I'll try to turn the course of history from evil to good! There is a law: if you behave as a human in the world of people, then your pursuers, no matter who they might be or how much power they might possess, are obligated to play by the same rules. Thus, the chase moves to another plane, into the lower world of people. It will cause them some trouble to find my trail. There will be a race to see who's first—either I'll change the course of world history or they'll find me and eliminate me. I'll have a final chance! A human is a minute midge, it's easy not to notice him, but History . . ."

Anna looked at Luka with dismay. "What about me? Will I be left alone in this twilight world?"

"Don't be afraid, they won't touch you! They're only interested in me. The cosmic law of cause and effect forbids direct interference in a human's fate."

"That's not what I'm afraid of!" She pushed his arm away angrily. "Why can't you understand that I can't live without you in this dull semblance of life among all these people who are human half-shadows and half-wrecks!"

"Is that your way of saying you love me?"

Anna broke into tears and clung to Luka. He comforted her, caressing her quivering body.

"It's very dangerous! In order to prevent our separation you have to return to one of your former lives, during a time when you lived on earth. It's a big risk. You don't know when you lived before, do you?"

Anna shook her head.

"There, you see! I can't help you extend the thread of memory through your former lives. We never met before and there's no single knot where our fates were woven together." He stepped back and looked into her tear-stained eyes. "Try to understand. The danger is that when you dive in your past you might end up in a cesspool of human history, in some dark land and godforsaken time when nothing was happening. In that case, no matter how hard I try I won't be able to change the course of world events and our escape into the past will serve only to delay our capture. This time not only mine but yours! I had wanted you to make this decision by yourself, but now I understand that I can't put you in such danger. Such a step would influence your next life in a way you cannot know." Luka hurried, sensing that a new wave of sobbing was about to begin. "Well, all right, let's try to remember. Tell me, have you ever had a recurring dream?"

"I have!" Anna sobbed, wiping her eyes with a handkerchief. "Sometimes I dream that I'm flying and sometimes I dream that people are demolishing a cathedral. It's so big and beautiful, but I can't see it in detail—it's as if in a haze . . . I'm standing and crying and there's nothing I can do!"

"How do they wreck it? Do they set it on fire or shell it with cannons, or take it down stone by stone?"

Anna thought. "No, I can't see anything. I just know they're demolishing it and I feel terrible."

"That could be anything!" Luka sighed. "It could be the temple of Herod the Great in Jerusalem, which the Romans destroyed in the year 70 A.D. or it might be some provincial Catholic church during the Middle Ages, the victim of feuds between petty local barons." He looked at Anna. "Well, God is merciful, isn't He?"

She nodded happily and began laughing. "I'll help you!"

"You are funny! Neither you nor I will even know that we've had this conversation. Everything will be a blank sheet. We'll place our fate into His hands! It's completely possible that you won't even know how our escape into the past will end. If we're not lucky, they'll see to it that all memory of me is wiped from the annals of human history. Someday you'll wake up in your apartment feeling both happy and sad from something you felt in a dream, but no matter how hard you try you won't be able to remember a thing! There, there, mind you don't cry—you and I haven't lost yet and I don't intend to render such a service to our cursed friends!"

He took Anna by the hand and led her to the window. The sun reflected on the gold of the cupolas and the colors of the day were joyful and pure. Anna raised her head and looked at Luka.

"Why are you smiling?"

"I'm thinking how wisely the world is made. Do you remember what the Bible says: 'He who increases knowledge increases sorrow.' I'm thinking about how grieved many people would be if they knew that when they are reincarnated they have a good chance of seeing the very same faces they saw in a past life. The karma of people is connected, and often it's a punishment for one person to have to exist in close proximity with another person. But man is not granted such knowledge and His mercy lies in this as well."

"Are you joking?"

"Perhaps I'm joking . . ."

The languid sound of a flute came from somewhere on the street.

"It's time!" He drew her close and kissed her. "You know, one thing has always amazed me—no matter what we do or how we act, it's all still called life."

He laughed and waved his hand through the air. Stepping into the space that opened, they found themselves in the Telyatnikovs' apartment. Despite the bright morning sun, the windows in the large room where Sergei Sergeyevich was working were fully shaded. A lamp was burning on the desk. Layers of heavy cigarette smoke clouded the room from floor to ceiling. Telyatnikov sat with his chest against the desk, writing something fast and feverishly. There was something childish about his pose, like an A student who out of spite is hiding what he's writing from his less intelligent neighbor. From time to time Sergei Sergeyevich's shoulders shuddered, but you couldn't tell if he was laughing or crying.

Anna crossed the room with decisive steps. She pushed aside the heavy curtain and threw open the window. As an ocean of sunshine burst into the apartment, the fresh breeze stirred the sheets of paper all covered with scribbles and spun them into the air. Not understanding what was happening, Telyatnikov threw himself at the papers in an attempt to save them. He gave his wife an angry look.

"What is it? What are you doing? Don't bother me, I'm working!" There was irritation in his voice, his strained red eyes raged. "Wait, I'll finish what I'm writing and come."

He wanted to go back to his work but Anna stopped him.

"Sergei! Take a break for a minute, we have a guest. We need to have a serious talk with you."

"What sort of a guest am I?" Luka bent over and picked up from the floor a sheet of paper totally covered with a large jerky handwriting. After running his eyes over the notations, he headed for Telyatnikov and handed him the paper. "Sergei Sergeyevich, where did you get this formula?"

Telyatnikov shuddered again, jerking his shoulder with obvious spite, and began crudely shouting in a squeaky voice, "Are you accusing me of plagiarism? I figured out everything myself!" He feverishly began collecting the papers that were scattered around. "Professor Shepetukha just suggested the external form, but I had felt the interdependence earlier."

"Shepetukha you say? So that's it . . . Sergei Sergeyevich, give up on all of this, travel somewhere, take a rest! It only seems that your equation connects the past and the future . . ."

"How would you know?" The scholar turned on him. "You're just jealous of me! All of you! Because I'm a genius!"

"Sergei Sergeyevich, the wave function doesn't describe the human soul," Luka started to say, but Telyatnikov interrupted him.

"Soul? Why are you bothering me with the soul? It's nothing more than a vibration in the world's information continuum. When a person dies, he radiates into space all the information accumulated and altered during the process of life—that's all! And you go on about the 'soul,' the 'soul'! As soon as I publish the first results of my research the scholarly world will quake!"

"Test your hypothesis, differentiate time by space, and you'll come up with nonsense, the worst kind of foolishness . . ."

But Telyatnikov had stopped listening. Luka took Anna by the arm and led her into the kitchen.

"You can't help him now," he said with a frown. "Sergei Sergeyevich won't abandon his work until he's convinced of the fundamental falsity of its initial hypothesis. But I think he's only a chance victim of theirs, the attack is aimed at me. The chase is being conducted according to all the rules: even if everything else falls through, they'll accuse me of disseminating secret knowledge to people. It will look very convincing: I drove a scholar mad with the purpose of possessing his wife. And I have possessed her." Luka smiled at Anna. "A dirty trick, but it works flawlessly. All of this confirms once more that we need to hurry. Wait here for me, and whatever happens—wait! I'll be back soon!"

Anna noticed with alarm how his face changed: the high cheekbones hardened, his chin became heavy as lead. Without saying another word and scarcely taking note of anything around him, Lukary stepped into the wall and disappeared from the three-dimensional world of man.

9

Once in the astral plane, Lukary looked around his studio suspiciously. He stood and concentrated on his inner hearing, but he didn't sense any immediate danger. In the distance some kind of warning note sounded like the light whir of a mosquito, but there was no time to analyze its source. He was not sure he was safe, so he acted quickly and decisively. The only thing that caught his attention was Monet's lady in a garden, which hung in an alcove. He paused before it as if seeing it for the first time, struck by the brilliant colors and the feeling of peace it radiated. The view of a garden lit by the sun and the figure of a woman in white always gave him joy. The image would dissolve into air saturated with the scent of flowers or into the soft touch of grass on his cheek when he used to lie in the cool shade of trees. With time he began to prefer a stroll in this garden to long walks in the damp London fog and he returned the canvas of *The Waterloo Bridge* to the museum. Now the figure of the woman reminded him of Anna and his need to hurry. With a wave of his hand Lukary returned the painting to the Hermitage museum and flung open the doors of the cabinet where he kept the most valuable part of his collection. It was time to part with them. He couldn't leave without first returning this priceless wealth that didn't belong to him. Taking scroll after scroll from the shelves, he held them in his hands as if to memorize them by touch, and then they disappeared from his hands and returned to their places in libraries and museum collections. When he had finished with the cabinet, he went over to the bookshelves, which began to empty, one after the other, as his hand passed over them. He hurried, but still couldn't refuse himself the pleasure of running his eyes over the gold-stamped folio spines one last time. These books were his true friends and teachers—he had conversed with them as he took each step along the path of knowledge and enlightenment. The last thing left was to sort through his own manuscripts. He wouldn't have had to write them down since he remembered their texts to the last comma, but he'd been captivated by the very process of sliding a pen over paper and the magical flowering of images from ordinary words. With pen in hand, alone on a swing, he would fall into the depths of despair, then rise to the heights of ecstasy.

"How unexpectedly, how quickly everything changes in this life," thought Lukary, making a pile of his papers. Quite recently the meaning of existence was contained in these pages, but now he was happy that in its inconclusiveness his work reminded him of Anna. Though still immersed in his thoughts, Lukary kept observing the emptied space of his study carefully and soon he noticed a faint luminescence behind the easel. It flashed with a reddish-brown color and immediately disappeared, but Lukary already understood—he hadn't been fast enough! A powerful net of energy hung over the studio like a scarcely visible haze, and, as before a thunderstorm, electric tension could be felt in the air. Without making any sign that he'd noticed an outside presence, Lukary finished gathering his papers and then destroyed them by laying his hand on top of the pile he'd made. He had a physical sense that a number of events had taken place somewhere very nearby and at any moment their repercussions might pour down on him. And, indeed, it *was* worth his while to get rid of the papers because at this moment Shepetukha was shoving his way through a crack in the astral plane. After making a sprightly jump to the floor, the *leshii* smoothed out the sparse gray hairs on his head with one of his paws and made a face as he passed by the emptied shelves.

"Hitting the road?" he wanted to know, gnashing his teeth for effect.

"Ah, Professor," Lukary greeted him. "With my simple soul I'd decided that I wouldn't see your vile face for at least a month. How's life in the open universe?"

"Philosophizing and discoursing as always!" Shepetukha slouched over to the table like a provincial Don Juan and wiped a paw across its smooth surface. "You've destroyed all those scraps of paper?"

"Listen, Shepetukha, why do you keep turning up before me? Not for anything good, no, not for good!" Lukary went over to the easel and removed the canvas stretched across it. "So, tell me, how did you manage to return so quickly?"

"I pulled it off somehow, old man, I did!" Shepetukha said casually, wiggling his sparse eyebrows meaningfully.

The *leshii*'s impudent look and familiar manner of speaking reconfirmed Lukary's guess that his affairs were in bad shape. For the last time he glanced at the portrait he'd begun, then that disappeared too, going into nonexistence with all the various canvases and pencil sketches. The studio was empty.

"I told you. When you work for the organization it will both feed and protect you!" Shepetukha lectured, wagging a finger patronizingly. "There aren't so many idiots left who live by the light of a distant star. It happens quite often that when you go a little closer and look harder it's no star at all, but the little hole the cat has under its tail! You've been striving and hoping. Well, it's much better to serve—find your little corner, settle down in it, and live your life while helping the system."

"You're telling this to *me*?" Lukary smiled, but with a steely note in his voice.

Frightened, Shepetukha recoiled from the table, but as if he'd remembered the role he had to play, he immediately stuck out his puny chest again. "Drat you! And what's that 'Professor' talk of yours?"

"Oh, wasn't it you who made a drunk out of the hapless Telyatnikov with that cheap port? You work without any imagination, without inspiration. You didn't even take time to touch up the equation to make it look more contemporary."

"That erudition of yours doesn't concern me at all!" The *leshii* waved a paw. "I'm a small-time rascal, a technical performer. They tell me what to do—I'm a flag in hand, a drum around the neck, and off to greet the dawn!" He looked at the master of the studio impudently and at the same time apprehensively. "All the same, where are you planning to go? Running off to report about the old lady's death?" His fat lips grinned mockingly. "They'll drive you so far away, Lukary, oh, yes, so far you'll never come back! Say, wasn't it a pity to part with that floozy?"

Lukary ground his teeth. "So tell me then, who ordered you to toss out that formula to Telyatnikov?" he asked, keeping his eyes lowered so as not to reflect the fire of hatred that suddenly gripped him.

The forest spirit shrugged his skinny shoulders, clearly underestimating the threat hanging over him.

"There are those who value Shepetukha . . ." He looked up and at once the hair on his scrawny body stood on end and his lower jaw dropped like the lid of a suitcase.

"No . . ." he whispered with lips only, and began to emit small and frequent hiccups. "I . . . I . . ."

"Well?" Lukary pressured him, noting from the corner of his eye that a red vibration in a corner of the studio was becoming more active. "Tell me, or you're risking your health!"

By now Shepetukha was hiccuping to the beat of his pulse. A cosmic cold streamed from Lukary's eyes, leaving the *leshii* with no doubt that his days were numbered. A mysterious force tore Shepetukha off the floor, pressed him against the wall, and, as housewives do with dough, began to roll him out on its flat surface.

"I, I'll make you . . ." Shepetukha made a last attempt to threaten.

"Oh, yes, you'll make me . . ." Lukary agreed. "But—later. Till then I'll make you . . . and right now. Tell me, my friend, would you like to become one of Siqueiros's frescoes?"

"Don't threaten me with Siqueiros!" Shepetukha began to wail with all his might. "I'll tell everything without him."

Once he was released, he crawled along the wall, lamenting, "See how I suffered for the cause!"

Working from a distance, Lukary raised him in the air and shook him vigorously.

"Well?"

"Let him alone, Luka!" A voice came from the corner, where the flickering that had gained in strength began to acquire a human shape. "I can see you're tormenting him especially in order to arouse me!" Shaking little sparks off himself, Serpina stepped out of the reddish-brown light. "And, Shepetukha, you ought to know that duty is inseparable from suffering!"

Like Lukary, the privy councillor appeared in his traditional human form. He wore a stylish suit with a pocket handkerchief that he had picked to match his bright tie. He looked fresh and elegant. His long, curly hair lent an artistic touch to his handsome round face, and the smooth manner in which he moved and spoke intensified this impression.

"No one, especially the bosses, likes complainers." Serpina spoke in a somewhat singsong voice as he moved toward the center of the studio with a casual stride. "It's tough for you, but you'll do your work!"

"Boss! At last!" The *leshii* rushed toward Serpina and stopped a few steps away, clasping his paws to his chest in a burst of joy. "He was torturing me, he wanted to make me into a Siqueiros. But like a true fighter I . . ."

"It was a bad job of torture, then." The privy councillor furrowed his brow in distaste and turned away from his agent.

"I started to taunt him like I was ordered." Shepetukha couldn't calm down, looking with devotion at the back of his boss's well-pressed suit. "But he nailed me to the wall! Then to cause great moral suffering he threatened to turn me into a tub at a women's bathhouse."

"Shut up!" Serpina ordered quietly but very distinctly, and a grimace of disgust contorted his professionally good-natured face. After wiping it off, as one might do with a dustcloth, he turned and held out both his arms to Lukary, who'd been watching this encounter from the wings. And as if he'd only noticed him just now, Serpina heartily exclaimed, "Luka! My friend! How glad I am to see you!"

The master of the studio was in no hurry to embrace Serpina, however. With arms crossed, he stood with a sarcastic smile on his face and watched as his childhood friend approached him. Meeting such a chilly reception, the privy councillor cut short his welcoming rush and asked, with some resentment in his voice, "You're not glad to see me? Remember what buddies we were. No, really, it's pure swinishness on your part!"

The senior privy councillor halted in the middle of the studio, his whole demeanor suggesting injured pride. Without even looking, he sat down in the chair that Shepetukha readily offered him. During the ensuing quiet Lukary heard the clocks strike in the lower world. Anna was waiting and the game had just begun—and its rules didn't depend on him. But playing by the rules, Lukary looked at Serpina coldly and asked, "To what do I owe this honor? I had no doubt that the Secret Operations agents would pay me a call, but I dared not hope for a visit by such a distinguished guest. It's a great honor for an ordinary *domovoi*!"

"Stop it, Luka, don't pretend to be so humble!" Serpina lay back in the chair and threw one leg over the other. "The disfavor will pass and you'll find a suitable position in your department. No one will question your high rank in the hierarchy of the Powers of Light."

"Did you come to return me from exile?" Lukary smiled.

"Not quite." The privy councillor fiddled with the gold chain on his watch. "But I can be of assistance. You know very well that I'm not just a cog in the machine. We have good contacts, including one of the leaders in the Department of Light Powers. There are sober-minded, practical politicians everywhere. For instance, something which earlier was practically considered apostasy can be presented as a fresh idea if there's goodwill. Think about it—life is the art of compromise, as they say."

"Oh, Serpina, why should I trouble you? You've done so much for me already!" Lukary forced his lips into a smile. "It's thanks to you that I wound up in exile."

"Please!" Serpina beseeched him, spreading his arms theatrically. "You shouldn't confuse friendship with official responsibilities. Whoever expresses a lack of faith in the correctness of his superiors' actions simply must be punished in any hierarchy. That is just as much a law of nature as the law of universal gravity. Further, I see that you think I provoked you. Do you think I'm capable of that?" The privy councillor placed his hands on that part of his chest where people usually have hearts. "Yes, I'm capable of that. Yes, I provoked you!" he continued in a completely businesslike tone. "But solely within the framework of official duties! Nothing personal and it was for your own good, by the way. Remember: if you don't sin you can't repent, if you don't repent you can't be forgiven." He laughed boisterously, turning everything into a joke. "Do I need remind you of this, Luka? The entire world plays by the same rules. Believe me, old man, if you'd been in my place you'd have done exactly the same thing because the nature of power dictates it. Power can neither be moral nor amoral, either it makes itself stronger or it destroys itself. Please, let's talk like old friends! You understand everything perfectly and understanding is half of forgiving."

"Be more careful with him, he's dangerous!" Shepetukha whispered fervently in the privy councillor's ear while casting sidelong glances at Lukary. "I reported everything about him in good time, I wrote down everything there was! About his tricks and his willfulness and the fact that he's been shirking his duties as a *domovoi*. And recently he's taken to going to the people like that . . . like that proletarian writer. I've distributed a special report about that to the organization. Another thing"—in his professional zeal the *leshii* was gasping for breath—"he fell head over heels for that woman in the old lady's apartment! I'm telling the truth—or," Shepetukha swore, "may I rot up to my head in a swamp before Judgment Day! Fine if he'd taken up with that little Lucy—the ghost—she's one of our own kind from beyond the grave, but, no, he up and falls for a gal who's alive! It's a transgression! A mésalliance!"

Serpina moved away from the *leshii* in disgust and squeezed out an "Out of here!" through his teeth.

Shepetukha had no time to bat an eyelid before his whole body turned to gray mold and he dissolved into the studio's quiet air, leaving the clearly distinguishable smell of rot behind him.

"Personnel problems. You have to work with all sorts of rubbish." The privy councillor turned to Lukary and gave him a bright white grin. "No training, no school, just dirty tricks, that's all."

"Listen, why did you slip Telyatnikov that old equation from the Academy?" Lukary sat down in his favorite work chair.

"Well, in any case, that doesn't have anything to do with you. You may consider it a coincidence." Serpina lit up and puffed a few times on his stubby goat-head pipe. "I was present at your last meeting with Shepetukha, as you noticed, of course. You've always been so devilishly gifted. I see now that this is what made you act so fast and energetically."

"What do you mean?"

"Oh, Luka . . ." Serpina threw up his hands in bewilderment, as if to excuse his interlocutor's dim-wittedness. "We've known each other for so long! I've been thinking a lot about you recently. If you disregard certain details, our fates are as similar as two drops of water. Don't you find it symbolic—after so many years and lives to meet in the same place where we spent our first childhood? Some cosmic cycle must have come to completion and now we are standing on the threshold of something new and unknown. Yes, this was a barbaric and dark and impenetrable land—and it remains so: whenever they start to build something, they choose to found it on blood."

"It seems you're in a melancholy state," Lukary noted. "Are you in a mood for memories?"

"Why not?" Serpina shrugged. "One doesn't have many chances to sit with a friend and remember the past. It was our first childhood: there was something simple and pure about it, something never to be repeated. The meeting with Cronus predetermined so much in the lives of all three of us."

"Don't bother, Serpina, it's not necessary. You're repeating my conversation with Yevsevy almost word for word, and I have no doubt that since you were on my trail you saw him and found out what I was interested in."

The senior privy councillor was silent.

Lukary waited for some time and then asked, "Did you upset his equilibrium?"

"No! For what reason? Such nothings as he, who are living, as it were, on earth, are extremely useful to us. You remember the words of the great proletarian writer: 'Who is not with us is against us'? The world has changed completely since then; we try to work more subtly now, without going to extremes. If the great writer were alive today he might write: 'Who is not against us is with us.' Serpina tapped his pipe against the heel of his shiny shoe and continued somewhat sadly, "Time has changed, old man, time itself. All told, it's only an inherited illusion, as if it were possible to maintain any neutrality between good and evil. In fact there are only two kinds of people—those who create good and all the rest. So all the rest are our people. It's a short step from not doing good to doing evil—just don't ask yourself who you are and why you've been born on this earth."

"You're strangely weary and sad today. I don't think I've ever seen you like this." Lukary examined Serpina intently.

"You're right. I am sad today," the privy councillor agreed. "Do you know why? I'm saying goodbye. I'm saying goodbye to you forever!"

"Isn't it too soon, Serpina?"

"No. To be honest, I liked the passion you displayed when you found out about the secret protocol between our departments to maintain a balance between good and evil in the world. Personally I wasn't enthusiastic about the agreement. It deprived us of competitiveness but, unlike you, I became reconciled to it. There are things that go beyond one's resources and one must accept them as a fact. You didn't understand that and you still don't. It somehow didn't get through to you that if He didn't take care to note your protest on two occasions, it means something might be wrong with you. Whose business is it what happens on a tiny planet in the backwoods of the galaxy? Not yours or mine. He created the world as it is and everything that happens happens with His knowledge and in conformity with His intentions. After He hurled the morning star from the heavens and turned the fallen angel into Lucifer, He did not take away his might and power. Haven't you thought about why? Because He needed the fallen seraphim in a new capacity. So ask yourself, then, against whom are you rising? Do you really think these small-fry, insignificant humans need your sacrifice? They have hope, and enough of it to get them to the grave." Serpina laughed shallowly. "The first time, I don't know why, you were only sentenced to exile. You can't expect such a soft punishment now."

"So you've come, as you did the last time, to create a pretext for my prosecution?"

"Oh, no." Serpina waved his hand. "The last time they couldn't try you for heresy because it involved a secret agreement, but now you've made such trouble that no pretext is required. You're not going to start denying that you stopped the Kissoeides of time?"

"All right"—Lukary evaded a direct answer—"if your appearance isn't a provocation, then why are you here?"

"Don't hurry me!" Serpina requested, lighting his pipe again. "It's not as simple as it might seem to you. We understand perfectly what a difficult situation you've put yourself in, and, though it might seem strange to you, we're prepared to extend a helpful hand to you."

"To me?" Lukary raised his brows in surprise. "Your hand, your help?"

"Don't be in such a hurry to refuse it." Serpina smiled. "You remember when we talked with Cronus and I said he was stupid? Well, I simply proved to be more honest than you and Yevsevy."

"You think so?"

"I know so! I said what you were thinking and couldn't help but think, because there's a maggot hole inside every human—it's the source of vile thoughts. Temptation lives there eternally and it's not a person's fault that he was made that way. With regard to humans, the Lord has proved to be a great trickster. People don't know where they've come from and have no idea of when and where they'll go. If someone figures out by himself something worth doing, then suddenly it's time for him to die. So, tell me honestly, isn't it mockery—to compel people to live in a world of ever-alternating hope and despair?" Serpina's eyes were sad. Lukary even thought that he detected something human in them.

"Imagine," the privy councillor continued, "if it's God who tempts people by allowing them to have certain thoughts and plays the fool by keeping Himself ignorant of every minute of their dreary, suffering life, then might He not have created people for His own amusement? What can you expect of them? They're foolish clowns putting on an act. And if that's so, then all your sacrifices and struggles are just silly—you're playing on the wrong team. Just think, you have an excellent opportunity to change sides, to join those who have understood His intentions and play up to Him by pouring oil on the fire of human stupidity. If you side with us, you'll become truly initiated in the great secret of human destiny. We'll see to it that they restore your high rank and position in the hierarchy of the Powers of Light. What a pleasure it is to know the true order of things, to feel yourself a giant among pygmies. With your talent you'll easily get into the elite of those who are admitted backstage in this theater of the absurd and who have a detailed knowledge of the mechanism that makes the world turn. Those who know—and keep quiet."

Serpina got up from the chair and casually walked around the empty studio. "You don't have to make a quick decision." The privy councillor smiled and winked meaningfully. "There's 'no time'—how often we use these words without considering their deeper meaning. Yet that woman in the lower world is waiting—and hoping. Incidentally, her fate also depends on your answer. How happy she'll be to see you again when you're strong and confident. And how upset she'll be if she finds out that you've let happiness escape out of your own stupidity. All told, we're not asking for much: just tell us exactly how you stopped the time machine and that will count for you. You can rest assured that our department knows how to appreciate a willingness to cooperate."

"So I did manage to stir up the hornet's nest?" Lukary gave Serpina a smile. "They started to worry that they wouldn't be able to hide such a thing from Him!"

"You overdramatize things. Of course, your feckless trick caused some trouble, but a joint team from both departments is already working on the generator." The privy councillor waved a hand tiredly. "Those who could turn His attention to what took place don't want to upset the Creator with such a trifle. You should understand this—no one in this world is ready for the hour of judgment."

"What if He learns about it nonetheless?"

"Enough, Luka, that's enough! Maybe it would be terrible, but there are so many with dirt on their hands. Another logic begins to operate here, my friend. When everyone around is clean, the soiled want to wash themselves, but when everyone is up to their necks in dirt it's much easier not to notice. That's a universal law of human existence, applicable to all other worlds as well. To be honest, I don't understand why you did what you did. Besides, why all these bare walls and shredded papers? It's romanticism, hollow romanticism! You've nowhere to run and no one will permit you to go. It's all vanity, Luka, pure vanity! You know as well as I what resources the Department of Dark Powers has at its disposal."

"You think it's time for intimidation?" Lukary inquired.

"Why bother to intimidate? Let me just tell you what you should expect if you don't accept my offer." Serpina came to a stop behind the back of the chair and looked almost sympathetically at the friend of his past youth. His voice was steady and indifferent, but Lukary could easily detect the note of triumph and superiority. "You'll go directly from this studio to stand before the joint high court of both departments and be tried for theomachy and crimes against the system. You raised your hand against the foundation of foundations, which God granted to each and all, and that is time. In a fit of pride you wanted to take away His supreme mercy, and for that you must pay. Don't smile—I know what you're thinking. Out of ignorance you think you can take advantage of the trial in order to expose the interdepartmental agreement. Nothing will come of it . . . Forgive me, I forgot to tell you about the preliminary treatment your being will be subjected to immediately before you're taken to court. There are great experts in our department: you'll be a little lamb when you leave their tender hands. You'll forget about your obsession with secret agreements and confess that you turned to crime out of love for a woman on earth—that you wanted to be with her forever! Well, you're not the first, and you won't be the last. Someone from the hierarchy of the Powers of Light did a similar thing—if you remember, it's even described in the Bible. Your sentence?" The privy councillor raised his brows dramatically and paused. "The sentence will be the usual: capital punishment—complete disintegration of your being, after which every trace of your existence will be obliterated from the world's memory. Theomachists don't exist and they cannot exist physically—that is one of the system's fundamental postulates, and in this matter the system will not deviate from the letter of the law. Every structure makes self-preservation its first line of business. 'Lukary? What Lukary?' they'll say. 'No, you're confused, there never was any such being!' "

"Who's taking me to trial? Not you, by any chance." Lukary smiled.

"Imagine that. I'm aware of your supernatural might and haven't forgotten my defeats, but this time I'll manage." Serpina was absolutely calm and confident.

Lukary got up from his chair and stretched his shoulders. A cheerful fury sparkled in his spirited glowing eyes.

"How about fighting like we did in our youth—one on one? Do you remember how we fought until the first one bled?" He took off his jacket . . .

10

Kolka Burov knew about hallucinations firsthand. "To tend the common flock," he explained to his pals, "takes a lot." Here he'd make a face and thrust his sinewy neck to one side. "In every house they pour me a glass. I'm like their real father."

Whatever wasn't finished in the day Kolka would drink up in the evening as he sat with his old lady in the wooden shed attached to the house, at the table beneath his grandfather's large icon. When the small figures of saints around its edges began to bustle about by themselves, Kolka knew that was it—he knew he'd had exactly the right amount, and tugging at his sunburnt cheek, as was his habit, he'd go take a leak before sleep. At such moments he would stand for a long time and breathe in the fresh air from the river, he'd look at the stars and think about life. Burov loved all of this terribly. Everything was going around in circles—the cottage and the shed, too, but if you lay down in the grass the stars stood as if they were rooted down and they helped Kolka a lot. Not just to maintain his balance, but in his life in general. There was a reliability in the stars and a solidity that was lacking on earth. In his wanderings around the area he relied especially on the North Star. "A wee and trusty little star," Kolka thought, "and, my goodness, you can't go anywhere without it—it's in such a steady place." He was so happy to think like this, because by some side route thoughts about himself would make their way into his meditations on the stars.

That night he'd already taken his breaths and done up the buttons on his fly, and he was just about to head for the cottage when something unusual made him prick up his ears. The white moon, pale as a faded shirt, hung high over the edge of the forest; its cold light reflected on small drops of the mist spreading along the river. A large black bird silently traced a path above a strip of the distant forest, but it was not from this ordinary sight that his heart began to palpitate and suddenly tightened in pain. What he saw astounded Burov beyond measure, but later, no matter how he vowed, no matter how he swore to God, no one believed him. Who would believe that right there in the sky two enormous horses were rushing along pulling a green covered wagon along an invisible road leading to the stars, and then, after describing a circle, they returned with dogs only to dissolve in the white fog on their way. After wiping his eyes with his fists, Kolka crossed himself with sweeping movements and deep conviction. The tipsiness flew out of his besotted head all at once—he couldn't remember when he'd felt so clear and lucid. But the real spectacle lay ahead. Against the deep starry sky Burov suddenly saw a cock flying over the dark strip of forest. As it sped upward it flew stiffly, without the slightest movement of its wings; it flew by flexing its rich plumage, like an arrow released from a bow. Directly behind it an infinitely powerful force moved into the sky; at its head was something shaped like a knight's helmet, which then turned into a long cigar-shaped body. On the sides Burov made out two outstretched arms covered up in armor. The rest was lost in a raging squall of fire. So in the radiance of his own glory might a Demiurge have gone to battle, but Kolka didn't know such words. Before his very eyes the cock lit upon the crown of the knight's helmet and then was immediately transformed into the helmet's battle feathers. The next moment the vision vanished. Burov stood there for some time and watched the sky, and then sank onto the wet grass with a quiet moan.

White light was pouring onto the empty world, shining on the fine drops of mist. Lukary traveled farther and farther from earth; the bliss of free flight flowed through him and the joy of his own power was intoxicating. He thirsted for battle, his armored muscles tensed in anticipation of a mortal fight, and he aimed himself into space, into the cold world of stars, which was open to the forces of good and evil. Freedom! Somewhere far away the moon dissolved into a vanishing white dot. The sun, luminary of the world, turned into a tiny star, and still he flew on, greedily devouring space, stringing space onto the invisible thread of his own rapid flight.

Any moment now out on the edge of the galaxy he would see a vivid flash, and, gathering speed, toward him would rush, as black as the cosmic night, the one who had sold his soul to the devil, the one with whom he must contend in his last battle. Serpina! It would be an open battle, a duel in which all doubts would be discarded and only the cold intellect and the cocked pistol would remain. "Lord," Lukary pleaded. "Don't take the joy of battle from me!" He waited, and the salty taste of sweat and blood reached his lips and his chest rose in anticipation of battle, but only the black of galactic night and cosmic solitude surrounded him. He had rushed here, he was exhausted, his enemy had tarried. Imperceptibly, with a touch gentle as muslin, a most delicate net covered his entire body, which was corseted in burnished steel. Lightly at first, then more and more strongly, it embraced him, it squeezed and squashed, and as it pressed, his armor began to shatter. He understood. Hell's embrace was closing upon him; he could see the gaping depths of the black hole ready to swallow him; and with each instant he felt its horrible inescapable pull more clearly. The steel crunched like thin fall ice, the coat of mail groaned, unable to bear the strain. Lukary tore himself away with all the strength he had left. Skirting the insatiable jaws of the black hole, he headed for earth. He knew that only after he fell there and lay stretched out on its silky meadows would he find salvation.

That night all of the world's observatories recorded the appearance of a previously unknown comet flying to earth at an incredible speed. A collision was inevitable, its consequences apocalyptic. When he saw it, an old scholar rushed to call home and give warning . . . Of what? He laughed, lit a cigarette after a thirty-year break, and walked to the window. In the observatory garden a cherry tree blossomed, the spring night was quiet and mild. The academician looked up to the sky, the comet was already visible with the naked eye, it was approaching at enormous speed. The old man crossed himself and closed his eyes: one! two! three! He counted to ten and ran to the telescope: the view of the starry heavens disappointed him with its ordinariness. He stood beside the most powerful apparatus in the world, as if he'd been struck by lightning, clearly realizing that he didn't understand a thing, not only about life but his own science. The old man knew only one thing for sure—he was happy.

Subsequently, at a specially convened international congress the most prominent scholars were at a loss. There were extremists among the young who proposed to pass a resolution that no such a phenomenon could exist in nature, but they were persuaded to give up this idea and the scholars went home without any resolution. Journalists scoffed as much as they could, naturally, but they didn't know the truth about what had happened either.

Only Kolka Burov knew.

After running to the spot where the star fell, he saw a man sprawled on the ground. Completely covered with bruises and cuts, the man was pressing his whole body into the loamy soil, half crying and half laughing.

"Oh, what a job they did on you." Nicholas slipped off his padded jacket and put it over the unlucky fellow. "Be patient, brother, I'll run and get vodka, that will make you better."

Burov rushed at a trot to his cottage but when he returned the only thing lying on the flattened ground was his jacket.

"Well, I'll be . . ." said Nicholas, and that's all he could say.

• • •

"Childhood's over, Luka, we're playing by entirely different rules now." Serpina looked with narrowed eyes at the battered Lukary. Picturesque rags, which once were a suit of high quality, covered his bruised and slashed body. His face was soaked in blood, and his eyes burned like coal. "You just didn't understand that time has changed and all those duels and other Don Quixote tricks went out of style long ago. It's cold calculation and pragmatism—there's no room for sentimentality. Today the whole world lives by different laws. As the human has evolved from the beast, he hasn't come closer to the divine, but lives like a programmed automaton. You're just breathing the dust of bygone centuries. You and I live in a cruel world and you have to adapt, whether you like it or not." Serpina smiled patronizingly. "You've succeeded in setting all the forces of hell against you, my friend, and the fact that you broke out of its embrace can only be ascribed to a miracle. All right, that's enough"—he cut himself off—"let's accept that you've learned your lesson. Tell me what you did to Cronus's Kissoeides and you can go to Anna, she's waiting."

"But you'll cheat me, Serpina!" Lukary was pronouncing every word with difficulty. His smashed lips bled.

"No, Luka, not this time. I know you—once you've started on this path you won't revert. Only the weak in spirit think it's never too late to leave the game, but you know full well that it's impossible. The road must be taken to the end. You have no choice, even a spirit of light endowed with your resources can't break free from the powerful nets of the underworld. You've done too much . . ."

"And I'll return to my place in the Department of Light Powers?"

"I promise!"

"And you won't touch her?" Swaying on unsteady legs, Lukary took a step forward. The senior privy councillor was waiting, standing by a chair and smiling as he watched his rival's broken stride. Lukary finally managed to get closer, pausing directly in front of him. His eyes were empty and sad.

"Shall we shake on it?" Serpina could not control the satisfied smile that surfaced on his round face.

"We'll shake!" With a light touch Lukary pushed aside the hand extended to him and, quickly, without his full strength, hit the privy councillor in the solar plexus. Serpina's eyes slipped out of orbit. The secret service man doubled over and started to gulp for air. The second swing landed a knockout blow on the Black Cardinal's subordinate.

"Well, it's quite a different matter now!" Lukary wiped the blood from his face. "So much for 'the forces of hell,' 'the forces of hell' . . . Very different laws operate in this world, my friend. There are some advantages to working in the human form."

He looked at the body lying on the floor and, still not steady on his feet, stepped out of the astral plane.

"If you separate the variables in the equation and take the gravitational constant out of brackets . . ." Sergei Sergeyevich whispered, biting his tongue from his efforts. He was ecstatic and at the same time indignant at the need to make intermediate transformations. "And then . . ." He chewed the end of his pencil with excitement. "Then multiply both parts by the speed of light squared."

Behind his back an irritating movement was taking place. Telyatnikov swung around sharply and looked at the door in a sudden burst of anger. Anna stood there as pale as a sheet holding on to the doorframe.

"Seryozha," she said almost inaudibly, "I feel terrible."

"Terrible? Why terrible?" Sergei Sergeyevich said in alarm. The thought "But you can't put 'terrible' in the formula because of its incorrect dimensions!" flashed in the assistant professor's inflamed brain. He was going to tell his wife this, to ask if there wasn't some other, more suitable variable, but she suddenly left the doorway, stepped into the room, and collapsed onto the rug as if she'd been shot. Not quite understanding what was happening, Telyatnikov got up from the desk in complete confusion and stared in amazement at his unconscious wife. A gust of wind blew the window open; the white curtain flew up in a frightful way, knocking a vase with dried-up flowers onto the floor. The terrified Sergei Sergeyevich looked around the room. It suddenly seemed to him that a man covered with blood and rags walked straight out of the wall, took Anna by the arm, and immediately disappeared. And yet his wife remained there on the rug, and he, Sergei Sergeyevich, by some strange force was returned to his place at the desk. Then, from the corner of the room his old friend Professor Shepetukha jumped into view; he was naked for some reason, and his gray skin was covered by sparse green hair. The professor went up to Anna with trembling paws and a knee-jerking gait; he looked at her face and immediately fell back with a horrible squeal. "Ambulance!" shouted Telyatnikov, who'd just come to himself. "Ambu . . ."

The sounds stuck in his throat on their own. A doctor appeared from nowhere and began fussing over Anna. In an agitated state he began constantly poking her, now in the jaw, now in the stomach, then walked around the prostrate body, gesturing in despair and cursing in Latin. The woman's eyes had rolled back, she was not breathing, and only the slightest trace of a pulse spoke of a flicker of life remaining. Shepetukha minced along behind the doctor, trying to look over his shoulder, and mournfully lamented, "She's dead! Quite dead!"

Sergei Sergeyevich saw now that he was not a professor, but more likely a medical attendant or even more probably an orderly. "What's wrong with my head today?" Telyatnikov wondered, getting up and cautiously approaching his wife's body. Little pieces of formula kept falling in paper flakes from the ceiling and circling in the air, though this did not stop him from observing the medical practitioner's behavior. Meanwhile the doctor from the ambulance straightened up, threw back his long curly hair, and turned to Sergei Sergeyevich.

"Well, have you finished playing, Assistant Professor?" he asked in an irritated voice, keeping his palm on the jaw, which had become quite blue and swollen. "Your wife's been taken away! You fool!" Unable to contain his indignation, the doctor shoved the unfortunate Telyatnikov in the chest so hard that he flew back against the wall, and then the doctor turned to the orderly, spat out a pair of teeth that apparently were superfluous, and went on. "You let her get away, you big-eared scum! I'll beat you to a pulp! Don't you see, the lady's in a lethargic sleep! They're gone, they're both gone, now go and find them!"

Moving with difficulty and pursued by the fussing orderly, the doctor left the apartment through a window. He vanished into the still air right in front of the speechless Telyatnikov's eyes. The Professor Shepetukha look-alike also started to disappear but suddenly returned and shook his small bony fist at Sergei Sergeyevich.

When the ambulance crew that had been called finally arrived, they found two bodies in the apartment and several extremely frightened kindhearted neighbors who were trying to help.

Anna turned around. Somewhere far below, in the time and space she had left, she saw herself lying beside Telyatnikov on the floor of her apartment. Some unfamiliar anxious people in white smocks were taking out their gear and preparing injections. Strangely, she felt no pity or sorrow but only an unexpected new freedom: she hadn't the slightest desire to return to the world she'd left behind. Yet anguish still dwelt within her, an inexplicable soul-rending anguish for that meaningless and bitter absurdity that her life had been. With extraordinary speed she was flying through a dark, seemingly endless tunnel. Someone cried out to her, calling her to come back, he was laughing wildly, hysterically; she heard fragments of strange, senseless, scary talk; a cacophony of sounds swept over her in waves from head to toe. The howl of a jackal mixed with a hyena's wail and laughing call, and moans of ecstasy gave way to the screams of victims being tortured.

"Luka!" she called out into emptiness, and immediately sensed his powerful, calm energy near her. "What happened to me? Did I die?"

"Don't be afraid." He was right beside her. "The astral plane is scaring you. Death is beautiful and free, it is gentle and merciful, but what you are experiencing now is still not death. You will return, you'll return to the human world again."

"Will you return too?"

Anna raised her head and everything around her had suddenly changed, the voices that frightened her had fallen behind and an enchanting, marvelous chorus of beautiful clear voices flowed above her, quietly at first, then more powerfully and triumphantly, and she floated in their gentle sounds. A star . . . In the boundless heights a distant star flared with a radiant, emerald light, penetrating all.

11

September isn't the best time of year in Moscow. Especially the start. Sometime in the middle of the month Indian summer begins, but the first few days are usually pallid and overcast, if it doesn't rain. A dreary gray hopelessness fills the city to its rooftops, and the heart sinks in expectation of the long cold winter. If it's not the rain or the tiresome gray, then it's the wind. In the early morning hours it pushes the garbage that has piled up during the day along the empty streets together with scattered leaves, tin cans, and shreds of newspapers. What's in this news that's managed to grow old? The summer's gone, no more summer—that's the top story.

Lukin bent over to pick up a rumpled sheet of newspaper from the sidewalk. He smoothed it out in the swaying light of a wind-rocked streetlamp. Yes, the fascists in Germany were craving power . . . The latest data on the fulfillment of the first Five-Year Plan . . . The Red Army private Suchkov got a watch engraved with his name for valor during a fire.

What a sad and dark scene! Freedom—Marx's "understood necessity"—as realized in the proletarian system. Lukin crumbled the newspaper and threw it down on the street. The wind caught the ball of paper and sent it hopping over the pavement. Luka pushed his hat down on his forehead, wrapped himself more tightly with the flap of his macintosh, and lit a cigarette. Straightening up, he looked down the end of the street.

"In all circumstances," he said out loud, "no matter what happens—a fire or a dictator's last struggle—you can always find people who'll benefit by it. Such is the human animal, it seems—he can turn anything to profit."

After sharing these thoughts with the empty street, Lukin thrust his hands more deeply into his coat pockets and walked down the pavement, pursued by gusts of wind. Without a streetlamp the night closed in; dampness and the smell of benzine wafted from the nearby river. He came within a few yards of the corner and turned around. The entire street was visible—it was empty and dark. The watch on his arm showed two o'clock. In a clearing between the buildings the Cathedral of Christ the Savior stood silhouetted against the dark sky. Somewhere on the square a police whistle blew. Moving with a catlike softness, Lukin stepped back against a wall and listened. There was a rustling that seemed very close. His hand slipped into his coat pocket and rested on the handle of a gun.

"Hey, comrade!" came a voice from a gateway. "Come here! Hurry, hurry, there might be shards on your side!"

Moving sideways without taking his eyes off the black opening of the alleyway, Lukin crossed the street and approached a gate that led into a maze of courtyards. He stepped into its darkness, briefly entering a passage through which he could see down the entire alley. As he came into dim light from the street, he could make out two figures pressed against the wall.

"Where are you? I can't see you!" said the same voice, which seemed familiar to Lukin. Somewhere he had definitely heard that bewildered tone, which sounded like a call for help. The air smelled of a nearby rubbish heap and cats. Lukin drew closer, keeping to the wall, and came to a stop a foot away from the man who had spoken.

"We were coming back home from our friends' place," the stranger said. "By any chance do you have cigarettes? I don't smoke, mind you, but for some reason I really want one now."

Lukin took a pack of French cigarettes from his pocket and held it out in the darkness. The man felt around and pulled one out.

"Thanks! If you can, give me a light too."

"I do know this man," Lukin decided, striking a match against the box—"and I know him well." Shielding the weak flame with his palms, he raised it to the stranger's face. Against the darkness the quivering light brought to the fore round spectacles and a neat, almost totally gray goatee.

"Sergei Sergeyevich? Telyatin?"

"Lukin! By God, Lukin!" The man straightened, forgetting about the cigarette. The match went out and he peered intently into the dark. "No, I don't believe it! It's impossible!"

"It's possible, Sergei Sergeyevich, it is possible."

All of a sudden an explosion of enormous force rent the quiet of the night. Something immeasurably heavy, like the weight of human sin, crashed onto the earth, and the ground began to tremble. The walls of the buildings shook and a handful of small stones clinked on the cobblestone pavement. The abrupt stillness that followed was broken by the trill of a police whistle, painful to the ears. A car's engine roared and the weak beam of its distant headlights slid over the wall of a building on the other side. They made their way across the ground on legs that felt suddenly numb, exited through a gate, and stopped at the intersection. Through clouds of dust that had not yet settled a frighteningly shapeless pile of debris could be seen in the place where the cathedral had stood.

"They won't get away with that so easily!" Sergei Sergeyevich kept saying as he comforted the young woman crying at his side. "God will never forgive them this! Never! I didn't think they'd dare try a second time; I thought He wouldn't allow it."

Telyatin was also crying, he didn't hide his tears. The arm that was around the woman's shoulders trembled, his fingers moved nervously.

In the beam of headlights they could see some people rushing about in the cathedral's ruins. The windows in the buildings surrounding the square were all black.

"Most likely they dynamited it from under the bridge," Lukin surmised, his attention directed upon a row of streetlamps that had been knocked down on the other side of the river. "Today in the streetcar people were saying that Lazar Kaganovich personally pressed the button the first time. 'We'll yank old Mother Russia's hem!' he said, then pressed. The bastard!"

The young woman sobbed loudly.

"All right, let's go." Supporting his companion, Telyatin turned and wearily walked up the street. "Today in the institute they said that the police had cordoned off the square and there might be arrests at night. I wouldn't have come to look," he went on, addressing Lukin, "but my niece Anya persuaded me. It's hard on my heart, it's all so ugly."

Lukin fell behind a little; he looked back a few times, but the street remained quiet and dark. There was only light in a few windows of the huge Government House that rose on the other side of the river. They turned into the midst of courtyards and walked through a maze of alleys. Sergei Sergeyevich stopped unexpectedly and turned around.

"Lukin, is it really you, Lukin? I can't believe it!" He stepped forward somewhat uncertainly, embraced Lukin, and kissed him three times. "Alive, you're really alive!"

Somewhere above their heads a window banged and a man's deep voice promised to tear off the head of anyone who kept him awake. "A working man's on the first shift tomorrow," the guy hollered to the whole street, "but some idiotic moron fools around at night and doesn't let you sleep! Damn fucker!"

"Let's get out of here! Hurry," Telyatin urged. "God spare us from the police!"

Taking Anya by the arm, he practically ran into the nearest alley. Lukin followed, surprised by the quickness of a man no longer young. On the way Telyatin mumbled, "That's all I need—if they find out in the institute, I'll lose my job. I said we shouldn't go, didn't I?"

"Why are you so upset?" Lukin caught up to him. "If the police come, just tell them who you are—that will take care of it."

"Listen." Sergei Sergeyevich came to a halt. "Did you just come from the moon? What are you doing here anyway?"

"The same thing as you—being a witness to history. Do you suspect me of something?"

"Of course not, what do you mean?" Telyatin wiped the sweat from his forehead. "My nerves are acting up. Forgive me, Lukin, I didn't mean it! Where do you live now?" Sergei Sergeyevich panted as he spoke. "The next streetcar stop is far away, come with us. We're almost there, we can sit down and remember the old days. There's something to remember, isn't there?"

Telyatin threw his arm around Lukin's waist and pulled him close. Lukin didn't protest.

"I just arrived today," he said, trying to stay in step with Telyatin. "So I decided to look around and see what you folks in the capital are up to."

"Good, thank God for that! To be honest, we had you buried. The field hospital reported that you were dead."

"Almost." Lukin smiled. "I really got a good-sized hole in me."

They stopped at the corner of a public garden, looked around in all directions and ran quickly across the open space, then dove into the entrance of a once privately owned large apartment building. The broad staircase and hall were empty. Trying not to make any noise, they made their way to the right door. Telyatin opened it by touch and let Anya and Lukin into the apartment's stuffy interior. In the dim light of a dusty lamp Lukin saw three iron mailboxes hanging in a row and three bells on the doorpost.

"Everyone steals," Sergei Sergeyevich was saying in the meantime, locking the door from inside. "They stole before too, of course, but not so much. People had consciences and knew some limits."

When he'd finished with this important matter, Telyatin walked to the end of the narrow high-ceilinged hall and, taking out a large key with a massive bit, unlocked the door to a room. The room that came into view at first reminded Lukin of a furniture warehouse.

Sergei Sergeyevich knew the impression his living quarters made and immediately explained, "Our living space was reduced to a single room. We had the whole apartment before."

While the hosts prepared a late meal—putting on the teapot, cutting bread, herring, and sausage, Lukin sat down in a tall chair with a carved back and leather seat, lit up a cigarette, and with curiosity began to observe the peculiarities of other people's life.

"Why, I haven't introduced you yet," Telyatin suddenly remembered. "This is Anya, my niece, the daughter of my late sister. Anyuta, this is my old friend—one might say, colleague—Lieutenant Lukin."

Lukin rose and kissed the hand the young woman extended to him.

"I'm very happy to see that the captain has such a charming relative." He gave Telyatin a sidelong glance. Sergei Sergeyevich shuddered like a frightened child.

"What did you say? Captain? Ah, yes! Excuse me, I was lost for a second. He and I haven't seen each other for more than ten years," he explained to Anya. "One unwittingly thinks in terms of the past. But just think about it, my friends, what an extraordinary meeting!"

A pile of books lay on an enormous carved sideboard. Lukin picked up the top one and read the title: *The Physics of Electricity*.

"You're a student?"

"No, if I may say so, she's an actress," Telyatin answered in her stead. "That's my book, I earn my bread with that kind of work. Our Anya's been an actress from birth," Sergei Sergeyevich continued while slicing the herring with a knife. "True, until now, for the most part lines from offstage and bit parts."

"Oh, Uncle! You'd best talk about yourself."

"Well, in general, there's nothing to tell." Telyatin drew himself up and looked at Lukin. "I teach physics at the Water Supply and Management Institute. What can I do—we need to live. I'm hiding in a remote corner so that no one will bother me. It's just our bad luck to live in vile times like these."

Lukin casually went to the door and looked out into the hall. Sergei Sergeyevich wrapped the herring entrails in a newspaper and wiped his plump white hands with a rag. He opened a door in the sideboard and with some ceremony took out a small bottle of vodka and placed it on the table.

"You should tell about your discovery." Anya brought some small glasses and wiped them with the end of a cloth. "You know"—she turned to Lukin—"I don't understand any of this well, of course, but he proved that Einstein was wrong! Uncle even wants to write him a letter."

"Well, it's not that I proved it," Telyatin said, raising his eyebrows, "and it's not that he's wrong—however, there are certain considerations . . . Well, we won't go into it now, it has to be weighed and calculated properly. Why hurry when the topic is eternity? Let's sit down instead!"

After dislodging the sealing wax from the neck of the bottle with the handle of a knife, he pulled out the cork with its tip, and poured vodka into the glasses.

"To our meeting, Lukin, to our meeting! I'm happy to see you alive." Telyatin drank his glass and put a piece of sausage on his bread. "The last time we saw each other was . . ."

"October 1, 1918," Lukin prompted. "Almost fourteen years ago. At Zhutovo Station south of Tsaritsyn. It was a remarkable battle, Sergei Sergeyevich, I remember! We attacked for more than a day and night and we took it in the end. They were a special Red infantry division—but we cleared them out like rabbits. They abandoned their armored train, the special trains with provisions, the wounded. You aren't by chance a member of the Bolshevik Party now—I'm not hurting your tender feelings, am I?" Lukin inquired. "Times change, and you don't have to list your White past when you fill out personal forms."

"Why are you talking like that? Do you want to scare Uncle?" Anya looked up at Lukin.

"Don't get excited, dear," Telyatin calmed her. "Our guest simply has that charming way of speaking! As a matter of fact, I certainly didn't list the Volunteer Army on any forms. But I do answer honestly—that I taught at the General Staff Academy before the Revolution."

"Yes, Sergei Sergeyevich, your face shows that you're the most civilian of creatures. To this day I wonder how you happened to be fighting with us then."

"You wonder? That's strange. I thought it was my duty to what I used to call my country. Enough about that. Instead, tell me how your life has turned out. I don't even know how exactly you were wounded."

Telyatin raised his glass and clinked Lukin's. Lukin drank the vodka in one gulp, tossing back his quite gray head.

"How has my life turned out?" He lit a cigarette, released smoke from the corner of his mouth, and bit his upper lip. "Probably the same as everyone else's . . . I was wounded in a stupid way—it's always stupid when people get wounded and killed. You remember Colonel Sotnikov, of course? He ordered us to investigate the special trains left standing on the tracks. I climbed into the first car and opened a compartment door. I managed to get a look at him. A Red Army soldier, just a boy, his entire chest wrapped in bandages. His face was as white as chalk, his eyes a pure cornflower blue and glowing from fever. He didn't even have the strength to raise the revolver—one leg was bent and he rested the barrel on his knee. I opened the door and he pulled the trigger. It was all very simple. The hospital was next. Odessa. I don't know why but for some reason I was unable to leave. Then I made my way to Samara. I was a stevedore, I made shoes, and later I managed to enroll in an accounting course. My education, so to speak, made this possible." He made a wry smile, reached for the bottle, and filled his glass. "Now, as you see, I've come here, I want to seek my fortune in the capital." With a look at the door Lukin asked, "Why can't I hear your neighbors? Don't you have two of them?"

"You need not worry about them. They're not here now. Pashka the proletarian"—Telyatin pointed to the closest wall—"went off on a job. He signed up for a yearlong construction project and he's gone, but he left us his key so that we'd guard his interests. He's a good man—he drinks, of course, but everyone drinks today. The second neighbor," he said, giving Anya a quick glance, "she works nights, comes home in the morning, and catches up on her sleep all day. Also a good woman."

"For you, Uncle, everyone's good, you're like some kind of little Jesus! You live thinking how not to offend anyone. She's a prostitute, a common prostitute, one of the chic women for foreigners."

"Why do you talk like that? There's nothing wrong with Lyudmila Nikolayevna working in a foreign-currency bar, she serves our guests . . ."

"That's exactly what I'm saying—she's a prostitute!" Anya insisted. "You'd better be quiet."

Sergei Sergeyevich suddenly turned red. He began to cough and started wiping his glasses with a felt cloth.

"It's good that the neighbors are quiet," Lukin remarked, trying to relieve the tension. "They don't bother you."

"Tell me what happened with the Red soldier," Anna asked at once, "the one who shot you?"

"For obvious reasons"—Lukin smiled—"I don't know exactly. I think they finished him off right there in the car. It was a brutal time, Anechka, an extremely brutal time. Human life wasn't worth a red cent. But if you look at Russian history . . ."

"You know," Sergei Sergeyevich said, looking at Lukin thoughtfully, "you'd better think again about Moscow. There are persistent rumors that after New Year's they're going to introduce passports and residence permits and that means they'll be checking on everyone. At such times it's best to be where people have known you for a long time. A new wave of purges is coming, and even in our institute—a godforsaken place, something is simmering and stewing all the time . . . And the scum . . . You can't imagine how much scum comes to the surface here!"

Outside the window the sky turned almost imperceptibly lighter. A car passed somewhere below.

"Well now, I need some sleep. I have to teach tomorrow." Telyatin let out a deep sigh. "What a long, hard day! Some moments are like mileposts, you know—a new epoch begins with them. I have the feeling that we lived through one of those today. Remember my words: we'll pay for the cathedral's destruction." He raised his glass. "Lord, forgive us!" After drinking his vodka, he turned to Anya. "Put Lukin in Petka's room. Until he makes living arrangements he can stay in the proletarian's room—he'll be none the worse for it . . ."

Telyatin was quiet until his niece left the room, then, still looking uneasily in the direction she'd gone, he continued. "I'm sorry for her. I've had a life, but what's in store for her? . . . She wasn't admitted to the institute—she's not of proletarian background and she has no reliable profession. Just in the past few days she's become rather nervous, as if expecting something. A girl needs to get married, but on the other hand, it's terrible—people have sunk so low, they've become petty, and something beastlike has appeared in them. While she just goes on and on about the theater! Listen, Lukin." Sergei Sergeyevich leaned across the table and began to whisper. "You're not too old yet—take Anka and go somewhere. Nothing good will happen here. Go to America! They're rich, they're promising us a loan worth a billion dollars. If you're lucky, maybe they'll let you out, or else you can escape across the border . . . And I'll get along here somehow, I'll feel better." He looked at Lukin. Behind the glasses his eyes were red, and there was a note of mad hope in his voice. "Just don't say no, think about it, think it over well!"

The door opened and Anya came back into the room and disappeared behind a screen into her part of the room. Lukin followed her with his eyes.

"Let's go, we won't disturb you. Good night, Anya!" He got up, took his coat and hat from a hook, and followed Telyatin into the hall. A dim, dusty bulb hanging from the high ceiling flooded a tall narrow chest with its cheerless light. Sergei Sergeyevich sat down on a small nightstand. Lukin remained standing. They smoked in silence.

"Why are you looking at me?" Telyatin raised his head and stretched wearily. "Have I changed? I know I've changed. It's hard to remain human in a herd of swine. Just try to build a new life for yourself out of fragments of the old. You can get your fill. But even though you hold up your head, you'll sink lower and lower until you start gobbling up the dirt beneath their feet like everyone else! 'Oh, you wear glasses, oh, you speak three languages—here take this, here—a boot in the gut!' I'd have shot myself long ago had it not been for her . . . Why are you quiet?"

Lukin squatted down beside him, and lowered his voice to a whisper. "Do you think if I hadn't been wounded then, if I had remained in the unit, maybe everything would have turned out differently? If we'd taken Tsaritsyn that fall, it would have been the end of the Bolsheviks! Sometimes I think that we needed just one more bayonet in this whole story—mine." From very close up Lukin looked into Sergei Sergeyevich's eyes without a blink. "Everything was going according to plan, even the big whiskers was sitting there in the city just so that we could hang him on the first post . . . No, I don't believe that shot was arbitrary or accidental—do you understand, Telyatin, I don't believe it." Lukin smiled and his smile frightened Sergei Sergeyevich. "But it's not over yet," Lukin said thoughtfully, "it's far from over. In classical tragedies it takes a minimum of two acts."

He winked at Telyatin. A tiny and disagreeable shudder struck Sergei Sergeyevich.

"I thought I was crazy." He spoke with difficulty. "Now I see it's you who's crazy. Keep in mind that I won't withstand torture."

"Oh, Sergei Sergeyevich"—Lukin gave Telyatin a friendly hug—"you've completely misunderstood me. But let's sleep now, you have a hard day ahead."

Lukin took several steps down the hall, then hid behind the neighbor's door. Telyatin remained in the corner for some time, clearly confused and frantically trying to understand what he was thinking about. Then he turned and looked at the portrait of Comrade Stalin that Petka had pinned to the wall.

After a restless night Lukin allowed himself a good sleep in the morning. The absent proletarian's worn-out couch didn't lend itself to euphoria in the arms of Morpheus, but that didn't stop Lukin from lying around till noon. He finally got up and began pacing the tiny room, curiously observing the trappings of a very modest life. Two keys had been shoved under the door and a note with instructions about where to find food and what to eat for breakfast. Anya had written in a childishly round script that she and Telyatin would probably return late and he shouldn't wait for them for dinner. In a postscript, bearing obvious traces of hurry and, so it seemed to Lukin, of hesitation, Anya asked to speak with him, "as an old friend of Sergei Sergeyevich." After reading the message, Lukin neatly folded the paper several times and put it in the pocket of his suit trousers. Her request made him happy for some reason. Trying not to analyze his feelings, he nonetheless realized that he had woken up eagerly awaiting a meeting with Anya.

Pulling his trouser suspenders over his naked trunk, Lukin stood up and looked at himself in the cracked, yellowish mirror attached to the old chiffonier; he inserted the round black radio speaker into the wall socket. They were broadcasting a review of the day's news. With the announcer's droning voice in the background, he walked over to the window and looked out at the street. Overnight it had turned colder and the wind had picked up; at times an amazingly bright blue sky showed through the breaks in the clouds which were gliding rapidly over the city. Below, a small truck rumbled as it raced over the cobblestones; behind it, black and shiny as a beetle, a long government limousine rolled past on big wheels. A streetcar rang at the turnaround and then went by. For a moment the sun peeked out—a dazzling cheerful ray reflected on the glass. There was a crowd gathered at the entrance to the bakery. Someone in a cap was cursing in despair and flinging his arms about, but he was thrown out of the line nonetheless, and, insulted, he dragged himself off in the direction of the streetcar stop. Lukin glanced after the limousine; he estimated the distance and bit his upper lip, deep in thought. In the meantime the announcer continued to read the news.

"The twenty-fifth of September marks forty years of Maxim Gorky's literary and public work. The entire country is preparing for anniversary celebrations honoring the first proletarian writer. In order to mark this event and the contributions of the man who fought to give the proletarian press a role in raising the cultural-political level of the working people of the Soviet Union, on the initiative of the editorial board of the journal *Ogonyok* a meeting of editorial workers and literary contributors to thirty-nine journals and newspapers has resolved to launch a collection of funds to construct a multiengine giant propaganda airplane, the *Maxim Gorky*. Elected to the committee for the management of the collection of funds and the construction of the agitplane were Comrades Alksnis, Baranov, Mekhlis . . ."

Lukin went over to the chiffonier and pulled the speaker out of the socket. Picking up a well-used, chipped green teakettle from the table, he headed for the kitchen. In the daylight from the small window the room seemed neglected. The large room, which was painted a dirty rose, had three tables—corresponding to the number of families in the apartment, as was the practice in every communal apartment. Two of the tables were graced by kerosene stoves. A thin stream of water flowed from the faucet into the sink. Squinting as he looked around the squalid interior, Lukin lit the stove closest to the window and put on the teakettle. Through the unwashed soot-covered glass he could see the roofs of neighboring apartment houses. Beyond the river the gray bulk of the Government House, the newly settled apartment house for high officials, hovered over the older buildings. It seemed alien to Moscow's urban landscape and only irritated Lukin. It was unpleasant just because it reminded him of the destruction of the Cathedral of Christ the Savior, in whose place, according to plan, a four-hundred-meter-high Palace of Soviets, crowned with a sculpture of the leader, was to be built. The newspapers reported that work on the project was underway and the finished Government House would form part of an entire complex meant to beautify the capital's center. "Not much of a beautification," Lukin thought, looking again at the huge gray rectangle, and suddenly he felt that someone was standing behind his back. Pretending still to be studying the street, he listened attentively, but the apartment was quiet.

Lukin turned around. A woman stood in the doorway, separated from him by the space of the kitchen. The light from the window illumined her figure. She was tall, with a fashionable smooth hairdo which emphasized to her favor the graceful carriage of her head. She wore a short loosely tied flannel robe, worn from many washings, and black silk stockings and heels. In her right hand the woman held a small pistol. Lukin knew the weapon: a tiny Browning for women, no doubt silver-plated, with a pearl inlaid handle. If it didn't shoot, it could almost have been a toy. In the meantime the barrel of the pistol was aimed at his chest, and its repeating upward movements suggested that it would be a good idea for him to raise his hands. Lukin did so, though rather slowly. As if to encourage his understanding, the woman smiled, and stepping into the kitchen, leaned her back against the dirty rose wall.

"So, you got caught." Her voice, slightly hoarse, was beautiful and deep. "A voice for singing romances to a guitar," Lukin thought.

"Did you decide to have a bite before busting the apartment? Of course, why should good food go to waste?"

She continued to examine him. Her large eyes with their dilated and somewhat alarmed pupils lingered on his face, slipped down his broad chest, taking note of the long white scar, and stopped at his well-made suit trousers and good leather shoes.

"Well, why don't you talk? Say something in your own defense before I put a hole in you!"

Lukin shrugged his shoulders. "It's all happened to me before . . . including the hole. But you can see for yourself that I don't fit the description."

"True." She smiled. "You're dressed very exotically. When burglars do a job, they don't strip to the waist, and you're not at the doctor's." She took a long thin cigarette from her robe pocket.

Lukin saw that the woman's index finger was slowly and irreversibly pulling back the gun's trigger. He stopped breathing—he couldn't tear his eyes from the pistol's black muzzle. There was a flick and a flame shot out of the Browning's end. The woman lit up and put the lighter in her pocket.

"You can put them down . . ."

Lukin lowered his arms and took a breath.

"What if I'd been armed?"

"Who knows?" The woman drew the robe over her breasts and inhaled greedily. "What's there to lose?" She walked up to Lukin, coming very close, and focused her *rusalka* eyes on him. "Tell me, what's there to lose? This garbage dump?" She gave a nod toward the window, and twisted her lips contemptuously. She smelled of wine and something artificially sweet. "OK"—she waved her arm—"what's there to say? I understand you're staying with those Telyatins. You certainly don't look like a friend of our local proletarian." She rocked back on her heels and sent a thin stream of smoke toward the ceiling. "I've been living here three years and haven't seen anyone visit them."

Wearily, she walked over to the kerosene stove and turned the wick with a practiced hand.

"That's my stove . . . No, go ahead, use it—I don't care! These days everything belongs to everybody, even me." She tried to smile but the face she made was pitiable. "You might even say I'm a symbol of their shitty socialism, you can put me on a pedestal. I'm the anvil on which foreign currency is forged for the land of the Soviets. And all these . . . They take money from me and want me to sleep with them for free. It won't work. No, I tell them, go chase after dollars, and not for me, but for the needs of heavy industry. Citizens, when you get pleasure, you're helping to industrialize the land of the toiling proletariat. But to the last one they're all skinflints and swine . . . I'm ready to do it for free, though, to help the victims of the Volga region famine. Do you want to?"

The woman flung open the flaps of her robe, showing Lukin her small rounded breasts.

"Well, why don't you say something? I like you, I love men like you. You can call me Lucy, like the rest." She yawned. "Let's put it off till evening, though, I want to sleep—I'm dying. You're not in a hurry, are you?"

She put on bright lipstick and ran her hand tiredly over her face, then walked out of the kitchen, rocking on her heels. Lukin quietly watched her go.

When he returned to his little room, he ate his breakfast slowly, got dressed, and carefully arranged his tie in a large English-style knot like those pictured in portraits of Lenin. With a shoe brush he found in the proletarian's wardrobe, Lukin cleaned his shoes to a shine. He took another look in the cracked mirror on the chiffonier and was pleased.

After the stuffy, dust-filled communal apartment, he breathed easily and freely outside. He was startled by the number of people on the street. It was the height of the working day, but all the same a stream of people moved past him on the sidewalk: there were round-headed plainly dressed peasants and men with a businesslike air of importance who rushed about in high boots and jackets, beneath which you would often see round-collared embroidered white peasant shirts. A vision out of the past was attracting general attention—from his high seat a cab driver was picturesquely trading with a lady whose fat neck was wrapped in a fluffy fox stole of sparkling silver. While leisurely examining the drama of city life in the capital, Lukin sauntered up to the nearest corner with an expression of indifference, turned it, and began to take an interest in a hardware store window. Behind the large pane of dirty glass, padlocks were displayed on white paper; for the sake of realism beneath each of them lay a massive key with a heavy, ornamental bit. In the glass, as if in a mirror, Lukin could see the entire small street with its pedestrians and cars and a streetcar that gleamed in the sun as it approached the stop. After the warning ring sounded and the streetcar had started to move, Lukin rushed from his place; a minute later he was hanging on from one of the steps, smiling at the fat openly good-natured conductress.

"Aha, a street urchin, just like a little kid"—she spoke to him kindly—"then you should be hanging on the bumper in back! And dressed so nicely—a hat, too. Citizens"—she spoke in a loud voice—"whoever's just come on, pay for your tickets!"

Lukin stepped up onto the platform and closely watched the street as it vanished into the distance. No one had noticed his quick disappearance from the street. Convinced of that, he pushed his way to the middle of the car and got stuck, squeezed in from all sides by fellow citizens. He rode in this semi-suspended condition for about half an hour, got off at the Metropole Hotel, and walked from there. Despite the cold wind he was warmed by the sun, and in sheltered corners it was even hot.

Lukin walked slowly onto the stone blocks of Red Square, looked around, thought for a moment, and headed toward the Cathedral of St. Basil the Blessed. The new marble mausoleum that had replaced the provisional wooden one was sparkling to his right, but Lukin had little interest in Vladimir Ilich Lenin's burial vault. Instead of paying tribute to the leader of the world proletariat he stood for some time near the old execution spot, the Place of Skulls, then walked around the cathedral, leaned against its brick foundation, and started to wait. He had to wait a long time. The minute hand of the clock on Spassky tower covered three-quarters of a circle before an automobile exited from the gates. He was approximately a hundred and fifty meters away. Lukin began to count. It took six seconds for the car, whooshing over the stone pavement, to disappear from his field of vision. He couldn't say exactly who sat in the car or even how many people were in it. He bit his upper lip, then lit a cigarette and began to think. A large pack of Pioneer scouts, carrying an unfurled banner, was on its way to pay a call on Grandpa Lenin. A policeman stepped out from behind the monument to Minin and Pozharsky and headed straight for Lukin. His young, mustached face shone with good health; a soldier's shirt, gathered in folds at the back, clung to his strong body. Lukin prepared himself mentally and unfastened his coat with a natural movement: there was a holster with a gun under his jacket. The policeman drew near, stopping about a yard away, and looked sternly into Lukin's face.

"What are you doing, comrade! It's Red Square, and next to it's the mausoleum and you're smoking! That's not right!"

"Sorry," Lukin pleaded, extinguishing the cigarette with his heel. "I've just come from abroad, I haven't been here for a long time, and I was deeply moved."

"I understand." The policeman softened. "I was watching you. You've been standing here for an hour."

With a salute the policeman turned and slowly returned to his post near the monument. Lukin took a deep breath and folded in the flaps of his macintosh. He walked through the square and down to Okhotnyi Ryad, where he asked a polite old lady about the route. He got on the first streetcar that took him to Kalanchyovka.

Everything was in turmoil on the square in front of the station. Crowds of speculators who'd come to the capital were frantically asking anybody and everybody how to go here and how to ride there, and as soon as they got an answer, little trusting the tricky Muscovites, they'd immediately recheck the information. The enormous hall in Kazan Station was full of people. Stupefied from the stuffy heat and the pressing crowd, people were storming the railroad ticket counters in hopes of getting out of the insane city faster. From the side Lukin observed this mass display of human passions, then went and took his shabby doctor's traveling bag from the baggage room and returned to the ticket hall. He walked several times up and down the unending line with the worried look of an absentminded intellectual who was lost in the crowd; first he'd take out a fat wallet, then nervously stick it back into his coat pocket. In the intervals between these seemingly senseless acts, Lukin would put his bag on the floor and diligently wipe his damp forehead with a large handkerchief.

He didn't have long to wait. Just as once a shark smells blood it rises to the top of the sea and begins swimming in circles, so a certain unattractive type began to flash in Lukin's field of vision ever more frequently. Wearing a flat cap, crumpled trousers with baggy knees, and a rather tight stumpy jacket, the redhead circled him. Once, trying to be casual, he almost moved in on his victim, but apparently something frightened him off and he dissolved into the thick crowd. Finally, taking advantage of the fact that the man wearing the hat was staring at the train schedule and blinking more frequently, the redhead gently moored onto the lost fool and lightly slipped his hand into the coat pocket. He touched the wallet, his nimble fingers closed around the soft leather of an expensive foreign item—holding the promise of so many delightful things in life—when suddenly a terrible and inexplicable pain pierced his hand. The redhead still didn't understand what had happened, but with a professional's sixth sense he knew that he'd been caught. A moment later the thief discovered the reason for his discomfort, to say the least. He was standing within a closed ring of people and the man in the hat was gripping his hand, which still rested in a pocket other than his own.

"Citizens," shouted the "fool" in the heartrending voice of a man who hadn't expected such a dirty trick from fate. "What's going on here? A pickpocket! He wanted to steal my wallet! I have twenty-seven rubles there and a certificate that I'm on official assignment. Did you see that, did you all see?"

He pointed to the redhead's too curious hand in his pocket and then pulled it out, and, indeed, it was still squeezing the wallet. Some dozen men stepped forward as if on command, unambiguously rolling up their sleeves. The redhead shuddered, his entire puny self clenched in fear of a trial by a law of someone he didn't know, called Lynch. But Lukin cooled the justified anger of the working people toward this tool of world capitalism.

"Citizens," Lukin said in a loud voice, this time his natural one. "You're all witnesses, and now I'm going to hand over this sponge to the police. Stay here, don't break up, I'll be back in five minutes with a policeman."

"Where'd we be off to?" reassured an old man in a padded work jacket and out-of-season cap with earflaps. "We'll be waiting here for a ticket till kingdom come."

Holding the thief's arm more tightly, Lukin left the ticket line, but instead of heading for the police department as he had promised the working people, he went toward an exit from the station. Out on the street he pinned his unwilling companion to the building's wall, asking quietly and clearly, "Well, Red, do you miss the wooden bunks? I see you've forgotten the taste of gruel."

This said, Lukin could tell from his victim's eyes that he'd been wrong—the redhead hadn't forgotten the tastes of prison.

"Very well," continued Lukin, hypnotizing the thief with his look.

"Listen to me carefully and trust me when I say that the last time I joked was in the year 1917." With his free hand he pulled two cigarettes from his pocket and stuck one in the redhead's mouth. He grabbed the second with his lips and lit them both with his lighter. The thief smoked with pleasure, a flame of hope appeared in his eyes. "So"—Lukin rolled the cigarette to the corner of his mouth—"now you and I'll go to your hideout, you'll introduce me to the boss."

Red shook his head. "I want to live!" His voice was raspy and dry.

"If you want to, you will," Lukin assured him gently. "Your boss will thank you for bringing me."

"Oh sure he'll thank me!" The redhead made a wry face and Lukin realized that the thief had good reason to doubt. "A knife under your jacket—and you're dead meat!"

"It's a hundred-million job," Lukin was still working on him.

"OK," he agreed. "You wait here for me. I'll go there and be back in a minute. A hop, skip, and a jump! I'll get permission and return."

"Maybe we'll go to the ticket window instead—otherwise I'll stick out like a sore thumb here by myself. After all, they're waiting for us in there. We'll pick up a cop and the three of us will go write the report. Do I understand your decision correctly?" Lukin squeezed the thief's arm harder, making him wince.

"Oh, you're a strong one," the redhead uttered, barely breathing. "Let me think it over, don't push me."

"You'll think it over on the way," Lukin assured him. "As for my strength, it's from a special art the Chinese do—kung fu. If we get to be friends," he promised vaguely, "I'll teach it to you so you'll have something to do in your cell . . ."

With these words Lukin dragged the thief from the wall and through the crowd, heading for a cab that had just turned into the station's entrance.

They rode side by side in the droshky. Lukin smoked and kept an eye on the redhead, while trying to decide whether or not this was the same cab he'd seen that morning at the Telyatkins' building. Lukin had a clear memory of the lady with the fox stole, but he'd slipped up with the driver and his carriage. At last he decided that even if it was the same cab it might be a coincidence, though he was left with an unpleasant feeling of annoyance at himself. The thief sitting beside him was tense, his skinny rear fidgeted on the leather seat and from time to time he bit his nails. Lukin didn't want to carry on a polite conversation and kept silent. Meanwhile they were traveling more and more by back streets and only once did they cross a lively broad road where streetcars passed and a cheerful policeman, wearing bell-shaped white gloves, stood in the middle of the intersection. They entered the Marina Roshcha area without noticing it. The buildings surrounding them had turned black with age and many looked ramshackle. They all seemed the same to Lukin and he didn't try to memorize the meandering route but just took note of their general direction. They surprised a large group of gypsies on the road.

After paying the cabdriver and waiting until the cab vanished from sight, Lukin and the redhead walked shoulder to shoulder down a long and especially unsightly narrow lane the sides of which were grown over with burdocks and thick waist-high grass. One of Lukin's hands held on to the thief's wrist, the other carried the doctor's bag. They walked three blocks this way; one time the redhead began to fuss and whimper, but after a friendly squeeze he continued on toward a tall gateway, once painted green, where a small door dangled on one hinge. Squinting from the bright sun, he entered the courtyard and stopped in a last hope of escaping the coming turn of events.

"Well?" Lukin looked at his companion gravely, raising his brows in expectation.

"Over there, do you see those stairs going down?" The thief motioned with his head toward a corner of the courtyard surrounded by buildings on all sides, where there actually was a small slanting door down a few steps. "Wait here, I'll go see if the boss is at home."

"Oh, why should we disturb him," Lukin objected. "Let's wait together, on the off chance someone will help us. I'm not in a hurry to go anywhere, the cops at the station toil like mules around the clock, so we'll manage to . . ."

As he spoke he drew the redhead close and sank down next to the wall on a log that had been polished by bad weather and the rear ends of innumerable sitters. He spoke the briefest of warnings: "One move and I'll shoot!"

Lukin leaned his back against the wall, which had been partly eaten away by bugs and was warm from the sun. He blissfully narrowed his eyes and looked out from under the broad brim of his hat at this neglected corner of old Moscow. The redhead kept fidgeting, staring from time to time at the basement windows. From the side they looked like two old friends who had sat down to get warm in the sun and chat about life. Time passed and the courtyard remained empty, except for a mangy red cat which had crawled out of the building to keep them company. Finally the little door that was cut into the gate squeaked on its one hinge and into the yard, moving softly with a slight spring, came a bulky tough wearing a cowboy shirt with rolled-up sleeves and wide-bottomed trousers of unprecedented dimensions. Of medium height, he was almost as broad in the shoulders as he was tall. The tough hesitated for a moment in the doorway and looked around the courtyard suspiciously. His eyes came to rest on the idyllic picture of two friends relaxing.

A second later the little door in the basement opened and a scrawny man looked out. He was dressed in a military jacket and riding breeches and wore slippers over bare feet. From far off, the way his head tilted on his wiry neck made him look like a rooster as he peered out. A Central Asian, Lukin realized, and didn't fail to note that the slant-eyed man's hand remained in his pants pocket, obviously gripping something that could shoot. In the meantime the tough came closer, stopped a few yards away, and gave Lukin an impudent stare, paying no attention to the redhead. So as to make the process of introduction easier, Lukin rose and, grabbing his bag from the log, walked slowly across the courtyard toward the waiting fancier of military uniforms. The redhead trudged behind him with a downcast head. Lukin passed the slant-eyed man, who had stepped aside, and went down the steps; he pulled the wooden door open and bent to enter the low-ceilinged basement room. In the center of the room, beneath the light of a bare electric bulb, two men sat at a table heatedly playing cards. A third man lay on a wooden bunk at the back of the room, covered up to his head by a padded jacket. Next to him was a door that led, Lukin could see, to the inner recesses of the basement. Skirting the players, Lukin went to a far corner and sat down on a chair.

The tough approached the redhead. "Did you go and squeal, you scum, and bring this snoop with you?" With his powerful hand he jerked the thief off the floor and held him up as a warning, but decided not to finish him off with a blow.

"Wait, Sailor, don't get excited," the slant-eyed man stopped him. He didn't come over, but watched what was happening from the door. His bleating voice completely fit his appearance. "When he appears, he's asked to enter."

He chuckled and pointed his stubbly chin toward the door near the bunks. The tough called Sailor gently lowered the redhead to the floor, half dragged him across the dirty boards toward the door, and shoved him into the next room. Lukin could only see that it was much better lit there and that a bright kilim hung on the far wall. The door closed. Silence followed, broken only by the sailor's heavy breathing and the smack of cards on the small table. The Asian was still hanging out by the door, watching the room in his roosterlike way and keeping a hand in his pocket. Lukin put down his bag, crossed his legs, took out a pack of cigarettes, and flicked his lighter. The stuffy room smelled of something sour, largely owing to some puttees drying on a cord above the bunks. Lukin finished his cigarette and began to yawn, but suddenly the inside door opened and a man of medium build with a head of extremely curly gray hair entered the room. His rugged good looks didn't go with his round granny glasses, but he took these off right away and put them in the pocket of the white shirt he wore under a warm wolfskin vest. The man conducted himself with dignity: his movements were unhurried, and you could tell with one glance how strong and fit his body was. Lukin guessed that he was about fifty, perhaps a little older. His clean expensive clothes were especially conspicuous in the squalor of the basement.

"I think someone's been smoking in here," the man said, wrinkling his nose and chasing the cardplayers from the room with a casual gesture. "Ah, our guest? Well, a guest's allowed to! I've heard about you,

I've heard a lot about you," he continued, going up to the table and sitting down on the freshly vacated chair. Settling into its curved back, he stared at Lukin for a long while. Lukin was surprised to see that there was a certain similarity to himself in the man's bearing as well as his external features. Meanwhile the man went on talking.

"Red told me how you caught him and related a fantastic story of how you tortured him and forced him to bring you here. Well, here you are! Tell me to what we owe your visit. Oh, Sailor," he ordered lazily, barely turning his head toward the tough, "frisk this snoop—I believe he promised to shoot Red. I wonder what you've brought us in your bag."

Obeying the command, Sailor walked over to Lukin, shoved him aside as a general warning, and reached for the bag. Later he was probably sorry for his haste, because the next moment, remaining silent as a real man should, he crashed to the floor and stayed there, inhaling the fumes of the spit-covered boards.

"Not bad," the man commented, "not bad at all! But you're getting excited for no reason. He'll come to, of course . . . But until then you have time"—he smiled—"we'll go have a talk! Let's have that gun of yours."

Threatened by Slant-eye's pistol and that of the figure on the bunks who'd just come to life—a bruiser with a beard, it turned out—Lukin pulled out his revolver and put it on the table.

"And now, if you'll be so kind, the bag," the man ordered.

"Maybe I should open it myself?" Lukin proposed.

"Oh, why should you go to the trouble." The boss grinned wryly. "Slant-eye, go get it!"

The skinny Asian thrust his pistol into his breeches, circled Lukin, and took the bag. He placed it on the edge of the table, fiddled with the lock, and quickly opened the metal-rimmed sides. What met his gaze jolted him: his eyes turned glassy, his bony face became whiter than a sheet. Scarcely moving his lips, he muttered, "A grenade! Without a pin!"

Everyone knew he was telling the truth because the pin was hanging on the chestnut bag's threadbare side, tied to the lock by a string. The next moment all save Lukin were lying on the floor covering their heads with their arms and counting to three.

Reaching across the table, Lukin grabbed the bag and pulled it over, closed it, and took out the revolver. He stepped back against the wall so that he could see everyone lying down. Three seconds passed, five, seven. The boss was the first to stand. Brushing off his pants with his palms, he gave Lukin a sideways glance and curled his thin lips.

"You're a joker, I see!"

"Life's made me one," Lukin noted enigmatically, keeping the muzzle pointed. "I offered to help, after all. Listen, Grisard, I believe that's what you're called, let's get down to business! You and I are playing games here, but these things shoot. I really don't want to have to explain who squeezed the trigger first. Besides, neither one of us is eager to get the police involved. Shall we talk?"

"Let's talk." Grisard sat in his chair and issued a command. "Take Sailor out for air, let him freshen up, it got a little hot in here. Don't go far, you might be needed."

Lukin waited until they dragged the tough out the door, then sat down on a chair, placing it so that he could see the window and both doors. He put the gun in his pocket, but his hand held on to it for company.

"The grenade's a fake?" Grisard asked, examining Lukin from close up.

"Why do you say that?" Lukin smiled kindly. "It's the very best kind—English. It's just that the grenade comes separately from the fuse." He spoke slowly, then took out a cigarette with his left hand and lit up. Narrowing his eyes, he inquired, "The Volunteer Army . . . Odessa . . . poverty . . . a crowd of brutes?"

"Let's not disturb the past." Grisard grinned. "Personally I'm not absolutely convinced that it actually existed . . . Why did you come?"

"I want to practice my marksmanship with a rifle. I need the barrel of a Mauser issued in 1930. With a collapsible butt, a semiautomatic firing pin, and a small shoulder support."

The gray-haired man looked at Lukin suspiciously, chewing his lips as he thought. "The Volunteer Army . . . Odessa . . . poverty . . . a killer for hire?"

"Let's not disturb the past." Lukin smiled. "Unlike you, however, I have no doubt it took place."

"Sorry, I'm very sorry." Grisard leaned back against the chair and put his arms behind his head. "I'm really very sorry, but I don't deal in guns. If you'd like, I can offer gems, family treasures, if you don't have your own, of course. I see that you don't. Buy some, you won't regret it."

"Oh, I neglected to say," Lukin interrupted. "Pick a good silencer and a German telegraphic sight. The magazine has to take three cartridges, and be sure that the cartridges are in excellent condition. I'll take a dozen."

"A magazine for three cartridges, you say." Grisard nodded sympathetically and chewed his lip again. "That's for when one might not suffice and there isn't enough time for a fourth shot," he reasoned out loud. "With rapid firing being somewhere in the range of thirty shots a minute you're counting on having six seconds at your disposal. Judging by the fact that you've chosen a Mauser rifle, the shooting will take place from a significant distance . . ." Grisard whistled lightly. Keeping still, Lukin looked at the boss in expectation. "It won't work out—I don't plan to have any dealings with the secret police. I've had enough of cops! If you have other wishes, drop by, you know the way. I can't vouch for my boys, though—you've offended them greatly."

"You've got two days to prepare. I'll pay with American dollars—two thousand rubles' worth."

Grisard raised his eyebrows in amazement and let out another whistle. He was quiet for some time, musing in a concentrated way. Then he spoke, smiling at his own thoughts. "Who knows? Maybe there's a possibility! Call it a sign of fate . . . To live it up in my old age like the white man. Ten thousand. In cash. That's pretty cheap, by the way, if you consider the cost of kerosene needed to burn this bug-infested place."

"For that money you could buy the whole city of Moscow and burn it." Lukin laughed. "Five. Five thousand! But spare me from your slaves and, what's more, abstain from provocations yourself. It's big money and serious business, why take an unnecessary risk?"

"All right," Grisard agreed. "A thousand in advance."

"I don't have a thousand, I'll give you two hundred." Lukin pulled two green bills from his pocket. "You should know I wouldn't carry big sums on me."

He got up and took the bag from the floor. Grisard stood up too; he picked up the money with two fingers and casually stuck it in the pocket with his glasses.

"We'll meet the day after tomorrow at noon in the little park by the Bolshoi Theater. You'll hand me the goods in a storage tube and you'll get an envelope with the money. No tricks, please. Accompany me to the gate and moderate your gang's ardor. If I find out I'm being shadowed, consider the deal off." He went to the door but stopped suddenly. "Since I've taken an interest in your safety for a certain period of time, I want to offer you some advice. The easiest border to cross is near Nikolsk-Ussuriisky, about fifty miles from Vladivostok. A bit far, of course, but safe. You can easily find Chinese guides and they don't cost much . . ."

"Right, thanks for the advice." Grisard smiled. "I'll pay you back in kind. For some reason I like you. I even think that had the cards fallen a different way we could have been in each other's place and I'd have been requesting your services."

"Let's put it this way. I didn't ask you for anything—we made a deal!" Lukin cut him off. "As for your conjectures, no matter how the cards might have fallen, I would never have been in your place."

"As you please." Grisard curled his lips into a bitter grin. "But I'll offer you some advice anyway. For the same reason of mutual safety." He came closer and stopped right in front of Lukin. "Change your clothes the first chance you get for something more Soviet. Maybe no one would pay attention to you in Paris, but in this blasted Land of Soviets you should be more plain. In general, the rule here is: the grayer, the safer."

Grisard skirted Lukin and went into the courtyard. Slant-eye was hanging around not far from the door, Sailor and the bearded bruiser were resting on the log. When he saw Lukin, Sailor got up on shaky legs and reeled in his direction, but Grisard stopped him with a nod of his head. The boss took his guest through the courtyard and silently opened the door and let Lukin out the gate. At this pre-dusk hour the narrow lane was quiet and empty and tufts of gray clouds drifted across the sky heading somewhere to the south.

12

Lukin returned home around six. Remembering Grisard's words, in the Krasnaya Presnya district he dropped in at a department store and bought a heavy dark blue worker's overshirt and a cap with a stiff lacquered peak. As far as he knew, such caps were worn by law-abiding shock-brigade workers and railroad engineers, who have always been attracted to uniforms. After hanging around the counters for a while, Lukin slipped into the shaft of a freight elevator on the landing and quickly changed into his new clothes. He rolled his hat and coat neatly into a large sheet of wrapping paper that a salesclerk had thrown away, tied up the bundle with string, and strapped it to the handle of his bag. This simple operation done, Lukin walked down the stairs into the store's courtyard, which was full of boxes and garbage, and in order to escape a potential tail went through a gap in the gate to a side street. He stopped a passing taxi and asked the driver to go to the Belorussian train station as fast as possible, but halfway there he changed his mind and called out the address of the Government House. When they reached the gray bulk, he paid his fare, bought a pack of

Kazbeks at a kiosk, as well as several papers and the latest *Krokodil* magazine, then headed for the apartment on foot.

A fine lazy rain began drizzling from the gray sky; near the river a cold wind was gusting. Lukin stopped in the middle of the arch on Bolshoi Kamennyi Bridge and looked at the ruins of the Cathedral of Christ the Savior. A few walls were still standing and some people were puttering about in the piles of debris. The sight created a feeling of unsheltered loneliness that grieved his heart. Someone touched his sleeve. Lukin turned quickly. An old woman beggar stood rooted there with her arm held out. Her face was as wrinkled as a baked apple, her eyes full of sorrow.

"Give a penny to the poor, dear! I used to stand on the church porch, but now there's no place for me, I'll go begging." She clenched a coin in her withered palm and gave a toothless smile. "The first time the devils smashed it right before New Year's . . . It was bitter cold. I thought it's the end, I won't last the winter. In the morning I go out to look and my precious is standing, it didn't give way to the devil's might! Thanks be to God, I think, He protected it. But no, likely we wronged Him, we don't have His blessing! They say the great prince Konstantin Pavlovich bestowed twenty-seven pounds of silver on the cathedral and Demidov sent two hundred gold coins for the altar cross . . . No good will come, no good . . ."

Still muttering, the old woman turned around and shuffled away in her tattered shoes, dragging herself down to the embankment. Lukin followed her with his eyes. There was something frightening and awful in the sight of this solitary figure on the bridge in a flurry of wind. Whom had he met—was it Russia? Lukin sheltered the flame of his lighter with his hands and lit a cigarette, then walked to the opposite side, trying not to look at what was left of the great monument to the war of 1812 . . .

In the Telyatins' apartment it was dark and quiet. The light from the small window, reduced by the dusty air in the kitchen, barely reached the hall. From the opposite wooden wall the portrait of the leader of the people, hard to discern in the semi-dark, watched Lukin.

"Lenin's best disciple," Lukin recalled the title the ruler had assumed in accordance with the table of ranks. If someone wrote "Ilich's renowned companion-in-arms" it was understood he meant Vyacheslav Mikhailovich Molotov, while the epithet "steadfast Bolshevik-Leninist" signified Voroshilov. Lukin smiled; lifting his arm, he aimed his finger at the place where the eyebrows met above the crooked Caucasian nose.

Back in his room Lukin unpacked the bundle, hung his jacket and macintosh on wire hangers, and turned in front of the mirror in his new overshirt. Now, at least as he saw it, he looked more like a skilled worker. The clothes looked too new, of course, but if he crumpled and roughened them a bit, they'd do fine. He pulled the revolver from his jacket pocket and stuck it behind his belt, barely managing to cover it with the hem of the shirt before the door opened without warning and Anna appeared in the doorway. Her fashionable pleated skirt of soft satin and expensive, delicate shoes gave her a sporty look.

"Well, finally! Where were you? I was waiting for you." The young woman walked into the room and only later examined Lukin with surprise. "Are you going to a masquerade? What did you put that on for?"

"I . . . it seemed . . ." Lukin was taken aback by her force. "I didn't want to stand out, you see. I'm a modest person on the whole, not used to . . ."

"All right, all right. Take off that ugly thing!"

"To be honest, I wanted to think that I'd look like a cultural worker in a printing shop in this shirt. It has its charm, you know."

"Perhaps," Anna agreed. "Couldn't you move a little faster, we'll be late to the theater. You found my note, didn't you? We need to talk without making Uncle suspicious."

"Are we going to see Shakespeare, I hope?" Lukin stepped behind the open door of the chiffonier, quickly changed the shirt for a jacket, and put the gun in its pocket.

"I'm afraid not. Tonight it's Pogodin's *Tempo*. I took two complimentary tickets. Not long ago we staged *Hamlet*, but the theater was attacked for political vagueness and aesthetic formalism."

"Of course." Lukin shut the door of the chiffonier and took his hat from the hook. "In this country princes and their fathers' ghosts are not held in high esteem."

They decided to go to the theater on foot. The streetcars were overcrowded—at the end of the working day people hung from the steps. Lukin took Anna's arm and opened his umbrella. Anna was silent.

"You know"—she finally spoke—"yesterday you went to sleep, but we still talked for quite a while. Uncle trusts you. Help him . . . I don't know how, but help him. He's perishing . . ."

She grew silent again. The rain ended. Lukin closed the umbrella, but didn't let go of the young woman's arm.

"Sometimes I wake up at night and hear him walking around the room, then he stops by the window and stands still, as if he's trying to hear whether a car is coming. He doesn't have any friends. There was one, a professor and chemist, but he hanged himself. Before he died he caught Uncle in our entrance and told him he'd been called in to the secret police and that he'd signed everything. About himself, about Sergei Sergeyevich, and others. He confessed that they had distributed a letter written by eighteen Bolsheviks accusing Stalin of establishing a regime of personal rule, and something else, but he no longer remembered what it was. The professor was a Party member, but Uncle's afraid just because he knows that such a letter exists."

Anna took a deep breath. She was breathing hard from the fast pace and her hurried words.

"He has troubles at the institute too . . . A team of inspectors is there—they're reviewing all the textbooks. One swine, Uncle's best student, reported that his instructor, Telyatin, was not trustworthy, because in his work on methodology he didn't cite a quotation of Stalin's in full and thus distorted the leader's thought. They called Uncle up before the authorities—we didn't sleep all night. We kept searching for that unfortunate quotation and couldn't find it. Apparently he copied it from some place, but doesn't remember where . . ."

"Life is amazing," Lukin thought while listening to Anna. "It's like a jug into which you can pour the nectar of sublime thoughts and love or the slop of vile acts and denunciations. That same word can describe a bestial hatred toward creatures like yourself or a sublime flight of feelings." He smiled to himself. "When you depart life, you really must wipe your feet."

"Are you laughing? Did I say something funny?" Anna gave Lukin a puzzled look. "You probably don't care about any of this."

"No, Anechka, no! It just hurts me to see what life has done to Sergei Sergeyevich. He was smart, a man of talent, an officer . . ."

"Why do you say *was*? Do you think they'll arrest him? Are you burying him? Though I've thought many times that Uncle and I are outcasts."

"No, no, I didn't mean that at all! I simply remembered how he was fifteen years ago. You're asking me to help him." Lukin stopped and looked into Anna's eyes. "How? I don't know. Wait a little while. I hope that everything will change soon. Sometimes if you just touch a stone it's enough to start an avalanche. I also want to tell you"—he smiled—"I can't help but tell you that I like you very much. Please don't ever tell anyone what you told me today. It's our lot to live in a terrible age, but unfortunately you can't choose the time you live in." He took her hand in his and pressed it to his lips. "I've lost a lot in this life, I wouldn't want to lose you!"

"I believe you."

They took a narrow street to the Arbat. In the distance, on the opposite side of the street, the gray theater came into sight.

"I need time to look around," Lukin said, adjusting his hat as he walked. "I have some money saved up so I don't need to hurry to find work. I can finally allow myself to live like a free artist." He looked at Anna's face. She was smiling. A small shiny Ford, black as a beetle, with the steering wheel on the right side, was driving toward them. People were flowing to the theater from all directions and crowding in front of the entrance. Several government Mercedeses drove up, and a group of foreigners got out accompanied by some citizens who looked like bosses and their fussing aides. Lukin recognized Yenukidze. Making a path for Anna, Lukin pushed his way closer. There were no guards, if you didn't count the clod in the cap who kept some distance from his charge. As he stood in the crush, Lukin saw the group with the foreigners enter through the theater doors. The cars drove off. The crowd droned as it moved into the theater.

The old woman who took the tickets smiled at Anna cordially and looked at Lukin with interest. After standing in line to check their coats, they went to the second floor. A group of men wearing somber business suits and fixed official expressions stood by themselves near the center arch leading into the auditorium. Lukin's eye was caught by a man of average size with a large forehead and straight combed-back hair. His face, with its high cheekbones and tightly closed lips, had a determined look. He was standing somewhat to the side and didn't take part in conversation. His gaze slid indifferently over the faces of people who entered his field of vision.

"Ah, Anna Alexandrovna." He smiled with reserve when he saw Anna and Lukin coming toward him. He stepped toward them and spoke as if he were continuing a conversation begun long ago. "I'm sick to death of all this heated and empty babble about the theater!"

"Hello, Boris Yevgenievich." Anna was happy to see him. "Meet a friend of our family." Lukin stepped forward and shook the strong hand extended toward him.

"All around there's just chatter—I'm tired of pointless talk." Boris Yevgenievich continued to complain about fate. "We need to have rehearsals, but here comes a whole delegation."

"Comrade Lukin came from Samara to visit us. He wants to find some suitable work." Anna switched the conversation to a more general topic. "I brought him to see our theater."

"Do you also indulge in acting? I've been in your theater, though long ago," Boris Yevgenievich said, and studying Lukin, added, "I can see you as a character actor, or maybe you work with production? Come visit, you can look at our stage sets. The premiere's soon, and we've hardly begun! All in all"—Boris Yevgenievich got worked up again—"I have the impression that the entire company spends half a day looking to see where on earth Dmitriev has gone. Like it or not, we have to assemble a staircase for the first and third acts . . ."

"Dmitriev's our set designer," Anna explained. "Boris Yevgenievich," she began, but a glowing young man had just come up to them in order to take Boris Yevgenievich away. Boris Yevgenievich spread his arms in a gesture of helplessness.

"Well, see there, I already have my first job offer." Lukin smiled. He led Anna off to one side and asked who the man was.

"Boris Yevgenievich Zakhava, our director. He and Vakhtangov, who created this theater together. Now he's staging *Yegor Bulychov* for Gorky's anniversary—that's probably why he's nervous. The production's been put under the control of the Central Committee, and they've had a hell of a job getting the play through. First they had to convince Gorky to redo everything and now they're running out of time. There's the socialist competition to deal with, the daily control over rehearsals, notes in reports—in short, there's plenty to despair about. Rumor has it that Gorky will come to the opening on the twenty-fifth, and with him . . ." Anna stood on tiptoe and whispered in Lukin's ear, "Stalin." She gave Lukin a meaningful and slightly frightened look. "Gorky has already been coming to rehearsals, but he doesn't interfere with the production—he just sits and watches. The whole burden falls on Boris Yevgenievich and the actor Shchukin—he plays the title role."

While listening to Anna, Lukin carefully examined the men exchanging greetings with the foreigners. The Germans, he understood from certain shouts that carried over to him, were members of an official trade delegation.

"The other man, the one who led Zakhava away," Anna continued, "is Kirshon, a big name in the literary world. His plays are artless and dull, but in real life he's capable of doing anything. One of the playwrights said that last year Stalin himself ordered Kirshon to stop persecuting writers who aren't Party members—Stalin himself, imagine that!"

The third ring sounded, later than usual, because of the guests, Lukin realized. Everyone moved into the auditorium all at once. Lukin and Anna had just taken their seats in the orchestra when the lights slowly faded and the heavy curtains parted. The audience applauded. The first act of the play began. Lukin didn't follow the story. While looking at the stage he was thinking about his own matters, though he didn't forget to clap with the others. During intermission Lukin led Anna to the edge of the stage and turned to examine the auditorium carefully, especially the side opposite him where the director's box was located. After the show was over, they lingered in the aisle, letting the people in a hurry go ahead of them.

"Is it really Indian summer?" When they were outside Lukin threw back his head and looked at the clear sky. It had indeed become warmer by night, the north wind had quieted down, giving way to the gentle breezes of the distant southern steppes. "I love this time of year. It has a pure sadness, and something else"—he snapped his fingers—"that goes straight to the heart. Probably some vague fear before the long autumn and imminent cold. Man has the nature of a wild animal, he doesn't like bleak winter."

They walked slowly to the side of the boulevard and turned off onto a narrow street. In the light of scattered streetlamps the trees seemed hushed, couples were kissing on the benches.

"Have you seen Gorky?" asked Lukin. "From close up?"

"I have. Nothing special—an old man like the others. Tall and round-shouldered; for the most part he's quiet. Once at a rehearsal he burst out in tears—they say he's very sentimental. His eyes? I don't like them, they're sort of colorless and worn out."

"Does he come often?" Lukin stopped under a lamp and lit up. The cone of light filled with puffs of white smoke.

"Yes, perhaps . . . You know that the premiere of *Bulychov* is coming soon and it's being given special importance—like a crown topping his work of forty years. Alexei Mikhailovich is in great favor now. Many people think that it's because of him that Joseph Vissarionovich is favorably disposed to the theater. It's true, he often goes to the Bolshoi and to the Moscow Art Theater, but he was at our theater once too."

"Long ago?"

"Long ago. Long before I joined the company—in 1925, I think. Lower-ranking officials from the Central Committee come here more often. You know"—Anna became animated—"I heard one of them say that Nizhny Novgorod will be renamed Gorky and the anniversary will be celebrated throughout the country."

"That was to be expected." Lukin smiled. "One has to pay generously for loyalty and support of the regime."

"You don't like him?"

"No! He let the authorities turn him into a living icon, he has found himself among those who serve the politics of the moment. 'What can I do for you?' People who are attracted to power can always be bought, the only question is the price. Don't think that I'm condemning him—who am I to condemn? In such matters everyone must decide for himself. Our time divides everyone into lackeys and those who close their eyes to what is going on. There are saints, of course, but few of them . . ."

"Why are you talking this way? You must be angry about something." Anna stopped and looked up at Lukin. "The Russian intelligentsia have never been lackeys!"

"Oh, the Russian intelligentsia!" Lukin mimicked her. "By and large the Russian intelligentsia has always been infantile and cowardly and has never gone beyond dreaming of a good Tsar. They're good at being completely immersed in themselves and poisoning themselves with self-pity and pity for people of their kind! But when it's a matter of defending human worth, of truly living according to their convictions, or simply of defending their own property—then they take an ostrich's stand. Read our great literature and you'll see that I'm right! In our decline we all come out of Gogol's story 'The Overcoat.' The 1917 Revolution comes from there too. Everything that happened and is happening to us proceeds logically from the past. From the inability and lack of desire to defend your own worth it's only one step to becoming a slave and parasite, and our creative intelligentsia has taken this step. That's why it's not clear where our messianic literature ends and the secret police begins. It explains the competition among our writers as to who will first and most faithfully reflect the Party's latest decision in his works. For the one who succeeds the fun begins—a fast life with vodka, restaurants, and women. Forgive me, Anya, I shouldn't be telling you this . . ."

"I don't want to believe everything you say is true! A person needs hope in order to live, and this . . . How can one live?" Anna walked with her head down, looking at her feet. "Is it really the same everywhere?"

They walked down a flight of steps and up a narrow street.

Lukin was silent. Anna didn't know if he was listening or thinking about his own matters. She felt safe beside him—there was a pleasant sense of peace that she hadn't felt since childhood. "What will happen tomorrow," she thought, "will happen tomorrow, but today, right at this moment, I feel well." She stopped in the entranceway. Lukin turned her to face him and he looked into her eyes thoughtfully and sternly, she thought.

"Today was a long day and you're tired," he said, "but I still must tell you something. Let's start with Sergei Sergeyevich. No matter what, he must be put in the hospital. Heart, lungs, liver—any reason you like, but he must be taken out of the institute at once. That will be your job! If you need money tell me. Second," he turned and glanced around the empty street. "Don't discuss anything we've talked about with anyone. Think about when, with whom, and about what you're speaking. It's much more serious than you might imagine. Somewhere someone spilled a pitcher of evil and it has flowed into people's hearts. Or perhaps it's like in Hans Christian Andersen—you remember, the slivers from the mirror that fell as it flew around the world."

Anna smiled. "It would be wonderful if a magician would turn up and change everything at once and restore a humanity to people."

"Unfortunately it doesn't happen that way. There is one road—whoever has let himself be pulled off it must climb back on his own. That is the immutable law of life. No one, no single magician, can change it. And there's something else . . ." Lukin unexpectedly gave her a big smile. "I'm probably going to take up your director's offer and go to work in your theater. If you don't object, of course."

Anna thought he wanted to say something more, but Lukin was silent.

It smelled of cats on the stairs. The apartment building was asleep, dreaming empty dreams about Soviet life. A light was on in the kitchen, filling the dirty rose space with a dim haze. Anna tiptoed through the hall. She opened the door to her room, stopped for a moment, and looked at Lukin. He was standing in the front entrance looking at her. The door closed. Still smiling, Lukin undressed in his room and, instead of pajamas, put on the shirt. In the neighboring apartment a clock struck twelve. Lukin warmed up some tea on an electric hot plate, then sat down with glass in hand in an old worn armchair. He moved over the pile of newspapers he'd bought during the day. He began his survey of the press with the issue of *Krokodil*, which he found boring and not at all funny. Of everything he read, the two best "jokes" put you on guard and made you think. "If a fellow plays the violin well," Lukin read, his forehead furrowing with displeasure, "this still doesn't prove that he's politically correct." The second one had to do with foreign policy; it claimed that when the League of Nations was closed for a lunch break, Japan would dine on China. There was also such a bad joke about Communist bragging that you had to feel sorry about the impoverishment of humorists. The monotony of the news in the press exhausted Lukin—it even seemed that the same person had written everything from the first to the last page. Nothing important had taken place in the world that day. The German Parliament was expected to be dissolved again, Hitler was still thirsting for power, and at the same time the Land of Soviets was fighting to create cadres of its own cultural intelligentsia. Lukin liked the expression "cultural intelligentsia"—he was sorry it wasn't from *Krokodil*.

In the newspaper *Pravda*, which he'd left to read for last, the headlines were clearer. They sounded warnings: "We shall intensify our struggle with the right-wing lack of discipline in grain procurement!" "Relentlessly unmask the plunderers of socialist property!" All the newspapers mentioned the new attack on Mukden by Chinese volunteers and they all published materials relating to Gorky's anniversary. Lukin finished his reading and unceremoniously threw the papers on the floor. He lit a cigarette and thoughtfully began to examine the bookshelf hanging next to him on the wall. The proletarian's library didn't seem to be of much quality. It consisted of half a dozen crumpled paperbacks, all looking the same, from an adventure series, and the first trial edition of the short biography of Stalin, the leader of the people. Lukin reached out and took the hardcover book from the shelf and opened it. There was a glossy picture of a man with a bushy mustache drooping over a heavy chin. The man was squinting as if he wanted to examine Lukin better and remember him; his narrow forehead was furrowed beneath his thick combed-back hair. What was there in this face? An unbending will? Cruelty? The cunning of a wild beast?

The door squeaked and Lukin looked up. Lucy stood there, wearing a full skirt and gaudy short jacket. Her straight hair was held back with a comb, revealing a painfully beautiful face, pale to the point of blueness. It was as if someone had intentionally wiped all the color from it, likening it to a white canvas on which a portrait of a woman was still to be painted. But some of the portrait's features already showed through—the large feverishly glowing eyes.

"Am I disturbing you?" Lucy closed the door behind her, walked into the room, and sat down on the mattress, which had been put on a block of wood and covered with a blanket. "You know what? I haven't had a drink today!" She crossed her legs, showing her pretty round knee, and continued in a deep, enticing voice. "I didn't go to work . . . Because of you. I woke up in the afternoon, as if from a jolt, with just one thought—it's him! Please don't laugh, don't hurt me. Yes, I know that it's funny and sad, but I've fallen in love with you. You're my salvation, my only chance in this life. Really, I'm not lying." Her eyes bore into him and she pleaded with a smile, "Lukin, take me away from this pigsty! Take me away, you won't be sorry. I'll be everything for you—lover, cook, dog, just take me away. I have some foreign money—I'm not foolish enough to give them every cent."

"Did Telyatin tell you about me?"

"Did he tell? Yes, a little . . . For instance, that everyone always calls you Lukin. Take me away from here—really! All day I've been imagining you and me strolling around Paris. If you like, we'll go to the country, but far, far away. You'll plow the earth, and I'll sit at the window and wait for your return . . ."

"Cocaine? Morphine?" Lukin looked into her eyes.

"Yes, to make me feel better, so that I don't hang myself. I don't know how you feel but I don't like the idea that I'll be found cold and stiff in a noose, and they'll take me out and just let me fall down . . . It's all stupid and disgusting—like life itself!" She broke down and started to cry; tears poured from her open eyes and she didn't wipe them. "I have no strength left," Lucy whispered. "There's dirt and brutishness everywhere. They force me to sleep with foreigners and write down what they talked about. I know French and German, I studied at an institute for girls from the nobility . . ." She sniffed and blew her nose into a kerchief. "They take the money from me and tell me that prison is crying out for me, while they just keep trying to crawl into bed with me. Beasts, dirty swine . . ." Lucy dropped her hands on her knees and, staring into the space before her, in a weak voice said, "I'm tired."

Lukin picked up a pack of cigarettes from the mattress and offered it to her. For some reason she smelled the cigarette before she lit it. "French." She sank back and blew a thin stream of smoke toward the ceiling. "Look there in the proletarian's stuff," she requested, pointing a long finger with a blood-red nail at the chiffonier. "He always has something to drink. If they're not drunks, then every last one of them's a greedy boor."

Lukin bent down, fumbled in a corner of a sliding drawer, and pulled out a bottle of vodka sealed with wax. Lucy handed him a cup with a broken handle that was standing nearby.

"Pour me some! A full cup! Keep on pouring and pouring. Petka and I have our own worker-peasant accounts!" She laughed and raised the vodka to her lips. She drank in small sips, tossing her head back slowly. "Now your turn! Don't you want any? Are you disgusted?"

Lukin saw that she was getting drunk fast—a smooth and half-contemptuous smile appeared on her beautiful lips.

"Did you know a countess is sitting before you? And all things considered, I'm leaving for Paris tomorrow and you'll be rotting here until your nose collapses because in this country everyone has the same proletarian syphilis. So, what are you waiting for? Throw yourself at me, tear off my clothes and take me. You're the leader—you can do anything." The expression on her face changed, becoming haughty and scornful. Lukin thought that she was probably telling the truth about her background.

"You don't want to? Then we'll make a report!" Lucy began shaking, she jabbed her cigarette stub forcefully into a saucer that served as an ashtray. "You're just an impotent dud like the rest of them! And you look like a typical secret service man, the same scum. I see now, I understand everything . . . They sent you especially to check on my loyalty to the regime." She became silent; her face, distorted by a grimace, reflected the titanic effort of thinking. "What was it I said? That they're impotents and scum, but I said that about bed and not about the Soviet regime. You can't . . . can't put anything over on me! And tell your Sergei Sergeyevich that I'm not going to sleep with him anymore. For political reasons . . ."

Stepping uncertainly along the creaking boards of the parquet floor, she went toward the door, turned, and looked at Lukin with vacant unseeing eyes. "I treated you like a human, like a man! But you . . ." She waved her hand in despair. "You ass! I see, yes, I see, I'm not blind—you're running after Anka. The theater . . . holding her by the arm . . . You think she's different? We're all the same, all! But she doesn't know anything about life yet! They'll beckon with a finger, call out, and she'll come like a sweet young thing! If I put in a word for her, that'll be good, then she won't be shot right away." Lucy smiled crookedly. "She had an admirer here, she considered him a suitor. They went to concerts too, and he conversed on lofty themes, gave her flowers . . . Then suddenly he disappeared! He had asked about her in the theater and found out what kind of standing her uncle had at the institute—that was the end!" She almost burst into laughter, but instead simply said, as if she were establishing a fact, "It's a terrible time. These aren't people, just ghosts. There's no life and they're not alive."

Lucy pushed the door and went out into the hall, but came back right away.

"I'll probably die soon. Today I had a beautiful dream. An enormous empty cathedral, and I'm like a little girl, and there's a patch of mosaics on the stone floor. The organ is playing and my soul feels peaceful and well, and there's nothing I need . . ." Lucy became silent and he suddenly thought that she wasn't drunk at all. She raised her big *rusalka* eyes at him. "Don't push me away, Lukin, I do love you. You don't believe me? Do you want me to get down on my knees? No . . . It's a shame that everything turns out so stupidly."

Lucy made a painful, crooked smile. Slowly she raised an arm and aimed at Lukin with her finger. "Bang!"

13

If someone with free time on his hands had decided to watch how Lukin spent the next day, he surely would have concluded that this tall middle-aged man had come to Moscow to flit about. Clearly drawn to the capital's historical sites, Lukin spent hours on end examining Red Square in full, then with the same meticulousness he got acquainted with the small public garden in front of the Bolshoi Theater and the buildings and streets adjoining it. He sat on a bench for a while, smoking and admiring the facade of the world-renowned citadel of opera and ballet, and with the air of a man who enjoys his own idleness, he aimlessly roamed around the center of town, peering at one thing after another. He ended the day at the theater, but didn't stay there long. After making a note to himself that the main guest box was located at a level much higher than the stage, Lukin left the box and once on the street again headed toward the Moscow Art Theater. He waited for the intermission, then took his seat in the orchestra, and after looking around to see the layout of the hall, he settled down and watched the rest of the play. Kirshon's piece *The Trial* was playing and Lukin was curious to see what the polished young man he'd seen at the Vakhtangov had written. He hadn't liked the man's sleek good looks, and Lukin was listening to the words carefully, trying to overcome his prejudice. He thought the dialogue was boring, the obvious political message of the play was offensive, and the whole thing was limited and contrived. "Well, at least, I've made my acquaintance with a piece of socialist realism," Lukin thought while returning to the Telyatins' apartment. That evening, after refusing tea and making a date with Anna for later, he went to bed early but couldn't fall asleep and listened for a long time to the internal sounds of the apartment house.

The next day, an hour before noon, he was at the theater square again, walking around and observing what was taking place in this tiny piece of Moscow. Life flowed with its usual rhythm: people ran to and fro doing their business, street vendors in white aprons poured out glasses of carbonated water, young mothers slowly pushed unwieldy baby carriages, which somehow resembled cars. The streetcar that pulled up to the stop sounded its warning ring and Lukin looked at the round city clock on the post. The hands showed two minutes to twelve. At the same time out of the corner of his eye he saw Grisard entering the public garden. He was carrying a black tube and a shabby briefcase, and in both his bearing and his dress he looked like an engineer who had been forced to do his work at home. Without any fuss Grisard sat down on a bench, settling himself in a solid and respectable way, and from the briefcase took a sandwich wrapped in brown paper and a bottle of milk and began eating his lunch. "Well done," Lukin thought, "he's sticking to the image—everything is psychologically right. What an actor is being wasted—he's as good as Ktorov!"

Lukin walked around the public garden at a leisurely pace. Everything seemed normal. In the meantime Grisard had finished munching his sandwich; he leaned back against the park bench with satisfaction and started to smoke. The city clock showed ten minutes to one. Lukin loosened his shirt, touched the handle of the revolver, and with a vacant look headed toward the center of the garden. He took a cigarette from his pocket and glanced around from side to side looking for a light; when he found himself a few feet away from Grisard his face lit up and he headed straight for him.

"Mind giving me a light?"

Grisard held out a box of matches, seeming displeased. Lukin lit up and sank down beside him on the bench.

"Great weather!" Nodding his thanks, he returned the matchbox and brought the tube closer to himself. Putting it between his knees, Lukin opened the top and looked into the black interior. What he saw satisfied him completely. From his pocket, in just as measured and relaxed a way Lukin pulled out a small parcel wrapped in newspaper and placed it on the bench between himself and Grisard. The edge of the sun came out from behind a cloud and gently warmed the little garden. Two young mothers holding their children's hands walked by on the side of the theater with the mighty columns. Grisard bent his arm and looked at his watch; nervously throwing down the cigarette stub, he got ready to leave. He neatly folded up the greasy sandwich paper and stuck it in his briefcase along with the parcel and the empty bottle, and then, as if he had lost something, he began to dig around inside it, checking the money. Their glances met for an instant, reflecting nothing but caution and attentiveness. A traffic controller in a white soldier's shirt walked past, waving a striped stick. Grisard snapped his briefcase shut, got up, and straightened his stumpy engineer's jacket. As Lukin watched him leave, he saw how Grisard changed his gait, assuming the active purposeful air of an important official carrying a briefcase.

Lukin got up from the bench, casually grabbed the handle of the tube, and lazily went off in the direction of Tverskaya Street. After traveling all around the city for about an hour and changing streetcars several times, Lukin took a taxi and returned to the Telyatins' apartment. He'd picked a good time—it was empty at this time in the middle of the afternoon. He shut himself in his room, pulled the rifle out of the tube, and painstakingly examined it. It wasn't new, but it was in good condition, cleaned and oiled, and on the whole it looked like something that had been treated well. Lukin opened a case that was inside and from it took a thick rod with a support on one end, which he screwed onto the breech of the gun; then he screwed the round silencer onto the muzzle and fastened the optical sight with a screw. All the parts fit perfectly, and when the assembly was done the sight of the finished construction gave him great pleasure. All the same there is something unnatural in the beauty of a murder weapon, Lukin thought, putting the rifle to his shoulder and taking aim. He was ready to swear that he wouldn't miss a five-cent coin at two hundred meters. The only problem was how to get within two hundred meters of his target. Lukin smiled; he checked the cartridges lying in the little box—there were ten. After he'd dismantled the rifle and carefully wiped off his fingerprints, picking up each part with a rag, he packed them into the case and shoved them back in the tube together with the barrel. Then he climbed up the back stairs to the attic and hid the tube behind a thick beam, piling some trash that was lying around there against the beam as a precaution. When this operation was over, Lukin washed his hands carefully, changed his shirt, and combed his hair before the mirror on the chiffonier. He set out for the Vakhtangov Theater, where he'd arranged to meet Anna.

As soon as he got to the lobby he realized that he'd come at a bad time: something was going on. The administrator who met him at the door was extremely agitated and for some reason demanded to see Lukin's ID and admission permit. Lukin explained that he had arranged to meet Zakhava, but the administrator nervously waved his hand and said, "It's not the time, not now!" He lowered his voice to a confiding whisper. "Comrades from the Central Committee. They're holding a meeting in the auditorium with the theater company. I saw you a few days ago with Boris Yevgenievich, but believe me, my good fellow, he's in no mood to see you right now! Find a seat somewhere and wait!"

The administrator quickly forgot about Lukin's existence and ran up the stairs. Lukin took advantage of the freedom and slowly climbed to the third floor. As he walked down the hall he slipped behind the heavy curtain covering one of the entrances to the balcony. From the height of the circle he could only see the stage, which was lit up and on which a table, covered with something velvet and red, had been placed for the committee. Several men with concentrated expressions sat in a row at the table. Lukin recognized only Zakhava. A fat man, in a tight-fitting semi-military uniform, stood at the podium and, constantly stroking his shaven head, addressed the audience, which Lukin could not see. In the large empty hall his words sounded hollow. Lukin pressed against the wall and listened attentively.

"Thus," the fat man was saying, "the first performance of *Yegor Bulychov* must become the central event of the nationwide celebration honoring the anniversary of Alexei Maximovich, whom all of us so ardently love. The Party has entrusted us, one might say, with the high honor and responsibility to fight at the front lines of the ideological struggle for a new proletarian art!"

Lukin looked up over the podium. Hanging over the entire width of the stage was a banner with the slogan: "For militant tempos! For works of high intensity!"

"In conclusion, comrades," the speaker went on, "once again I want to summon you to vigilance! Comrades, the enemy does not sleep. We live during a time when opportunists of all kinds, who are angry at our successes and achievements, have stuck their beastly mugs into the light of day. In this connection I want to warn you that we in the Central Committee have put everything concerning your theater production under the strictest supervision. I do not exclude the possibility that Party and government leaders will attend the premiere, thereby placing a special responsibility on your collective. I wish you clarity in your work, comrades, and great creative successes."

The fat man in the semi-military uniform rolled out from behind the podium and took his seat at the table with the presidium members. His place was taken by a nervous middle-aged man who wore a black business suit and necktie. He spoke in abrupt, though smooth, phrases, for the most part addressing the people sitting at the long table.

"Under the leadership of the Party and the Frunze District Committee of the Communist Party our young theater has become one of the most prominent cultural units in the capital. We are patrons of the Kauchuk factory, two military units, Moscow School No. 27, and our country's Minusinsk District, from which three of our brigades have just recently returned. All of us in our young theater highly value the trust the Party has shown us and we are fully aware that the obligation we have taken upon ourselves has great political importance. The anniversary of the great proletarian writer Alexei Maximovich Gorky, whom all of us fervently love, is an event of world significance, and the collective of the theater will hold the banner of socialist art high. We have placed the production of the play under closest supervision, and are publishing a special newsletter about our work on this performance; we've entered a socialist competition with that part of the company that is busy staging Comrade Slavin's play *Committee for Foreign Affairs* for the anniversary of the Revolution; and in the lobby of the theater we're organizing an exhibit entitled 'Forty Years of Gorky's Work.' "

Lukin slipped out into the hall, walked one floor down, and sat on a plush-covered bench. The voices from the hall didn't carry this far and he could wait quietly for the political presentation to end. The center doors of the auditorium opened rather soon, however, and the important guests left the theater in the company of the local leaders. After waiting another five or so minutes to be sure, Lukin walked down a side stairway and sat in the last row of seats in the orchestra. The meeting had ended, only those who were taking part in the production remained in the hall. No one sat at the committee's table, and Zakhava was pacing up and down the aisle near the stage by himself. He was talking in that even style which was characteristically his, as if reasoning with himself and sharing his thoughts with his colleagues.

"No one is free in this life, and the plot, by virtue of its static character, imposes restrictions on us. There's no action, no development of events, and the play can only be helped by the psychological depth of its imagery. It is up to each of us to provide that depth. I realize I'm uttering commonplaces, but I'd like us all to understand the problem we face in an identical way. As the committee has correctly suggested to us, the strength of the play lies in the revelation of the political conditions of the age in which the Bulychov family was reared. Consider these words of mine as an overture to the rehearsal and let's still begin with the first act and try to get through it and the second act as well!"

There was movement in the hall, several people came onstage as Zakhava went to the orchestra and sat down on one of the end seats. Taking advantage of the pause, Lukin came to greet him.

"Oh, it's you! Anya talked to me and, I must admit, I'll be grateful for your help. Just imagine, we don't have enough menial workers! We're shamelessly behind on the scenery, and I'm too tired physically to be chasing after either the head of supplies or Dmitriev, who's always disappearing. He's our set designer," Zakhava explained automatically, obviously concentrating his thoughts on the stage. It seemed he had forgotten about Lukin, when he suddenly turned to him and added, "Go and meet the man in charge of the workshops. Akimych is a real grouch, but he knows his business and has never let us down. And tomorrow—go to the personnel department with an application . . ."

Boris Yevgenievich got up from his chair and began waving his arm. "No, no, do the opening arrangement like yesterday, and please let's not waste time . . ."

Taking these words to mean the end of his audience, Lukin left the director and set out in search of Akimych. He found him in a room next to the shops, which was completely crammed with all sorts of frames covered with canvas and wooden screens daubed with paint. Akimych was a stocky and elderly gray-haired man.

"You say Boris Yevgenievich sent you?" He raised his bushy gray eyebrows slightly. "Your name's Lukin, you say? Fine, then—Lukin it is. We know what we're doing and we were at the meeting too. You don't look much like a laborer, but that's none of my business—the bosses know better! Sit over there on the side and watch."

Lukin just smiled and didn't say anything at first. Then, after asking to see sketches of the scenery, he became absorbed in studying the drawings. After a while he set them aside, took a pack of Kazbeks out of his shirt pocket, and offered Akimych a cigarette.

"You live in style!" Akimych narrowed his eyes. "We'll use our own, thanks, more true to life."

He took out a pack of cheap tobacco and put it on the table. The label pictured a man sitting on a sack. Under the picture Lukin read the inscription: "Smoke a Makhorka from KTK. Your gloom will quickly go away!"

Akimych handled the cigarette paper skillfully and rolled a smooth thick cigarette, which he stuck into a long ivory mouthpiece.

"So, are you hurrying with the scenery?" Lukin started to smoke. Leaning back against the chair, he observed the master's well-built, solid figure. "You don't have enough working hands?"

"Enough—not enough." Akimych shook his head enigmatically. "What's the hurry?"

"But supposedly the premiere is near at hand!"

"That depends on whose hand," Akimych noted philosophically. "Our creative workers keep changing their minds. Do this today, tomorrow it's that, but when the time is pressing they'll agree about everything. Let them run crazy—it'll be clear later that I still know better than they do what should go where on the stage!"

He hadn't yet managed to elaborate on his approach to working with the artistic elite when a woman's tousled head showed up in the doorway and she commanded in a military tone, "Akimych, get to Zakhava! He and the designer are at each other's throats!"

"There, you see," Akimych commented, "they're getting into shape."

He gathered the pile of sketches from the table, put them neatly into a folder, tied it up with laces, and with a slight waddle set off for the auditorium. Lukin hurried after him in pleasant anticipation of the spectacle of a bullfight.

"I'm exhausted from explaining it to everyone," said a man wearing an artistic shirt and pacing back and forth in front of the stage, his arm beating out the tempo of his speech. "The tree has to be moved! It shouldn't poke into the window. So, my friend, so, old man"—he rushed down the aisle when he saw Akimych—"so do *quelque chose* with Bulychov's study—one can't turn around in it!"

"Listen, Akimych," Zakhava interrupted the artist, "I still think that the staircase to the second floor must be located onstage! The actor can't go off to somewhere in the wings and appear upstairs only later. This very 'later' interrupts the action—it contradicts the psychology of the performance's inner development."

"Because of your stairs it's impossible to enlarge Bulychov's study," the artist disagreed. "It's yet to be seen if this interrupts the action or not, but if there's no room for the actor to stand erect, excuse the expression, then it's no longer a matter of psychological exploration. Besides there's no time for your staircase, and no one to build it. Akimych, do you have enough time to make a staircase? There isn't time!" The artist kept on talking, not giving Akimych a chance to open his mouth. "And the premiere's just around the corner!"

Akimych sensibly kept silent and watched the battle. Lukin drew closer and said behind his back, "The staircase is essential even from the point of view of balancing the scenery. Everything arranges itself around it, as around a central element. I was comparing two of your sketches—it's much better with the staircase!"

"There, you see what a new person has to say," Zakhava crowed.

The artist stared at Lukin, but then just shrugged. "Oh, do what you like!" He turned and faced the stage, where part of the scenery had been mounted, and with a final outburst said, "But do me the favor of taking the tree out of the window. I won't let you win that one!"

"Well"—Akimych grinned slyly into his whiskers—"you proposed a staircase, so go ahead and make one!"

"I'll need boards and material. It doesn't take great skill."

"There are boards piled up in the storehouse. Go over there tomorrow. As for skill, that remains to be seen."

They returned to the workshop in silence. Lukin sat down at the table and sketched out an outline, estimating the measurements on the sketch. Akimych was walking around in circles; he was breathing hard, but his pride didn't allow him to go and see what was taking shape. After suffering this way for about an hour, he changed his clothes and, standing before the door, growled, "Turn off the light and lock up everything, the tools could get stolen. People are thieves and thieves they shall remain."

Lukin sat and worked on the sketches until about nine o'clock. He measured the scenery that was made, marked down the dimensions, and estimated the new arrangement. He inserted the staircase so that it looked as if it had been planned from the very start. The entire section of the two-story house immediately acquired a look of authenticity and a fundamental persuasiveness. Satisfied with the result, Lukin locked the room and set out for the auditorium in order to see for himself how everything would look in full scale. But the stage was still being used. The rehearsal of *Yegor Bulychov* had ended and they were running through separate scenes from other plays by Gorky, which they were planning to show on the small stage and in the lobby. Anna was busy with one of these; she was sitting in the middle of the hall supervising the progress of the rehearsal. Noticing her from the door, Lukin went over and sat down beside her.

"It looks like you took to work right away." She smiled, seeing the sketch of scenery in his hands. "How was your talk with Zakhava?"

"Fine! Tomorrow I go to the personnel department," Lukin responded. "I've received an assignment of state importance: building a staircase."

"Today I placed Uncle in Botkin Hospital. I have a friend who's a doctor there; she says he really does have something wrong with his heart."

The director who was working with the actors turned around and looked tiredly in their direction. They stopped talking and sat quietly until the rehearsal ended. They went home on the streetcar, standing on the rear platform. An enormous white moon flooded the world with its silver radiance, a light warm breeze stirred the leaves of the trees, and black lacelike shadows quivered on the ground. The bitter smell of withering nature crept into the soul and made it weary; one wanted to stop decaying summer, one wanted love. Somewhere a gramophone was playing and, as if on waves, the words of a romance floated by, imbued with a southern languor: "The weary sun bid tender farewell to the sea . . ."

"What a marvelous night!" Anna said. "I feel its tenderness and the sorrow of dying. Look, the roofs of the buildings are so white, as if they were covered with snow. On such nights for some reason I feel sorry for myself and I'm on edge—my heart longs for those cold boundless heights. Tell me, do you know any terrifying stories?"

"One. About my own failed life . . ."

"Are you sad? Don't tell sad stories. Tell me something interesting."

"I don't know if this will interest you." Lukin smiled. They were standing very close. The streetcar turned around and pushed Anna against him. He embraced her and didn't let go. "I love you! I probably shouldn't tell you this. My life is absurd, it's not settled . . ."

"Don't say anything else." Anna pressed against him, barely holding back tears. "I was waiting for you, I waited for you so!"

Lukin bent down and kissed her on the lips. Then he moved back and looked into her eyes.

"I have no right to expose you to danger! Promise me one thing: the time might come, and very soon, when we will have to escape. Without any discussion, leaving everything behind. Promise that you'll do as I say, otherwise I must disappear from your life right now."

Lukin looked her straight in the eye. Alone on the back platform of the streetcar they rushed through space and time, through a range of rising worlds.

"I always believed you would come," Anna said simply. "I prayed and you came. Lord, thank you for the happiness you've given."

In the morning Lukin ran off to his own room to shave and change his shirt. On the way he met Lucy, who darted into the kitchen like a ghost. Lukin greeted her but she didn't answer; she didn't even look up at him. When he came back to have breakfast he put down a wad of money in front of Anna and said, "You'll need it. Memorize the address." Lukin wrote something on a piece of paper and handed it to Anna. "Memorize it well, then write it on the back!"

Anna silently memorized what he'd written, turned the paper over, and picked up a pencil. Lukin crept to the door and threw it open with a jerk. No one was in the hall, but he sensed a quick movement behind the slightly opened door to Lucy's room. He waited a while, then returned to the table, took the paper from Anna, read it, and tore it into small pieces. As neatly as possible he heaped them into a tin ashtray and put a match to the pile.

"Also . . ." He mixed up the ashes with the end of a knife and whispered into Anna's ear, "Go there only when I tell you. Immediately, leaving everything behind, and without any discussion. You'll wait for me to come for a day and night; if I don't, then make your way to Nikolsk-Ussuriisky. It's on the Chinese border, not far from Vladivostok. There you'll find an old man named Chen. Everyone knows him. Show him this." Lukin took a small cross from his neck and placed it in Anna's hand. "He'll understand everything, supply you with money, and see that you get to Europe . . . I suppose that's all."

"Have you planned something dangerous?"

"Not at all." Lukin smiled. "I just have to finish something that Sergei Sergeyevich and I didn't manage to do in 1918."

"What about Uncle?"

Lukin looked her in the eye. Anna saw alarm in his look.

"You'll tell him at the last moment. If he doesn't want to leave, that's his decision. Oh yes, I almost forgot—you must always have the cross with you, and carry the money in a special belt . . . Oh, Anna, why are you looking at me like that? Say something to cheer me! What's going on at the theater?"

He sat down across from Anna, spread some butter on his bread, and put a piece of sausage on it. She watched how he ate, energetically working his jaws, and tears were in her eyes.

"Yesterday," she began, "yesterday men from the Central Committee came, they had a meeting with the company . . ." Anna took out a handkerchief and daubed her eyes. "They said how important and crucial the matter was and for some reason they accused us of being ideologically lax. I don't understand it very well, but afterward Boris Vasilievich said that it's serious."

"Boris Yevgenievich," Lukin corrected her instinctively.

"No, Boris Yevgenievich is Zakhava, but Shchukin said it. Don't you know Shchukin?" Anna was surprised. "He and Zakhava are staging the play together, and Boris Vasilievich is playing the role of Bulychov. They also said that Alexei Maximovich promised to bring Stalin himself to the theater!"

"Oh really, why would he go to some theater?" Lukin questioned, and sliced off another piece of sausage.

"Not to 'some' theater, but to the Vakhtangov," Anna said, about to take offense on behalf of her theater. "Everyone knows Gorky is very close to Stalin and he allegedly serves as Stalin's link to the creative intelligentsia. Thanks to Gorky, Joseph Vissarionovich has become an inveterate theatergoer and his wife even organized some sort of salon for people in the arts. She serves them tea and . . ."

"No, I didn't know that," Lukin answered absentmindedly and got up from the table. "Let's go or else you'll be late for your rehearsal! Today I must get a truck from the supply manager and go to the storehouse to pick out boards for additional scenery . . ."

On the corner, while waiting for a streetcar, Lukin bought a newspaper from a young paperboy. On the first page, set in large type, the headline "Fire in Marina Roshcha" caught his eyes. He quickly skimmed through the story. It reported that a fire had broken out the day before, late in the morning, and had continued for about five hours. It had burned an entire block of old Moscow houses in which, according to the police, two thieves dens were located. This fact was supported by the discovery in one of the basements of burned corpses with characteristic bullet holes in their skulls. The criminal investigation suspected a settling of scores between gangs of burglars followed by arson in order to cover up the traces.

"Did something happen?" Anna looked over his shoulder. "Are you really interested in that?"

"Of course not, only out of curiosity." He folded up the paper and stuck it in his shirt pocket. And it was with curiosity that the people waiting at the stop observed a scene unusual for Moscow—a trim man with graying hair bent down and tenderly kissed a slight, pretty woman.

There was another witness of this scene, however. Standing with a cigarette at the kitchen window, a woman watched how carefully Lukin helped Anna onto the step of the streetcar, and how he climbed up himself and protected her from the crowd bearing in on all sides. A telephone call interrupted these observations. When she picked up the receiver of the phone hanging in the hall, Lucy heard a familiar man's voice. Within a minute, after hurriedly getting dressed, she was leaving the building. Lukin was just sitting down in the truck in order to get the boards from the storehouse when Lucy, having passed by the building on Lubyanka Square that everyone in the country knew about, walked into the entrance of an unremarkable neighboring residential building. She climbed to the fourth floor, rang a familiar door, and began waiting. It didn't open right away; someone fussed for a long time with the lock. When the door did open, a stranger stood in the doorway. He had a well-built body and a round face; his artistic-looking wavy hair was long, down to his shoulders. There was a vague, almost cordial smile on his full lips, and it would certainly have seemed cordial if his brown eyes had not betrayed a guardedness.

"Excuse me, apparently I've made a mistake," Lucy said, puzzled about how this could have happened, and she started to turn around and leave but the man stopped her.

"No, Lyudmila Nikolayevna, there hasn't been any mistake! I've been waiting for you. Please come in and take off your coat. As soon as the tea's ready, we'll have a cup and then a little talk. It's unusually warm outside," the man continued as he closed the door and led the woman into the room. "In a word, Indian summer!"

Continuing this light banter, he brought in a teapot from the kitchen and poured the tea into glasses that had been set out earlier. He placed a small bowl with ring-shaped biscuits and lumps of sugar on the table.

"Well, you're a bit surprised, I can see." The man sat down across from Lucy, put a lump of sugar in his glass, and mixing the tea with his spoon, went on talking very simply and in a relaxed manner. "I recognized you right away from the description. I would have recognized you on the street: you have a striking and memorable appearance. Like it or not, I have to envy our colleague who works with you—to meet such a beautiful woman is a pure pleasure." He sipped his hot tea, broke a biscuit in his hand, and stuck a piece in his mouth. "I asked him to call you so that you could elaborate on something in your last report. It has yesterday's date on it, and I looked at it as early as last night. Oh, excuse me, I haven't introduced myself yet! My last name's Serpin, I investigate especially important cases in the central political administration."

Serpin opened a folder that was lying in front of him and took out a paper covered with Lucy's small handwriting. "But go on and drink your tea, drink it or else it will get cold! Have a biscuit . . ." He began leisurely looking through what was written there. "Yes . . . here you describe your meeting with two Germans very, very vividly—you have real literary talent. Later you tell in passing about a rendezvous with a Frenchman." Serpin broke off his reading and looked at Lucy. "Tell me, are Frenchmen really such first-class lovers? All right, all right, I'm joking!" He became absorbed in reading again. "There! I found it! You write: 'In answer to the request to note anything unusual I am informing you that two days ago a Lukin arrived from Samara to visit my neighbors the Telyatins (I gave information about them earlier)—he came either to look for work in Moscow or simply on a visit.' "

Serpin put aside the paper and took a sip of tea from his glass.

"Well, explain to me, please, what is so unusual about this comrade's coming to see his friends in the capital? So he came—so what?—why did you consider it necessary to mention him in your report?"

Lyudmila Nikolayevna shrugged her shoulders and took out a pack of German cigarettes from her purse. Serpin leaned across the table and gallantly clicked his lighter.

"How can I put it . . ." Lucy began, letting a stream of smoke flow up toward the ceiling. "I just thought this man was a little unusual. There's nothing special about him, but still he's sort of . . . not like others. I haven't been in Samara, of course, but I don't think the people there are like him."

"In short," the investigator interrupted her argument, "did you begin to suspect that this Lukin is pretending to be someone else and has something to hide? Be more concrete! What was so striking? What caught your attention?"

"He dresses well"—Lyudmila Nikolayevna narrowed her eyes, as if observing Lukin's intelligent gaze before her—"and he behaves confidently . . ."

"You're speaking rather strangely." Serpin grinned crookedly. His eyes fastened on Lucy's face, searching for weaknesses. "The country is completing its Five-Year Plan, the well-being of the workers is improving, and it seems strange to you that our man acts confidently and is well dressed. If you rely on our newspapers, for example, the efforts of the Party and government are directed precisely toward this goal."

"Yes, yes, correct," Lyudmila Nikolayevna hurried to say. "I didn't want to say that at all! Understand, you notice him on the street—nice hat, foreign coat, very well-made suit. Yes, and he smokes French cigarettes—Gauloises. And, in my opinion, you know, he realized he was being extravagant and now he wears a simple worker's shirt . . ."

"Yes, and what else?" Serpin marked something in his notebook. "Tell me, Lyudmila Nikolayevna, tell me everything! As if you were confessing to a priest! You're one of us, there's no reason to be shy. Perhaps there are some intimate details we can use to entrap him? For example, something in a foreign language might have burst out in a moment of ecstasy. The time we're living in is such a cruel one, Lyudmila Nikolayevna, that we must know everything in order to protect the state from the enemy."

"I don't think there's anything else . . ." Lyudmila Nikolayevna wavered. "Otherwise he's an ordinary, though noticeable, man."

"Age? What does he look like? What does he talk about with those"—Serpin checked on the paper—"those Telyatins of yours?"

"A little over forty. Rather tall, dark hair with some gray, regular features, hooked nose. I heard them talking about the theater . . ."

"Is that all?" The investigator stared hard into Lucy's eyes and got up from the table. Going over to the window and looking somewhere out on the street, he continued in an angry and harsh voice, "You bitch, you blabbed too much, and now you're trying to change your story. 'I don't know anything, leave me in peace!' Certainly not! You'll crawl on your belly for hard drugs—coke and morphine. You're appropriating hard currency from the state. And do you know, you spy whore, what a file we have on you?! No, in your case you won't get off with the Northern Camps of Special Designation, this calls for the death sentence! So, did you two come to an understanding, did you sleep with him? Answer, when you're asked!"

Lyudmila Nikolayevna could not look away from Serpin's solid back, which was wrapped in a snug-fitting service jacket; she was in no condition to make any sound. Her lips were shaking; there were tears in her eyes. She tried to smoke but her fingers wouldn't obey. As if nothing had happened, Serpin returned to the table, sat down, and looked at Lyudmila Nikolayevna almost tenderly.

"So, what were we talking about just now?" He broke a biscuit into pieces in his hand and started to chew on them while loudly sipping his tea. He leaned across the table and patted the woman's hand reassuringly. "Oh, come, come, what is it? Get a grip on yourself! Things aren't as bad as you think . . . they're much worse. We value you, and as long as we're on friendly terms—you remember, like in childhood—nothing will happen to you! It's necessary, after all, to remember trivial things. What kind of things did he say and do? Well!"

Lyudmila Nikolayevna sobbed. She wiped her red nose with a handkerchief and took a swallow of tea, which had cooled a little.

"I . . . I went to his room at night. Somehow I couldn't sleep, you know . . ."

"Of course, of course," Serpin encouraged her, smiling, and skeptically raising his brows. "He turned you down, I see, thereby insulting the woman in you. That was a pretty good try, but it won't work. Moreover, he really insulted you by preferring that neighbor of yours. Women don't forgive such things, do they? For his part that's very inconsiderate."

"How do you know? Are you following him?"

"Yesterday you told our colleague over the phone that they were most likely at the theater together, and inasmuch as no one was in the apartment he could drop in for the report. Of course, he made you come to him, but he gave me the information along with your note. You see, it's very simple, one just has to know how to listen and draw conclusions."

Lyudmila Nikolayevna looked down at the floor and was silent.

"He wanted me to go to Paris with him," she continued after a pause.

"My dear Lyudmila Nikolayevna, that's just a fantasy! Here's what the matter's about, it seems." Serpin struck his forehead with his palm and snapped his fingers. "You fell for him. Oh, don't deny it, I can see that you fell in love and therefore you're shielding him. And in the meantime he's fooling around with the Telyatin woman. Isn't that right? As a fellow human, I understand you—hope is the last thing to die. Ah, Paris—the white acacia, the flowers of emigration! But all that's the past. Lukin won't be traveling anywhere anymore—but you can, if you're smart! You underestimate yourself, Lyudmila Nikolayevna, and, by the way, we need people like you not only here but also abroad. You have an excellent education, two languages, you're beautiful—such people are few . . . If you like, I can take care of your career. A place in the embassy or the wife of a successful diplomat . . ."

"He's living with Anka." Lyudmila Nikolayevna bit her lip. "I saw him leave her room this morning!"

Serpin thought it best to be quiet. Inhaling voraciously, Lyudmila Nikolayevna finished her cigarette, then crushed the butt into the ashtray with her long fingers, the nails of which were painted blood red. The sky over the roof of the nearest building was wonderfully blue. It suddenly seemed to her that she was standing on the steps of the Sacré-Coeur church, and Paris stretched beneath her: houses, a maze of streets, roofs, a sea of roofs beneath the blue fall sky.

"Somehow a few days ago . . ." Lyudmila Nikolayevna began in a hollow voice, and then she grew quiet. "In our apartment at the far end of the hall," she began again, "my neighbor hung a portrait of

Joseph Vissarionovich cut out from the magazine *Ogonyok*. The day Lukin came he stood near the front door and looked at the picture. Then he did this."

Lyudmila Nikolayevna stood up and extended an arm, pointing with her finger, as if from a gun, and aimed this imaginary pistol at Serpin: "Bang!"

"Well"—the Soviet secret police investigator smiled—"now we have something!"

14

On the way back from the lumber storehouse Lukin asked the driver to go past the Telyatins' building. He didn't go into the apartment but climbed up to the attic by the back stairs. He pushed aside the pile of rubbish and pulled out the black tube. After some consideration, Lukin opened it, took out the telegraphic sight, then put it back, and put the lid on the tube. He returned to the vehicle. The phlegmatic driver, who was waiting for him at the wheel of the truck, didn't pay the slightest attention to the tube. Within about twenty minutes, the small truck drove up to the theater, making a roaring noise because of its damaged suspension. Lukin carried the boards into the workshop and set them down on top of the tube in a stack next to the wall. Akimych found Lukin at work when he dropped in around lunchtime. Examining the boards, he blurted out, "They cheated you with those boards, fella. Those are just knots over there. You don't have a good eye!"

Lukin didn't bother explaining that it had cost him a lot of trouble to pick out several boards with knots. But the old master didn't show any more interest in what Lukin was doing: just as he'd promised, he didn't touch the staircase. Lukin worked hard the whole day—he finished all the preparations and got home around midnight. The next day he appeared in the theater at the crack of dawn and started to assemble the structure, fitting it to the scenery in the room. While covering the spaces between the steps, he nailed on a piece of wood with two knots at his own eye level. After dislodging the knots and then slightly evening out the holes, Lukin put the knots back in place. Now whenever he wanted he'd be able to take them out instantly and have an excellent view of the auditorium. These operations wouldn't be noticeable from the auditorium, since the openings were located under the step and far back in its shade. When he finished the flight of stairs, Lukin put together four hollow rectangular columns and connected them together, forming something like a frame to which the flight of stairs was attached. He nailed plywood onto the sides of the frame and added a platform made of planks at a level even with the floor of the second story of scenery. In this way, he came up with a cablike structure, with enough room, one side of which was the staircase. While admiring what he'd made, Lukin smoked a cigarette, then went out into the hall to see what was going on in the huge empty building.

It was close to eleven o'clock. The night watchman was peacefully dozing in the storeroom by the stairs; the theater company, tired out from the day, had gone home. Lukin returned to the shop, locked the door, and pulled out the tube from behind the boards. He took out the rifle parts. After he'd gathered them all, he screwed the round silencer case onto the muzzle and inserted three cartridges in the magazine. He picked up the screen he put together earlier and carried it out into the service hall that stretched along the entire theater. Lukin rested his target against the far brick wall. Somewhere a clock struck eleven. He stopped and listened. Stepping quietly, he walked around the neighboring rooms—they all were empty. After waiting a while, he went back to the shop for the gun. He stood about fifty yards from the target. In the turbid light of the night lamps Lukin pulled back the bolt, hoisted the rifle to his shoulder, took aim, and pulled the trigger three times. Three muffled shots rang out in the empty building. Without wasting time he ran into the shop, hid the rifle behind a cabinet, and went out into the hall again, waiting to hear voices or steps. But everything was quiet; the watchman was sleeping and dreaming. Lukin stood there for a minute, then returned to the spot where he'd fired the shots, picked up the empty cases, and only then walked over to the target. Grisard hadn't cheated him: the rifle was aligned perfectly. All three bullets sat in a small dark wooden knot, clearly visible against the background of the light boards. After returning the wooden screen to the workshop, Lukin pulled the knot out of the board and put it in his pocket along with the empty cartridge cases. Then he loaded the magazine with three new cartridges, wrapped the rifle in a piece of canvas, and hid it in a hollow recess in the frame's support, covering it with a piece of board that fit in well. He moved the whole construction a little to be sure that the rifle was fastened tightly and wouldn't make any extra noise. He only had to take away the tube, which he did, blocking it with pieces of old scenery in the storage room. Lukin carried the little box with the remaining four cartridges with him. That night he fell asleep immediately, forgoing his habit of smoking a cigarette and analyzing the day's events.

Late in the evening of that same day a light was burning in one of the windows of the building on Lubyanka Square. Two people were in the room. An elderly carefully dressed man, small in size, was pacing from corner to corner; the second man, an investigator for the Soviet secret police, stood and waited, leaning against the windowsill. The silence lasted several more minutes, but Serpin had no intention of interrupting it. The boss had to think through every decision and issue a concrete order. Serpin's job was to provide facts and suggest ideas, but the small gray man had to make the decisions—the price of a mistake was too great, its consequences too serious.

The old man, who looked like a bird of prey, stopped in the middle of the room and looked at Serpin intently, studying him carefully. He held his head proudly, eaglelike, whether because of his small stature or his high position in the Party hierarchy.

"So, you don't think it's Paris?"

"No, Comrade Ergal," the investigator replied respectfully. "I would like to formulate my thought in a different way. According to our agents' data, he doesn't belong to any of the émigré organizations founded in Paris. Besides, as far as we know not a single one of those organizations is engaged in acts of terrorism."

Ergal shrugged his shoulders almost imperceptibly and walked over to the table. He pulled some yellow sheets of paper out of a briefcase and handed them to the investigator.

"Read this!"

Serpin took the papers and carried them over to a round table lamp. It was an issue of the émigré paper *Struggle*, published in Paris and dated March 1932. On the first page a paragraph was marked off; it began: "Yan Rudzutak, the profligate who frequented all the bordellos in Paris using Party money, has been named by Stalin as Chairman of the Central Control Commission—the conscience of the Party, as it is usually called."

Further on there was an appeal issued by the "Struggle" group. Serpin read it.

"Workers, peasants, members of the Party! The Stalinist dictatorship has discarded its mask in the face of threatening events in the Far East; with a cynical lack of principle it is making a deal with the Japanese military clique that has already swallowed up Manchuria. In Germany a gang corrupted by the subsidies of Stalinist officials is coming out against the interests of the German proletariat and in support of Hitler's fascist dictatorship. Wherever the forces of reaction are struggling in open battle against democracy the Stalinist lackeys join the ranks of those who are destroying the unity of the workers and preparing a victory for the reaction. Look around you! You'll see a system of Asiatic despotism, the dictatorship of Stalin, the 'infallible teacher.' Arise! Demand the restoration of your rights!"

Serpin raised his eyes from the paper and looked at Ergal, who stood waiting with his arms crossed.

"This is one more proof of their weakness," he said firmly. "They're only capable of making appeals and not at all capable of terrorist acts. The White emigration in Paris isn't coordinated, it has fallen apart. The All-Russian Military Union, successor to the Volunteer Army, headed by General Miller, is simply in its death throes. They fantasize that the White struggle isn't over; they carry on conversations about patriotic duty, and in fact it's only snobbism strangely combined with poverty. We may not know other things, but we do have a thorough knowledge of the situation in Paris: hunger makes people compliant very quickly!"

"In that case"—Ergal put the papers back in the briefcase—"in that case, we're doing business with a loner. Did the surveillance give you anything?"

"Nothing, although they're sticking close. At the same time I warned them: it's better to let him lose you than notice you and get scared off ahead of time."

"Smart." Ergal nodded and was silent. Serpin deferentially examined his finely chiseled aquiline profile and the thin capricious lips above a protruding chin. "Perhaps"—Ergal groomed his wispy mustache with a fingernail while thinking—"perhaps this is good! If only we have an irrefutable fact, we can put together a group of accomplices to join him. You and I have some experience in this business, don't we?" He smiled and looked at Serpin. "Proceed according to plan, and as for Alexei Maximovich, it's not necessary to bother the old man—find a stand-in. It might lead to a leak of information and besides it's the man's anniversary!"

He molded his lips in the semblance of a smile and took the briefcase from the table. Serpin stood at attention. Ergal walked over to him and for a time they stood and observed each other in silence.

From his window the Soviet secret police investigator watched his guest settle into a large black car that had been waiting below; the car took off and headed in the direction of Old Square.

For Lukin the next two days were marked with increasing stress. The newspapers announced that on the day of *Yegor Bulychov*'s premiere there would be a special conference at the Bolshoi Theater honoring the glorious jubilee, which would be chaired by Kalinin. Naturally all the leaders of the country were expected to gather right in the theater to honor Gorky. This news distressed Lukin, but it had no effect on the people working on the performance. Only a few days remained till the premiere, and rehearsals went on almost uninterruptedly with the finished stage sets in place. True, it turned out that there weren't enough sources of light, rheostats hadn't been installed, and Lukin still had to busy himself with that work, spending days on end in the theater. When it looked like everything was finally done, Zakhava called him aside and said that it still wasn't right and he needed to get more props.

"You have to understand," Boris Yevgenievich said as he walked Lukin down the hall, "in essence you are just as much a creator of the performance as I or the actors. The objects that the audience sees onstage must convey an inner meaning. Take the Gospels, for instance, or a Mother Superior's staff or even a bunch of mushrooms—they're not just things in themselves, they provide the best characterization of their owners! So, my friend, make an effort so that it doesn't turn out to be a joke."

With that in mind, Lukin went to the secondhand market and bought the picturesque old objects that were lacking. A man strolling along not far from the traders' stalls seemed vaguely familiar to him; he'd seen his face somewhere before. This put him on guard and on the way back to the theater Lukin checked to see if he had a tail, but he didn't notice anything. A vague feeling of alarm stayed with him, however.

Because the stage was so busy Anna's rehearsals took place right in the lobby, and they saw each other several times a day. They ate together in a cafeteria close by. In these meetings, as they touched hands, both avoided talk about the future; there was some of the same sadness of the fading Indian summer. Anna didn't ask anything, but their reticence stood between them, lending to each meeting the poignancy of parting and the joy of seeing each other in the present moment. Lukin furtively kissed her temple and she shuddered and he knew he was happy. And they still had the nights.

On the morning of the third day Lukin was fiddling around on the stage, adjusting a panel of scenery that had come off its frame. The rehearsal had started; they were running through the play's first act and he was trying to work quietly, without distracting the actors. Akimych tiptoed over to him, bent directly over his ear, and whispered in a voice constrained by excitement, "The Master's come!"

"Who?" Lukin was at a loss.

"Who, who? Stalin—that's who!" Akimych mimicked. "Alexei Maximovich brought him in order to show off."

A moment later Lukin looked through a crack between panels of scenery and saw that in the box closest to the right of the stage a door had opened and against the background of the hall light, one after another, two very recognizable figures appeared. First came a short man with a large head and narrow erect shoulders; after him, stooping and as if embarrassed by his own height, a tall older man. Any schoolchild would have known them at first sight. Looking to the sides, Lukin noticed movement by both doors of the orchestra and on the balconies—the secret police guards. In the meantime the rehearsal was going on as usual. Zakhava, who was sitting in the first row of the orchestra, didn't even turn around.

Lukin got up from his kneeling position and out of habit brushed the dust off his trousers. He walked casually over to the stage exit. But just as he moved the curtain, a heavy hand settled on his shoulder. A man who looked Caucasian was standing there and staring questioningly at the man next to him—an administrator, who was practically shaking from fright.

"Who's that?"

"Our stagehand . . ." the administrator said, stammering.

Lukin let himself be searched and then went down the stairs to the lobby. Paying no attention to the rehearsal going on there, he bent down over Anna, who had been waiting for him.

"Leave! Immediately!"

Then he went back up to the shop just as casually and took a chisel from the tool bench. With the tool in his pocket he returned to the stage but the dark-haired Caucasian blocked his way.

"Scenery," Lukin said, speaking the way you speak to people who don't understand Russian well. "I must work."

The guard shook his head. He was standing half a yard away from Lukin, dangling his heavy arms; his square muscular shoulders blocked the passage.

"Look," Lukin said, taking the chisel from his pocket and holding it out for the man to see, "I went for a tool."

The guard shifted his weight to his right leg and moved as if to take the object being held out to him, but Lukin let go of the chisel and dealt a quick blow to his throat with the edge of his hand. The man began to wheeze, his eyes rolled back, his sunburned face turned a sickly blue. Lukin caught the lifeless body, dragged it to one side, and pushed it behind the curtain. He went back to the stage and looked around. No one was there. Crossing the stage floor quietly, he went to the recess under the staircase and stepped under the planks. There was a smell of warmed oil paint. The voices of the actors seemed to be very near to the plywood partition; he recognized Mansurova, who played the role of Shura. Working with the chisel, Lukin lifted off the board on the support of the frame and pulled out the rifle. The touch of the weapon calmed him. He unwrapped the canvas, gently seated a cartridge in the barrel without making a sound, and pulled the knot plug out of the board. A blinding bright light hit his eyes and he blinked. On Dmitriev's orders they had installed a lamp on the edge of the stage and its light aimed directly below the staircase. Lukin could hardly make out the dark pit of the orchestra behind this wall of light, not to mention the theater boxes behind it. He cursed. His heart was thumping in his chest like a bell, blood pounded in his temples. Right near him Shchukin was speaking Bulychov's words: "What do you think? Will I die?"

"That can't be," answered Glafira, whom Lukin couldn't see.

"Why not?" Bulychov asked. "No, brother, my affairs are bad. Very bad, I know!"

Trying to keep the sharpness of his sight, Lukin narrowed his eyes, so as not to look directly into the light from the lamp. In the wings where the immobile guard was resting, voices could be heard.

"I don't believe it!" Glafira said.

Lukin knew that after this came Bulychov's last lines in the first act and the curtain would fall. Placing the rim of the silencer on the edge of the opening, he directed the barrel toward the invisible target and pressed more tightly against the support.

"Stubborn woman," Shchukin began his last lines. "Come on, give me that kvas! And I'll have a drop of orange vodka too, it's healthy!"

The voices at the far end of the stage grew louder; Lukin knew they had found the guard's body. In the meantime Glafira, whom he couldn't see, drifted along the stage toward the footlights, her skirts shielding the light that had been in his eyes, and at the very same moment Lukin could clearly make out the two silhouettes in the box. He chose the left one, the one who was smaller, with the large head on narrow shoulders, and gently pulled the trigger. A dull shot rang out. The man in the box jerked and began to collapse to the side. As if respectfully accompanying him with the sight on his gun, Lukin moved very slightly and shot a second time. The next moment Shchukin, who was moving across the stage, covered up his target. He continued playing his part, not paying any attention to the unusual noise.

"The devils locked up the vodka! What swine! You'd think I was a convict, a prisoner!"

Something heavy fell onto Lukin's head from behind; his arms went limp on their own and let go of the rifle. A bright ray of light suddenly shot through the small hole, it curved and started to float the way everything around him was floating. Lukin took a step backward, trying to keep himself on his feet, but his legs no longer obeyed him and he fell onto the smooth, warm boards of the stage floor. That feeling of smoothness and warmth was the last thing—a moment later the world no longer existed for Lukin.

When he came to his senses he was in a cell. From the cot where he'd been thrown you could see an iron door with a peephole, a wall painted a dull gray, and a table attached to the wall. At the table, his hands properly crossed on top of his belly, sat a round-faced small bald man with thin whiskers and an equally sparse tufted beard. A bare electric bulb dangled from the ceiling on a braided cord. Lukin involuntarily moaned. He had a splitting headache, red circles sailed before his eyes, and snatches of words and incomprehensible phrases sounded in his brain independently of his will.

"Ah, you've come to," the little man rejoiced. Rising from the attached chair, he walked over and stood looking down at Lukin, who was lying on his back. "Here, drink a little water, sip it slowly! It's clear they gave you a healthy pounding, if the medical attendant was even sent for to feel your pulse. Oh well, it will all come out in the wash," he noted philosophically and settled down on the opposite cot. Lukin turned on his side and blocked the light from his eyes with his sleeve. His head had eased up a little, though it still rang like a copper bell.

"Have I been here long?"

"Long or short—no one can know. The only place on earth where time doesn't flow is in the Inner Prison at the Lubyanka. If you think about it, then it's probably day right now since there's light, but there's no guarantee—sometimes they burn the lights around the clock on purpose and throw you off balance."

Summoning his strength, Lukin sat up on the cot and took the aluminum mug held out to him. It was warm but he drank it greedily, taking a mouthful and spilling it on his rumpled shirt. Now he remembered everything, he remembered in detail—the figure that collapsed to one side and the calming sensation of the polished cock beneath his index finger.

"My name's Sheptukhin," the bald man said meanwhile, and the name seemed strangely familiar to Lukin. "My surname. Maybe you remember—if not, it's no great misfortune. I'm a secret informer. Well, something like a decoy duck. They jail me especially so that they can get confessions even faster—'break a man,' as we say. I use my own method in this work, a psychological one—I tell a person right away who I am. Of course, people can employ all their wits, tell tall tales, or play all kinds of dirty tricks, but that's not my way. I'm a humanist, my goal is to diminish the suffering of the prisoner under investigation. One way or another, sooner or later, he'll confess—man is a weak beast—so why be stubborn and take additional suffering upon yourself."

"Where's Anna now?" Lukin thought as he listened with half an ear to the informer's revelations. "It's certainly been more than twenty-four hours and she's probably already outside of Moscow. And ahead lies Vladivostok, Nikolsk-Ussuriisky, and the border . . ."

"I even became convinced of my higher destiny," Sheptukhin was saying in the meantime. "My place in life is here, in the prison, and in this respect Article 58 spells justice. I struggle against human suffering and this is precisely what a Christian should be doing on earth!"

"Listen"—Lukin looked into his cellmate's watery eyes—"have you been seeing a psychiatrist?"

"There, you see! I talk to you with an open heart, and you're rude to me! But I'm not touchy; what's more, your question is common, everyone asks it in one way or another. Let's forget it, let me rather tell you what awaits you. You've no doubt heard something about it already, but the work of this establishment today is not at all what it was in the twenties. New investigators have come—the most educated and cultured people, by the way. They're given lectures on psychoanalysis and introduced to the latest ideas in the world: no, these aren't your former sailors from the Cheka with mere revolvers. Each of the new ones has his own specialization—devilishly subtle and finely tuned. There are the psychological approaches, for instance; then there's one that works on sentimental people; and, of course, there are specialists in brutal interrogation—they would make the Brother Inquisitors look like beginning amateurs! And all of them know that if anything goes wrong they'll be treated just as mercilessly as those on the outside. If you refuse to talk, you'll get a chance to meet them all. The interrogation can work like a conveyor—the investigators change but the suspect stands for twenty-four hours a day. Listen to me, fella, listen—I wish you well!"

Sheptukhin stretched out and picked up a pack of cigarettes that had fallen from Lukin's pocket; he started to smoke, letting a thin stream float up to the ceiling and narrowing his eyes in pleasure.

"Good luck!" he stated. "And now I'll tell you how they shoot people here!" Sheptukhin inhaled deeply again, and an ecstatic smile appeared on his thick lips. "They strip you naked," he said with relish, "so that the clothes don't get damaged, then they put a thick felt mask over your head—you understand, the blood and brain can spurt out, and they shoot in the head . . ."

"Listen, Sheptukhin," Lukin interrupted him, "you've dispatched many to the other world, right? You argue with knowledge and desire and that repulsive mug of yours makes me sick! I think I just might do a deed that will please God—pick you up right here and now and strangle you!"

Fear flashed in the informer's eyes, but a moment later his blubbery lips were smiling.

"No, you won't—you don't have the guts! In my lifetime I've seen your sort—dandy little officers. You'll sooner lay hands on yourself! A few days ago I shared a cell with another one like you, called Yevseyev." Sheptukhin crossed himself. "He boasted too. He called me Mister, then threatened to strike me down, but when they brought him back from the interrogation he . . ." He took his hands off his round paunch and spread them sideways. "He groaned all night, ground his teeth, and regretted that he'd understood too late what to do . . . I tell him, 'So, what would have happened? Nothing at all! Our nation consists of little Yevseyevs—if something doesn't concern them, they won't lift a finger!' Oh yes, you all have an intelligentsia rottenness, you're weaklings! That's why you pissed away Mother Russia, but you didn't manage to crush the rabble!"

"Oh, Sheptukhin, you're being naughty." Lukin grinned. "And you said that you don't indulge in trivial provocations! Your little neck is so thin," he went on, thinking hard, as if weighing it over. "Who knows what will happen, whether I can control myself . . ."

The informer little by little began to sidle away from Lukin, but just then a key clanked in the keyhole and in the doorway stood a man in a leather jacket with a holster on his side. Lukin saw another escort behind him, a tall rural type of fellow with a round face and large cornflower-blue eyes that had a puzzled look in them. In his hands he clenched a rifle with an attached bayonet.

"Lukin, to interrogation!" The man in the leather jacket stepped aside.

Lukin got up and with a slight stagger went to the door. Sheptukhin looked at the convoy with a servile expression.

"Good luck," he wished to Lukin's back, "don't overwork yourself! If you don't come back, I'll smoke up your tobacco!"

They led him down long gray corridors, then up a flight of stairs. At one of the landings a ray of the low evening sun thrust itself through a barred window. After they passed a heavily guarded post the conditions changed sharply: a kilim runner appeared on the floor, the walls of the corridor were covered with wood paneling, and they saw men in military uniforms with similar expressions and tense eyes. The convoy stopped behind tall doors that reached to the ceiling; they placed Lukin face against the wall. The man in the leather jacket knocked and began to turn the round brass handle.

The escort behind Lukin shifted from foot to foot and breathed noisily into the back of his head. From so close up Lukin could see all the small cracks in the wood paneling. How many faces distorted by fear had faced this wall; how many people stood in this spot waiting for the interrogation to begin? The door opened, he felt a nudge in his back, and Lukin stepped into the office, which was lit by the setting sun. Directly in front of him was a barred window so well cleaned that it shone like a mirror; the massive leather furniture and the dimensions of the room showed that the office belonged to someone at a very high level. On the walls two portraits faced each other: Stalin and Dzerzhinsky.

"Take off the handcuffs and wait in the hall!"

A sturdy round-faced man with long wavy hair got up from his desk and straightened the semi-military jacket that squeezed in his full chest. Freed from the handcuffs, Lukin rubbed his hands with pleasure and stretched his shoulders a little.

"Come in, Lukin, have a seat." The man pointed to a chair that stood in the middle of the room. Blinking from the abundant light, Lukin went over and sat down on the hard seat. It was surprising that the chair wasn't screwed onto the floor. A strange feeling seized him suddenly: as if this had all happened before—this solid good-looking man, this conversation, and even the reflected red light of the sunset spread in the air . . . The hallucination disappeared as fast as it had sprung up; the man said, "My name's Serpin. I'm an investigator for Soviet state security for cases of special importance. And this"—he gestured with his hand—"is Comrade Ergal from the Party's Central Committee. Comrade Ergal came for the special purpose of attending your first interrogation."

Lukin turned around. In a corner of the room in a massive chair sat a short elderly man, who held his head in a birdlike way. The Central Committee man met Lukin's glance with his intent black eyes; he got up and moved to a chair by the window so that he could better see the prisoner's face.

"I'd rather not call this meeting an interrogation," he said in a deep voice at variance with his frail appearance, "let's consider it simply a conversation."

Serpin leaned over the desk and offered Lukin an open pack of Kazbeks. Lukin took one and lit it with the match Serpin held out. The investigator settled back into his chair and from there examined the prisoner sitting before him.

"Do you know"—he tapped the top of the box with the end of the cigarette—"I pictured you exactly as you are. Yes, you gave us a lot of trouble! I'd like to understand what incited you, what you were hoping to achieve by making an attempt on Comrade Stalin."

"I didn't miss, did I?" Lukin stared at Serpin.

"No, your shot was excellent! And it was creatively planned. But why did you take this step?"

"You won't understand." Lukin smiled wryly. "Let's say that for me he embodied absolute evil . . ."

"Well, that is an explanation, although the overwhelming majority of Soviet citizens wouldn't agree with you. People have only just begun to breathe freely; life has gotten better; and they connect this with the name of Stalin. Yes and the fact that we caught you so quickly is also not an argument in your favor. In our country you can't do anything secretly—the people are keeping vigil! The people may be uninterested and lazy, but if someone lives differently than others, they will notice! As for the attempt on Comrade Stalin—that will rally people even more, evoke a wave of protest and intolerance toward plots by enemies of the people!" Serpin looked at Ergal as if checking his own words with Ergal's opinion. The man from the Central Committee got up from his chair, and with his hands authoritatively clasped behind his back, he walked around the office, stopped in front of the leader's portrait, and looked at it attentively through narrowed eyes.

"I'd like to talk a bit more precisely about the consequences of your step." Ergal paused, grooming his wispy mustache with a fingernail. "In any case you didn't accomplish anything. What kind of man is he?" Ergal nodded his head toward the portrait. "He is a symbol, and it's impossible to kill a symbol. Imagine the Columned Hall, a body in a coffin, flags at half-staff. Everything covered with funereal drapery . . ." Ergal turned and looked at Lukin. "His comrades-in-arms make speeches and each one vows to take the place of the fallen warrior. And they will carry out this vow! The pantheon will be increased by one more deity and a new sovereign will be seated on the throne. In this country it's senseless to kill leaders because there's an incubator working at full capacity to produce them. It selects the cruelest and most ambitious young children and nourishes them with a poisonous elixir of power over beings like themselves. A Pioneer scout is always prepared! A Komsomol youth is the Party's trusty helper! If you kill one, ten will rise in his place; if you kill ten, crowds will form at the base of the pyramid, thousands will clamber over others' heads! Someone will rise to the top, the rest will be crushed—and it's no tragedy—in Russia a man's life has never been worth two cents. A linguistic construction like 'human dignity' sounds artificial and unconvincing in Russian. In general, the word 'dignity' is rarely used in our language, and for 'human' we're accustomed to use some term having to do with class: workers, peasants, in short something relating to the workingman and not to man in general. We're getting into the field of linguistics now, but I want to tell you that when a power structure has been created and the country has been entangled in a strong net, it's not important who's at the head—either Molotov or Voroshilov would do . . ."

"Don't be so sure." Lukin sat up in his chair and flicked off the ashes from his cigarette into the ashtray. "They're of low quality."

"High quality isn't necessary here," Ergal objected, simply and informally. "They might not be able to succeed the way Dzhugashvili did, but they won't be any worse than the boss at holding on to the power they get. Mediocrity always makes the best dictator, because it tries to lower everyone to its own level . . . By the way, I'm telling you this only so that you can better understand the situation in which you've put us all. The choice is very small, Lieutenant."

"Lieutenant?" Lukin raised his eyebrows in perplexity.

"You didn't serve after 1919, did you?" Serpin inquired as if collecting incidental information. "According to our facts your rank hasn't changed! And please be so good as to stop your show of surprise. If not everything, we know a lot about you. Sergei Sergeyevich warned you honestly that he was not a fighter. It's amazing that such a weakling had worked his way up to a captain. He's clever, of course, but has no character!" The investigator nodded sympathetically and lit the cigarette he'd been rolling in his fingers. "You didn't live in Samara; you likely came here from Paris. However, it suits us that you worked alone and aren't connected to any of the émigré organizations—this gives us room to maneuver. We'll think up a group of co-conspirators for you!"

"You have experience." Lukin smiled and put out his cigarette in the ashtray. "My case must seem ordinary in the production line of so many deviationists and counterrevolutionaries."

"I wouldn't say that!" Ergal interrupted him. "There's something theatrical about the political trials of the past, you can feel the artificiality. People seem to have accepted the rules of the genre and followed them. On the one hand, it seems to be reality, but in fact it's a play. By virtue of fate, the role of defending the purity of the doctrine fell to some; to others, the role of evil conspirators; and to the people, as always, the role of a herd being fed specially prepared ideological cud. Everything changed with your appearance on the scene. A tragedian among comedians disturbs the general harmony. Now it's necessary to try to attain the level of a full-scale tragedy or else remove the tragedian. I'm making myself clear, I hope? It's precisely because of this circumstance that our choice and yours is limited."

"I must say you are unusually candid." Lukin smiled.

"Why not?" The man from the Central Committee shrugged his shoulders. "You don't know about this, of course, but in the place where important policy is decided people are candid to the point of cynicism. Everyone knows what everyone else is worth. We might not love one another, we might even hate, but there's something greater uniting us—power! And there's nothing to fear: I won't take you into account, for obvious reasons, and as for Serpin . . ." He didn't finish, his lips formed what looked like a smile. "It's an astonishing thing, the personnel file of people who execute decisions, as a rule, is thicker than that of the people who make them. Whether we like it or not, we're taking part in a race with casualties. And we simply aren't left with enough time for diplomatic subtleties . . ."

"If I understand you correctly, you're proposing that I play the role of the goat who leads the herd to slaughter," Lukin said, looking straight at Ergal. "You'll take care of the composition of the herd yourself. Then there'll be a trial at which I, as the assassin in the plot, will implicate the others, and after that will follow an all-Union hunt for the enemies of the working people . . ."

"You grasped the idea correctly! This time there'll be no tricks—an attempt on the leader's life is serious . . ."

"And if the tragedian doesn't agree, you get rid of him? Well, I think that variant suits me better." Lukin smiled. "I accomplished everything I wanted, and what's left doesn't alarm me. The death of a tyrant will rouse the people, a sobering up will inevitably set in."

"You have an exceptionally high opinion of the people." Ergal laughed. "In the best case they're a crowd. I think of them as a herd. The human animal is capable of surviving under all sorts of conditions. As for the death of a tyrant, as you deigned to put it"—Ergal looked at Serpin—"show him the photographs!"

The investigator pulled a drawer of the desk toward himself and took out a packet of numbered photos, which he handed to the prisoner. Lukin looked at the top photo with interest. Taken from a distance of approximately one meter, it captured Stalin lying on the floor with a neat little hole in his forehead, exactly between the eyebrows. There was no doubt that he was dead, but something in the very disrespectful manner in which the leader's picture had been taken put Lukin on guard. He took the second photo. Everything looked the same, but the mustache familiar to all was missing from his face. A terrible thought jolted Lukin; he pulled the last photograph from the packet. The man there had features similar to Stalin's, but that was all. A long scar ran across his shaved head.

"In Kolyma, where he was jailed for gangsterism, his nickname was Joseph." Serpin took a second packet of photographs from the drawer. "Here, if you're interested in taking a look, is Gorky's double—an actor in the Leningrad regional theater, by the way. We could, of course, have asked Alexei Maximovich himself, but we decided not to risk it . . ."

Lukin looked at the investigator with a lost expression.

"A game's a game!" He shrugged his shoulders. "You were busy with the scenery and we took care of the actors. However, I must admit that until the last minute we didn't know how the attempt would be carried out or whether there'd be one at all."

"Now that you know everything"—Ergal entered the conversation— "you must make a decision quickly, practically on the spot. We can break you, of course, but we need you full of strength and the desire to collaborate—in that case we'll announce the attempt on Stalin's life to the whole nation and set things in motion. We won't guarantee you freedom, but we can promise a long and comfortable life. Otherwise, there never was an assassination attempt—and you never existed."

Serpin poked the end of his cigarette into the ashtray and said, "Decide, you're a strong man! Personally I even envy you: to be so much in love with a woman and not to ask about her fate, not say a word. But here you've also erred: a man of your profession has no right to a private life. And she loved you . . ." A note of dreaminess sounded in the investigator's voice, but he quickly stopped himself. "It's clear I'll never get accustomed to such sights, in matters of female beauty I'm weak! She truly didn't want to die . . ."

Lukin was on his feet right away. With one motion of his arm he overturned the desk on Serpin; a chair hurled with inhuman strength cast down Ergal. Lukin tore for the door. It flew open to meet him; the escort stood on the threshold with his rifle up. Lukin took one step. The astonished cornflower-blue eyes looked at him from above the sight on the gun. Lukin could clearly see the young man's lips shaking and trembling from fear.

"Don't shoot!" Serpin thrashed about, trying to get out from under the desk, but it was too late. The shot rang out. Lukin was thrown back, he caught his balance for a second, then took another step back and toppled onto the floor. A red shroud, like blood on water, spread past his eyes. Suddenly he saw the Red Army soldier in the train car, his bandaged head and the barrel of the gun pointed at his chest. That soldier had young cornflower-blue eyes too . . . Had the outcome only been postponed?

Warmth rose from the parquet floor; Lukin suddenly recognized the familiar smell of heated wax that carried many memories of childhood. In a white gazebo high on a steep riverbank a young woman turned her head to him and, biting her lips so as not to cry, said, "The shadow of a bird on the waves of time . . ."

"What?" Lukin tugged at the collar of the grammar-school uniform that was strangling him. A breeze from the river soothed his feverish forehead. "What did you say?"

"I said: This is your life," the young woman answered, and he saw that tears were slowly rolling down her cheeks.

"Anya!" Lukin shouted, but the cold of death stole up to his throat and locked his frozen lips. "Anya . . ."

15

In the warm and gentle Black Sea, at the foothills of the volcanic ridge Kara Dag, is an underwater cavern. In the most narrow part of this passage the walls are so close that they scrape a diver's body. Horror dwells in this cavern. You can find daredevils who go and dive through it, but in the evenings, sitting down with a glass of light Crimean wine, they confess: there had been a moment when a terrible animal fear had grabbed them by the throat, when their eyes had jumped from their sockets and their only thought was—go back! They were saved by the words of the old man: *just keep going ahead to where a faint light glimmers*. Sometimes the old man sits at the table, too, and silently sips wine, but then, unnoticed, he'll disappear, only to reappear the next morning in his place by the cavern's entrance. He is withered and black from the sun, and no one has ever asked him to save the lives of these young and healthy men—he does it on his own. Apparently that was the fate that fell to him.

Anna opened her eyes with a primordial horror which she'd had before that she wouldn't be able to see the sunlight. As then, her chest tightened in pain; patches of sunlight, as if through a deep wall of water, reflected on something white high above her head. Gradually a lusterless lighting fixture and the corner of a wall emerged from the iridescent haze; a curtain as white as everything around her stirred in the wind. Outside the open window it was spring. Anna knew this instinctively—there was no other way to have known. A ray of sun, refracted in the crystal of a vase, reflected multicolored spots on the spare setting of the hospital ward. Anna took a full breath and sat up in bed.

"Did you wake up, dear? Thank the Lord!" An old woman's kind, gentle face floated forth from the side somewhere. She had the clean smell of old age. "I'd had my doubts, I'm ashamed to say, for what kind of diagnosis was it they gave you—lethargic sleep!"

Slowly turning her head, Anna took in the ward with her eyes.

"Where am I? Was I wounded? Don't hide it from me, I know they shot at me!"

"Lie down, daughter, lie down." The nurse was worried. "You're just seeing things, you must not be fully awake yet. Don't think about anything, just rest. Everyone here loves you." The old woman helped her settle back on the pillow and put her light wrinkled hand on Anna's forehead. "See there, what beautiful flowers he brought you!"

Anna squinted at the bouquet.

"Lukin, my precious Lukin!"

"No, love, he had a different name . . ." The nurse fastened her glasses on her nose and read on a little piece of paper lying there on the bedside table: "Te-lyat-ni-kov . . . Sergei Sergeyevich. He left his phone number just in case . . ."

"Telyatnikov? . . ." Anna wondered. "Telyatin! That's my uncle. But for some reason Serpin said that they'd shot him."

"No," the obstinate old woman disagreed, "I wouldn't have let any uncle in to see you! He showed me the stamp in his passport, all done the proper way: he's your lawful spouse! You're just babbling, it seems, dear—and you don't remember your own husband! Look, don't say this to our professor, or he'll be angry at you! Remember, if you're asked—Telyatnikov's your lawful spouse!"

The old nurse stroked the sick woman's cheek, trying to soothe her. A painfully familiar smell drifted in from a small decayed garden. Anna closed her eyes. Something strange and unusual had happened to her, and an inkling of this gradually entered her consciousness. The world in which a falsely gentle Serpin had expressed his views, the world of people in black leather jackets and soldiers with rifles, where an enormous bureaucratic-gray city loomed over her, exuding fear from its dark alleys—this waning world started to lose its distinct outlines, it shifted somewhere to the side and anxiety took its place. Anna suddenly understood quite clearly that everything most dear, everything she lived for, was in terrible mortal danger. "I have to escape!" she decided. "I have to hurry and do it no matter the cost."

Anna quickly sat up in bed and lowered her legs over the side.

"Evgenia Ivanovna," she said, having not the slightest doubt that that was the nurse's name, "dear Evgenia Ivanovna, bring me my clothes. I have to go!"

"What are you thinking of?" the nurse said in amazement. "Tomorrow the doctors are doing rounds, they'll look you all over, examine you, after that you can be off. Besides, you're still weak, daughter, where do you want to go?"

"To church. I want to go to the Cathedral of Christ the Savior . . ."

"They blew that up sixty years ago! I was there when they demolished it. A piece of a marble slab flew into our window. It was good they made everyone leave or else it would have killed us for sure. When I came back toward morning the slab was lying on my bed, and there was a name on it in gold letters—the poor thing had perished in the war with the French . . ."

"Yes, I remember now." Anna frowned. "We were standing in an alley then—Uncle and Lukin and I . . . Where did I go then? Understand, Evgenia Ivanovna, a man vanishes from sight and he's my whole life. I don't want to live without him. I want to be in a place where it's light and holy. It's absolutely necessary for Him to hear me! He must hear me, it isn't possible that He won't, is it?"

"Somehow I've gotten all muddled along with you," Evgenia

Ivanovna honestly confessed. "My head is going in circles. First they were shooting at you, now you saw them destroy Christ the Savior . . ." She looked into Anna's eyes with her kind eyes. "I'm not blind, I can see that you need to go!"

Anna silently embraced the old woman.

"All right, I'll take the sin on my soul." Evgenia Ivanovna crossed herself quickly. "Take Maroseika Street to St. Nicholas in Kleniki. It's an old church, the place is clean and light. There to the left, in the heart of the side chapel, is the miracle-working icon of the Mother of God—pray to her. Ask our protectress for help. She'll help you herself, and she will intercede for you before her Son. A mother is always a mother, holiness dwells within her." Evgenia Ivanovna made the sign of the cross over Anna. She hurried, grumbling, "Impatient, you can't wait till tomorrow!"

Finding herself on the steps of the hospital, Anna stopped and looked around. Her head was spinning from the unfamiliar world of Moscow. From one end to the other the street was flooded with bright spring sun, and people and cars seemed to sail through its rays. The withered city nature gloried in the sun, elated sparrows were flying around the hospital garden. Anna's heart contracted in pain from a premonition that whatever she was about to do would change her life.

"Lord," Anna whispered, "have mercy upon me!"

A bell rang somewhere in the distance and its sound floated above the city. Fastening her raincoat as she walked, Anna went down the steps and hurried along the street. An uninterrupted stream of people was moving toward her on the sidewalk. There was something frighteningly inexorable in its flow—the compulsiveness of a mechanical machine, heartless and pitiless, destroying everything on its path. "Why are they all so sullen and anxious?" Anna thought as she shoved her way through and looked into their faces. "Are they all really suffering from misfortune? Such a bright cheerful day and they're so lifeless!" Suddenly she began to feel pity for all these people with their eternal problems, struggling in a closed circle of hopes and anxieties; she became afraid. If there was so much suffering and unhappiness around her, how would He hear her weak voice in the chorus of mass suffering? She raised her eyes in dismay and unexpectedly laughed. In the dark glass of a store window her own face was looking at her and the expression on it was exactly the same as the ones on the faces of people she'd passed on the street. Several pedestrians darted to the side but Anna didn't even notice. She rushed along the street and entered the gates of a small churchyard. "The Church of St. Nicholas in Kleniki . . . the Church of St. Nicholas in Kleniki"—repeating these words as if they were a mantra, she pulled the tall door toward herself and climbed a circular staircase. Somewhere from far inside a priest came out to meet her. A dark curly beard framed his young face; his eyes were light and clear.

"The church . . ." he began, but when his eyes met Anna's he stopped talking at once.

Taking a candle from a bench, the young man made a sign for her to follow with his hand. In a side chapel to the left beyond a heavy rectangular column, he placed Anna in front of an icon, then lit a candle, which he used to light the icon lamp.

"The miracle-working icon," the priest said quietly, and crossed himself. "Pray. No one will disturb you . . ."

Anna smiled gratefully, took the candle he handed her, and knelt before the icon. The face of the holy woman holding a child was dark, its features softly rounded; her enormous Eastern eyes looked sad, understanding everything and forgiving everything. The candle wax was dripping onto Anna's fingers; she didn't know the words of a prayer.

"Our Lady, most Holy Virgin Mary," she finally uttered, and the deep emotional intonation of these first words, gave her strength. "Help me! Forgive me for your Son's sake! In the crush of life I don't think about you often—because our existence intimidates us. And it's not a question of all the sorrow and suffering around us—although this occurs too—it's simply that out of thoughtlessness we accept the daily turmoil as our life and mistake the absence of misfortune for happiness. You see yourself—the soul hardens when it isn't given work. I'm that way: I wander around, always wanting something, always striving for something, but in fact all that I have in life is love! In this mournful chorus hear my voice, Mother of God, intercede for the one I love! There's no one I can count on anymore, only you! He's a sinner, of course, as we all are sinners, but he's not indifferent, he wants to help people. It's hard for him, he's alone, and his burden is beyond measure . . . You see, I don't even know what to ask for him. Pray to your Son that He show him mercy and justice! Forgive me, I am unworthy, I'm a sinner in all things, also in love, but you understand how this happens. It's for you to decide, Holy Virgin, but a man shouldn't be punished for his love!"

Anna prayed. The candle in her hand had completely melted. The smell of heated wax floated in the still air, the small icon lamp flickered. The holy woman on the icon looked at her with wise Eastern eyes . . .

The cold brought him to consciousness. There was no pain in his chest, but the memory of it endured in a strange way. The cold came from the stone slabs on the floor, the cold had dissolved in the air, like crystals of salt in water, cold was filling the whole world. Behind the narrow windows, which were set in deep recesses, stood majestic mountain peaks; the snow on their slopes was colored with the bloody glow of the sunset fading into night. Red patches of light crawled along the high ceiling as if alive; they sparkled on the oak beams that had blackened from soot. Somewhere at the other end of the large oblong hall a fire burned, but Lukary didn't feel its heat, only the rather sweet smell of birch logs reached his nostrils. Pressing down hard with his arms, Lukary pushed himself up into a sitting position and with difficulty turned his neck, which had become stiff from the uncomfortable pose. He looked around. The torches stuck into the walls dispelled the darkness in the hall, their light flickered on the polished plating of knights' armor. Looking up from below, from the slabs on the floor, he saw a long table built for banquets and two massive armchairs with high backs, where dark figures sat motionlessly. The red glow of the fire behind their backs made the picture more sinister.

"So you've returned?" Serpina got up from the chair and crossed the hall. He was still dressed in a short, semi-military khaki jacket, riding breeches, and boots. The senior privy councillor came to a stop over Lukary and studied him coldly. "I'll ask you please not to try any more foolishness. We've had it with your antics! He rubbed the edge of his hand across his heavy neck.

Having trouble controlling his numb body, Lukary got up on his feet and straightened his rumpled blue shirt. In the area around the left outside pocket the fabric had crinkled from the blood that had soaked through.

"James!" Serpina called out. "James, old man, be so kind as to look after our guest, because the last time he fell into the strange habit of throwing pieces of furniture."

The giant Moor who'd been standing in the background approached; he was smoothing out the white gloves on his enormous hands. With his escort Lukary crossed the knights' hall and stopped in front of the chair where the small elderly man who looked like a bird sat waiting for him.

"You know each other, I think." Without asking Lukary to sit, Serpina settled down in the other chair and crossed his legs. "Enough of this masquerade, however! Before you, Luka, sits the Black Cardinal, the head of Secret Operations in the Department of Dark Powers!"

Nergal bent his head very slightly and twisted his thin lips into a smirk.

"You almost killed me . . . With a chair! Not good, my friend, not good."

"Our mutual friend simply overestimated his ability, Monseigneur. I'd warned him about this, by the way. I pleaded with him to heed the voice of reason! And what does he do? He goes on the lam. Sustaining the illusion that he could save himself, he dives headlong into the lower world of people, thereby foisting new rules of battle upon us . . ."

Serpina paused and smiled sarcastically. "We accepted them and, as you see, acted toughly, according to the rules of the game. You have nothing to complain about and no one to appeal to, because even your death was in compliance with the law of those days. You lost, Lieutenant Lukin." Serpina began laughing shallowly, in such a way that the medals on his chest jingled a little. "See—I played the role so well that I was even recommended for an award. Kalinin himself gave it to me. And Cronus's machine works just as it did before. It was a complete fiasco, a defeat on all fronts!"

Lukary raised his head and looked at Nergal.

"Tell me, all of the horrible things that Russia has suffered—were they your doing?"

"Oh no! That was just one of those most rare cases when it's best not to disturb people," Serpina answered on Nergal's behalf. "If self-degradation reaches a critical level in the masses, then the dark powers no longer have any reason to intervene. Pride, thirst for power, a fanaticism insistent on demagogy are able to bring about the kinds of things we in our Department simply wouldn't have enough imagination to do. It's necessary to possess an especially refined depravity in order to put your whole nation under the knife in the name of an abstract idea. It's a cruelty you might compare with the deeds of the prophet Moses. No, Luka, in this case we played no part, the situation had been developing for a long time on its own. But I know why you're asking—you've had a love for that country since your childhood. Alas, my friend, alas!" The privy councillor threw up his hands. "It exists no more! With your stubbornness you mistake a mirage for reality and you can't resign yourself to that. Ah, the Russian people! Ah, Russia! All the smart people long ago joined the ones who won . . ."

"And who won?"

"Drabness and mediocrity—as always." Serpina shrugged his shoulders, exhibiting surprise at the naiveté of the question. "They destroyed the best people—those who still wanted something for the country; they exterminated them, like cockroaches . . . In short, genetically, a nation of conformists came into being, the descendants and spiritual heirs of prison guards and informers. The people will have to start everything anew, but Russia will be a completely different country then. The continuity with the old Russia has been broken; from the former nation only the name is left. Seventy-five years, three generations of a completely different life—that's enough to make an abyss. None of this has any relevance for you, though. I'm sorry, Luka, I'm very sorry! I'm going to miss you . . . An intelligent and energetic rival keeps one in good working form; moreover, it was great fun to watch your escapades." The privy councillor got up from his chair and looked at Nergal inquiringly. "Is it the time?"

"Before we go on our way"—the head of Secret Operations stopped him—"I'd like to clear up one small matter for myself. Tell me, Lukary, how do you explain such a bad choice of time and place for your activities in the human world? From the very first step it was clear to us that it was your intention to swing the pendulum of history from evil to good and, by so doing, try once again to attract His attention to yourself. The idea's not very original, but let that be . . . So," the Black Cardinal continued, "we were waiting for you at the beginning of the century in Zurich and Geneva; then we feared an attempt on Lenin's life later on—in 1917, when the fate of the revolution was hanging by a thread. But you go and turn up in 1932!" He threw up his hands again. "If only you knew, for example, what it cost us to secure the False Dmitri and Mazeppa, Ivan the Terrible and his men . . . All the forces who worked for us in all countries for as many as twenty centuries were mobilized. But 1932—that was absurd! I seem to remember that Ergal explained to Lukin how completely senseless it is to make an attempt on the lives of Russian leaders."

Nergal looked at Lukary expectantly, but Lukary remained silent. The sunset glow outside the window had faded; outer darkness had swallowed the mountaintops.

"If Your Excellence would allow me"—Serpina respectfully rejoined the conversation—"I think it's unlikely that our friend can give you any logical explanation. He's too proud to admit his own mistakes, and in essence there was only one mistake—he doesn't know how to handle women! Incidentally, that's a typical shortcoming in the entire Department of Light Powers, which endows these creatures with excessive energy. As for Lukary, he completely failed to understand how dangerous love can be. Two women . . ." Serpina paced the length of the table with the air of a professor giving a lecture. "Two women played a fatal role in his destiny. Not wanting to part with one of them, our friend, without reflection, threw himself into the maelstrom of the past, into a time where she had spent a previous life. That's why it was Moscow, that's why 1932! The rest of his behavior was all dictated by circumstance. The attempt on the leader was his only chance. By this time Stalin's power was absolute, but political killings on a mass scale hadn't begun yet, and theoretically an attempt on his life offered a chance to turn the course of history away from evil. Lukin sincerely believed that he could prevent a tragedy, but the human image he chose determined the precise form in which he had to act in order to achieve his plan. We don't know how everything would have turned out had he not permitted a second mistake to occur . . . He rejected a woman's love—many impudent men have paid with their life for such carelessness! This time the means of revenge corresponded to the time—a denunciation. It's conceivable that Lyudmila Nikolayevna acted on impulse, yielding to her offended feelings, but a denunciation, regardless of circumstances, remains a denunciation, and it was precisely that which gave us the thread we needed. So, we took our time, but we unraveled the whole thing!"

"Yes, the operation was carried out artistically in the literal sense of the word." Nergal smiled. "You deserve full credit, Serpina!"

The senior privy councillor bowed and modestly lowered his gaze. "It's an old rule, Monseigneur—search for the woman . . . All the same, it's a pity that we didn't manage to talk Lukin into appearing as a witness at the trial. In that event the years 1932–33—not 1937—would have been remembered in Russian history!"

Lukin raised his head. "All right, I understand everything. I lost, but I can't grumble over my fate. I was happy and did what I considered necessary, and there are not many who can boast of that. The only thing I don't understand is why I made the attempt on that beast by myself! His whole circle, all those who were close to him and were later liquidated, understood very well what awaited them, but no one raised a hand against him. Blyukher, Tukhachevsky, Ryutin—they knew the whole truth about the pockmarked Joseph, but they waited like sheep for him to kill them. If they didn't care about the fate of Russia, they might at least have thought about their own fate. Why didn't they?"

Nergal drummed his thin fingers on the arm of the chair. "It's a complicated question, but still a lot simpler than it seems . . . Blood explains everything. Blood was on the hands of everyone close to the dictator; blood was synonymous with power, it intoxicated them all. After they had organized a civil war, they couldn't help but know about the reality of the law: blood begets blood. They knew about it, but always thought of themselves as exceptions. For them Stalin was a phantom because the real Joseph Vissarionovich lived within them all. Believe me, Lukin, I know this breed of beasts thoroughly—it was I who bred them. There is nothing in this world more attractive than power over creatures like you. If you can't catch a man through love, if you can't buy him for money, then try power—that's the most reliable advice that I give to my subordinates. You also acted alone, Lukin, because Russia is a Christian country. The destruction of the masses has always been a policy in Russia, whereas the murder of a single person is a sin—it violates the Christian morality that has been beaten into people's heads. If Orthodox Christianity had understood the concept of karma as a burden not only of deeds and thoughts but also of what you should have done but didn't do, then Stalin would have been shot like a mad dog. But it's already been said—'a land of slaves, a land of lords'!" Nergal tapped his palm on the armrest, signaling that the conversation was over. "It's not a bad thing that people believe that history had to happen the way it did."

The head of Secret Operations stood up and adjusted the sword at his side, which embellished his snug-fitting Spanish nobleman's costume.

"It's time! Alastor is giving me the sign. The Prince of Darkness's court executioner shouldn't be kept waiting. He'll give your substance a working over and afterward you'll appear before the bar of the United Supreme Court on the charge of crimes against the system. You'll have to suffer, Lukary, and, in comparison with what you'll experience, physical suffering will seem like a birthday party. But I don't feel sorry for you! As a bright spirit, as a disciple in the hierarchy of the Light Powers, you knew what they were doing: you knew that the reverse side of supreme justice is supreme cruelty. It wasn't us—He made the world that way. We are but His servants and slaves!"

Nergal came to Lukary and stood by his side, and Lukary felt a powerful invisible net enmeshing his whole body and binding his breath. A moment later the slabs on the floor around them began breaking apart; the earth opened to reveal the abyss of the inferno. Nergal raised his arm and tongues of flames leapt from the depths of hell, showering them with the heat and stench of fire and brimstone. Lukary felt a terrible force penetrate him, like millions of thorns; it hurled him in the air and in the abyss below he saw a river of boiling lava . . . Then suddenly everything around them was illumined with a pure light blue glow and a mighty angel, spun from the radiance, materialized before them. His angel's face was majestic and beautiful, his high forehead slightly furrowed from weariness.

"Lukary," the mighty angel said in a tender, deep voice that resounded like a love-filled flute. "I've been sent for you."

"No! It's a mistake," Nergal shrieked, instantly losing his Spanish nobleman's tranquillity. "That can't be! Lukary's a criminal, he must appear before the Supreme Court! The highest punishment awaits him! He's not going with you!"

The angel lifted his huge, radiant, and, at the same time, sad eyes. A light veil of sorrow seemed to hover around his luminous figure. Against their will, Serpina and the Moor fell to their knees; the Black Cardinal began backing up, filling the castle with his curses.

"You're getting old, Nergal." The mighty angel spoke almost affectionately, but this time a menacing peal of brass sounded in his tender voice. "You're getting old . . . You're no longer capable of recognizing my rank. Know, then, Nergal, I am Anael, the head angel of the order of Principalities, and not just a messenger. Please do not compel me to resort to force."

"But hell awaits this man, the very memory of him will be wiped from the records of history! He turned against the most holy of holies—the system!"

"Of course, if you want"—the mighty angel did not heed the Black Cardinal's agitated speech—"I can grant you a rest for a couple of millenniums in a world of lunar solitude. If you'd like . . ."

Pronouncing these words in a quiet, tired voice, the mighty angel moved through the air to Lukary, picked him up, and placed him at his side.

"Be damned!" Nergal snarled, backing up, not able to endure the proximity of the heavenly messenger.

"*Vade retro, Satanas!*" the mighty angel hurled, without turning his head, and at that instant the head of Secret Operations and both his servants were turned into ash. Still keeping their shape, their bodies stood for a moment and then crumbled onto the floor, raising clouds of gray dust. The castle walls began to shake, then crashed to the foot of the cliff with a horrible din.

"Let us go. He wants to see you." The mighty angel took Lukary by the arm.

"Wait," Lukary pleaded. "I want to take her with me."

"Do you want her to die and never return to earth?" Anael's voice was deliberately flat, but Lukary felt a reproach in the aloofness. "The law of cause and effect is inexorable; by having broken the order of reincarnations you are condemning her soul to eternal wanderings in the astral plane. Is that what you want?" With his enormous radiant eyes the angel regarded the man standing before him. "I see that you have expressed a wish without thinking. Let's go!"

"But then I'll never see her again . . ."

The mighty angel didn't listen. Directly above their heads the clouds parted, and Lukary saw an infinitely blue joyful sky, permeated by golden rays. A bright burst of light enveloped their bodies, and they disappeared from the three-dimensional space of the lower world of man. Aiming their flight toward the spheres of brighter worlds, which were filled with a magical radiance, the mighty angel carried his companion high above the poor, sad spaces of purgatory and over the shadows of people shuffling along in an endless line, trying to comprehend the path of their life. Far below in the pitch-black haze, remote fires of low-burning coals revealed places of suffering and worlds of atonement; beyond them you could divine the dense monolith of hell's core, which was immensely gray, and reminded Lukary of hardened lava. In their unrestrained flight to the higher worlds, the angel and Lukary took a path into the highest expanses of universal will and intelligence, there where His mansions begin.

"You'll go the rest of the way by yourself," the mighty angel said, and Lukary saw himself standing on a staircase spun from radiant light. He wanted to thank the angel for saving him, but the angel frowned and, without raising his marvelous eyes, said, "I must ask your forgiveness, Lukary. I envied you and that is a terrible sin. We angels must answer for the purity of our thoughts and feelings. Forgive me, Lukary, for the sake of our Lord!" Anael bowed his head more deeply.

"I'll gladly forgive you." Lukary spoke in surprise. "But tell me, what could you, a mighty angel, envy in my unfortunate fate?"

"Don't speak that way—you don't know your own fortune." Anael raised his shining eyes. "I envied you because a woman loved you, with a love so strong that it could turn His attention to you. I'd like to know the words of her prayer . . . I must leave you now. Please don't tell anyone about my sin, I will master it on my own. Farewell!"

Lukary watched as the angel disappeared into the depths of space. Ahead, sparkling with all the colors of the rainbow, was the staircase woven from rays of light. He began to climb it, heavily at first, and then more and more easily, barely touching the steps and feeling a growing freedom of movement with each step. He was no longer walking, he was flying over a river that rushed below, overflowing with inner light, and all around him floated enormous translucent spheres, which passed through one another in an intricate dance. The faint singing of children's pure voices gradually filled all space; and peace and acceptance of the world poured into his soul in purifying silver streams. External forms dissolved, disappearing by themselves, and an azure light with a tint of gold merged with the heavenly singing and music, forming one whole. Without the slightest effort, and intoxicated by his abundant happiness, Lukary floated into this world without any sense of time or limits of space, only feeling that something wonderful and tender embraced him and he knew that it was unconditional forgiveness, just as he knew love. All at once joy swept over him like an ocean wave and his entire being, rippling with pleasure, was enclosed in pure ecstasy. An exquisite brilliant light permeated the world. It wasn't blinding, it caressed and comforted, and—Lukary knew this was true—God was in this light and He was this light.

"You wanted to speak to Me," the voice said. Lukary heard it in the depths of his own self, and he suddenly understood that no thought and no knowledge could be secret from Him.

"Lord!" Lukary felt neither fear nor servility, just the pure joy of absolute openness. "Forgive me! I wanted to tell You something which I considered extremely important, because of the limitation of my vision, but now I see that my undertaking was completely unnecessary."

"Yes, I know everything. You rose to defend what you sincerely considered My idea. I thank you for that! You were defending Me, while risking the loss of your very soul. Usually it's the other way around: people ask Me to defend them. Thank you!"

"What I sincerely considered Your idea? Does that mean I was wrong? Does it mean that man's highest destiny doesn't consist in his increasing good in the world through the work of his soul?"

Everything Lukary believed in and had lived by, which he had moved toward through his life and suffering, immediately collapsed and was scattered into dust; his being, seized by an inhuman and devastating bitterness, contracted in pain. His soul didn't grieve for itself—the fate of a small, insignificant midge beating against the glass of life doesn't matter, he thought; but the life of billions of those beings who call themselves people had suddenly become so hopeless and senseless.

"Don't despair, there's no need—you were right. You were as right as people can be," said the voice, and Lukary felt the warming wave of His compassion. Suddenly he understood that He was smiling. "You are still at the beginning of the path . . . As a human you're able to understand only part of Truth. In its simplicity and harmony the world is incredibly complex, and it isn't given to people to imagine it in all its diversity—only to accept it with the soul. When you're climbing a hill, you can't see the top of the mountain range. If you possess only literary style, it is impossible to retell the contents of the Bible—you'll get something either bitter or sweet." The One who is Light began to laugh. "But there's no need for that! To God what is God's; to Caesar what is Caesar's. If you believe, you must travel the chosen path and Truth will be revealed to you. Faith is the high road that leads there. But every person must climb alone—you don't go to Golgotha in crowds!"

"What about Cronus's machine? You commanded that it be made!"

"When a child asks you for a toy, it's hard not to give it. People are also children; they just imagine their childhood has ended. In truth they've just become sad and stopped believing in fairy tales. It doesn't occur to them that life is a game and the single thing required from them is to know on whose side they are playing. Whoever lives cheerfully and lightly will be saved, one with an open soul, who is able to find joy in this life and is not afraid to laugh at himself. Such a person will not pursue false values."

"Is the flow of time determined by the relations between good and evil in the world?"

"You're a funny man, Lukary, you've thought up so many things!" He laughed deeply. "And the funniest thing about it is that it's all true. Through the work of their soul people destroy evil in themselves and create good, and the course of their time is determined by how and by what they live. What presents itself as good and evil on earth is, in fact, two universal principles that form the basis of the action of the cosmic law of cause and effect. A human, who lacks the ability to comprehend their movement with his intellect, simplifies everything, as usual, and reduces it to a scheme he can understand. Human fantasy endows these principles with its own images, and they, by virtue of the subtlety and receptivity of their matter, accept the forms that people have created. Young forces and turbulent desires still dwell on the tiny earth in the boundless universe, just as in Russia on the earth itself. None of this means that good and evil are a fabrication; they do exist and act, and no one can protect people from meeting Nergal or Serpina. You only need to know about yourself, what you are doing and to what you aspire. Now you can see you were right, absolutely right!"

"Lord!" Lukary cried out in his heart. "You're so kind to me, but I am a sinner, I have doubts! My soul doesn't understand—why must a person renounce desires and feelings on the path to enlightenment? You denied death with death; I cannot accept that eternal life denies life on earth!"

"That's what you say!" The voice was silent but Lukary knew that He still was there beside him. "How is it possible to turn away from life when there's so much grief and sorrow in the world! Don't turn from life, but remain merciful there, remain with your help and give hope to those who suffer and are unhappy. There's only one road, but, indeed, each chooses his own way . . ."

"I have another great sin." Lukary was quiet, but the One who is Light, did not hurry him. "Punish me for lack of faith! In the churches, in the worship for You there is so much that is vain and human, so much hypocrisy . . ."

"Judge not lest you be judged," the voice interrupted him. "Each one serves Me the way he can, and I speak with each in his language. Be open to the world, as children are, love your Creator, not like an icon, but like life, a whole of which you are only a part. Now, Lukary," and Lukary understood that his fate would be decided now, "you will return to the world of bright powers, to that same place which belongs to you by right. I could reward you for devotion and courage, but I have nothing to give you—for a bright spirit the only reward is everything he has done. Whoever understands life knows that only each person himself can evaluate what he or she has experienced. Justice doesn't set in by itself; it inevitably comes through the development of the inner world. There's a difference in whether you live with a pure soul or internally bear a cross you've built with your own hands. Therefore I cannot reward you. If you have a request, speak!"

"Lord!" Lukary did not feel any fear but only the joy of asking the One who can do anything. "Be merciful, I want to return to earth as a man!"

He expected to be punished for ingratitude now, but nothing happened. He who is Light was silent and Lukary felt that He might also be sad. He still could feel His love, but a touch of sorrow had been added to the spiritual peace and harmony within Lukary. Of course, His feeling was vastly larger and more colorful; in it sounded the pure melody of autumn in crimson, sunset forests, and there was sorrow there as well.

"Well, you made your choice," he heard the voice of the Light. "You will see all of its consequences. You were and you remain a human; you still cannot part with the hope for human happiness and you're not able to understand that time brings sadness. By my will you will return to the world of people, the world of dense matter, whose name is ignorance. The path of enlightenment—the ascent to truth—you will have to begin all over again. You know this path is difficult, it's hard for a human to travel in both joy and sorrow toward that distant star—for you it will be difficult a hundredfold. Because you once achieved the heights of enlightenment, you'll never be able to lose your emotional vulnerability and your intense capacity to feel compassion for others; you have willingly given up the protection that a hardened soul provides. You'll meet ignorance and malice on earth, you will be tormented by the vulgarity of life and by the lowliness of human aspirations. There is nothing I can do to help you. By the cosmic law of karma you carry within yourself not only the burden of what you have created but also the wealth you collected—to love and to embody compassion. Life is an exhilarating but also a cruel game. You haven't changed your mind?"

"No!"

It is said that when a person first appears in the world, he possesses supreme knowledge of it, but, in order to protect him from suffering, a guardian angel passes a hand over him and the child enters life without any foreknowledge. A wave of tender warmth passed over Lukary, and as it washed over him he heard a voice of love and sympathy quietly recede.

"Then go . . ."

16

September isn't the best time of year in Moscow. It's slushy, you feel dreary, and, what's more, rain drizzles dismally and winter lies ahead in all its cold inevitability. You have to lie to yourself again—that fall rains are elegiac, they wash away illusions and the summer's unrealized hopes, and that once purified you will solemnly enter the temple of your own sublime sorrow. You have to invent holidays for yourself, call your anguish a poetic mood, not feel sorry for yourself under any circumstances, and, above all, value the mind's rational coldness. On Tverskoi Boulevard they're sweeping leaves from the walks, and the depressing drabness of the overcast day makes the Arbat utterly boring; even the violinist in his thick wool coat which has soaked up the wet has put aside his instrument and is smoking still another cigarette under the portico of the theater. Daily life . . . On this side of the street, and on the opposite side it's daily life as well, and it's no holiday even in that tall building with the tasteless relief on its facade. Turning on the lights in the daytime is always bad. There's some kind of hopelessness in it, as if people were struggling and hoping for something, and then they got tired and became resigned: they let autumn into their hearts. In order to hide what has happened from themselves, they've drawn the curtains. Deep in their souls, of course, they know that it's all only a game and that summer is gone for good, but people never admit to their dissembling—if they did, they might not have anything to live for. And so, full of significance, their shadows will keep on moving in the yellow light of a dim lamp, as in the deceptive murk of an aquarium, and their lives, in concert performance, will never end. Don't call out to the sleepwalker, you won't be any the better for it, and he might fall and be badly bruised. "Hey, you there, close the blinds more tightly!"

"Lukin, do you hear me? I'm talking to you!" He felt someone shaking his elbow.

"Huh? What? Excuse me, I was thinking. It's a rainy day . . ."

The secretary shot him a brusque look and flung the tall door open like a master of ceremonies.

"The academician is waiting for you! And now you've found time to look out the window . . ." she continued disdainfully, then let him into the office, as if doing him a big favor. On his own Lukin opened the inner door of a small internal hall and then entered a room flooded with electric light. Everything inside sparkled with a festive shine and sheen; with the openness of courtesans the glass cabinets along the walls exhibited their property—long rows of canonized works. The frail man who sat behind an enormous desk raised his head from his papers and looked up over the top of his bifocals.

"Come in, Lukin, come in!" Rising to greet him, Nergal shook his hand quickly and pointed to a chair beside a small attached table. "Have a seat. How are things, how are you?"

The academician sat down in a revolving leather chair and pulled up a pile of folders. He opened one of them. The words he muttered didn't make any sense and Lukin chose to ignore them. However, the master of the office wasn't expecting an answer. In a show of how busy he was, he got down to business right away.

"I looked through your article. I found it interesting, like all your work."

Nergal fastened his eyes on that part of Lukin's forehead where, had he been an Indian woman, a colored dot would have sat. Lukin had long ago noticed the academician's habit of focusing just a bit over his interlocutor's eyes, and it still irritated him every time they met. "There's something birdlike about him," he thought as he looked at the man behind the desk, "he's like a small, delicate bird."

"However," Nergal went on without lowering his gaze, "I don't regard it as publishable. I'm speaking as the editor-in-chief of the journal of the Academy. Your reflections on how the outcome of the Civil War and the country's fate were related to the fighting for the station at"—he checked with the text in the folder—"Zhutovo are not devoid of originality and appeal, especially your assertion that a dozen or two White soldiers could have reversed the course of history . . . Very, very entertaining and probably it would generate a wide polemic, but"—Nergal raised his finger—"it's not the right time for it! To promote the subject of civil war at such an unstable time . . . We might be misunderstood. There will be people who'll consider such a step a provocation. As a Russian, of course, I'm for it with all my heart, but it's necessary to wait a while, to see how things turn out . . ."

"What familiar words!" Lukin exclaimed suddenly. "And the situation is repeating itself." Before his dissertation defense they had kept him waiting exactly the same way. Nergal was a big man even then, a full-time Party secretary at the institute. Everyone in the department was working to put a doctoral dissertation together for Nergal at the same time, and his candidacy for membership in the Academy was pushed through, but that was later. At that earlier time, for some reason everyone was gossiping behind closed doors—and Lukin's fate hung by a thread. No one knew how it would turn out: some said that he'd get kicked out just for raising the question of who was responsible for the Civil War; others claimed that Lukin's work would be recommended for a doctor's degree immediately and he'd get a position at the Party Central Committee office, where they needed fresh blood.

Serpinov, a man of experience, who was close to the leaders, took Lukin by the arm and explained as they walked the long corridors of the institute that it all depended on how *they* would look at it. It wasn't clear who would be looking. He uttered some evasive words, with a mysterious significance, but in any case the decision was to come through Nergal, and he was avoiding him, although he still would exchange greetings. It was at that time that Serpinov told Lukin something that jolted him: some academicians are selected on the basis of their scholarly work; others come from the Party. Time passed, and Party headquarters was clearly not interested in him, but after sitting on it for a while, the bosses did give him permission to defend the dissertation, and without further ado he got his degree in history. "Why does everything turn out this way?" Lukin thought. "On its own there has emerged a breed of human that parades out in front on a white horse no matter who's in power!"

"Of course," the academician was saying in the meantime, "you have a new approach and you did a fair amount of work in the archives, but"—here Nergal smiled conspiratorially and his voice took on the tone of a fellow plotter—"history is an applied science, and you must not make a mistake about when and where to apply it." He laughed smugly, and Lukin was suddenly afraid that this small and no longer young man would come over now and as a means of encouragement give him a fatherly pat on the cheek.

But instead the academician frowned and cut short his laughter.

"As a matter of fact, there's another question I called you here to discuss." He paused dramatically. "We'll speak man to man. You've no doubt heard about the coming staff reduction, and I wouldn't want people to accuse me later of not giving you warning. No, nothing's been decided yet, but anything might happen . . ."

"But I've been working for fourteen years in this institute!"

"Oh, who counts these years, my friend! There's no longer any Party committee, no one to complain to. And it might be the best thing for you—you're still not old, you can find something else to do, something in business, for example. At least you'll have money. But history, that's like a hobby for all of us . . ."

The academician stood, a sign that the conversation was over. Lukin mechanically shook the hand that was extended to him and walked back into the receptionist's room. His steps echoed resonantly in the long corridor and grew quiet in the enclosure of the stairway.

His heart sank for some reason and empty, meaningless words swirled in his head. Without quite understanding what had happened, he put on his coat and cap and left the institute. The rain persisted and streams of water flowed over the road. "Damn nonsense," Lukin thought as he shuffled around puddles indiscriminately. "But something must be done, measures must be taken immediately!"

Anna was standing by the window, looking into the courtyard. She saw Lukin right away, he had only to walk under the arch. She saw him but didn't recognize him at first. It's always terrible not to recognize a person who's close to you, because during that short moment when he or she seems a stranger to you, you're able to perceive the most cruel truths—you can recognize things that at another time, in a state of relaxed familiarity, the brain simply refuses to accept. The merciless eye doesn't spare a stranger; it notices everything down to the last little wrinkle. Suddenly the old woman walking down the street turns out to be your mother, and your beloved is that round-shouldered man with the tired face who's wearing worn-out shoes. "That can't be!" something bursts out deep within you, but now, poisoned by knowledge, the brain coldly corrects you: "It can be, it certainly can be . . ."

Anna wiped her hand over the window that had quickly fogged up, but the courtyard was empty and there were only drops of rain outside beating down in fine streams and running onto the tin of the windowsill. As if she were afraid that she'd be caught standing by the window, she sat down at the kitchen table and opened a book. The key was turning in the lock, the door squeaked, the chain clanked as it fell. He fussed about in the entrance for a while, then appeared in the doorway.

"You're here? I expected you later." Anna dawdled and then abruptly, as if she'd come to some decision, looked up at her husband. He stood there in the checked jacket he always wore with his hands in his pockets as usual. She didn't remember when he'd gotten into the habit of wearing a shirt over a thin sweater, but now it irritated her. "I phoned the institute but they said you'd left . . ."

Lukin crossed the kitchen and stopped next to the window.

"What a miserable day . . ."

Anna put down her book and scowled. How long can you go on wearing the same things—those trousers should have been taken to the cleaners a long time ago, or at least ironed. Her eyes took in her husband's stooped figure . . . Lord, how long it had been! On the day they met he had worn a light gray suit and a blue shirt with a bow tie. He loved wearing such ties, and only later, somehow unnoticeably, had he switched to dull turtleneck sweaters. That day . . . that day he was walking down the street, smiling happily, and she knew right away that this striking young man was heading for her, as she stood waiting in the Wedding Palace.

"My name's Luka," he said with a kind of boyish mischief, taking her hand and kissing it. "That's what my friends call me."

Everything that had happened to her before their meeting suddenly became trivial and unnecessary. Surrounded by the crowds on the street, they spent the day alone with each other in a city flooded with spring sun. And later, no matter how hard they tried to remember, no matter what kind of hypotheses they put forward, it remained perfectly unclear why he had come that day to the Wedding Palace in a strange, distant district of Moscow.

"Fate plays with man," Lukin would say, "but man plays a trumpet."

He didn't tire of repeating this remark, and with time Anna simply began hating it: empty, completely meaningless words and that light, casual tone he said them in . . . Where had the feelings gone? When did the honeymoon turn into daily life?

"Do you know who phoned me today?" she asked, pushing aside the self-pity that had begun to rise in her. "You'll never believe it—Telyatnikov!"

He turned around and looked at Anna with bewilderment. His face was like a white spot in the light of the gray day that fell from the window behind his back.

"Don't you remember Telyatnikov?" Anna asked in surprise. "Sergei Sergeyevich? The day you and I met I was waiting for him; we were planning to get our marriage license. Later he came over a few times, begging me to return . . ."

"Oh, yes, now I remember." Lukin ran his hand through his gray-flecked hair. "What does your Telyatikov want? Does he still insist you get back together?"

"Please don't act like an idiot! You know I can't stand it when you make fun of other people's feelings. By the way, Sergei Sergeyevich has made some kind of colossal discovery and he called sort of to say goodbye. He's been invited to give lectures in America, and, I remember now, there was something about it in the *News*. I even meant to check if it was really him, but I guess I was too busy."

"What was it he discovered?" Lukin asked with a grin.

"Something about time connections. He said that if you use his formula you can predict the future . . ."

"Do you want to try? Or maybe you're sorry? You could be going with him to America now, live somewhere in California or the Bahamas . . . Bahama, Bahama mama!" he sang, not troubling very much about the right melody.

"Lukin, don't talk to me that way, you shouldn't. I can see for myself that you're in a terrible depression." In the half-dark of the kitchen she tried to make out the expression on his face. "Did something happen?"

"No, nothing special. What can happen in our life?" He shrugged his shoulders.

"Don't lie, Lukin, you're no good at it!" Anna got up and went over to her husband. "Troubles at the institute?"

He turned and looked sideways out the misty window.

"You know, ever since we moved into your aunt's apartment I've had a strange feeling. I feel as though we should be able to see the Government House from here, but if you look it's not there. It's exasperating . . ."

Lukin looked at his wife. She stood waiting with her arms over her chest. He took a cigarette from his jacket pocket and started to smoke. A grayish-blue stream of smoke drifted out the small opening in the window.

"It's really been a strange day . . . I was fed up with everything at work, and I walked home over Kamennyi Bridge." He shook out the few ashes on his cigarette into the ashtray. "Just imagine, I'm halfway across and all of a sudden in the place where the swimming pool is I see the Cathedral of Christ the Savior. It was all white and seemed to be flowing into the rainy fog. My whole body shuddered and the center cupola began to list terribly and then it collapsed. It was like a delayed razing, but in absolute silence, you see, absolute! If the explosion had made a sound, it would have been easier . . ."

He brought the cigarette to his lips and inhaled quickly. "I stood there and couldn't rouse myself from what I'd seen, and suddenly behind my back came a screech of brakes. I turned around. An enormous foreign car had stopped by the sidewalk and a rather despicable type of fellow crawled out. He had thick lips, and a face like a pan, a bald head with a few gray hairs, and the cocky manners of an informer, but on the other hand he was wearing a smart suit and flashing a big ring. Behind him was a beautiful, statuesque woman in a sable coat, somehow gaudily made up, like the nouveau riche. I stood and looked, and the bald man dismissed me casually with a wave of his hand: 'Go on, get lost . . . What are you staring for—haven't you seen the new Russia? Well, take a look then!' He pushed the woman forward, and I went off to the side, but I looked and saw she wasn't wearing sable at all but tattered shoes and a padded jacket, which had the fur of some small wild animal crudely pinned on it. The bald man and his car vanished somewhere, but the woman turned around and looked up at me from under the scarf tied around her forehead: she looked and was silent, but there was grief in her eyes. Everything inside me turned over all at once; I couldn't breathe, and I felt so terrible and sick that I might as well have hanged myself—I felt as though I had wronged her!"

Lukin greedily inhaled again and then put out the stub. Anna was quiet; the pity in her eyes was mixed with fatigue. It was the way you look at a person who is close to you but hopelessly ill.

"Otherwise she was a beautiful marquise." He winked.

"Lukin! What are you doing to yourself, Lukin? You're killing yourself." Anna caressed his cheek. "Lord, who would have guessed how tired I'd get of your suicidal moods and fantasies! We're only human, but you can't get along in this world. Please tell me—what's happening to you?"

"What?" Lukin thought for a moment and looked at his wife. "Nothing. Probably I'm tired of being a person . . ."

He moved away from Anna and stepped out into the hall. He came back with a briefcase that had seen better days.

"For a long time I've wanted to give you a present." Lukin put the briefcase on the chair, flicked open the locks, and took out a flat rectangular object wrapped in paper. He removed the packing material, leaned the painting against a vase on the table, and stepped aside. On a framed piece of cardboard two dancing pink flamingos were captured in elegant poses. "Here, it's to replace our abstract still life . . ."

Anna held her breath as she looked at the picture.

"You know, I just got the feeling that all this happened before . . . These birds and the rainy day. Luka, dear Luka, what's become of us?" Anna walked up to her husband and pressed against him. "Are our best days behind us already? I feel that we're growing apart from one another, that you're going away somewhere. What will happen to us?"

"We'll live." Lukin gave his wife half an embrace. "Considering the lack of an alternative . . ."

"Always joking! Sometimes I think you haven't changed at all, you're still waiting for life to bring you a miracle. Don't do it, Luka, don't wait—when the miracle doesn't come it will hurt terribly . . ."

The old clock suddenly wheezed and began to strike. Lukin shuddered: something in its strike alarmed him and summoned him, too.

"You know," he said, becoming nervous, "this morning Yevsei called. He's in a mess again. I promised to drop by . . ."

"That Yevsei of yours is always in a mess." Anna threw her husband's arm off her shoulder. "You feel sorry for everyone! Who'll feel sorry for you? In any case, your hapless friends are better off in life than you. Just remember that whole business with Serpinov! You knocked yourself out making speeches at meetings just so they'd make him department head, and as it turned out, he hadn't needed your help at all. On the sly, while you were busy giving speeches in his praise, he got himself elected to Parliament. As it turned out, he and

Nergal had planned everything earlier. Everything's been like that, Luka . . . How long can you go through life acting like a simpleton!"

"It's still a pity they didn't admit you to the Shchukin Drama School." Lukin smiled. "They lost quite an actress!"

"All right," Anna quickly agreed, "go and indulge Yevsei, but go to Masha's straight from there. I called to warn you about the invitation. We're being invited to take a look at her husband . . ."

"No, I'd rather go to work! Why should I look at him?" Lukin shrugged his shoulders and seemed annoyed. "I've known him for fifteen years and, to be honest, I'm not burning with the slightest desire to see his glum face."

"What? Didn't I tell you what happened?" Anna clasped her hands. "Mashka left him, she found someone else!"

"Maria Nikolayevna?" Lukin asked. "Your overgrown Mashka?"

"Just imagine. It doesn't matter what her size is, what matters is love! She met a fellow philosopher at a symposium and fell in love. She says he's very smart and unhappy and has a shock of curly hair. She calls him Diogenes and assures me that in the summer they're going to rent a barrel for two by the sea. Only three couples are coming tonight and a French colleague of theirs who's at the university on an exchange. We'll spend the evening and get acquainted—her Diogenes should be interesting to talk to. So, please dress a little more respectably, since it's a party and a foreigner is coming . . ."

Begovaya Street isn't one of the sights worth seeing in Moscow. It was green once, with lots of small gardens in front of two-story cottages built by the German war prisoners; now it's turned from a nice place for people to live into a dirty main artery of the capital. Still, even though it's covered with spit and soot, it's dear to Lukin's heart, as a part of childhood living on in the soul is always dear to someone. Their old building had been demolished long ago, the friends he'd played with had moved to different parts of the city and their tracks had been trampled underfoot by millions of bustling feet, but Yevsei still lived there in a large, gloomy apartment with windows overlooking the courtyard, and this made Lukin feel better. He remembered so much: how he would always meet people here; the large, fake-leather suitcases in all the rooms, like animals in the zoo; how the guests would all be wined and dined at the table. But then, without practically anyone noticing, it's painful to think, Yevsei's relatives died one after another, the apartment emptied, and the tradition of an extended family came to an end.

"Times have simply changed!" Yevsei would explain. "We're fools, we don't want to understand that the time we live in imposes an order on our lives and participates in them. You study history, you're racking your brains over why there was a war, why there was a revolution? But the answer's simple—the time was right!"

The period of those words was long ago, however; it had vanished into thin air. Their heated discussions were forgotten, and only three of them remained—and then two. Serpinov distanced himself, and again somehow without anyone noticing, and although he lived nearby, they only saw him on television. Once he had called and offered Yevsei a position in his political party, but Yevsei turned him down—it was too easy to get one's hands dirty.

The rain stopped. As in childhood, the door to the dilapidated entrance banged with an energetic spring. The familiar worn steps took him automatically to the third floor. The window covered with cobwebs on the landing seemed as opaque as ever. Lukin rang. Two short rings and, after a pause, a long one. The door didn't open for a while, the apartment seemed unoccupied—you might have guessed as much after only one ring—but now a bang came from somewhere, something crashed, and there were shuffling steps behind the tall doors. The door opened and Yevsei hesitated in the doorway. Over a cheap sweat suit, worn out at the knees, he wore an old Army coat with its collar raised.

"It's cold!" he said in place of a greeting. "Don't stand there, come in!"

He wasn't drunk, but his speech didn't sound right, and the way he swallowed the endings of words could have misled anyone.

"Love appears suddenly, when you're not expecting it at all," he sang as he led his guest into a large room, which was cold as a crypt. Yevsei sat Lukin down at the table and slapped him on the back. "Don't be afraid, my love won't be coming now! Lyubka's at her mother's. Early this morning she took the children and drove off. Look at me, Luka, I'm not a beast, am I?" He turned and presented himself full face and then in profile. "Why does she say I'm a beast?"

"They've left you again . . ." Lukin saw the meager provisions on the table and the crumpled pillow and blanket tossed on the couch.

"No one left me. Why do you always take things to extremes?" Yevsei walked around the table and sat across from Lukin. "They went away, that's all! They're free people in a free country. Anyway, why are you so dressed up today? A suit and a tie—my, what a diplomat! Perhaps you decided that I invited you to my own wake?" He took a bottle from the table and opened it with the end of his knife. "Look, I haven't touched it, I was waiting for you. I even dozed off for a while . . ." His puffy face was marked with lines.

"Don't drink, Yevsei," Lukin begged.

"Not you, too." Yevsei filled a small glass. "I'm not getting drunk, but drinking in order to enjoy an artistic perception of the filth we mistakenly call our life . . . Did you ever hear about alcoholic impressionism? Or, perhaps, you know what a torment it is to feel yourself living in time every second of the day? That's what it is . . ."

He raised the glass and clinked Lukin's. He drank cheerfully, with pleasure, grunting energetically and taking bites of pickle.

"Old man, you just don't want to admit it, but you and I are totally engaged in a struggle with inner emptiness. And we're not alone, everyone lives that way!" After one glass his love of talking got the better of him, as usual. "It's impossible to travel through the wilderness of one's own existence without settling it with mirages, without convincing yourself that the indifference and weariness we feel before life and the female is real love. In its essence the world is drab, like a urinal wall, and we paint it so that it will be more amusing to live. They're mirages, old man, mirages—I paid tribute to them too, I welcomed them with my arms out for the sake of Christ, I went with my last hope. I wanted so much to believe in them! But alas . . ." Yevsei made a face and opened his fist, which held nothing. "Of course, you can ask, what about love? But the train doesn't stop at that station anymore! I've been married seventeen years, love doesn't last that long. It can bear every adversity and hardship—but it can't tolerate time. A woman must be loved from a distance, my friend . . . In general man is a toxic substance, he must be taken in homeopathic doses . . ." By now he was thoroughly drunk. "So, why don't you say that man needs to live through his work? Say it! I'm no longer affected by trivial ambitions and worthless aspirations—all of that ended a long time ago. And what's left? Not a thing! Life ends like a theater performance, Luka. There's nothing more to show, but the curtain still doesn't fall. I didn't want much, however, and I achieved still less, and who the hell cares! You get tired from the senseless stupidity of the surrounding garbage, tired of being a witness to your own life . . ."

He reached for the bottle and poured two more glasses.

"You know, I've been thinking, and one thought stunned me. You can pick up some music and play Chopin for the whole evening, but no one would ever think of retyping Pasternak for pleasure! God be with him, Pasternak—and by the way, I've started to write a little myself. Tell me what you think: "It was the third day of the end of the world. Radioactive snow silently whirled down, thoughtfully covering a pile of dog shit!" Some image, huh?"

"Listen, you really shouldn't drink any more." Lukin tried to take Yevsei's glass from him but Yevsei caught his hand.

"Don't make a fuss, Commander! When I drink I get inspired. You want to make big money? Then think up a way you can go crazy quickly and without any problems. Believe me, you won't be able to stop the flood of those who'll want to do it. Suicide's a great sin, but in the case of madness, it's one-two and you're out of the game, and none of the vileness in this best of all worlds can touch you anymore. His greatest mistake"—Yevsei pointed toward the ceiling—"was to let beasts know that they're beasts! A pig doesn't have any complex about being a pig, and humans should strive toward such a state . . ."

Scowling, Yevsei drank up his vodka and tossed some canned meat on his plate.

"Above all, we need to accept our own bestiality and nothingness. Instead of thinking that we're the crown of nature!" He grinned sarcastically, picked up a piece of the compressed meat with his knife, and started to chew. "Life's a simple thing—you have to live through it and then you can spit and forget it! I can imagine how insulting it will be when you die and don't find the slightest little thing beyond the grave. That will be a joke!" He laughed loudly.

"I know why you're talking like that." Lukin had finished his glass and he started to slice a round of the meat. "It's all because you're afraid of life and are running away from it . . ."

"Me? Afraid?" Yevsei stood up. "Look who's talking—someone who's been digging all his life in the garbage dump of his country's history! If you'd like to know, all your studies are masochism pure and simple. You're the only one who needs them, and it's you, not I, who's looking for asylum in the past."

He got up from the table and stared at Lukin. Lukin had turned and was gazing out the dark window. Yevsei bent down and looked into his face. "Listen, forgive a son of a bitch, I didn't mean it!" He reached out and covered Lukin's hand with his own. "Honest to God, I didn't . . ."

"I'm not offended. Unfortunately you're right. I've thought the same myself." Lukin reached for the bottle and filled the glasses. "You know, I'm probably not going to finish my book about the White emigration—who needs it? . . . Even to propose such stale goods is funny. What do all of us care about gentlemen officers, the flower of the Russian nation, those who remembered Russia as they lay dying as mercenaries in Africa or polished the sidewalks of European capitals with their worn-out shoes."

"That's right. Don't finish it! Who gives a damn about someone else's trouble?" Yevsei leaned his head to one side and chewed with his lips. "Don't write about them, Luka—really. By his nature man is incapable of telling the truth: he'll either blacken something or praise it to the skies. Existentialism, my friend, is pure existentialism . . ." He moved his fork around the plate, trying to spear a small pickled tomato. He couldn't do it. "Maybe they got exactly what they deserved?" He raised his head. "Maybe it was retribution for cruelty and ambition; after all, it's not enough just to love one's country. But if they're to be judged, the only judge is God! Let's pray for that."

They drank without clinking glasses. Lukin watched Yevsei. After the outburst of emotions he had softened and relaxed; he looked sullen. Lukin hesitated a while and then decided to speak.

"Listen to me carefully! We've been drinking, but what I'm going to tell you is very important to me. True, life is empty, I know that, and I know about spiritual weariness and the pain of losing mirages. But just think—what if it's not all for nothing? When a baby grows up, the rattle he no longer needs is taken away. So a person doesn't have love, no longer has many friends, no one needs his or her work. Maybe it's all part of a plan and someone higher up, who separates the wheat from the chaff, is giving the person a last chance to make the only correct decision—to set out on the path of enlightenment and make the ascension to the true self."

A sardonic smile appeared on Yevsei's swollen face. "Another mirage? Let fools be blessed—it's easy for them in this world because they live in a realm of fantasy! Thus are we cast about between future castles in the air and the cemetery of yesterday's hopes."

"Wait, you haven't heard everything! I have glimpses of something significant, more and more often now, something that exists very near to me, though independently of me. In order to see the sky above, you just need to learn how to hold this world in your soul. I feel I've reached some kind of border and, if I step across it, I'll start on a difficult and tiring, but very happy path . . ."

"I know that path, I took it." Yevsei was having trouble keeping his eyes open. A pitiful smile floated on his sodden face. "It leads to the cemetery! Don't deceive yourself, Luka, nothing will come into your life now except old age, and that will be long and loathsome, humiliating you with countless sicknesses and the petty nuisances of senility. Our life is a great misunderstanding inside a bright candy wrapper, but there's a happy ending—we all die . . . Our Lord must be a great joker to have created such an entertaining little animal as the human species, one so imaginative in sin. I forgive you all your sins in His name. Now drink up and leave. Go, Luka, go, don't keep me from mourning for humanity. I want to fall asleep and have my bright fairy-tale dream!"

Doors . . . why does life have so many doors? How nice it would be to find one that would open to the enchanting garden of childhood, the old Moscow courtyard where you are loved and people wait for you and Yevsei is sitting on the fence, eating an apple and making faces at you . . . But, alas, there are no doors like that in adult life. You keep on opening the other ones; you open them and behind them find the same thing, and you really don't want to go in, but you have to—the door's open. Lukin looked at the number of the apartment on the expensive fake-leather wrap over the door and checked it with the address on his piece of paper. His whole life had been this way—he sighed and pressed the buzzer.

The door opened. A graceful woman wearing a tight black dress stood on the threshold. Her smooth hair, which was combed back, revealed her classic features; her large *rusalka* eyes looked at him without blinking. Lively voices drifted out from the apartment but Lukin didn't understand what the words meant.

"Is your name Luka?" the woman asked in a deep vibrant voice.

You could tell she was a foreigner by her strong accent and the way she softened her vowels.

"I know everything about you, Mashka told me. Perhaps you heard—my name is Lucy!"

Lukin felt a jolt in his chest from something powerful and as inescapable as fate. He swayed and closed his eyes, and when he opened them the woman was still looking at him with delight.

"No, I'm not a ghost." She laughed. "I'm a French woman from

Paris. Smile, Luka! In France we say that a life without a smile is one lived in vain."

Lucy stepped over the threshold like a child rejoicing at a present and ran her hand across his cheek.

"Luka! I've waited so long for you. I shall love you with all my strength."

Lukin backed up.

"No!" He took several steps back into the hall and turned around. "My life's over, I still have something very important to understand, I have to set out on the path of enlightenment . . ."

A subtle smile, like that of the all-seeing Buddha, touched the woman's lips.

"Do you want me to tell you what awaits you at the end of the path?" Their eyes met. Her gaze was hypnotic. "Love!"

When he was on the street again, Lukin took a deep breath. An enormous white moon flooded the world with its silver light, a soft warm breeze stirred the leaves, and the black lace of shadows quivered on the ground. The bitter smell of early fall crept into his soul and woke his memories. It seemed it had all happened before: on a warm evening like this he had embraced a woman and together they flew through time and other worlds to where a distant star beamed an emerald light. And now, without warning, everything burst—and an incomparable longing swept over him, a passionate longing to live, shattering his thoughts and filling the entire world . . .

FEBRUARY 1993, MOSCOW

notes

p. 2 *Vladimir Vysotsky* (1937–80)—popular Russian actor, composer, and singer, whose sudden, untimely death shocked the country.

p. 5 *Hermann*—the gambler in Pushkin's *The Queen of Spades*, who does see and believe in a ghost.

p. 30 *The "Internationale."* The line quoted is the first line of the Communist anthem.

p. 32 *Diogenes*—Greek philosopher of the Cynic school and moralist (c. 412 B.C.–c. 323 B.C.), said to have lived in a barrel.

p. 47 *Rusalka*—a water sprite in Russian folklore. *Rusalkas* are sometimes thought to be the souls of unbaptized or stillborn babies, or of drowned maidens.

p. 71 *Communism within the borders of one insane asylum*—a play on the slogan "Communism within one country."

p. 75 *Perun*—pagan Slavic god of thunder.

p. 79 *Rod*—another pagan Slavic god.

p. 83 *Saltychikha*—Darya Saltychika, a landowner in the eighteenth century who was put on trial for killing a large number of serfs.

p. 84 *Cathedral of Christ the Savior*—the large cathedral in Moscow, a monument to the war of 1812–14, which Stalin ordered destroyed in December 1931. He planned to build a large government building, the Palace of Soviets, in its place, but the ground proved impossible to build on. Finally, a swimming pool was put there. After the breakup of the Soviet Union, plans were made to rebuild the cathedral and in 1995 the cornerstone was laid.

p. 84 *There's a temple for you!* Refers to the mausoleum where Lenin was on view.

p. 134 *The great proletarian writer*—Maxim Gorky (pseudonym for Alexei Maximovich Peshkov, 1868–1936). Novelist, playwright, and poet. Participated in the 1905 Revolution and later joined the Bolsheviks. His novel *The Mother* is considered the first major socialist realist work. In his last years of life he helped to establish socialist realism as the only acceptable Soviet literature and became an apologist for Stalin's regime.

p. 152 *Lazar Kaganovich* (1893–1991)—an early Bolshevik, Party chief in Moscow in the early 1930s, member of the Politburo (1930–57), and one of Stalin's closest aides.

p. 154 *Our living space was reduced.* In an attempt to solve the housing crisis in Moscow at this time, large apartments were broken up into communal apartments. Six or seven families, sometimes more, shared the common areas of the kitchen and bathroom, but had only one room for themselves.

p. 179 *Molotov; Voroshilov.* Vyacheslav M. Molotov (1890–1986), Bolshevik politician and close aide of Stalin's. Foreign Minister in 1939 when the Nazi-Soviet pact (the Molotov-Ribbentrop pact) was signed. Kliment Ye. Voroshilov (1881–1969), Bolshevik and close Stalin supporter. Supervised purges in the Red Army as Commissar for Defense.

p. 179 *The crooked Caucasian nose.* Stalin was from Georgia, in the Caucasus.

p. 181 *Yenukidze* (Avel Sofronovich, 1877–1937)—Georgian Bolshevik, secretary of the Central Executive Committee of Soviets, and a man close to Stalin.

p. 183 *Boris Yevgenievich Zakhava* (1896–1976)—well-known Soviet director and actor.

p. 184 *Joseph Vissarionovich*—the first name and patronymic of Stalin.

p. 186 *Hans Christian Andersen.* From his tale "The Snow Queen."

p. 216 *Old Square (Staraya ploshchad)*—where the Central Committee's headquarters was located.

p. 216 *Kalinin.* Mikhail Kalinin (1875–1946), Party activist, became President of the U.S.S.R. in 1938.

p. 221 *Article 58*—of the Criminal Code, which covers anti-Soviet activities.

p. 221 *Cheka*—the secret police organization established in 1917.

p. 225 *Columned Hall*—in the House of Unions, near the Bolshoi Theater, where the show trials were held in the mid-1930s and where, after his death in 1953, Stalin lay in state.

p. 226 *Dzhugashvili* (Joseph Vissarionovich)—Stalin's real surname.

p. 240 *1932–33—not 1937.* Stalin's purges and terror took place over a long period of time, but 1937 is generally considered the worst period of terror.

p. 241 *Blyukher, Tukhachevsky, Ryutin.* Marshal Vasily Blyukher (1890–1938) and Mikhail Tukhachevsky (1893–1937) were Soviet military leaders who were executed during Stalin's purges of the Soviet high command. M. I. Ryutin (d. 1937) was a district Party secretary in Moscow who opposed Stalin and was also purged.

p. 241 A *land of slaves, a land of lords*—from Mikhail Lermontov's poem "Farewell, unwashed Russia."

About the Author

NIKOLAI DEZHNEV is a novelist, a playwright, a physicist, and a specialist in international economic affairs. He worked at the UN Industrial Development Organization in Vienna for six years, and his first novel, *International Civil Servant*, was published in Russia in 1987. *In Concert Performance*, Dezhnev's first work to be translated into English, was first published in Moscow in 1995 and reissued in 1997. He lives in Moscow with his wife and son, where he is at work on a new novel.